Harlem

Harlem

Len Riley

DOUBLEDAY *New York London Toronto Sydney Auckland*

30825 2145
(A)

PUBLISHED BY DOUBLEDAY
a division of Bantam Doubleday Dell Publishing Group, Inc.
1540 Broadway, New York, New York 10036

DOUBLEDAY and the portrayal of an anchor with a dolphin are trademarks
of Doubleday, a division of Bantam Doubleday Dell Publishing Group, Inc.

Book design by Bonni Leon-Berman

Library of Congress Cataloging-in-Publication Data
Riley, Len.
  Harlem / Len Riley. — 1st ed.
    p.   cm.
  I. Title.
PS3568.I3795H37   1997
813'.54—dc21   97-1363
                                                                        CIP

ISBN 0-385-48508-5

To my Mom, Thelma McDaniel Riley.

To my Dad, William Benton Riley.

And to my kids, Lia, Laurence, and Leonard Riley, Jr.

With all my love.

In Appreciation

Over ten years ago, I asked my Dad to send me a cassette of his old 78 RPM records, Duke, Earl "Fatha" Hines, Fats Waller, etc. He did. And after hearing them once, I decided to write *Harlem*. So Dad, you started it all, and I will be forever grateful for your nurturing and encouragement from the very beginning.

But this page is mostly for my other family, my nontraditional family; those who urged me to finish, to complete what had been started. And I will be forever grateful to them:

Bud Slocomb, who told me to write about the people and things I love.

"Brock" Brockington, Maureen Cotter, Chip Miller, Travis Miller, Diane Moore, and Stephan Shikes—my buddies.

Vinnetta Cole, the first person to read this book in its entirety, the first person to make me cry from her response.

Jodi Brockington, who placed *Harlem* in the right hands.

Marc Brogdon—the "right hands."

And to:

Barbara Avedon

Josh Avedon

Denis Bastian

Scott Bennett

Michael Binns

Yona Brand

Bon Brown

Alan Budde

Wilda Budde

Cynde Caraway

Kathy Caraway

Lee Cartwright

Ceapach Choinn

Steve Dane

Joyce de la Cruz

Eddie Ferrer

Anita Fry

Alan Greenberg

Jeanette Greenberg

Ed Gustin

Michael Haupt

Michelle Haupt

Jane Hauser

Pete Heine

Barbara Hubbard

Mary Lou Johnson

Rosemary Johnson

Martha Kaplan

Roz Kern

Mary Beth Kremmel

Jimmy Laatch

Laura Leyva

Jennifer Ann Macchiarella

Rich Maxwell

Joel Asa Miller

V. Quinton Nunn

Cher Oakes

Pete Osterhaus

Elaine Peck

Larry Peck

Gary Phillips, Jr.

Steve Posner

Maurice Prince

Nick Radin

John Rehr

Ramon Romero

Karen Rosenhoover
Jan Saddler
Alan Saunders
Steven Andrew Slater
Jeff Slocomb
Margaret Smith
Murrie Speight

Joseph Suber
Audrey Tatum
Suzanne Thompson
Curtis Tureaux
Lorna Tureaux
Renée Valente
Argentina Zepeda

And I thank God for putting them in the path of my life. When I was homeless and everything looked hopeless, their food, shelter, feedback, patience, encouragement, and love kept me going.

Words cannot express my love and appreciation to all of you.

Harlem

Harlem's flyin',

Me-oh-myin';

Mister, you can always find,

Anything you've got in mind

Come on up with your buttercup . . .

Or mingle if you're single

In Harlem.

Music and Lyrics by Dandy Reed

Prologue

August 15, 1926

Six o'clock.

IT WAS AN HOUR GENEVA USED TO HATE BACK home because it meant dim smoky light from the oil lamps and kitchen work that went on indefinitely until it was time to fall into bed exhausted.

Here, it was different. The city came alive when lights began turning on. She looked out the window of the second-story office and marveled at the street lamps, which cast a soft glow all up and down 125th Street. The muted sounds of trombones and trumpets and saxophones would soon bounce and wail their way up and out of the cellar speakeasies, spreading along the sidewalks, sneaking into the back alleys, and drifting up through the open windows of apartment buildings.

Soon, people from downtown would be spilling out of subways, hopping out of cabs, stepping out of limousines—boisterous, brazen, already a little high—looking for more excitement, more bootleg, more fun, and more jazz.

Geneva smiled to herself. Back home they still probably didn't know what jazz was.

She returned to her desk thinking how lucky she was to have escaped. If it hadn't been for Adam and Virginia, she'd be there yet. They didn't know it, but they'd done Geneva a favor. She hated both of them. Well, she thought to herself, not exactly both. She could never hate Adam. But now, all those lies she had written to get even with them suddenly might come true. She bent over to adjust the seams in the new silk stockings she'd bought during her lunch hour. She wanted to look her best that evening.

"Aren't you the pretty picture."

She didn't have to turn around to know who was appraising her, even though she hadn't heard him open the door to his inner office. She was tempted to make a wisecrack, but held her tongue instead. She didn't want him to change his impression of her.

She slowly straightened up and simply said, "Thank you," imitating the demure tones of his well-to-do friends. She made herself busy tidying up her desk. From the corner of her eyes, she could see him contemplate her body as she moved. She stretched just enough to let the crepe chemise dress pull tightly over her breasts.

Lester Noble sauntered toward the desk with a grin of appreciation.

Geneva smiled with the memory. They had spent nearly half the previous night at the Bamboo Inn, dancing the Camel Walk and Charleston to that song. Every time the band stopped to go into another number, Lester flashed another bill, and sure enough, they started playing the song again.

He danced up to her and hummed "Ain't She Sweet?"

"Don't remind me," she said, letting her dark eyes glance up flirtatiously. "If my mother knew . . ."

Lester's face went serious. "She doesn't approve of dancing?"

"Dancing's all right—at least the *nice* kind of dancing," Geneva explained, with a good deal of thought between words. "It's not the dancing that would worry her. It's her daughter's staying out until five-thirty in the morning."

Lester placed a hand protectively on each of Geneva's slim arms. "The lady doesn't have to worry. I'd never let anything happen to her daughter."

Geneva pushed her lips together and gently kissed the tip of his nose in what she hoped was the right combination of girlishness and encouragement. It was a gesture Clara Bow made in her last movie, and Geneva had spent hours imitating it in front of the mirror, wanting to get it just right. The soft look in Lester's eyes told her the practice had paid off.

Geneva switched to her business voice. "I suppose we should close up. It's after six. Everyone else is gone."

He continued to eye her, not answering. Then he walked to the window and stared down at the street.

Geneva placed papers in the desk drawer, pencils in their holder. She still wasn't exactly sure what a receptionist was supposed to do, other than answer the phone and greet prospective clients. She knew Lester had hired her for her supposed gentility and peach-colored skin more than anything else, so it really didn't matter. It was only important that she continued playing the role she'd played the day she applied for the job.

Fortunately, Geneva was a quick study and a good imitator. Between plays at the Lafayette and Alhambra, and Lester's successful real estate clients and his refined circle of friends, it was easy enough to pick up the correct language and manners of the black *bourgeoisie* that was so important to him. Since he ran one of the few colored real estate companies in Harlem, Lester expected anyone connected with it to give a good impression. Lester's father had gotten into the real estate business when the Dutch, German, and Jewish residents of Harlem began fleeing the area after the influx of black families in the first decade of the century. Buildings were often left vacant, and Mr. Noble began renting to colored families in many sections that had previously been white. Strivers' Row, for instance, a beautiful street with many brownstones designed by Stanford White, had slowly been vacated by its former residents and was now inhabited by the cream of Harlem society, many families having been placed there by Lester and his father.

Lester had inherited the family business at age twenty-six, when his father passed away, and he'd increased its profits exponentially in the years since. Lester's mother had always stayed out of the office, but it helped that clients knew she was part of Harlem's upper crust, being a benefactress of the arts and heading up many charity boards and fund-raisers. Geneva had seen photographs of Lester and Mrs. Noble in the society sections of both the colored newspapers and the *New York Times*. It amazed her that a white paper would report on the doings of colored people, but this was New York, not Jacksonville.

In addition to Lester's connections, each of his employees came from families with impressive social credentials—all, that is, except Geneva. But Lester didn't know that; at least not yet, and Geneva was determined that he never would.

Geneva had been blessed with a light complexion and an iron-clad determination to make something of herself. She'd used her fertile imagination to concoct a suitable background for herself on the day of her first interview.

"Where's your mother now?" he had asked.

"Somewhere in Europe," Geneva lied, crossing her legs at the ankle in a ladylike fashion. "I was brought up in boarding school."

"I see," Lester said. She watched him stare at her shapely ankles. "And your father . . . ?"

"Dead," she answered, with a sorrowful look.

"I'm sorry," Lester said.

Geneva waved away his concern. "My mother was from New Orleans originally. Her family was very strict. She was considered one of the town's great Creole beauties. When she was sixteen, my mother developed a crush on a man her father didn't consider worthy, and she was shipped off to England. She met my father at Oxford. His family was said to be one of the foremost colored families in Europe before their fortunes reversed and left them nearly penniless. My mother fell desperately in love with him and married him anyway. They named me after the city in Switzerland where I was born. He died soon after."

Lester gazed at her intently. He was buying her fable better than she'd anticipated. She decided to put the lid on her story.

"My mother's father disowned her after she married my father, but he sends her the proceeds of a trust fund each month, so she is far from destitute. She has to stay in Europe though, and neither she nor I may make any demands of the family or expect any of them to acknowledge our existence."

That story was straight out of a movie she'd seen several years ago.

Geneva lied about her age as well. On the job application, she carefully pruned herself from twenty-seven to twenty-one. She knew Lester was a bachelor. And when a bachelor starts adding up a woman's debits and credits on a matrimonial balance sheet, a woman's age must sound young enough to let the man think she can still be easily molded into the partner he wants.

The first time Lester had asked Geneva out, it was at the end of a long day at the office, and Lester was exhilarated after closing a big sale. It seemed he asked her on an impulse, but Geneva knew he'd been eyeing her whenever he thought she wasn't looking, and they'd had many talks that bordered on being flirtatious. She was disappointed that she didn't have time to go home and change clothes, as she hadn't done laundry that week and wasn't wearing one of her newer dresses. Still, she was proud to be seen with him as they walked down 125th street to Frank's Restaurant, the most expensive eatery on the block.

As they ate their dinner, Lester laughed and dropped names, casually slipping in questions about Geneva's background. She had expected this, and had long prepared for the moment. She knew that families like the Nobles wouldn't take strangers in without first making sure they came up to the mark; particularly one who was female, and attractive.

Although Geneva had lived in Harlem only four years, she had met enough men of Lester's position to know what snobs they were. They looked down on dark skin, on Negroes from the South who had migrated North, on laborers, on street slang, on dialects, on just about everything that didn't sound, look, or smell white. For most of these men, even the love of ragtime or jazz didn't develop in their hearts until after the whites started clamoring for it.

Aware of this, Geneva responded to Lester's casual questions during their first date with answers just as casual—and with not an ounce of truth in them. Lester possessed the brass ring of upward mobility, and Geneva was making a grab for it. She knew any hint of her real background would disqualify her forever.

The only thing she didn't have to hide was her coloring. In Lester's world, her pale skin was something to boast about. It was her badge of belonging. You either had it or you didn't. The rest of it—the manners, the precise diction, the slight English enunciation, the soft tones, the straightened hair—could be acquired. But not light skin. Not only did a light complexion receive the admiration and envy of the darker-skinned multitude, but Geneva knew it was the surest available passport into colored society—a society far more ensconced in discrimination than most of the world was aware of.

Sitting across the table from Lester that first night at Frank's, Geneva once more thanked her lucky stars for her good fortune. She had stood out from the others back home, and she stood out up here in Harlem. Frank himself had given her the royal treatment when she and Lester arrived at the restaurant, and she couldn't help noticing the admiring glances that darted her way from the other diners. Lester was aware of them, too. That was the icing on the cake; it told her she was successfully carrying out her charade.

After dinner, they had strolled over to Lenox Avenue and up to 133rd Street, the block everyone called Jungle Alley. Here was the heart of Harlem's nightlife—the Cotton Club, and

Connie's Inn—both of which allowed only whites as paying customers—and many other cabarets and nightclubs. Neon lights flashed gaudy invitations to hear jazz and dance, and to watch revues such as the Hot Chocolates, a chorus line of beautiful, half-naked women. They walked past the Clam House with its sign advertising Gladys Bentley's risqué act, and Pod's and Jerry's Catagonia Club, where Willie "the Lion" Smith played. As they strolled along, Lester made derogatory comments about the other couples, black or white, who he felt weren't up to his standards. A group of white downtowners were overdressed. A black couple looked as though they were just off the bus, dressed for the cotton fields. That group in front of the Clam House was uncouth.

Geneva agreed with his comments, although she could have cared less. Her mind was set upon keeping Lester's interest in her building.

A crowd had gathered on the sidewalk up ahead, and Geneva momentarily forgot her prime objective. She pulled on Lester's arm. "Let's go see," she begged.

The crowd—a lively collection of sight-seers and nightclub hoppers—was having a good time drinking from flasks, good-naturedly pushing and shoving, laughing at outspoken comments from the more extroverted among them, staring and pointing at the swells entering the clubs. Fun and excitement seekers seemed to come from everywhere: some from other cities, some from other countries, but most of them from right here in New York City. Black skin and white skin mingled freely on 133rd Street and in those cabarets where blacks were allowed to be paying guests. In many clubs, only whites could attend the performances. But here, it was as if there had never been a color barrier. It wasn't like back home, Geneva thought. No wonder they called Harlem the center of the world.

"It *is* her," a white man wearing a black homburg stage-whispered to the people around him.

"Hey! And *he's* with her!" someone else added. The whispering and giggling became louder.

Geneva's eyes followed the stare of the crowd. A long, white Pierce-Arrow was slowly pulling down the block toward them. Sitting on the fenders—on opposite sides of the hood—were a dark gentleman garbed in top hat and tails and an equally elegant colored woman wearing an elaborate headpiece of egret feathers and rolls of white fox fur over a red-sequined evening dress.

Lester pressed Geneva's hand, which lay on his arm. "Let's go," he muttered in her ear.

The white limousine stopped beside the curb where a photographer had set up his tripod.

"Who are they?" Geneva wanted to know.

"Just some entertainers trying to get their pictures in the paper," Lester remarked derisively.

Not wanting him to suspect she was one of those gawkers, she said, "They think they're so hot. What a laugh." Still, Geneva made no move to leave. The crowd had its collective eye on the two figures draped over the hood of the limo. Then a flash of light told everyone a picture had been taken. The couple jumped off the car and ran hand in hand down the sidewalk toward Geneva and the crowd.

At that moment, Geneva sensed something strange about the

pair. She couldn't quite put her finger on it. Suddenly they stopped short, glared at the onlookers, and simultaneously stuck their tongues out.

"Boo-ooo," cried the crowd enthusiastically in a friendly, good-natured sort of way.

"You silly bastards!" called out the man in the top hat and tails. His voice was shrill, like a fingernail on glass.

"Are you coming?" Lester asked, tugging on Geneva's arm insistently.

She didn't want to alienate Lester for something as unimportant and foolish as this, but she took one last look at the stylish couple, convinced their identities would finally come to her.

It was then that it happened. The woman—her egrets swaying in the night air—swooped long arms down and lifted the red-sequined dress halfway up her hips. A mass of black skin glistened in the glow of the garishly neoned street. The crowd hooted and hollered its appreciation. Only Geneva seemed confused by the male genitalia on display beneath the hem of the dress.

Then the dress dropped, once more covering its secret. The top-hatted escort lifted one arm to his bogus lady. With the other, in a sweeping gesture to the crowd, he removed the top hat and shook his hair free. It was clear that he, too, was bogus—a woman, not a man.

The couple, arm in arm, swung away from the assembled sidewalk crowd and strutted regally to the Drool Inn. They stopped at the entrance of the club, which was well known for showcasing blues singers, then the strange couple disappeared inside as the crowd spontaneously applauded their exit.

Geneva now let Lester's hand pull her away from the pushing

bodies and back to the comparative freedom of normal sidewalk traffic.

"Trash will do anything for attention," was his clipped observation.

"But they looked so sophisticated. So . . . so high Harlem."

Lester's eyes studied her face. "You haven't been to the Clam House?"

Geneva knew exactly how to respond. "My mother doesn't like me to go into nightclubs."

He nodded approvingly. "The woman who wore the tails sings there. She never wears a dress. The other one, the one in the red dress, calls himself Theda Barer."

Geneva used her girlish, anticipatory voice. "I wouldn't have missed seeing them for the world. Particularly the naughty part."

"It's people like them that are giving Harlem a bad name. No wonder the decent whites have all mostly moved away. Some of the decent coloreds are starting to leave too, from what I've been noticing."

"Your business is cleaning up," she ventured.

He shrugged off her statement. "That's different." He nodded at Mexico's doorman, who was dressed in a light blue bullfighter's uniform decorated with gold braids. The doorman bowed graciously and smiled solicitously. Lester waited until they passed the jazz blaring from Mexico's open door, then continued.

"All those no 'count Negroes coming up here for jobs. That's why rents are sky high. Not enough places, too many of the wrong kind moving in. Most of the white owners are selling out to less particular whites, who turn what used to be white-renting apartments into black-renting apartments at five times the rent." He squeezed her hand to emphasize what a big, financially secure man he was. She squeezed his hand back to let him know she understood.

He added, "That's why white folks like to do business with me. They know we understand real estate, and we understand the people they're planning to make their money from."

By the time he concluded, they were passing Connie's Inn on Seventh Avenue. Geneva drew Lester over to a poster for "Jazzlips" Richardson playing the latest revue. "Can we go inside?" she asked. "Look, Fats Waller did the music." She'd read about the fabulous gold and black tapestries in the club, and the famous raised dance floor. "Please, Lester?"

He shook his head. "Not in here. Even if we wanted to. They don't let coloreds in, except to work." Seeing her pout of disappointment, he quickly added, "But I tell you what. We'll go back to Seventh. We'll go to Small's."

Geneva loved the streets of Harlem after dark. The stone pavement seemed to sparkle from the glow of nightclub signs and from lights in the apartments above them. Streetlights illuminated the milling people, all looking so high Harlem and handsome, a feast for the eyes of feathers and furs, tight vests and bright spats, sparkling spangles and shimmering fringe.

From the High Hat Club, a few doors from Seventh Avenue, came the throbbing lament of a blues singer.

> My man's like an engine,
> once he ran so sweet and hot.
> My man's like an engine . . .
> yeah he ran so sweet and hot.

She glanced sideways at Lester's profile. He was so light, one could easily mistake him for white. *Another one of the lucky few*, she thought. She knew the two of them made what was called by most Harlemites a ritzy couple. And by the pride in which he held on to her arm, he knew it too.

> *Then just like an engine . . .*
> *His piston froze and he's all shot.*

His features were carefully formed—his nose a trifle too small, perhaps, and his lips a bit too thin—still, it was better to appear overrefined if one wanted to move up among the important Negroes of Harlem than not refined enough.

She affectionately patted his arm as they rounded the corner of Seventh Avenue. He swung his head and smiled at her. *Don't let anything spoil this*, she prayed. Then she asked herself, *What could go wrong?*

Geneva wasn't worried about anyone she had met up here. Her private nature kept her from confiding in people around her. When she took a job she wasn't proud of, and that included all of them before she landed her receptionist position with Lester, she simply used an alias. No problems there. Nor did her lodgings present any. The rooming houses she'd lived in may have been cheap and not in the best sections of Harlem, but they were always respectable.

Lester suddenly slowed his stride, then stopped and faced her, his eyes searching her face. A swarming group of downtown white revelers, dressed to the teeth and shedding their inhibitions along with their downtown manners, spilled stridently out of the Ambrosia Club, an all-white venue, and swirled around them, laughing merrily, poking and nudging Lester and Geneva closer together. For a moment, Lester's body was firmly pressed against hers.

"C'mon, chaps!" one of the revelers called out. "Ethel Waters is doing her stunt at the Cotton Club!"

As fast as the revelers had surrounded Lester and Geneva, they disappeared around the corner. Only the smell of perfume and gin and cigarettes lingered behind. Lester quickly moved a half-step back from Geneva, self-conscious and awkward. He seemed to have lost his usual cool demeanor. Then, unexpectedly, he stepped forward again, his body almost touching hers. His thin lips, slightly open, drifted closer to Geneva's red bow of a mouth. She felt his breath on her skin. It was warm and held a hint of the scampi he had eaten at Frank's.

"Instead of Small's, how about my place?" he asked. His voice was deeper than usual.

All her life had prepared Geneva for this moment when an important relationship stood at a crossroad. The wrong answer would stop the romance cold. The right answer moved you a point closer to your goal. The trick was to figure out what the man expected, what he wanted, what his plans *really* were. This time, it was easy for Geneva to answer.

She averted her eyes. She wanted to appear ladylike but not too indignant. "You know I couldn't do that." There was just enough wistfulness in her voice to imply his suggestion wasn't totally out of the question; it merely required the right circumstances. Like an engagement ring, for example.

"I'm sorry," he said, sounding disappointed and pleased at the same time. She knew her assessment of his intentions had been right.

Thank God! she thought, breathing another silent prayer of relief as they walked across the street in the direction of Small's Paradise. "Thank you Jesus for steerin' me right," she muttered under her breath. "Just don't let it drag on too long," she added, half-aloud. Time, she knew, was not on her side. The longer things took, the greater her chance of being found out.

"Don't let what drag on too long?" Lester asked.

"Oh, nothing," she mumbled sweetly. She felt snug and warm, as if the father she never knew had suddenly appeared and thrown his arms around her, comforting her, the way she used to dream he would when she was small and felt nobody wanted her.

Geneva clung tighter to Lester's arm. She was positive things were going to work out to her advantage. She made a vow to herself. She would use all her ingenuity to force Lester to come to a decision as soon as possible—a decision from which he couldn't escape.

Now, remembering that first night together—and all the nights that followed—Geneva glanced across the office at him and wondered if tonight might not bring the decision she wanted so badly.

He was still staring out the window, down on to 125th Street. He'd always been noncommittal—never again making even the slightest sign of a pass since that one time outside the Ambrosia Club, never sounding her out about anything more serious than how to spend a night on the town, never involving her with his cigar-smoking men friends—and always a gentleman.

As if sensing her eyes boring into his back, Lester turned and faced her. His small nose and thin lips seemed smaller and thinner than ever. A few beads of perspiration had broken out on his forehead. "I've found out something about you," he said. His voice was serious, filled with accusation.

Geneva's heart sank. *The game's over*, she thought. He might as well have hit her with his fist. She could scarcely draw her breath.

His words came out in a rush. "You're much too fragile and precious to be living unprotected. Harlem isn't safe for a young woman alone. My mother wants to meet you. Is that all right with you?"

At first she didn't understand. Her mind was still mourning the dreams she thought destroyed. "I . . . I don't . . ." she stumbled. "I'm not sure . . ." For a second she almost began to defend herself as she desperately searched for some lie that would make her position still appear respectable, no matter what he'd learned. Then it came over her. No explanation was needed. He hadn't found out anything at all.

She began breathing again. She stopped fidgeting with the pencils on her desk and forced an expression of composure back on to her face. *Don't appear too eager*, she warned herself. *Be careful.* "If that's what you want, Lester."

"I do," he said.

"And does she?" It was a question she really didn't want to ask, but she had to know.

"She asked me to invite you over for dinner."

Geneva's spirits soared. "When?"

Lester still hadn't smiled, his eyes continuing to seek something in hers. "Tonight . . . if that's agreeable with you," he said.

Geneva wondered if she was ready. She had been hoping for this moment, and still she dreaded it. What if something went wrong? She would never have a second opportunity to redeem herself.

Lester finally smiled, sheepishly. "I know it's last minute. I was trying to get up enough nerve to ask you all day long but . . ." He turned back to the window and again stared fixedly down at the street. "Frankly, I was afraid you'd think it was too old-fashioned . . . you know. Like I was cornering you into something."

She turned around for his inspection. "Do you think this dress is a little too . . . too racy?"

"She's not exactly a stick, you know. She likes the latest fashions. In any case, she knows we're stopping by on our way to what she calls the trash bins of town, and she knows one doesn't go to those dens of iniquity dressed like one's ready for a Sunday sermon from Reverend Powell."

Lester took each of her hands in his and held them out to her sides. He leaned forward and kissed her mouth solemnly.

As he pulled away from her lips he said, "If all goes well . . ."

He turned and walked into his inner office, leaving Geneva alone to contemplate the sentence he left dangling in mid-air.

Chapter One

Between Lenox Avenue and Madison Avenue, a two-block-long square of brownstones neatly faced a beautiful, small park that was tucked away from the noise of the crowds on 125th Street, one block away. Two white men—Charles Payton and his next-door neighbor, Ralph Hingham—were drinking an early evening highball in the Payton brownstone. Charles Payton stared out on the park's lush summer foliage while listening intently for a sound from upstairs.

"It should be any minute now," Payton said, finally breaking the silence. He was a nervous man, but prided himself on never letting it show. "She started labor a good hour before I returned from the office."

Ralph Hingham was a practical man. "I still say you should have taken Rose to a hospital. Everyone does nowadays."

Payton strengthened his drink with more scotch. "I was born

in this house. My father was born here. My sons will be born here."

Hingham shrugged. "Suit yourself. I say it's more sanitary in a hospital."

"Nonsense," was Payton's reply. "Next you'll be telling me stocks and bonds are bad investments and you're selling your house."

Hingham let a smile light his face. "How did you know?"

"Know what?" Payton's question was harsh. He hated guessing games.

"I *am* selling the house." He faced Payton's astonished stare with a glow of self-satisfaction.

"Jesus H. Christ!" Payton exploded. "Joining the rats in the other blocks!"

The remark put Hingham on the defensive. "It's merely a matter of common sense," he said weakly.

Payton slammed his fist on the table. "Do you realize you're turning this block—our block—into a sinking ship too?" He poured himself another drink and took a swallow to calm himself. "You grew up in that house, for Chrissake! Who bought it?"

"A broker I know."

He was hedging. Payton could always tell. He bore his steel gray eyes into Hingham's. "Who did the broker buy it for?"

"You should be a district attorney, Charles, instead of selling investments," Hingham commented.

"Cut the crap. Who?"

At that moment, an infant's wail sounded from the floor above. Hingham felt a temporary respite. "Congratulations," he said. He raised his glass and emptied it.

Charles Payton stood up and started toward the hall. Then he checked himself and swung around to face Hingham again. "It's going to a nigger, isn't it?" he said.

"I decided it was time to be sensible," Hingham explained carefully. "They're offering unbelievable prices. There'll never be another chance like this. We're taking the proceeds and moving up to Irvington. Ada and my mother are tired of the city anyhow."

"Swell. That's just swell. You're a great friend!" Payton didn't care if he sounded caustic. He'd seen it happening to the blocks to the north and more recently to the blocks directly to the east. One black face moves in and the next thing, the block is swarming with them. He didn't want it happening to his block. He couldn't part with this house. His grandfather built it. He had lived his first thirty-five years in it and he expected to live his next thirty-five in it. It was a white neighborhood then, and he saw no reason why it shouldn't remain one. "Sell it to a white man!"

Payton looked at his friend from boyhood with new insight, as Hingham tried to worm his way out of a tight spot. He'd thought Hingham was someone you could count on. But he was beginning to learn you can't really depend on anyone but yourself.

"They're really quite nice," Ralph said in a timid tone.

"Sure they're nice. Everybody's nice. But for the most part, they're a bunch of uneducated, unprincipled, unruly savages. Now, don't get me wrong, it's not their fault they're like that. But when they get this close they start interferring with our world—the way we want it!"

Payton caught a glimpse of his scowling face in the sunburst mirror at the bottom of the stairs. "We haven't finished this conversation." He wanted Ralph to know how disappointed he was. Maybe he could still change his mind.

He stopped in front of the mirror and arranged his bland, open face into a smile before going upstairs. He wanted to look happy for Rosie and for the baby. His son. His firstborn. A surge of pride swept through him. He wished his parents were still alive to meet their grandchild. He wished things were different. He wished Harlem wasn't changing. He was thankful for one thing though. The stock market kept going up. He was fast becoming a well-to-do young man instead of a struggling Wall Streeter trying to pay off his father's debts. His own son would want for nothing. He swore it. Never.

He hurried into the bedroom. Rose was sitting up, lacy pillows propped behind her, a pleased but weary smile of accomplishment on her face. She held the bundled infant in her arms. Dr. Peterson and the nurse were standing off to one side watching Charles, their eyes smiling congratulations.

"Darling," Rose said. "Come look." She held the mound of blue baby blanket in his direction.

Payton stepped closer, apprehensively. "We'll name him Daniel, after his grandfather," he said.

"No, darling," Rose said. There was a lilt in her voice.

"Charles Junior, then," he said with dogmatic insistence, afraid she might come up with a name from her side of the family.

She laughed. "Don't you understand, dear? She's not a boy, she's a girl."

"A girl?" It had never dawned on Payton his first child could be anything other than a son. His expression reverted to a scowl.

"I thought we might name her Evelyn," Rose said. "After your mother."

She buried her face in the blanket, nuzzling the baby. She missed Payton's look of unhappiness. Nor was she aware that he never took a close look at the baby that first visit.

Payton kissed Rose on the cheek and went downstairs to the study. He was glad to find Hingham gone. He poured himself another strong slug of bootleg scotch, experiencing a fleeting sense of well-being that at least he was able to buy the good stuff and not the poison.

Then his disappointments returned. They swept over him so strongly for a second he thought he might cry. First Hingham's news about selling his house. Then Rose's news about the baby. A girl!? Christ!

Chapter Two

Much farther south of 125th Street—almost two thousand miles farther—a non-franchised bus heading north was doing its best to speed along a Georgia road. Already it had been plagued with two flat tires and a faulty water line since leaving Jacksonville, Florida.

The small bus was three-quarters full. In the first four rows of seats sat white passengers. Then there were three rows of vacant seats. The last eleven rows contained coloreds. Almost all the whites and coloreds alike were asleep; Virginia, in the backseat, was the only passenger awake.

"You okay, missy?" a voice asked.

The bus swerved for a split second then straightened itself. Virginia jerked her eyes in the direction of the driver, realizing he'd asked the question. She smiled apprehensively, hoping she hadn't done something wrong. "I'm fine, thank you," she quietly called back. She didn't want to disturb Adam or the babies or Billie now that they finally were all relaxed and at peace for a spell.

The driver seemed satisfied and Virginia lost the little tremor of fear that had come over her when she realized he was speaking to her. Now that they were finally on their way, she was petrified that some small thing, something she hadn't planned on, might crop up and send them back home before they ever got to where they'd have a chance to lead dignified lives. And if it was too late for her and Adam, at least it wouldn't be too late for the boys.

Thinking about them warmed her. She looked at her two boys, huddled up close to Billie as they slept. Their brown faces were still soft and innocent. If only she and Adam could keep them that way. Almost all faces back home turned hard and mean before they reached ten or eleven. By the time they reached twenty—Virginia's age—if they were girls, they weren't pretty anymore. Or if they were males, they looked like old men with nothing to hope for. Virginia didn't want that to happen to Chick and Dewey. She wanted something better for them than what they could expect growing up around Jacksonville.

Her eyes shifted to Adam, who lay sprawled out beside her. They'd been fortunate. They were first in the colored line when the bus loaded up, and the five of them had the long backseat all to themselves. Adam made a barely audible grunt as he brushed an imaginary fly from his forehead. His sleep, as usual, was fitful. He turned his head so he faced the seat's back. She smiled encouragingly at the nape of his neck, wishing him pleasant dreams. Virginia was a deceptively frail-looking woman, considering she had worked like a man from the time she was five and first went with her father and mother into the fields. She let her thoughts wander as the rickety bus bumped along the road and she watched her family sleep.

Adam had been against the idea of going up North from the beginning. "Things maybe ain't so great here," he had said when she brought the subject up, "but they ain't so bad a man can't live with 'em." He was referring to the last two years with the lack of rain and then all of it coming at once and flooding the crops, ruining all the hard work.

"Besides," he pushed on, "it's the way things are. The way things'll always be, for that matter. They was like this for our grandaddies, they was like this for our pa's, and they's like this for us."

The family had been in the middle of dinner. Adam's young stepsister, Billie, was putting Chick and Dewey into bed in the alcove of the makeshift two-room house.

Virginia hated this kind of talk. She had heard it from the men around her for as long as she could remember. "That's not so," she shot back at him, her voice louder than she normally let it be.

Adam laughed. "I sure got me a high-spirited one, I'll say that."

Virginia glared at him. "Maybe you got more'n you bargained for, Adam Lambert."

He tapped his fingers beside his bowl on the table. His voice was overly patient. "No black man's gonna be able to make things any different. Even if he knew how, you can bet your last bushel of turnips, the white peoples ain't gonna let him."

"White people," Virginia firmly corrected him. Her mother had taught her to read and write, and Virginia was becoming a stickler for proper grammar.

"Okay," Adam said, sounding good-natured. "White people, then."

"And don't say ain't."

"Aw c'mon, Virginia! Everyone says ain't." He threw his spoon on the table and strode out of the house. The conversation was over as far as he was concerned.

After that, every time the subject came up about things being different up North, he said more of the same. "Nothing's any different anywhere," he stubbornly maintained.

Virginia guessed he might be saying it to himself even now as he slept on the backseat of the bus. His face restlessly swung back toward her. His eyes were still closed, but pained worry lines were wrinkling the brown forehead of his handsome face— a face that still made her heart jump whenever she saw him. She laughed to herself. It was funny that she, and not Geneva, had wound up with Adam. Geneva was the one with the smooth light complexion, the luscious figure and pretty face. Virginia had always been considered plain, and too thin to be interesting to a man. But one day Adam had stopped by their house alone, without Geneva. He'd asked her to go for a walk, and had explained that Geneva and he had had a big argument over her behavior toward one of the women in their church. "Geneva was jealous of Hattie jus' because I helped her carry some stuff home one day in the rain. She went around whisperin' about her, sayin' things I knew wasn't true. She jus' got a bee in her bonnet and wouldn't let it go. I tole her to stop it, but she had to keep on bad-mouthin' Hattie, who never done nobody any harm. I had the wool pulled off my eyes," Adam said. "I never knew she was that mean. I couldn't trust her no more."

Virginia just listened. She'd heard several of her female rela-

tives complain from time to time about Geneva and her uppity
airs, but she'd never given it much thought. Geneva was always
friendly enough whenever she ran into Virginia, even if she
didn't ever spend much time talking to her. Soon Adam
changed the subject and began describing his plans for his farm.
They stopped by the creek bank and talked for hours. On the
way back home, he asked her to go to a picnic that following
Saturday. Virginia, hardly believing her luck, answered yes.
They'd been together ever since.

Not that Adam was everything a woman could hope for in a
man. He was never one to upset the apple cart like she was. "Do
it this way," they'd tell him, and he'd do it. Not Virginia. She'd
find a better way to do it. Easier. Quicker.

She realized after living with him and having his two sons
that he might never make a wave in the duck pond—a ripple or
two from time to time perhaps, but no waves. So Virginia would
do the pushing and the prodding, and she'd do it with such care
Adam would never catch on. She knew his pride in being the
man of the family was fierce. She'd have to prod softly with a
butterfly's touch, so quietly and persistently that in the end he
would imagine it was his idea to begin with.

That was how she managed to get them on the bus.

One evening, Virginia pulled out Cousin Geneva's stack of
letters from an old Fanny Farmer Candies tin box she jealously
guarded them in and selected one.

" 'I'm having the time of my life,' " Virginia read aloud to
Adam. " 'Colored folks and white people are all treated the
same up here. I live in a big apartment with lots of room. The
streets are always filled with famous people. We all drive around

in fancy cars and wear the latest clothes. I spend every night in a different nightclub. They call Harlem the Negro capital of the world because everyone is rich and there's more jobs than Negroes to fill them.' "

Virginia stopped, looked up, and commented, "It sure sounds a lot different from down here."

That was the end of the passage she had marked in that particular letter. Virginia always marked the best parts of Cousin Geneva's letters, the parts that were the most exciting and made her yearn to move up to Harlem. This way too, it was easier to point them out to Pastor Coleman whenever he wanted to borrow them. He liked to read the best parts of the letters to his congregation to illustrate the freedom colored people enjoyed once they got away from the South. His goal was to convince his flock that this was the sort of freedom they should strive for in the South as well.

Adam thought about what Virginia had just read. He rubbed his square jaw. "Yeah," he finally conceded, "I guess maybe you got me on that one. Maybe things *is* different up there. But that don't change the facts. We still got the rights to farm my land. I can't just . . . give it up."

Virginia had gone over this with him before. "You said yourself the ground hasn't got enough strength to maintain us anymore. What's the good in struggling with it year in and year out, if that's so?"

"I dunno," he said wearily. "I just think it's fittin', that's all. My grandaddy worked it, my pa worked it, I should work it."

"And where does it get us? The few crops we were able to get above the ground this spring rotted in the flooding."

Adam took another tack. "There's a lot of new companies springin' up 'round the river. Maybe I should mosey on over there and get me a nice payin' job with one of 'em."

Virginia laughed. "Those places haven't got any good paying jobs for folks like us. Not even any bad paying ones. You know as well as I do how many have gone there lookin'. Willie Boy, Junior, Leroy—I can't name all of them." Virginia gently unfolded another of Cousin Geneva's letters.

Adam frowned. He was only twenty-eight, but when he frowned, he sometimes looked to Virginia to be twice that old. It was the worries that had done it. Worries because Virginia's father wouldn't speak to her even after all this time, as if they were the only young couple to ever start a family out of wedlock, as if getting married after Chick was born didn't matter; worries that little Chick's and Dewey's lives wouldn't be any easier than his; worries that Billie might get into trouble because she was too pretty; worries that there wouldn't be enough to eat or enough money to buy manure and seeds or enough wood to warm them through another damp winter.

"This is home," he said firmly, convincing himself. "A man don't just up and leave where he was born."

"He does when he's got no chance where he is," she answered, and she pulled out another letter from Cousin Geneva. " 'I'm so glad I came up here,' " Virginia read. " 'I dread thinking of what my life would be if I had married someone down there and got stuck in some shack with a bunch of yelling kids at my heels.' "

Virginia hadn't meant to read that paragraph, and she hurried over it. "Oh, here . . ." she explained, "here's the part I wanted to read. Cousin Geneva says even the little colored kids live like kings up there. She says most of them go to private schools and they all have nannies to take care of them. Some of them even have white nannies!" She looked at him and smiled. "Doesn't that take the cake?"

He didn't smile, so she read some more. " 'The men I go out with are all good-looking and earn over two hundred dollars in a single day. Almost all the men do. You should see the way they deck themselves out and sashay along the avenues at night with their fine ladies. The stores on 125th Street are better than the best downtown stores in Jacksonville.' "

Virginia stopped for a moment. "She must be talking about the white stores. We don't have any downtown." Then she continued. " 'Some of the men run their own businesses, but all have good positions. The worst jobs and the ones that don't pay so well go mostly to the poorer whites. And believe me, there's more of them than there are poor colored people up here.' "

Virginia paused to let Cousin Geneva's words sink in. Then she added, "She says she feels sorry for all of us who are stuck down here and won't ever know how different it is up there."

Virginia felt she had made enough points for the time being. She neatly refolded the letters and placed them back in the candy box.

Eventually, Virginia's persistence paid off. One afternoon, Adam came home early and slammed the door of the frame cabin so hard it shook on its stilts. "You win," he shouted. "We're goin' up North! My mind's made up."

At least she thought it was her persistence. It wasn't until sometime later that she discovered more than her prodding was involved in his decision. It turned out that earlier in the day, Adam had been forced to watch helplessly while three white

men beat a colored boy half to death because, according to the
men, the young man had looked funny at the sister of one of
them. The police kept Adam and the other blacks who were on
the scene from interferring. It wasn't the first time Adam had
witnessed this kind of senseless hatred and it probably wouldn't
be the last. But coming when it did, the poor boy's beating
swung the pendulum in Virginia's favor.

After that afternoon, they scraped their pennies together,
scrimping in every way possible until there was bus fare for all
of them. Naturally, Billie would be coming. Adam had cared for
his stepsister for all but the first three of her fourteen years. He
was more like a father to her. Besides, Billie's coming made it
easier for Virginia. Billie loved taking care of the boys.

Virginia had been brought up to respect religion. It was an
important and necessary part of her existence. Sitting on the bus
after all the months of struggling to make it, she whispered a
prayer of thanks and then added, "Watch over us, dear Lord.
Keep us safe . . ."

She abruptly broke off the prayer. For the first time since the
notion of moving North got lodged in her head, a flicker of
doubt assailed her. What if Adam was right? What if things
weren't so different after all? Then what? At least it was safe
back home, as long as you did what you were told and didn't
attract anyone's attention. The doubt built and turned into fear.
It oozed from the pit of her stomach up into her chest. At home
she had her friends and relatives around her to help whenever
there was trouble. Where they were going, there was no one
except Cousin Geneva.

Virginia clenched her teeth together and squinted her eyes
tight. She was determined to push the fear out of her body. It

was a trick she learned when her papa was beginning to preach on Sundays after six days of work in the fields, and he was always too busy to read to her. She was afraid he didn't love her anymore. She used to sit in the corner of the room where her bed was and watch him studying the scriptures. Then she'd force the fear away with her physical exertion. In a few minutes he'd turn and say, "Come over here, Virginia, and Papa will read to you."

"What we're doin' is right," Virginia muttered through her clenched teeth, daring the heavens to disagree.

Instead of the heavens, it was Adam who responded. Another grunt escaped his lips.

"You'll see," Virginia said to him in her imagination. "Chick and Dewey are going to get a good education. They'll sleep in a room of their own. They'll wear nice clothes. You'll get a good job, I know it." The fear dissolved. A warm feeling swept over her.

She moved her eyes to the black landscape outside the window. The silver sliver of moon hung just above the silhouette of a dead pine tree.

Virginia made a wish. "Make Harlem better than it is even in our dreams," she said, remembering a time when her mama was alive and her papa still looked on her kindly and she was a little girl lying in bed, wishing on a new October moon before contentedly sinking off to sleep.

Virginia must have dozed off this time, too. The next thing she remembered was waking up as the bus slowed down. It lurched off the road, rattled across a stretch of hard-packed Georgia clay, and rumbled to a stop in front of a dimly lit gas pump.

She looked about the bus. Everyone else was still sleeping. Billie opened her eyes for a brief flicker, then let them lazily close. Adam rolled to his other side, dead to the world.

She couldn't blame him. For the past few weeks, he'd been working day and night to get things ready. He'd leased the family's farming rights to Cousin Joe. He gave the remaining months due them in the cabin to a penniless family who had arrived from Everglade City with no relatives to help them out.

After paying for the bus tickets, they still had some money left over to purchase new outfits for Adam and the boys and buy enough fabric from the general store to run up a new dress or two for herself and Billie. Virginia knew they were splurging on the clothes, but she wanted her family to look nice when they arrived in Harlem. She wished they had more money to tide them over, but she knew once they got there, everything would be all right. Cousin Geneva would take care of them until Adam got his feet on the ground and found a job. She was sure of it.

She needed to stretch her legs and get a breath of air. The bus driver had opened the door and was outside, gabbing with the pump owner. Virginia carefully tiptoed her way down the length of the bus, making sure she didn't disturb anyone or cause any inconvenience. She had been taught all her life not to bother people, especially white folks. That didn't mean she didn't do what she felt was right; she just did it without starting up a fuss or making a fool of herself in front of people.

She was hoping to ask the driver if it was all right for her to get some air because she didn't want to do anything that was against the rules, but the driver was too busy talking baseball to notice her. She quietly stepped off the bus.

Virginia's eyes finally began to focus in the dark after she left the lights of the bus behind her. The gas pump stood in front of a dilapidated assemblage of pineboard walls, counters, and makeshift lean-tos. A sign in need of repainting announced: GAS AND EATS. A rest room to the right was labeled WHITES and one to the left was labeled COLOREDS.

She sucked in the damp night air. With every mile they traveled, she knew they were getting closer and closer to a world hardly anyone knew existed a few years ago; a world where colored people had just as many chances as whites to make something of themselves. It was a world she couldn't imagine in her wildest dreams. It was almost like being on your way to heaven, only better, because when you got to Harlem, you were still alive.

As it turned out, the bus wasn't allowed to go all the way into New York City because, as the driver announced, he didn't have the necessary permits. He dropped off the passengers instead in New Jersey in a place called Weehauken where a ferry would take them across the Hudson River to Manhattan.

The ferry ride cost two pennies apiece except for the boys, who went free. It was afternoon and sparkling bursts of sun shone from the massive array of buildings that held them in slack-mouthed wonder. The Lamberts could hardly speak. Rows and rows of buildings climbed up into the sky for as far as you could see in either direction. Virginia felt she was coming home for the first time in her life, even though she'd never seen the place before.

"Look! Look!" she exclaimed to the boys and Adam, wanting

to share her excitement. She was the first to see the Statue of Liberty majestically standing guard far down at the mouth of the river.

"Oh, it's beautiful," Billie said.

"My, my, my," Adam added in his slow-tongued drawl. "What will them white peoples think of next? White *people*, I mean."

As they stared mesmerized, Virginia made two vows to herself. First she would take Dewey and Chick to the statue one day so they could see it up close. Second, she would keep after Adam until he lost that drawl and that thick tongue, by pounding correct grammar into his head as she'd been doing with Billie. She knew, next to the color of one's skin, that it was the way you spoke that held you back or moved you ahead as much as anything else. It wasn't Adam's fault he spoke the way he did. His family couldn't afford the luxury of letting him go to school past the sixth grade; they needed him to work the land with them.

Virginia, on the other hand, had been fortunate. Before Virginia's birth, her mother had been one of the first colored schoolteachers in the entire state—not that she was allowed to teach anywhere other than in makeshift sheds at her own expense. They didn't like colored children going to school in those days. It might make them uppity.

So from the time she was little, Virginia had been taught by her mother how to read, write, and speak. Occasionally Virginia slipped into what her mother called "gutter-talk." It made conversation easier with some people. And when she got emotional, it was easier to vent her feelings. But she made a conscious effort to always speak correctly in front of the children.

She was grateful for her mother's gift, remembering her marriage vow and the very moment she swore to Adam she would teach him everything she knew. Together, they would teach Dewey and Chick until it was time for them to go to school. Up here, she knew, colored children could be educated just like white kids. She trembled all over as she continued to stare at the Statue of Liberty. It was no longer a dream. Their lives were going to be different from now on. The whole world had opened up, ready to be explored, offering its opportunities.

By the time they got off the ferry, little Dewey had fallen asleep and Virginia carried him. Chick tagged along with Billie, holding tightly onto her hand. Adam carried their belongings. They finally reached a street where a jaunty, well-dressed colored gentleman who looked to be nearly ninety told them they should take a bus going uptown. He was going there himself, he told them, so all they had to do was follow him. Adam had enough money to pay the fares with a little left over. They weren't concerned. They knew once they got to Harlem and found Geneva there would be nothing to worry about.

Riding uptown on a street called Broadway, Virginia noticed how different she and her family looked from the mobs of people that crowded the sidewalks—more people than she'd ever seen in her life. Everyone looked so sure of themselves and well turned out. She decided all their thoughts and money must be centered on what they wore. As soon as Adam got his first pay, she knew what she'd do. She'd buy them all new outfits. She didn't want anyone saying Geneva's relatives were dumb country bumpkins.

The old man motioned to them to get off when the bus approached 125th Street. He pointed out the window at a trolley

car and explained it would take them crosstown to the address
Virginia had shown him.

They stood on the sidewalk and waved good-bye to the help-
ful old man when the bus drove away. People passing jostled
them as they stood there, overwhelmed. Gasoline fumes, the
smell of the river, and a variety of other smells they didn't recognize assailed their nostrils. Honking horns, clanging bells,
screeching brakes, hoofbeats from horse-drawn wagons, shouts
of playing kids, and the din of adult chatter vibrated in their
ears. People pushed by them without so much as a pleasant nod.
What if they couldn't find Cousin Geneva? Virginia clenched
her teeth. It would be all right. She smiled at Adam to prove it.

They boarded the trolley car and discovered they were two
cents short of the fare they needed. Panic started to hit Virginia.

The conductor looked at their clothes, at the bags they carried, at Dewey sleeping in Virginia's arms, at Billie's big, beautiful, open smile. He shook his head in mock despair and smiled
back at Billie. "You folks can ride this time," he said. "Y'see, we
city folks ain't all that hard-hearted."

After they sat down, her panic dissolved. She decided God
must have His eye on them. "Thank you," she murmured so no
one but Him would hear.

The conductor showed them where to get off after Adam
handed him the envelope with Geneva's return address. "You
take good care of yourselves," he called as they left, sounding as
though he really meant it. Right then, Virginia knew everything
was working out exactly as she had dreamed.

It was dark by then and the streetlights were on. They glowed
up and down the street as far as they could see. Black men and
white men with fine-looking ladies on their arms strolled by

them, mingling freely. The sounds of jazz floated through the air. Music was everywhere. It was better than anything Virginia imagined. No wonder Cousin Geneva loved it so. Virginia silently thanked her for writing about all the wonderful things here. Virginia suddenly realized, if it hadn't been for Geneva, they wouldn't have known about Harlem. They wouldn't be standing here now across the street from where she worked. Virginia could hardly wait to see the surprise in Cousin Geneva's eyes when she saw her. She was going to be so pleased to have kinfolk around again.

Chapter Three

That morning, a self-confident Geneva had awakened late in her tiny, inadequate room—a room for which she paid an exorbitant weekly rent. She had moved into it the day she got the job with Lester's company, selecting it because it was adjacent to two blocks of fancy brownstones on 138th & 139th streets, bordered by 7th & 8th avenues, an area known as Strivers' Row. Strivers' Row was the most elegant address in Harlem. Only those Negroes of the upper echelon could afford a Strivers' Row address. A'Lelia Walker, daughter of the famous Madame C. J. Walker, who'd invented an enormously successful line of hair products, lived there in her Stanford White townhouse that she nicknamed "The Dark Tower." There, she held court in the company of European blue bloods, black musicians and writers, and Broadway actors and actresses. Others on Strivers' Row included Harlem's highest-ranking businessmen and leading lights of society. Once you got to Strivers' Row, you'd arrived.

Geneva's overpriced little room didn't quite have the same degree of prestige, but it was close enough to let Lester know she was not just any light-skinned colored woman. Not everyone in Harlem understood intangible class distinctions, or had the instinct to know which neighborhoods were acceptable and which were to be avoided.

Geneva knew the high price she paid for the one-room walkup was worth it when two days earlier Lester's mother had asked pointedly over dinner, "By the way, my dear, where does your mother allow you to reside in Harlem?"

Mrs. Noble had rich, café-au-lait coloring, silky gray hair, and the clipped speech of the Negro upper class that had been cultivated over many generations. She also had the same tight lips and small nose as her son.

"I don't take money from my family," Geneva responded. "I'm a grown woman and I plan to make my own way, not theirs."

Mrs. Noble's arched brows arched higher. She commented dryly, "An admirable quality, but not always practical."

"It's practical for me," Geneva said, letting strength and pride permeate the words. She had decided to appear independent, poised, and businesslike. She sensed it would appeal to Mrs. Noble's matriarchal nature.

"But you haven't told me where you live," Mrs. Noble persisted.

Geneva purposely sloughed over her St. Nicholas Avenue address in a singsong manner as though it was a matter of small importance.

Mrs. Noble smiled, and was much more friendly now. "But, my dear," she said, sipping her glass of bourbon, which she pretended was sherry, "even if your mother didn't select your place of residence, she most certainly must be pleased with it. It's as nice an area as any young girl on her own could choose."

After that, the rest of the visit was a breeze. Mrs. Noble laughed at every clever thing Geneva said. She admired Geneva's sensibilities, the way Geneva spoke, the manner in which she held her teacup. Mrs. Noble kept patting Lester's hand encouragingly. She petulantly complained because he hadn't brought Geneva to the house before.

It became obvious to Geneva after hearing some of Mrs. Noble's comments that Lester had told her all about Geneva's mother from New Orleans, her father from England, and the genteel, moneyed background. She hoped that Mrs. Noble and Lester had never seen a Vilma Banky movie of a few years back. If they had, they might come to realize that her parents' story was almost an exact duplicate of the movie's plot—except for the skin color of the principal characters, of course.

"I'm so pleased you came, Geneva dear," Mrs. Noble said as she and Lester were preparing to leave for their night on the town. "It's about time Lester brought around someone worthwhile."

Mrs. Noble emphasized the word *worthwhile*, and her hard glance at Lester as she said it told Geneva everything she wanted to hear. His mother—who could have been Geneva's stumbling block—was behind her, actually pushing on her behalf. And if Geneva knew anything about women, she knew as the days went on, she'd push even harder. A mother like Mrs. Noble wouldn't let Lester get carried away by some Cotton

Club chorus girl the way so many of the upper-class young Negro men did. She would know such marriages ended only in the
alienation of a mother and son. But a woman of Geneva's sort—
or at least the sort Geneva pretended to be—that was another
story.

When Geneva walked away from the Noble house that night,
her arm firmly entwined in Lester's, she could almost hear Mrs.
Noble's heavy sighs of relief.

Later, after a midnight supper at Happy Rhone's on 143rd
Street and Lenox Avenue, while they listened to Duke Ellington
play a piano solo of "Solitude," Lester made everything official.
He placed on Geneva's finger his mother's engagement ring of
what seemed like thousands of diamonds embedded in five
woven antique gold bands. He explained that his mother had
given him the ring that evening at the house, insisting he present it to Geneva before she came to her senses and married
someone else. The ring first belonged to his grandmother, who
had passed it on to his mother, who was now passing it on to
Geneva. What Geneva had been hoping for had finally come
true. She stared at the ring, hardly believing his mother had
acquiesced so quickly. Maybe these society types weren't that
stuck up, after all. Or maybe her act had been incredibly convincing, more so than she'd dared hope. She looked up at Lester, smiling, and as they stood to dance, she placed her arms
around his neck. "Darling," she sighed into his ear, "I'm so
happy."

As they moved to the slow song, Geneva had a fleeting pang
as she recalled Adam's face. She'd never feel for Lester what
she'd felt for Adam. But that wasn't what marriage was all
about; this was her step up into the life she'd wanted for so

long, and nothing was going to stop her from obtaining it. Adam belonged to her impressionable youth; the sooner she forgot him and the passion he'd inspired, the better.

Suddenly Lester pulled her out of the way as someone shouted, "Catch him!" One of the white men from a neighboring table swayed past them and fell, face down to the floor.

"Oh my God! Not again!" cried a tall blonde who seemed equally inebriated. With exaggerated poise, she poured her drink on his head. The man sitting beside her laughed convulsively, dropping his cigar from his mouth into his drink.

Lester disapproved of their antics. "They only come up here so they can get away with murder," he said. "They wouldn't dare act that way in their own clubs."

Neither Geneva nor Lester spoke for a while. They danced to the murmurs of trombones and saxophones making love to piano chords. Geneva was led across the dance floor on a cloud. Then, as the number ended, Geneva asked, "Should I wear it to the office?"

Lester pressed his hand between her shoulder blades. She could feel the perspiration from his palm seep through the fabric of her lilac dress. "Of course," he said. "Let everyone know."

She wished he didn't sweat so much.

"What shall I say if they ask me when?"

"When? Give them any date you like."

"I'd like tomorrow," she teased in a whisper, snuggling close to him, letting the innocence she'd been feigning dissipate slightly.

He laughed pleasantly, overjoyed by her new suggestiveness.

"Me, too, but two weeks is about the earliest we can arrange. Can your mother get here on such short notice?"

Geneva let her eyes go cloudy. "For health reasons she probably won't be allowed to make the trip. I thought I told you she hasn't been well."

Lester patted her back comfortingly. "We'll have a small wedding at my mother's house then. Unless you'd rather wait until she's better."

She shook her head sadly. "I'm afraid there's no point in waiting."

"Mother will be delighted."

And so was Geneva. She was still just as delighted now, two days later, waking up in her rented room. *No more vile bathrooms to share*, she thought to herself as she stretched luxuriously under the covers. No more going without lunch so she could buy a new pair of stockings. No more lectures from Uncle Tom idiots who accused her of acting so high falutin. She smiled at the thought of how she'd surprise the folks back in Jacksonville one day and flaunt her diamonds and fur coats. She'd laugh in their foolish faces. She'd make Adam grovel for running out on her. She'd make that sneaky little bitch, Cousin Virginia, wish she'd never been born. *No*, she thought grandly, applying her face powder. No, she wouldn't do anything of the kind. She'd go back down South with dignity. She'd play the elegant society lady bestowing a little grandeur and unwanted clothes on the less fortunate friends and relatives she'd left far behind. That was a much better role. For a moment, she wallowed in the satisfaction it gave her. Yes, it would burn them up even more than if she were merely spiteful.

All day long at the office, the delight in her good fortune
bubbled over. It had taken her this long to fully absorb the fact
that she and Lester truly were going to be married. Whenever
doubts crept over her, she had only to glance down at the glittering engagement ring to reassure herself.

Geneva's high spirits were such that even total strangers
seemed friendlier. Geneva was not a woman many men took to,
unless, like Lester, she wanted them to. Men didn't seem to like
it when a woman had a mind of her own. Women were even less
apt to appreciate her. But today, people at the luncheonette
around the corner from Lester's office, people at the bank, people at the cigar store, all seemed to like her.

Lester had left the office earlier for another meeting with a
man named Hingham, who had his brownstone on the market.
Unlike some of the other white owners, Hingham didn't object
to a colored sale. In fact, Lester told her that morning, Ralph
Hingham welcomed it because he knew he could get three times
the price than he could from a sale to whites.

After the meeting, Lester had plans to attend a bachelor party
thrown for him by a group of his male friends. They were taking over Pod's and Jerry's Catagonia Club, a popular speakeasy
on 133rd Street. "Little Jazzbo" Hilliard was playing, and the
men were having drinks on the house, as one of the owners was
to be an usher in Lester's wedding.

Geneva was relieved. She never felt comfortable around Lester's friends; they seemed aloof, and she wondered what they
said about her in private. Only Dandy Reed, a handsome singer
and lyricist who always had a different lady on his arm, went out
of his way to be friendly to her. So let them have their boys'
night. She'd go shopping in the nice stores on 125th Street,

then maybe take in a movie, or else just go home and pamper herself with a long, hot bath.

She was still thinking about the rest of her evening when a hesitant tapping sounded at the door leading to the outside hall. She realized she was all alone and checked her watch. Six-twelve. She usually locked the hall door as soon as the others left, especially if Lester had gone. An ounce of caution was Geneva's philosophy. But tonight, the excitement of her coming wedding made her forget all about caution.

She sat perfectly still. If she didn't say anything, perhaps the person would go away. The tapping stopped for a moment. Then it started again. This time it sounded a little more insistent.

Since all the lights were on, Geneva realized it was obvious that she was there. She decided to stop being silly. She might as well answer. Anyone could walk in easily enough. She'd just say the office was closed and to come back tomorrow.

"Yes," she called. "Who is it?"

The door opened partially. A head shyly poked inside and stared in at her.

Geneva's mouth dropped open. Four years had passed, but that face still haunted her. Blood rushed to Geneva's head. Her ears began to buzz. *What nerve! I won't allow that sneak up here! I won't let her ruin my life again!*

"Cousin Geneva? It's your cousin . . . Virginia."

"I don't know who you are!" Geneva suddenly screamed. "Get out!" Geneva rushed wildly toward the frail figure backing up against the door. "Get out, I tell you!"

Virginia stared at Cousin Geneva, wide-eyed, disbelieving.

Geneva grabbed her shoulders. She swung Virginia around

and pushed her out the door. She slammed it, and leaned against it, discovering she was breathing hard. She felt as though she had been physically attacked.

Geneva snapped the lock shut, then noisily fastened the bolt. "That'll keep you out!" she yelled to the world at large. "And don't you ever come looking for me again!"

Geneva remained pressed against the door. She lost track of time. Her only thought was to keep Virginia out.

After what seemed like an eternity, she heard the sound of footsteps walking slowly away down the hall. She wanted to scream at them to go faster. Then, finally, the footsteps were gone.

For a moment, she felt safe again until questions started flooding her mind. What was Virginia doing up here? What did she want? What if she came back when the other employees were in the office? Worse, when Lester was? What if Virginia sought out Lester and told him where they all came from? What if Virginia located Mrs. Noble?

Then Geneva forced herself to think rationally. Why would Virginia do any of those things? She couldn't possibly know about the wedding. And if Virginia did do something, she'd say Virginia's story was a lie; that Virginia was a complete stranger trying to squeeze money out of her. She'd say she never heard of the people from Jacksonville, and who could prove her wrong? She'd manage to think of something. She wouldn't let anyone spoil things now. Not Virginia. Not Adam. Not anyone.

Chapter Four

Virginia shuddered with disbelief. The encounter had upset her so, she wasn't able to tell Adam or Billie what happened until they were blocks away from the building. Virginia's entire body was damp when she finally got the words out. Cousin Geneva might just as well have thrown a bucket of water on her. Her pretty cotton dress stuck limply to her shoulders, to her back. She couldn't believe what had happened.

Adam and Billie couldn't believe it either. Adam came up with what he figured had to be the explanation. "She prob'ly didn't know who you was. Don't forget," he reminded her, "you changed a lot these past four years."

Virginia felt better, even though something told her this wasn't the answer at all. "You really think so?"

He reassured her. "Tomorrow morning, I'll go. It'll all be straightened out."

"But what do we do tonight?" Billie wanted to know. Even at fourteen, she was a practical girl.

Neither Adam nor Virginia had the answer to that. In the end, not knowing where to go and after walking around for hours, they stumbled into the waiting room of the railroad station and saw a vacant bench. Sinking down, they were overwhelmed by the relief this brought to their tired bodies. They were hungry, but even that didn't seem to matter now. Tonight they would sleep under a roof instead of in some back alley.

Sitting on the bench the next morning, waiting for Adam to return—letting Billie and the boys sleep while they were able—Virginia wondered again what was taking him so long. A million possibilities passed through her mind. Perhaps he got lost and couldn't find Cousin Geneva's building. Perhaps he saw Geneva but couldn't find his way back to them. Maybe the police picked him up for vagrancy, or—and this was something Virginia wouldn't let herself think about—what if Adam had been run over? It seemed like risking your life up here to get from one side of the street to the other.

The more she brushed that possibility aside, the more it came back. After a while she was so convinced it had happened, she pictured him lying on the pavement, no one caring, no one helping. Her fingers nervously opened and closed in her lap. She glanced at the clock again. Almost nine. A scream started to build in her throat. Every nerve cried out to him, "Be careful! Watch out! Don't let them hurt you!"

Hot and low-down,

Ain't no slowdown;

Bootleg, reefers, sex 'n beer

If you're lookin' for trouble,

One thing's clear,

You'll have no trouble finding it here . . .

In Harlem.

Revised lyrics by Dandy Reed

Chapter Five

The late summer sun lifted itself heavily up into a light blue Harlem sky. There was hardly a hint of the chilly fall air soon to come blowing down from Canada. At Mount Morris Park, small sparrows hopped about and twittered noisily on grassy knolls and granite out-croppings, and pigeons boldly searched for crumbs. A group of young boys were beginning to organize an early morning hike to the top of a three-stories tall mountain that had once served as a military lookout post. Later, in 1890, the park had been used as a racetrack.

Across the street from the park, Charles Payton, dressed in his usual dark Brooks Brothers suit, opened his front door and surveyed the weather. He was a well-built, vigorous man with light brown hair, carefully combed, and eyes filled with serious thoughts.

He stepped back inside and selected his derby. He decided

against an umbrella, though the forecast predicted rain by nightfall. He gave a few last-minute instructions to the Swedish woman he'd hired to help Rose with the baby.

"Mrs. Payton is sleeping," he said to her. "She wants you to wake her at nine when she has to feed the baby again. And bring her a little breakfast when you go up." He moved back toward the door, adding, "Oh, and keep this locked."

He closed the front door behind him, relieved to hear the bolt slide shut. *We'll have to be more careful from now on,* he thought. The neighborhood was changing.

His eyes stared straight ahead as he passed the house next door. Normally, he'd look up and, if anyone was at the door or front window, wave. Not today. Today, he was still burning over Ralph's decision to sell. He couldn't stand the thought of the slightest contact with Ralph, Ada, or Ralph's mother. Didn't they care anything for family or tradition? It was bad enough that speakeasies were springing up everywhere in the neighborhood, attracting high-living boozers and jazz-mad morons from all over town. Now it promised to get even worse.

The Lenox Avenue subway had been under repair all week, so he walked east along 125th Street toward the New Haven elevated station. Lately, he'd been taking the railroad down to Grand Central and switching over to the subway there, where he'd continue on to Wall Street.

Thank God for small favors, he thought, briskly striding past the neighborhood shops. As usual, the baker was fussing with his wife about a new cake they were displaying in their window. The tailor was busy pinning a businessman's jacket. A flashy woman was posed in the closed entranceway of the Starlight Room, a notorious bar noted for its loose women, and two dress shop owners were bitterly complaining about their business, completely ignoring the woman. Payton was amused by the thought that 125th Street formed a sort of borderline barrier between his own property and the coloreds. He knew the stores catered to the black as well as white trade—they had to if they wanted to survive—but at least the store owners were all white. One hundred percent. They didn't employ blacks, either. Even if the coloreds understood how to add up change and run the cash registers, chances were half the store profits would be lost in the process, Payton thought. *They're just not bright enough to be successful in business.*

A very light-skinned colored man in a natty tweed suit purchased a *New York Times* from the corner newsstand as Payton dug for a coin. "Mornin', Mr. Noble," the news vendor said to him. Payton watched the portly man dash across the street and into one of the office buildings that was renting space to black businesses. There weren't many like him, thank God, but there were a few, he had to admit to himself. "And only a few."

He thought back to the days when he was a young boy, before the hordes of black and Italian immigrants started moving into Harlem. Some of the ancestors of the original Dutch families who had settled the area were living in Harlem then. Many people still called it New Haarlem. But then it all changed. They'd tried to stop it, but slowly more and more blocks had succumbed to the black invasion. Negroes poured in from the South, escaping the backlash and lynchings that followed World War I, and from the West Indies. Now all the old Dutch and German families had been driven out.

Well, they weren't going to drive him out!

He bought a *Wall Street Journal,* tucked it under his arm, and reached the New Haven railroad station just as a trolley car clanged past on its way toward the Hudson River and the ferry that crossed to New Jersey. If he was going to move, Payton decided, he'd probably move to New Jersey. There, whites stuck together.

He entered the waiting room on the street level to buy a ticket. The eight benches in the waiting room were filled as usual with dozing black bodies—derelicts without shelter or money. Two or three lay sprawled out on the marble floor, their few belongings stuffed into cloth satchels and placed under their sleeping heads. Payton knew they were migrant farmworkers from small Southern towns or refugees from industrialized Northern states where there were few, if any, jobs for them. The industrial explosion that began after the Great War had brought a plethora of employment for white laborers in the new mechanized factories, but no one seemed to want to hire coloreds anywhere—North or South.

As he walked toward the ticket window, he realized he was one of the only legitimate passengers in the place. For the life of him, he never could figure out why these unfortunates all thought Harlem was the answer to their prayers. They came here filled with hope and ended up destitute; spending their days who knew where and their nights sleeping in waiting rooms, in back alleys, in subway entrances—anyplace where they felt the police wouldn't bother them.

Even as he resented their presence, he felt sympathy for them. Payton's anger spilled over when he'd think how they were crowding in on him, taking away a piece of his world, and at the same time, a less self-centered part of him wished they had a bed to sleep in and jobs to keep them out of trouble.

He purchased a one-way ticket to Grand Central and scooped up the change in a defiant motion. A coin slipped from his grasp, bounced on the marble floor, and rolled in a large arc, coming to rest finally between the shoes of a woman looking uncomfortable and unhappy, crowded against the end of one of the wooden benches by two young children.

He started toward her. Ten cents was ten cents. But he stopped a few steps away. The woman's eyes were open, watching him. She looked down at the dime, then quickly bent over and picked it up. Payton guessed he should have known better; the old finders-keepers rule.

Instead, she held it out to him. Her sad face made an effort to smile. "Here's your money, mister," she said in a soft, sweet way. She was prettier than he'd first realized. He stared, fascinated by her wide, innocent eyes. The children cuddled beside her were only babies. On the other side of the children was a teenage girl. Payton could see that she would be a beautiful woman, even half visible as she was.

He noticed the woman couldn't be much out of her teens herself. She and her companion were simply dressed in cheap summer clothes, but neat as a pin. Not the type he usually saw sleeping among the homeless derelicts. He wanted to cry out to her, *What in God's name are you doing here? Go home!* Of course, he shouted nothing of the sort. He returned her tentative little smile in his own abrupt way and stepped within reach of her outstretched hand to take the dime.

An impulse caused Payton to do something uncharacteristic. He dropped the rest of his change in her upturned palm. He disliked himself for doing it, believing people were supposed to make their own way without handouts, but at that moment, he couldn't help himself.

The woman's eyes opened wider. "Oh no," she said. "No, please."

"You ought to have some breakfast," he said gruffly.

Her hurt expression told Payton she was disappointed in him. It made him feel more like an outsider than ever. A train was pulling into the station overhead. It gave him the excuse to run, but even as he ran, he could feel her wide eyes staring at his back long after he was up the iron staircase and well out of her sight.

Chapter Six

Virginia looked down at the coins in her hands and moved them around in her palm. Ninety-two cents. She was thinking how much they could use it, but she hadn't wanted the man to know that. He'd have thought they were country riffraff, begging their way through life on the backs of others.

She was still examining the windfall when a patrolman sauntered in.

"Okay! Everyone out!" he shouted. He ambled about, banging his billy on the backs of benches, not viciously, just enough to make the wood reverberate and cause noise. "You can't stay here."

The vagrants—clothes wrinkled, hair in disarray, eyes aimless and lost—hurried out of the waiting room at the sound of his club. All, that is, except the four on the bench across from the ticket window.

"You too, lady," he said, walking over to them. "You'll all have to leave."

Virginia looked up, pleading. "Couldn't we please wait a little longer?" She spoke humbly, not wanting to offend him in any way. "My husband went to see someone. He told us to stay here."

The policeman frowned and slapped his billy in his hand. "What d'ya think we're running here? A flophouse?" he bellowed.

She couldn't leave just yet. Adam wouldn't know where to find them.

"You in some kind of trouble?" he asked, sounding almost concerned.

She thought for a minute she might cry, but pride helped her straighten her shoulders. "I'll be just fine if we can sit here a spell longer."

He rubbed his billy against his chin. "I tell you what. You can stay. But only till he gets back. And I don't want to see you here again."

"Thank you, kindly," she said, breathing relief.

"But if he don't come back . . ."

"He'll be back."

"In case something happens," he pressed on, "and he don't, promise you'll take your kids back home. This ain't an easy place for a woman by herself."

She was relieved when the policeman left, thankful they could stay there. She felt safer here than on the streets outside. The noise of the traffic and the pushing crowds intimidated her. Everything moved too fast. Even Saturday night back home was nothing compared to how busy this place seemed to be all the time. She wondered if she'd ever get used to it.

Then she thought: *Who cares if I do or not?* It was freedom and opportunity they were looking for, not peace and quiet. She looked at the clock above the train schedule blackboard.

Eight thirty-two.

Adam had been gone for over an hour. She prayed that when he returned, she'd know by looking at him, by the way he walked, that everything was going to be all right, that they wouldn't have to spend another night like the last one with no place of their own to sleep.

Then, like a miracle long overdue, Adam was there in the waiting room walking toward her. Virginia ran to him, afraid she was dreaming and he would vanish. She threw her arms around his neck. She sobbed with relief. "You came back!"

He laughed at her unexpected affection. "Course I has, girl. Wha'd'ya expect?" He patted her shoulders tenderly.

"You were gone so long."

"Geneva wasn't there no how. Some fancy hi-yaller man finally showed his face 'n told me no one by her name worked there. He looked at me kinda funny, like I done somethin' wrong. I told him I was related to her. Then he told me never to come there again or he'd fetch the police. So I high-tailed it out of there and on my way back, I saw this sign saying, 'Boy wanted,' so I went inside 'n waited for the boss to show up . . ."

Virginia's eyes brightened in anticipation.

"But when the boss showed up," Adam added, "it turned out they wanted a white boy."

Virginia's hopes faded. "What'll we do?" The question was directed more to herself than to him. If Geneva wasn't going to help them, they'd have to help themselves. Virginia was still puzzled by her bizarre behavior. Perhaps she really didn't want her country bumpkin relatives coming around, but she didn't have to be so cruel.

"Maybe we should go home," Adam interrupted her thoughts.

Virginia looked at the bench where the boys and Billie slept. "No. Once we get things straightened up, it'll all work out."

It began raining late that afternoon. In the morning Adam had earned fifty cents lugging potato sacks from a storehouse onto wagons that hawked them along the streets. He was able to mind the boys at the same time, leaving Virginia and Billie free to investigate job opportunities.

They walked about, taking note of places where men were wanted so Adam could check them out later. Whenever they ran across a notice that women were needed, they went inside. Each time they did, the people were either impressed by Virginia's ability to read and write—most of the new arrivals from the South had no education at all, they said—or were dazzled by Billie's fresh, young beauty. But, for one reason or another, the job was still never available.

"You should be on the stage," a white man who ran a laundry told Billie. It was the last place they had time to check out. The owner was looking for someone who could iron a few hours each day while the regular workers took their lunch breaks in fifteen-minute shifts.

"Forget about the stage," Billie quipped. "Right now I need an honest-to-God job. Do I get it or don't I?"

While Billie was saying this, Virginia tugged at her sleeve.

Talk like that always got colored people into trouble. Billie knew it too, and Virginia wondered why she was talking so fresh to a white man. It wasn't like her.

"You're too young to know how to iron right," he said, laughing at her smart talk instead of being angry.

"Maybe," Billie retorted, eyeing his employees, "but you'd have something nice to look at for a change."

The owner picked up a damp shirt from a hamper and tossed it at Billie. "Let's see what you can do with this."

Virginia watched while Billie laboriously ironed the shirt. Back home, Virginia chuckled to herself, Billie wouldn't go near an iron, so she was faking it, imitating what she'd seen Virginia do. Virginia whispered hints as Billie tried to show the man she knew what she was doing.

After Billie was finished, the owner picked up the shirt and inspected it. "Not so hot," he muttered. He tossed her a second one. "I'll give you another chance."

Each time Billie finished the ironing, he found something wrong. Then he'd give her another wrinkled garment to see if she could improve. This kept up until one of the laundresses sneaked over to them while the man was in an adjoining room. "Don't do no more," she whispered. "He does this every day to get free ironing. He won't give you no job. There ain't none." She hurried back to her tub.

Billie calmly collected the clothes she had ironed, rolled them in a ball, sat on them, and made sure they were well wrinkled again. "Oh look what I did," she said when the owner returned. "I slipped and all my ironing fell down with me." She grabbed Virginia's trembling hand and led her toward the door.

The man, livid with rage, hollered, "Don't you come back here no more, you whore!"

"Don't fret none 'bout that," Billie shouted back. "You could never afford me."

Once outside and a block away, Virginia felt secure enough to slow down. "You shouldn't talk like that to white folks," she said. "You know how they hate it when colored people stand up to them."

"Haven't you been noticin'?" Billie asked. "It's different up here. They let you speak your mind."

Virginia wasn't sure she liked Billie's new attitude. People should be nice no matter what, was her feeling. Just because some whites weren't, didn't mean blacks shouldn't be.

By the time the rain started to fall, Virginia and Billie had rejoined Adam. His temporary job hauling potatoes was completed. The man at the warehouse told Adam when he left that there might be another job for him in a couple of days.

With the fifty cents Adam earned and the ninety-two cents Virginia had been given, they walked north—ducking in and out of the rain as best they could—to a poorer, all-colored neighborhood where they'd heard they could buy food cheaper. They found a place that sold grits and collards and chitlins—just what they wanted—and happily, the cheapest items on the menu. They ordered and reordered until their stomachs were full again, almost feeling like they were back home.

After no one could eat another order, Adam's money was gone but Virginia still had nineteen cents left. They sat at the counter trying to sort out what to do next, not wanting to go back out into the rain. Adam and Virginia were too shy to ask any of the other customers questions. They didn't want to appear dumb, and the customers who came and went all seemed so busy and wrapped up in themselves, they were afraid to disturb them. Even the man who did the cooking and the woman who served behind the counter didn't seem to have the time or inclination for small talk.

Virginia finally got up the courage to speak to the woman. "Could you tell me . . . ?"

"Hams and yams with a side of greens!" the woman shouted at the man, ignoring Virginia.

The next time the woman was near them, Adam asked, "We was wonderin' where . . . ?"

The woman swung around with a plate in her hand and stared, as if she were seeing them for the first time. "You folks have gotta free up those seats," she said. Her voice was flat and disinterested. "The supper trade'll start pushin' in soon."

The benches at the waiting room were all filled up by the time they reached the station, and Virginia refused to let them sleep on the marble floor like cattle. "We'll find something better," she said.

They slept that night in Mount Morris Park. Adam found them a spot under an old watchtower staircase that seemed to be some kind of a monument, with Civil War cannons on each side. There was hardly room for the five of them to squeeze into and it was uncomfortable, but at least it was dry.

They slept in the same place the following three nights, congratulating themselves each evening that none of the other people without a roof over their head had yet discovered the dry spot. The rain continued to drizzle and pour down intermittently. During the days, they searched for work, gratefully accepting odd jobs when one came along, taking turns minding the boys. Somehow, between them, they managed to accumulate enough money to feed five stomachs.

On the fourth morning, the sun sneaked out through a thinning cloud cover. Although nothing had really changed, for some reason, Virginia felt encouraged. "This is going to be our lucky day," she whispered to Adam when they awoke.

Adam stretched tiredly. Once he got the sleep from his voice, he said, "I think it's high time you 'n me did some talkin'."

The seriousness in his voice made Virginia sit perfectly still. Adam never sounded like this unless he was about to tell her something he knew she didn't want to hear. She sensed, and dreaded, what was coming.

"I didn't want to say nothin' till I had to," he went on. "But my mind's made up. We're goin' back home. We'll never be nothin' but poor trash up here."

Virginia's dream started to disintegrate along with the clouds overhead. "We don't have the bus fare," she said.

"When I was checkin' along the docks yesterday, I came across a coal barge that's leavin' tonight," he said. "It stops at all ports 'tween here and Jacksonville. They told me we could work our way."

Virginia's heart slowed. "When we get back home, we won't have anything."

Adam had thought about it all night long, and he had the answer to that, too. "I can work my field with Cousin Joe. Maybe in time, I can buy it back."

"The boys'll grow up no better than us," Virginia reasoned. "They'll spend the rest of their lives fighting to get crops up for harvesting, hoping there'll be enough to keep from starving."

"It's a damn sight better'n starvin' up here in the cold with no friends around," Adam answered. "My mind's made up."

Virginia was depressed and saddened all day. At one point, Billie confided that she wasn't going to get on that boat, no matter what. She would stay and make something of herself.

"We'll see about that," Virginia said with disapproval. "When we go, you go. You're too young to be on your own."

Adam was hauling potatoes again for a few hours while Virginia and Billie were desperately going from store to store, hoping some job would come their way that might change Adam's decision. The neighborhood they found themselves in, 128th Street and Second Avenue, was shabbier than the areas dotted with speakeasies and clubs and theaters.

This was not a section where the downtown slummers caroused all night looking for exotic exhibitions of primitive passion. This was everyday Harlem, the reality behind the facade, a part only colored people saw. People on the street were hardworking, struggling to pay high rents and buy food. Most of the women who could find work hired themselves out to clean the houses of white folks living south of Harlem, downtown.

The few men who could find employment worked on the docks, at the bottom of the factory heap as menial laborers— jobs without any public contact but requiring the dirtiest and hardest physical chores. The light-skinned men—if they were pleasant enough and smiled enough—became downtown shoe shine boys, elevator boys, or, if they knew someone and if they were lucky, they'd become redcaps or porters at Pennsylvania Station. Little else was open to them.

Youngsters too old to play games lounged on the stoops with nothing to do. Women leaned on windowsills and called to people on the street. A group of men were crouched over in a crap game in front of a grocery store that displayed wilted vegetables.

It wasn't quite the picture of Harlem Cousin Geneva had painted in her letters. Still, Virginia thought, children weren't running around in rags and barefoot like they did back home. Colored people weren't cowed by police and the whites. More important—and it came over her that minute—there was an uplifting attitude even in this poor neighborhood. Freedom of spirit seemed to abound. That's why the people were so different than back home. She truly was glad they had come to Harlem, despite their current misfortune. *Things won't stay this way. We'll work it out somehow—if Adam only changes his mind. He'll eventually get a job. So will I. Billie, too, if that's what has to be done.*

Even as she thought it, Virginia knew it was impossible. Adam was not a man who changed direction easily, and his mind was made up. He was determined no member of his family would ever sleep in a park or on a bench again. He'd told her that this morning.

It was Billie who first saw the sign in the window of a small dry goods store. "Look," she said, pointing it out to Virginia. CLERK NEEDED, said the hand-painted sign. They peeked through the window. Among the bolts of fabric and ribbons and sewing paraphernalia was a chubby woman sweeping the floor with a broom as tall as she was. Their hopes rose. She was colored. White owners only seemed to want white help.

They walked inside and the woman stopped sweeping. "If it's about the job," she said, "you're too late." She removed the sign from the window. "I should've taken this down before."

The crestfallen expressions of Virginia and Billie touched a chord in the woman. She patted a stool in front of the work counter and cleared the space of a large pattern catalog. "Sit a little and tell me about it. I can see a mile away, you ain't at peace."

Virginia and Billie sat down and spilled out their troubles. The woman poured them cups of iced tea from a pitcher behind the counter, nodding her head knowingly. "Seven years ago, I was in the same boat. Believe you me, I know what it's like. No money, a big city . . ." She refilled her own cup. "My Henry and me was from a little fly speck of a place in Texas, and, honey—we didn't know from nothin'." She beamed and spread her thick arms to indicate the store. "Now look at all we got. It's ours—lock, stock, and mortgage. Ain't that a lark?" She laughed uproariously. "My name's Julia Mae Hopper! Pleased to meet cha."

She vigorously shook hands with Virginia and Billie and sat on a stool beside them, her tiny feet at the end of short plump legs not quite touching the floor. "Too bad I hired someone," she went on, "but I can't change that now. Julia Mae ain't one to go back on her word. Never. Neither is my Henry. But I got an idea for ya."

Virginia and Billie leaned toward her in anticipation.

Julia Mae pointed at Billie. "I always say there's more'n one way to skin a cat. If you don't have a pole to fish with, use a sledgehammer." She swung her eyes to Virginia. "Cotton to my train of thoughts?"

Virginia stared blankly. For the life of her, she couldn't understand what this peculiar woman was saying, and for the first time, she noticed her longer than normal fingernails. Three to four inches long, she guessed. She had a good mind to take Billie by the hand and lead her out of the musty-smelling store.

"You hold a Midas touch here," Julia Mae hissed, jabbing a finger in Billie's direction. "This young girl's got the Cleopatra sign." She picked out a piece of gnarled root from a jar on the counter and dropped it into Billie's tea. She then dipped her long fingernail in and stirred for a second. "Drink this," she commanded.

Billie looked at the cup with distaste. "Do I have to?"

Julia Mae slid from her stool and walked around Billie, making signs in the air over her head, behind her, and in front of her. "Drink up, gal. I've just chased off the bad spirits!"

"Don't drink it," Virginia whispered, but Billie was suddenly intrigued. She drained the cup, leaving only the gnarled root behind, and immediately began to cough.

Virginia was alarmed. "What did you give her?"

"Pipe down. It ain't gonna harm her."

When Billie stopped coughing, Julia Mae gingerly retrieved the root and dried it lovingly on a handkerchief. Then she slipped it back into the jar. "Brought this little baby all the way from Texas," she explained proudly. "My granny brought dit from Haiti when she married my granpappy. He was a cowpuncher over in Abilene 'fore he got himself killed in a shootout. That was some forty-odd years ago. Granny gave it to me when I came here—with Henry. She was ninety-eight then. She's a hundred and five now and still sharp as a tack."

She pointed at Billie again. "Look at this child," she said to Virginia. "Look at those green eyes with the little flecks in 'em. Honey, that's a sign. It means bucks—lots of bucks." She pointed out the tiny mole on Billie's thin, graceful neck. "See this? That there means a big mess of love. Maybe someone she'd least expect—I dunno, but I guarantee ya, it's gonna rock this child right outta her shoes. It don't guarantee happiness, though, not by no long shot."

Billie's eyes flashed signs of impatience at Virginia. "What we need is a job," she said, "else we go back home tonight."

"Hush up," Julia Mae muttered. "I'm gettin' to that. First off, I gotta point out that golden skin of yours. It's peach bloom, sweet and tempting. And the way you part that straight, fine hair of yours. It speaks both good and evil, depending on which side of the tree the peach falls when it's ripe."

Billie was getting bored. "We ain't got much time."

"Be polite," Virginia told her. "You're acting mighty uppity with folks."

Julia Mae shrugged off Billie's talk. "It's the juju root," she told Virginia. "Spirits hold her tongue. They're leading her on. She's got destiny behind her."

"We'd better go," Billie said to Virginia.

Julia Mae scurried behind them and rummaged through a cigar box she pulled out from under the counter. "If you jest hold yer horses . . ." She held up a slip of paper triumphantly. "Here it is! Here's where you go."

Virginia took the address and Julia Mae explained how to get there. Neither Virginia nor Billie understood what work was involved. Julia Mae spoke in vague, mysterious terms as if she wasn't sure either, saying, "He'll hire you, honey, you'll see," following them out to the sidewalk. "I put a work spell on ya so he's got to!"

The address led them to a shabby building at the end of Fifth Avenue, a block away from the Harlem River. Once past the doorway, the building's appearance dramatically changed. Brightly colored murals of street scenes, jungle foliage, seascapes, Western deserts, and religious rites covered the long walls. Whimsical signs were tacked onto the doors. POETRY SPOKEN HERE said one. BEWARE—WRITER AT WORK said another. An enormous line drawing of a saxophone was on a third.

Billie looked at Virginia. "Some destiny behind me," she said with a snicker.

"It's our last hope," Virginia answered somberly.

They climbed the stairs to the top floor where Julia Mae had directed them. There was only one door on that level. FLETCHER DEEL, the name they were looking for, was painted on it in a rainbow of colors. It was open slightly. They knocked and then opened the door wider, peeking in.

Inside reminded them of a large open barn. Cloth hung down here and there, separating it into areas. Rows of windows, reaching clear to the high ceiling, formed two walls. Against the windowless wall facing Virginia and Billie, a man stood on his head, his feet propped against the wall. He was watching them. "Come in, come in," he said.

Even upside down, it was obvious how tall and gaunt the man was. Virginia guessed he must be seven foot and bet he weighed no more than a hundred and fifty, if he weighed a pound. "Julia

Mae sent us," she said, a little scared of what they might be letting themselves in for.

"She said you were looking for someone like me," Billie chimed in.

The man's eyes rolled about. "What man in his right mind wouldn't be, my dear?" he said in a mock English accent. "Julia Mae may have sent you, but faces like yours are made in heaven. Someday you'll be a sorceress. But right now, you're a fresh mountain stream on a hot summer day."

Virginia wanted to get the conversation back to business. "She said you had a job open."

The upside-down eyes darted back to Virginia. "I have. And the young Mona Lisa can fill it perfectly." Virginia and Billie squealed happily with delight. At last something was coming their way.

"Unfortunately," the man continued, "I have no funds to pay for a model's services at the moment. If you could work on trust for a week or two . . . ?"

Virginia and Billie's shoulders slumped. Another worthless chase. They turned for the door. Fletcher Deel flipped onto his feet. He was almost as tall as Virginia had guessed. His skin was blue-black, the blackest Virginia had seen. He had perfect white shining teeth, a wide nose, and a wider smile of full lips.

"I can pay for the young lady's services as soon as I sell a painting or two or get another commission," he told them. "I pay two dollars a day."

Virginia explained they had no place to stay. They needed money now. Otherwise, they'd have to go back to Florida that evening.

Deel motioned to the loft around him. "That's easy to resolve. You two can stay here safe and sound. I sleep in the penthouse." Seeing their confusion, he explained, "In my little lean-to upstairs on the roof. I like open spaces."

"But there's others."

"Others?"

"My husband and my two boys."

His eyes didn't move from Virginia's face. She could almost hear him thinking about a crowd in his studio, the disruptions, the constant commotion.

"I see," he finally said. "You do realize this is my studio."

"We'll be so quiet," Virginia said, "you'll never know the boys are around. They're well behaved. And my husband will be out looking for work. I can cook and clean up and mend your clothes while Billie poses. You won't have to pay her anything."

Deel looked dubious. "I don't know . . ."

Virginia felt him weakening. Her words rushed out fearlessly. "It'll only be for a day or two. Adam's sure to find something steady by then. Maybe I will too. Then we'll move into our own place and Billie can come each day and work and you can pay her when you're able." *Please, please,* she prayed.

Fletcher Deel came to a decision. He clapped his hands with a sound of finality that startled the women. "Okay," he said. "We'll give it a little try."

Virginia and Billie half ran all the way back to the storehouse by the Harlem River where Adam and the boys were waiting. As they hurried, Virginia held imaginary conversations with Adam.

"Don't be stubborn," she'd say to him. "This is just what we need. A place to stay till we get our feet on the ground."

Sometimes Adam would smile and answer, "We'll stay." More often, he'd shake his head and, without a word, take them to the docks where the coal barge was loading up, preparing to leave. She knew how obstinate Adam could be.

Make him change his mind, she prayed aloud to the river breeze that had come up and was making tiny whirlpools of leaves at their feet as she and Billie ran along. *Make him see it my way. He just has to.*

Chapter Seven

Geneva still cringed whenever she saw a thin woman in a cheap summer dress walking along the street, sitting in the back of a passing streetcar, or shopping near her in a store. The fact that it was never Virginia didn't help in the least. Geneva couldn't believe for a minute she was free of her yet. She was convinced Virginia was searching for her, getting ready to swoop down and destroy her life. Geneva felt it in every bone of her body. She wouldn't be safe until the wedding was over. Not even Lester's mother could spoil things then.

Since the dreadful night Virginia showed up at the office, Geneva hadn't gone back there. She'd told Lester she had to prepare her trousseau, but actually she was afraid. The mere thought of the office made her stomach churn.

The night she'd sent Virginia packing, she'd almost run after her to ask about Adam. Geneva assumed he'd come North with

Virginia and their two brats. How dare Virginia come knocking at her door when she'd stolen the one man Geneva had ever cared about? It was possible, she guessed, that Virginia never realized Geneva was still in love with him. Certainly Geneva had acted coldly to Adam after their quarrel, and she'd simply laughed when her aunt told her Virginia was expecting Adam's child. She'd never let on to anyone back home that she still cared about him. Maybe Adam had never told Virginia what they'd meant to each other. Whatever she thought, she had some nerve just showing up at Geneva's door expecting a handout. And what timing! If only they'd come after the wedding, it wouldn't have mattered so much. As it was, Geneva was counting the days until the ceremony, just hoping Lester wouldn't hear anything to make him back out of it.

She'd made up a good story to tell him in case Virginia did come back to the office. She had told Lester that her grandfather, who was in New Orleans, had somehow heard of their wedding and wanted to stop it out of spite, since he was still angry with her mother. Disreputable people had been sent North to ruin her reputation, she said tearily.

Lester had pulled his stocky body up to full height—which wasn't much more than Geneva's—and told her not to worry. If anyone came looking for her, he'd know how to handle it. He gave her a comforting hug, a dry kiss, and told her to go home. Everything would be all right.

In spite of his words, Geneva didn't breathe easy. As the day of her wedding drew closer, she was more and more on edge. She became testy with Lester. Their cabaret nights were cut off. If she went out anywhere, she went alone. When she did see

Lester, it was at his mother's house with Mrs. Noble in attendance, talking about the wonderful days that lay ahead for her son and his bride-to-be.

Geneva explained her position by saying it was an old Creole superstition that bride and groom not be seen in public together the fortnight prior to the wedding. Lester smiled agreeably, but she overheard him explain to Dandy Reed one night at the house that "virgins can get real skittish before losing it."

At home in her tiny room, Geneva used her time to study up on French phrases that she knew were important to the bourgeois world she was entering. She worked on her enunciation. She read books on etiquette, checking out words she didn't understand in a dog-eared dictionary she had carried around for years.

The dictionary was one of the first things she had ever bought. She saved almost a year to buy it. Her mother's sister, the sister who raised Geneva after her mother ran away with that small-time preacher from St. Petersburg, thought she was demented wasting her money to buy a dictionary. Other than Cousin Virginia and her aunt, not many in the family could read, nor had they any interest in learning how. Their reasoning was, they could talk and that was enough. For the life of them, they couldn't fathom Geneva's time-wasting with a book, when she should have been working. From the very beginning, they had tried to stop Geneva from continually running over to Virginia's house whenever her mother was giving school lessons, but Geneva managed to do it anyway. Now all the studying was going to pay off.

Geneva and Lester made a lovely couple. It said so in the *Age*, the *Harlem Voice*, the *Harlem Home News*—even in the white newspapers, the *New York Times* and the *Herald Tribune*. The wedding was conducted before a full congregation at Mrs. Noble's church, Abyssinian Baptist on 138th Street. Well over four hundred attended the afternoon ceremony to hear the Reverend Adam Clayton Powell, Sr., with his white hair, kind eyes, and golden voice, preside. Mrs. Noble arranged for everything. She even selected a maid of honor and the four bridesmaids for the wedding party. It was a large and beautiful event.

The reception that immediately followed, however, was smaller by two hundred and all the more exclusive. It was held in the rectory of the church, a large wood-paneled room with stained-glass windows on one side and colorful old religious tapestries hanging against the high wall. Mrs. Noble had the place filled with baskets of white flower arrangements, with white and pink paper buntings streaming across the rafters of the Gothic room. The guests were from Harlem's *crème*. Lester arranged for Barron Wilkins's chef to cater the affair. Liquid refreshments were limited to tea and sherry, although Mrs. Noble poured her sherry from a special decanter that was hidden behind the buffet table. Geneva suspected it was bourbon.

Quite a few guests were celebrities—among them, Paul Robeson, Marian Anderson, and the conductor of the Harlem Symphony Orchestra, Mrs. Noble's favorite charity. Throughout the reception, Geneva was afraid she'd commit some *faux pas*. She kept a frozen smile on her face. When Mrs. Noble would say, "Geneva dear, this is our famous writer, Mr. Du Bois," or "Have you met Mr. Van Vechten?" Geneva would answer with a noncommittal, "How nice to see you," and then hurry away so there could be no possibility of saying the wrong thing.

Eventually, Mrs. Noble took her arm. "You're so frantic, dear. I want you to stop scurrying about like a chipmunk and enjoy your wedding. It's the only one you'll have."

"It's such a beautiful day," Geneva responded, dazed by it all.

Mrs. Noble patted her arm, leading her to Lester. "I'll see to the guests. You dance with Lester and have a good time."

Dancing a waltz with Lester to the strains of a three-piece orchestra playing "All Alone" was not Geneva's idea of having a good time. Lester, she had come to realize, was not a very good dancer. She wished he were taller, a little livelier. It wouldn't hurt him to lose a few pounds. Not that he was fat exactly, but she liked men on the slim side. She almost added to her wishes, "like Adam," but something stopped her short of it. This was no occasion to be frustrated by daydreams that should have been long forgotten.

Geneva and Lester went to Niagara Falls for a three-day honeymoon. Geneva thought it common—a honeymoon more suitable to the masses than members of Harlem's *haute monde*—but Lester insisted on it. His mother and father had gone there. So had his grandmother and grandfather and back through four generations. If they didn't go, Mrs. Noble would never forgive them. In the end, Geneva conceded to his wishes, and off they went on the *Toronto Flyer* out of Pennsylvania Station.

They had a compartment. Geneva had only traveled in coach before. She felt like the movie stars she idolized. She and Lester were the only Negroes in first class. Although the dining car, lounge, and observation platform were not open to them, the porters bowed and scraped whenever they brought food or drink to their compartment.

Geneva worried that Lester would notice she wasn't a virgin, so she made certain he was well supplied with cocktails the night of their wedding. By the time he stumbled into bed that first night on the train, she was sure he wouldn't remember any details about that part of the evening. The next morning, she whisked the sheets up off the bed the minute Lester got up. As far as she could tell, he had no idea she'd slept with a man before.

All through the honeymoon, visions of Adam kept slipping into Geneva's mind. She could almost feel him lying beside her the way he used to at Jordan's Creek, where they'd made love long into the night. One night, she even dreamed about him, and awoke to Lester shaking her.

"Are you all right?" His wet hand was on her shoulder.

"It must have been a nightmare," she explained.

"You were yelling," he mumbled. He rolled over and went back to sleep.

A week after the newlyweds moved into the house with Mrs. Noble, Geneva returned to work in Lester's real estate office. She couldn't stand spending another day with Lester's mother.

A new receptionist had been hired, and Geneva took over as office manager and Lester's assistant. She didn't know how to perform these duties any more than those of a receptionist, but being bright, she quickly picked up the important details.

She began to relax. Now that she was Mrs. Lester Noble, for the first time in her life, she felt secure. If Virginia ever showed up again, she'd snap her fingers under her nose. There was nothing anyone could say anymore to take away her safe new world. She had locked the past behind her and thrown away the key.

After being back at work a few months and still having seen no further sign of Virginia, Geneva reached a conclusion. Without Geneva available for handouts and lodging, Virginia had had no choice but to go back home to the fields where she belonged. Harlem was not a place for people like her. With that realization—other than a dream of Adam from time to time—they both disappeared completely from Geneva's mind.

During this period, Geneva more and more resented living in Mrs. Noble's house. She complained to Lester that they should have a place of their own; that Mrs. Noble, "sweet as she was," interfered in their social life, in their private life, and in their business life. One day they left the office to have lunch at a new little garden restaurant off Lenox Avenue, or so Geneva thought. Lester, instead, walked her down Madison.

"This isn't the way," Geneva said. Lester often went off in the wrong direction.

"Yes it is," he insisted.

"Chez Simone is that way," she pointed out.

"We're not going there."

"Where are we going then?"

"You'll see." A sneaky little smile jumped from one corner of his mouth to the other. "I've got a surprise."

Geneva loved surprises. She took hold of his arm in a burst of affection and held it tightly, something she hadn't done often since the day of their wedding. "Tell me, tell me, tell me . . ." she begged.

"You'll have to wait," was all Lester would say.

They walked along the edge of Mount Morris Park, finally

crossing over to a row of five nearly identical brownstones, the best-kept buildings in the block. Lester led her to the door of one and rang the bell.

A white woman in her early fifties opened the door a few inches and peered out nervously. "Yes?"

"I'm Lester Noble, Mrs. Hingham," he explained. "I told your son I'd be coming over."

Mrs. Hingham opened the door wider. "Oh, of course, forgive me. There's been so many things to think about. Come in."

A rush of anger swept Geneva. Lester was merely making a business call on their way to lunch.

"My son isn't here," Mrs. Hingham said. "My daughter-in-law will show you and Mrs. Noble around."

A colorless young woman came from a room at the back of the entrance foyer and introduced herself as Ada Hingham. She showed them through the four floors. Lester kept trying things, like opening closets and windows, asking Geneva for her opinion. Once they were back on the sidewalk in front of the house, he asked, "Well?"

"Well, what?"

"How do you like it?"

"Just terrif," Geneva said unenthusiastically.

Lester beamed. "Remember I said my mother's wedding present was being arranged? Well . . ."

Geneva didn't know what to say. A clomping horse-drawn wagon pulled to the curb near them.

"You mean that house . . . ?" Geneva gasped. Lester nodded with a wide grin.

"Potats! Nice-a-fresh potats!" yelled the swarthy wagon driver.

Geneva threw her arms around Lester and kissed his cheek. She knew all the houses in this neighborhood were owned by whites. They'd be the first coloreds in the block.

"You live-a here?" the wagon driver called to them. "Franco Donato's gotta cheap potats. Stock 'em for winter. You betta buy quick!" He sounded as though he had learned the words two syllables at a time. He displayed a toothy smile when he passed, and tipped his hat.

Geneva bubbled over. She turned to the driver and called back, "We don't live here yet, but we soon will!" She took Lester's hands and danced him around in circles. She could see heads curiously peeking out of the house next door. *Let them think we're crazy*, she thought, *who cares? Now I've got a house of my own without Mother Noble underfoot. Better yet—in a white neighborhood! Harlem's black elite will have to sit up and take notice of me now, if they haven't already.*

As a pleasant-faced white woman passed and ascended the staircase next to her new house, Geneva realized Harlem's white world would take notice, too. Her feelings of gratification all but submerged her in euphoria.

Her ecstasy didn't vanish until later in the day. That was when Geneva heard for the first time that Lester's mother would be moving with them.

Chapter Eight

Walking down Seventh Avenue to the barbershop, Fletcher Deel felt lighter than the drifting snowflakes. His feet seemed to skim over the damp pavement where the snow landed and quickly melted. He was thinking of the painting he had sold earlier that week at a higher price than he ever imagined. And to top it off, only moments ago, he heard the good news that a grant was on its way to him from the Davies Foundation. With the exception of Walter White and Alain Locke, everyone thought the organization that had become the one true artery of help for Negro artists was going to fold following the death of its founder, the philanthropist Jack Davies. However, the success of the all-Negro art exhibit the Davies sponsored at International House seemed to have reestablished its financial viability, and recently the foundation had been awarding more generous grants than ever before.

Everything good was happening at once, he thought. First Langston Hughes's piece in *The Nation* mentioned Deel as one of five dedicated artists adding "bright energy" to Harlem's Renaissance. Then a white critic for *Art News Today* wrote, "Fletcher Deel turns the Negro soul inside out, delving into deeper passages of the colored psyche than any other artist has dared journey before." He memorized the entire article. It was like poetry. After five years of ups and downs and never quite arriving, Fletcher couldn't help congratulating himself on his sudden burst of prominence, and his brushstroke was becoming more confident every day. Now, even Ernestine Rose was setting up an exhibit for him at her library on 114th Street. Miss Rose, as she preferred to be called, was a fussy elderly woman who knew every major writer, poet, sculptor, and artist in Harlem and had all the right connections with the art and literary world outside. When *she* paid a compliment to an artist, that was as high an endorsement as anyone could hope for.

Reaching the barbershop door, he paused for a moment and let his breath slow to normal after the brisk walk through the snow-filled air. His weekly ritual visit was the one luxury Fletcher allowed himself, even during his bad days. He loved chewing the fat and sparring with his creative peers. He loved the strong odor of witch hazel, the pungent soaps. They always reminded him for some reason of his early years back in St. Louis when his mother used to bathe him in the enormous old enameled tub in the bathroom above the family store.

Everyone who was anyone in Harlem's artistic circles hung out at the barbershop. So when Fletcher opened the door and went inside, it was no surprise to see Howard Dobbins, a playwright who borrowed money all the time; Lionel Tripp, an abstract sculptor who wasn't too good at it but knew all the right people; Dandy Reed, a composer who played stride piano at the Lafayette on weekends and played around with women the rest of the week; Countee Cullen, the well-known poet; and Booty Hay, an actor who consistently appeared in plays at the Lafayette Theater.

"Hey, my man!" shouted Booty, first to notice Fletcher in the doorway. "Been readin' good things about you."

"Hear Miss Rose is gonna hang you at the library," yelled Lionel from the back with a touch of envy in his tone.

Fletcher confirmed with a nod, hooked his topcoat on the wall, and sank into the only empty chair to await his turn with one of the four barbers. He wanted to brag a little about the grant, but he knew this wasn't the group to boast to. They'd pull him apart in seconds if he did.

"Speaking of hanging, how are they?" asked Howard in his sarcastic manner.

"Fair to middlin'," murmured Fletcher, offhand and casual.

"Keepin' your hand in?" This came from Booty.

"When I get the chance."

"That's what we heard," slyly intoned Dobbins with a snicker.

Fletcher didn't like the insinuation. "If you spent as much time on writing, Dobbins, as you do on bullshit, you might've won the Pulitzer for *Wild Pickin's.*"

The crowd hooted and hollered appreciatively.

At that point, Countee Cullen, who was being trimmed, broke in. "I still say *Wild Pickin's* should have won. Your play shows those pretentious, bourgeois, self-satisfied fools who read the *Age* exactly as they are—nothing but poor imitations of white society who turn their back on their own people."

"They turned their back on the play, too," fawned Dobbins at the tribute from Cullen, "but it's still selling out every night. And there's a good chance, in a few years after the run is over, you'll be seeing it return to Broadway. George Gershwin himself is talkin' about setting it to music."

"That'll be the day!" jeered Dandy as he loosened his collar. "Tell us another!"

"How would Fletcher know anything about what's going on?" Dobbins whined. "He's too busy . . . indoors."

"What do you mean by that?" Fletcher wanted to know.

He watched a wet towel slap down on Dobbins's owlish face, muffling any rejoinder he might have had in mind. Fletcher was miffed at his remark. He knew perfectly well what the man was referring to, but as far as Fletcher was concerned, his private life was nobody's damn business.

Dandy then turned his attention to Fletcher. "How come you never hang out at the Shimmy Room no more, with or without any available, unmentionable young pulchritude?"

"Who needs that cheap cellar!" Fletcher shot back. "Or your third-rate piano? The booze ain't worth shit and the whores even less!"

The shop broke into a roar of hooting laughter. "Seems like I hit a nerve!" screamed Dandy, slapping his leg.

"More like hittin' below the belt," snorted Countee.

The heat was beginning to get to Fletcher, although he usually took this group's harassing in stride. Then Lionel stuck his oar in. "They say you keep cooped up in your studio night and day . . . jus' strokin' and strokin', instead of paintin'. That right?"

That was all Fletcher needed to hear. He decided it was time to stop the conversation. "You can all go get fucked! You're worse than a bunch of old washerwomen!"

Fletcher was relieved to hear the gossip quickly switch to politics. It wasn't until after his haircut, while his barber was brushing off his shirt, that his situation cropped up again.

"Let's face it, Fletcher. We hear you got a hot piece of young Southern corn bread locked up in your studio and she's always begging for more 'n more butter . . . more 'n more corn . . ." By this time, Lionel Tripp's snide innuendos resounded through the shop. Even Countee stopped talking. Making matters worse, Tripp added, "She must be real hot for that corn of yours. Damn, man. She's not lettin' you come up for air!"

Ordinarily, Fletcher was easygoing, until he got truly upset. Then his temper went out of control. This happened now. He jumped from his chair and clutched Tripp's collar. Tripp's face turned to dark mustard as Fletcher tightened his grip. He lifted the shorter man out of his chair by the neck until Tripp's feet were off the floor. The surprised customers all stopped chattering at once. The barbers stopped their electric razors and posed like frozen statues beside their chairs. Every face turned toward Fletcher. The place was totally still.

"Take that back," Fletcher snarled in a whisper.

"Jeez, Fletch . . . I was only kiddin'," pleaded Tripp, gasping. "I didn't mean nothin'. C'mon, huh?"

Fletcher slowly let Tripp's feet return to the floor.

The shop remained quiet.

To save face, Tripp acted nonchalant. He took heavy steps to the mirror, throwing resentful looks at Fletcher's reflection, and adjusted his tie. Then he mumbled, "I ain't never saw a man make such a fuss over a piece of pussy."

Fletcher's large hand swung Tripp around and planted a heavy blow to his jaw. Tripp flew backward a good ten feet and landed between chair number four and a long settee where six men sat awaiting their turn. The faces turned away from Fletcher and stared at Tripp, who lay stretched out, unmoving. Then, almost immediately, aimless chatter began to fill the room as if nothing had happened.

"Next!" shouted the barbers at chairs one and two where Fletcher and Tripp had been sitting. Two customers left the settee and stepped over Tripp. When Fletcher left the shop, Tripp still lay unconscious on the floor, snoring.

The flakes were falling faster. The temperature had dropped and snow was now sticking to the sidewalks. Harlem never looked as exciting to Fletcher as it did under a coating of fresh snowfall. His blood still ran fast from Lionel Tripp's nasty remarks, but the clean look of everything outside seemed to help. By the time Fletcher walked to his old loft building, he had calmed down.

Even before he reached the top floor, he heard voices in the studio. Dewey and Chick were lying on the floor near a large table, making a mess of things with a set of watercolors Fletcher had given them. Billie was working under the light at the sink in the curtained alcove that sectioned off the kitchen.

He still couldn't get accustomed to the glow of Billie's skin. He'd never seen her kind of beauty before. It went far beyond the skin. It was in the green eyes with their oriental cast; the perfectly composed face, the high forehead, the straight nose; the sharply etched mouth and frugal lips; the firm jawline and the soft cascade of deep-black hair. Perhaps, he thought, it had to do most of all with the way she held herself, like a goddess. Her body suggested mysterious depths and unbelievable delights for the man who could win her.

Fletcher knew full well why his last paintings sold so quickly and received so much attention. It had little to do with his deft new brushstroke, which a number of critics had commented on. It was Billie's dominating presence in them.

She must have felt Fletcher's eyes on her. She looked up from the carrot she was peeling, a smile spreading across her enchanting face. "I didn't hear you come in." Even her voice held the faraway quality of a dream. He couldn't believe this woman was still in her teens. "It's snowing," Fletcher said.

"I know. We were up on the roof until Dewey got cold."

By the time Adam showed up, Fletcher and Billie had decided to go sledding after supper.

Adam was morose again and had little to say. Fletcher could tell he still resented Virginia for talking him out of returning to Florida. Adam once rambled on about it when they'd drank too much bootleg gin after the others had gone off to bed.

"There ain't nothin' 'cept shinin' shoes for folks like me," he had complained, filling his glass. "I don't speak good 'nough for porter 'n bellhop jobs they says, and my hands ain't fast 'nough for factory work. They says I ain't smart 'nough to be no janitor. Workin' on the docks is out 'cause they ain't gonna let a colored man in the union. In fact, I'm too dark to run an elevator."

At this time, Fletcher recalled, they started drinking straight from the bottle.

"Workin' the soil's all I can do anyhow. I never shoulda come here."

Fletcher could see pride was eating him up. Virginia and Billie were both earning money and he wasn't. He knew the only work Adam ever got was on days when the regular potato hauler at the storehouse went on another drinking binge. "Hey, it'll all be different once you land something permanent," Fletcher said, trying to lift Adam's spirits. "You'll see." After taking a swig, Fletcher suddenly had an idea. "Why don't you go to night school with Billie?"

"I's too old for that," Adam frowned.

"That ain't so. And it'll help you get a job," Fletcher pointed out.

"By then it'll be too late," Adam had obstinately maintained.

After that, Adam still hadn't found any permanent work. Fletcher knew he was hanging out most of the time at Mervyn's Pool Parlor. Whenever Fletcher passed the place, he'd see Adam inside cadging bootleg and hustling a game. Not that Fletcher blamed him. What else could the poor man do?

Shortly after seven, Virginia returned to the studio from her house cleaning job. Fletcher noticed that Adam hardly acknowledged her arrival. Fletcher hated to see Virginia's hurt expression. He felt sorry for her. Despite her cheerful banter, he could tell she was unhappy because Adam was so miserable.

During supper, Fletcher realized only Chick and Dewey were unaware of the tension around the table. They chattered endlessly about life in Harlem and their new friends. Throughout

their talk, Virginia's face smiled with interest, but Fletcher
sensed her heart wasn't in it.

After supper, Fletcher peered out a window. The snow was
coming down faster than ever. He looked back inside. Virginia
was getting Chick and Dewey ready for bed, and Adam was
solemnly lost in thought at the table. "I thought we were going
coasting," he reminded Billie.

"I plumb forgot," cried a delighted Billie. "I've never been
coasting."

Her enthusiasm made Fletcher feel like a teenager again instead of a man of twenty-eight. They wrapped themselves up
in their heaviest clothes and Fletcher took her hand and led
her down to the basement where he dug through trunks and
boxes until he found an old sled he'd purchased his first
winter in Harlem and never used. When they reached the
street, the snow was nearly six inches deep and beginning to
pack down. Fletcher insisted Billie sit on the sled, and he pulled
her along the sidewalks as if she were a child. They journeyed
crosstown past apartments with windows frosted from steam
heat through what seemed like a snowball fight in every other
block among the neighborhood kids. Finally, they reached
Morningside Heights where they joined other coasters, mostly
adults bundled in scarves laughing like children as they sledded
down the steep slope to the side of St. John's Cathedral, a large
square building that looked remarkably like pictures of Notre
Dame in Paris. It was an ideal spot that was bordered by the
black steel girders of the Ninth Avenue elevated trains that sped
around the corner of 110th Street with a singsong screech.
From the top of the hill you could see Central Park beyond the
train tracks.

Fletcher decided it was the exhilaration of the first snow that caused people to offer their flasks to him and Billie as if they'd known them all their lives. Everyone acted as though they were old friends. Even Billie, who usually never touched a drop, drank from each flask that came her way.

"You won't tell Adam," she made Fletcher promise. "He'd have a fit," she laughed.

The cathedral bell was ringing midnight as they coasted down for the last time. "We'll come tomorrow night, too," Fletcher shouted excitedly before they reached the bottom.

Billie shook her head. "I have school tomorrow night."

Fletcher's excitement dropped a few degrees. He'd completely forgotten.

The snow still fell while they trudged back across Harlem to the loft. Occasionally, Billie would pick up a mitten full of snow and playfully throw it at him. Whenever she did, Fletcher chased her and swung her around after he caught her. Once, they both slipped and fell together into a snowdrift, giggling like ten-year-olds. Suddenly their giggling stopped. Fletcher could feel the heat of her body through his clothes. He had an overwhelming urge to sink his face into her glorious halo of hair, to kiss her, to make all of her his.

He stifled his impulse. He was almost fifteen years older, a grown man. Billie was still a child, no matter what she thought. If he took advantage of her now, in a few years she might feel cheated and used. He'd seen it happen to other girls too young to know what they wanted. He wouldn't let it happen to Billie.

Reluctantly, Fletcher's arms released her. Her giggling began again as she scrambled to her feet. "I've never had so much fun in my life," she laughed, kissing his cheek and helping him up.

When they approached Jungle Alley, Fletcher was amazed that even in the storm, crowds still wandered about half-drunk looking for thrills to jolt them out of their daytime boredom and carry them through the night.

"One of these days I'm going inside one of those clubs and see what they're like," Billie threatened in a joking tone.

"If I were you," he teased, "I'd wait till I was grown-up."

Billie punched his arm. "Oh you! You're as bad as Adam!" Then she ran ahead of him, making Fletcher run after her until they reached the loft.

Fletcher dropped off Billie at the door, said good night, then walked up the steps that led to the roof where he had built his hideaway bedroom out of old lumber and stained-glass windows found in junk shops. When he got to the top, he heard Virginia's voice.

"Can I talk to you?" She had followed him up.

"Of course," Fletcher said, wondering what was on her mind. They stood on the landing. Through the open door, he could see the silent, peaceful snow blanketing the roof.

Virginia looked at him sadly. Her neck muscles were tight with strain, and small lines had formed at the corners of her mouth. She had changed considerably since she first brought her family to his loft and into his life, he thought. The soft, pliant quality seemed to have vanished.

"We owe you so much," she said in almost a whisper. Fletcher bent closer to hear her better. "But I'm worried about Adam."

"He'll be all right once he gets a job."

"He hates me for having one," she said. "I can feel his resentment. He wants to be the man of the family. Now he thinks I've taken *that* away from him." She turned her head toward the snow. "You'd think I *liked* cleanin' other people's places," she said with a bitter laugh.

Fletcher didn't know what to say. He knew how hard she worked, how much she wanted Chick and Dewey to have opportunities she and Adam never had, how much she believed in learning. He once heard her say, "We can't jus' hang back 'cause the white folks wants us to, and we can't fall in love with bein' poor and using it for a reason why we can't get ahead." Shortly after that, Billie enrolled in night school, but Fletcher had a hunch Virginia had said it for Adam's benefit.

"You don't owe me a thing," Fletcher finally said. "If it wasn't for Billie, things wouldn't be going so well for me and the painting now."

"We can't stay here forever."

All of a sudden, Fletcher wondered if this wasn't the heart of what she wanted to talk about. If it was, he didn't care to hear it. Once they moved, he would see Billie only when there was modeling work for her, and he dreaded that day. "We'll talk about it some other time," he said. "You can stay here as long as you wish."

He watched Virginia walk down to the studio, her shoulders tight and uncompromising. He thought, *Don't take Billie away. There's no reason in the world why you all can't stay here forever.* Then he turned and walked across the roof through the snow to his chilly homemade sanctuary. Once undressed, he hurriedly got under a heavy quilted comforter and lay on his secondhand mattress. Usually he fell asleep immediately, but tonight he lay

awake remembering the feel of Billie's body after they fell in the
snowdrift. He could still smell the young sweetness of her hair
as if she were close against him even now.

He realized with a start that he'd never been in love before.
He'd often thought he was, but now it was obvious that what
he'd felt with other women was merely some diluted imitation
of what he felt for Billie.

Early the next morning, Fletcher was awakened by a long,
piercing scream that floated up from the floor below. He
hopped out of bed, pulled on a pair of pants, and ran down to
the studio. Chick and Dewey were still in their bed. They stared
across the loft, frightened and unsure. Another scream echoed
through the apartment. *Oh my God*, he thought. *Something awful
has happened to her!*

At first he couldn't see any sign of Billie. He pulled back the
hanging fabric that partitioned off her sleeping area. She wasn't
there. He ran to where Virginia and Adam slept. It was then
that he found her. She was struggling with a writhing, kicking
Virginia.

"What is it?" he asked. "What happened?"

At that moment, Virginia let out another screeching wail and
broke free of Billie's grasp. She ran about the loft, crazed and
distraught. "He's gone!" she moaned. "He's left us!" She
dropped to her knees like a rag doll, spent and broken. "He's
gone," she whimpered hopelessly.

Fletcher helped Billie get her back to bed. Billie sat beside
Virginia and rocked her in her arms. "He'll be back," she comforted her, but Virginia didn't seem to hear.

"He's left us," Virginia sobbed. "He's never been happy
here."

Fletcher helped Chick and Dewey get dressed and fixed them bowls of oatmeal. He wondered what they thought of all this, if they were upset. Neither one had uttered a word since Fletcher came in, and now they were eating their cereal in uncommon silence. "Everything all right?" Fletcher asked them.

Chick spoke first. "I been thinking . . . Will Daddy be here when I get back from school?"

"You crazy or somethin'?" Dewey said. "Sure he will. Least-wise by suppertime."

"That's what I figured," Chick replied, gobbling down the last spoonful.

Billie was still rocking Virginia when Chick was leaving. Fletcher could hear him running down the stairs, then Chick yelling, "Hey! You got back sooner'n we expected!" Seconds later, Adam walked in.

Virginia dashed across the floor. She threw herself into Adam's arms. "You didn't go back home!"

"Back home? What's gotten into you, woman?" Adam laughed. "You think I'd jus' up and leave you an' Billie an' the boys an' go back home?"

"You weren't here when I woke up . . . ." Tears ran down Virginia's face. "That's never happened before."

"I jus' didn't want to bother you. You needed your rest. I had to see someone early." Adam kissed her while he beckoned to Fletcher, who was heading for the door.

"C'mon an' have some coffee with us, Fletch. I got somethin' to say."

While Billie made coffee, Fletcher sat at the table with Adam and Virginia and listened to Adam's news. His eyes, though, stayed on Billie's face.

"I got me a job," Adam said proudly.

"What kind?" Virginia asked jubilantly.

"Nothing to brag about, but it's a job."

Fletcher looked from Billie to Adam with the news. Adam's dour expression was gone for the first time in weeks, and he seemed more at peace than Fletcher ever remembered seeing him. Then another thought occurred to Fletcher. If Adam had a job now, the family would definitely be leaving the studio for a place of their own. He couldn't pretend to himself any longer that Billie would always be around. *Soon,* he thought, *men will be flocking after her, begging for her attentions, pleading for her favors.*

A cold sense of loss ran down Fletcher's backbone. *Not only will I be seeing less of Billie,* he speculated, *but someday soon, there's a good possibility I might not see Billie at all.*

Chapter Nine

With good reason, Adam decided to spare Virginia the details about the job he'd finally found. When she asked questions about it one Sunday afternoon, he said, "It's with a white company. They're kinda in the wholesale business."

Billie and Fletcher had taken Chick and Dewey for a walk so Adam and Virginia could have the luxury of being alone. They seldom had the opportunity these days, and now they were relaxing in bed.

"Many coloreds working with you?" Virginia pressed.

Adam sidestepped. "I haven't met them all."

"But what exactly do you do?"

He could see she was brimming with pride that after all these months he had located something. He wanted to satisfy her, but he didn't have the courage. He knew she'd disapprove and beg him to give it up. He also knew he wouldn't. He had vowed never again would he lose his manhood and sponge off his wife and Billie the way he'd been doing. For an uneducated, colored Southern farmer who was new in town, he'd soon discovered a legitimate job was impossible to land. It was bad enough for the educated colored men who had lived in Harlem for years. It was either this job or nothing. So instead of telling her the truth, he purposely became vague. "Oh, lots of different things. Helping the managers out . . . things like that . . ."

"Where's the office?" she asked.

"Not too far. Near the storehouse where I used to load the wagons." He pulled the blanket over his shoulder and kissed her, hoping that would get her mind on other things.

Virginia's soft, gentle manner had returned overnight. "I love you, my Adam," she whispered into his shoulder.

An hour later, the scent of oil and turpentine invaded Adam's senses. He let his eyes roam from Virginia to the high ceiling and realized why he smelled it. The odor was so embedded in everything, he was used to it and hardly noticed it. But now . . . "I 'spect we can get our own place," he said.

Virginia hugged him tighter. "Can't we wait till after New Year's? Fletcher doesn't want us to leave, and he'll feel better about it if we wait."

" 'Spect we can do that," agreed Adam, "but there's another thing on my mind." He knew Virginia wouldn't admit it, but she was working too hard. She held two cleaning jobs, which kept her hopping six days a week from eight in the morning until seven at night. Yet she still found time when she was home to bake sweet potato pies, mend clothes, iron and wash, and sew up new clothes on the sewing machine he and Fletcher found in the trash bin and fixed. She only allowed Billie to cook the meals and wash dishes. But that was all going to change. "Now that I got me a reg'lar job, my wife ain't gonna work outside no more."

He felt Virginia's body go tense in his arms. She sighed. "There's so much we gotta have. Let's talk about me not workin' some other time. Besides, Miss Best is nice, an' so's Miss Wilson. I couldn't just let them down now they're used to me."

The morning of Christmas Eve, Adam hurried to Broadway and 127th Street where it was arranged he'd meet his co-workers. Everywhere he looked, he saw old broken-down tenements that made Fletcher's loft building seem like a palace. At this point 127th Street became a dirt road, more of an alley than a street. Colored faces stared out from doorways and second-floor windows, looking suspiciously at everyone passing. Colored bodies in ragged clothes walked aimlessly about or sat hopelessly on curbs, already drunk on cheap hootch or high on reefers. He couldn't help thinking how lucky they were to have stumbled on to Fletcher's studio. *Thank God*, he thought. *Otherwise, we'd be here, too.*

As Adam approached the waiting crew of workers, he noticed that Charley, the boss of the Neighborhood Betterment Company, was already there. "Where the fuck you been?" Charley shouted at him. "You was supposed to been here five minutes ago!"

"So I's here, ain't I!" Adam shouted back. He refused to let Charley think he'd kowtow to him just because he was white. That was one thing Adam had learned. It wasn't the same as back home. Up here, if the whites didn't like what you said, they either fought you like a man, instead of hiding behind the

law and white robes, or they let it pass. Some of them even
favored you when you showed you had spunk. Adam knew that
for a fact because Charley told him so one day in the poolroom
when Adam hustled him into a game, won two dollars off him,
and almost beat Charley up after Charley tried to squirm out of
the bet.

"Hey, big boy! Take it easy! Slow down," Charley said that
afternoon, pulling out a fat wallet and throwing the two dollars
on the pool table. The next thing he knew, Charley was asking
him if he wanted a job.

Adam nodded that he did.

"In that case, meet us at five tomorrow morning. The company's gettin' together then and we'll see how the other guys
feel about ya." Charley gave Adam the address.

"Five's a touch early, ain't it?" It sounded like a funny time
for a meeting.

"For Chrissakes! You want the job or don't cha?" Charley
loosened his belt and belched.

"I'll be there," Adam told him.

The next morning, a little after five, Adam had felt uneasy.
No one said much. The meeting had been held in a dingy back
room located behind a narrow vegetable store that smelled ran-
cid from rotting tomatoes. Charley called it "headquarters."
Four other men stood around the room, stared at Adam for a
while, finally put their heads together and whispered a few
things Adam couldn't hear. Then they told him to start work
the next day. Since that day, Adam had spent most of his time
sitting around headquarters with little to do except occasionally
bullying small storeowners into paying overdue bills for bootleg
or simply collecting money they owed for insurance policies.

Today, however, he'd been told an important assignment was planned. "You do good on this operation and I might move ya up a notch," Charley promised, putting his arm around Adam's shoulder.

Adam stepped away from him. He looked over the assembled crew. "How come there ain't nothin' but coloreds here 'cept you?" Usually the men were mostly white, with only a sprinkling of colored faces.

"No reason. Just the way it worked out," Charley said evasively. He smoothed his greased hair. "We're goin' to the Bayou Club," he explained. "Ya know it?"

"Never heard of it."

Charley burst into an unpleasant guffaw. "That's 'cause it ain't opened yet, Lambert!"

Charley then turned to the group of jabbering men waiting for instructions. He raised his hand but they didn't respond. "Shut up, ya fucks!" he yelled. "Now listen to what I'm gonna say!" When the men went quiet, Adam noticed Charley's walk took on a swagger of importance. "We're paying a little visit on a buncha cheats who thought they could get away with screwing the company." Charley picked up a stick and smacked the side of his coat to emphasize his words. "They think Santa Claus gonna come down the chimney with a shitload of money 'cause it's Christmas Eve. Well, he ain't! Those cheezy wops stole the band away from one of our speaks an' for that . . . they're gonna pay." He snapped the stick in half. His face turned red. "The company's gonna teach 'em a lesson! They don't open tonight! They don't open never! Got that?"

The Bayou Club, Adam discovered, was in Jungle Alley, a block away from Connie's Inn. He and the other men followed

Charley to a red banner announcing: "Gala Opening Tonight!" which was stretched above a canopied entrance. As they stood looking up at it, a man in a business suit joined Charley. "Hiya, Lieutenant Baxter. Did Owney talk to ya yet?" Charley asked,

The man roughly grabbed Charley's arm. "Asshole! Why not tell the whole goddamned precinct!" He pulled Charley into a doorway a few buildings down from the canopy.

A few minutes later, a chagrined Charley soberly walked back toward Adam. "Everything's under control." He indicated the doorway where the man in the business suit stood watching. "Mr. . . . er . . . Smith, there, says no one'll bother us." Charley threw his shoulders back. "Okay," he signaled to the men. "Let's go."

For a split second, Adam wished he were somewhere else. Getting people to pay their debts was one thing, but this seemed nasty. Then he thought of the months when he hadn't earned any money at all, and he knew he couldn't return to that kind of existence. He had no choice.

He followed the others into the club and looked around the large room. Fake moss hung down from papier-mâché trees. A long bar that ran across the width of the room at the rear was supported by imitation bales of cotton. Varnished murals of misty swamplands and lazing alligators covered the side walls. At the front of the room stood a raised stage designed to look like a terraced levee. An orchestra with a bass drum that proclaimed "Jesse Davis and His Kings of Joy" was rehearsing there. Sandwiching the stage were huge painted tapestries showing black men in animal skin loincloths chasing nude white women with flowing blond hair. Adam had never seen anything like it. He started to chuckle.

"Shut up!" Charley hissed at him.

Adam cut off the sound in his throat and turned his attention to a man sawing wood in a far corner. In another corner, a man with a broom was sweeping to the tempo of the music while someone else was adjusting spotlights on the stage. Two men sat at a center table in front of the stage going through a card file and counting money. When one of them looked up and saw Charley, he nudged the other. The two men jumped up so quickly, the table tipped over, scattering the money and the cards on the floor.

"Whaddya' want?" one of them yelled.

"Nothin'," said Charley. To Adam, his voice sounded as cool as a cucumber. "We just wanta offer our sympathy, that's all."

"Yeah? Sympathy for what?" yelled the other.

"For not being able to open tonight," cooed Charley in what Adam had come to recognize as his most dangerous tone. "We stopped by to wish you a Merry Christmas!"

Adam and the others had been told this was the signal. Charley held a gun on the two owners while the gang followed his instructions. They tore down the Spanish moss. They knocked over the trees. They threw buckets of paint on the murals and tapestries. They ripped open the cotton bales with long knives and shattered bottles until the bar was a shambles of broken debris. After the chairs and tables were smashed, Adam and the others headed for the stage.

The orchestra had stopped rehearsing and its members stared out at the destruction with slack mouths. They looked scared to death, as if they didn't know whether it was safer to run or smarter to stay.

"Keep on playing!" Charley ordered. "And play louder!"

Shakily, the men lifted their instruments and did their best to continue, but for years after, whenever Adam heard "Wang Wang Blues," he'd think of that morning. He knew the band didn't have to worry. Charley had given everyone strict instructions not to hurt them or touch their instruments, boasting to Adam that they were needed in good condition since they'd be back that night at Connie's Inn. "That's where they played before the Bayou Club offered them more loot," Charley had said, "and that's where they're still gonna play. What they don't know is that tonight, they're playing for no money at all. They're donating their services 'cause they was bad boys. But you can bet your ass they never will be again."

Adam and his co-workers demolished the front of the stage and turned the levee into a pile of splintered wood. By then, there was nothing left to destroy. Charley fired a single shot into the ceiling. This, Adam had been told, was the signal to leave. Instead, Charley changed his plans. "Before we kiss this pretty place good-bye," he cooed, "let's have a little head crackin'!"

The band players fled the stage. Adam and the others balked. This wasn't what they'd been hired for, and they didn't like it.

"Fuck off!" Adam shouted. "We done our job an' we's goin'."

Charley pointed his gun at Adam, then fired. The bullet whizzed a few inches above Adam's head. "You may have done ya job, but ya ain't going nowhere. You wait, everyone of ya's, until I'm good an' ready."

With these words, Charley shot a bullet into the feet of each of the two club owners. Adam refused to watch and moved off by himself.

A cloakroom was near the entrance. In a flash, the man who

was sawing wood leaped out of it, brandishing a broken table leg. "If it's head cracking you want—" Adam heard him saying before everything blurred.

It was Charley, on his way out, who first saw Adam on the floor. Blood ran down his face from a cut on the forehead. "What the fuck happened to you?" Charley asked.

Adam was just coming to. "I don't know. This guy . . ." He tried to touch the stickiness on his face, but his right arm felt numb and wouldn't move.

Charley helped him up. "You're pretty dumb," he joked.

By the time Adam got back to the loft, he was feeling more like normal. His arm wasn't numb anymore and he breathed with relief. He had been sure it was broken. The studio was empty. Virginia was working. He guessed Billie and Fletcher were still out Christmas shopping, and he gathered from the conversation at breakfast that Chick and Dewey were off playing with the Donato kids.

Adam patted cold water on the cut in his forehead, trying to make it appear less ugly. As he inspected it in the partially oxidized mirror that hung above the kitchen sink, he laughed. "At least I ain't got a black eye."

Virginia was the first to return. As soon as she got a good look at him she shouted, "Oh my goodness! I had a feeling somethin' bad was goin' to happen today."

"It ain't so bad. Some guys jumped me," Adam lied, "but they didn't get nothin'."

Chapter Ten

The New Year's Eve party at Corky Johnson's was the first party the Lamberts had been invited to up North. Corky was an aspiring poet friend of Fletcher's who lived on the street floor of Fletcher's building.

"It's mighty convenient," Virginia had said when Adam waved the invitation. "But we hardly know the man. Why is he invitin' us, I wonder . . ."

Actually, the invitation had come to Adam through Fletcher, who'd picked it up that morning at his barbershop where they'd been left to distribute among the patrons. "It's a rent party," Adam explained. "Like we have down home . . ."

Fletcher was hauling some new canvases into the studio at the time. He could tell Adam was trying to stir up some enthusiasm from Virginia, but it didn't seem to be working.

He read the invitation aloud. "Hey! Jive and pig's feet! Gut buckets and chitterlin's! Hot brown mamas and rice! Bring your own dice! A social strut at Little Corky Johnson's Place on New Year's Eve. Come on over and shake it till you break it!"

"How much does it cost?" Virginia queried.

"Fifteen cents apiece."

"Guess we can afford that," she commented after thinking it over, beginning to warm to the idea. "And the boys are spending the night with the Donato kids. But what about Billie?"

Adam thought a minute. "You're right. We can't leave her alone."

Fletcher was at the doorway. "Why can't she come?"

"She's too young . . ."

"No she isn't." Fletcher interjected. "Corky left stacks of invitations at beauty shops, stores, all over. There'll be plenty of girls even younger. Besides, I'll be there to take care of her."

Fletcher seemed to hold his breath until Adam agreed Billie could go.

Billie appeared first that night. Fletcher hoped she couldn't tell how nervous her beauty made him. She wore a pink satin dress, a hand-me-down from one of Virginia's employers. She couldn't have looked better if the dress had been made for her, Fletcher thought.

When Virginia parted the bedroom curtain and stepped out, Adam whistled. She smiled self-consciously, and twirled around to model a dark green dress she'd made over the holidays. "How do I look?" she asked.

"Good enough to eat," Adam said. "Let's skip the party and stay here."

Virginia laughed, then remembered that Fletcher and Billie

were within earshot. "Hush up. You're not going to get out of taking us, now that we're dressed."

"You ladies are the berries," said Fletcher.

"What?" Virginia asked.

"Jazz club lingo," he replied. "You look great. Now let's go and do some struttin'!"

W hen they arrived, the party was going strong. Blue lights glowed from all the lamps, casting an eerie, dreamlike atmosphere on Corky Johnson's apartment. All of his furniture, with the exception of a few straight-backed chairs, had been removed to make more space. Swaying bodies were packed together everywhere—some in elaborate costumes, some in elegant evening attire, others in erotic near-nudity. A couple of women wore white tuxedos and smoked cigars; a few men reeked of perfume. Everyone, though, seemed to be having a hysterically good time, and everyone knew Fletcher.

"This is my crowd," he explained to Billie. "The Harlem Bohemian set. Most of them are creative pretenders, but a few of us are the real thing," he joked.

"I hate phony balonies," she said with an amused expression.

Corky Johnson, a slightly built man who looked as if he didn't have to shave, popped up in front of them with a cigar box in hand. Fletcher dropped in their admission money. "This one's on me," he said as Adam protested.

"Proud to greet you and glad to meet you," rhymed Corky in a loud shout to make himself heard above the ear-shattering din once Fletcher introduced the Lamberts. He pointed at the old upright piano in a nearby corner. "At the ivories sits young Dandy Reed, playing all the music you'll ever need."

Fletcher explained to Adam and the others, "Corky talks only in couplets at parties. He thinks it proves he's a poet."

Corky was pleased by Fletcher's good-natured ribbing. Then he stared at Billie in her satin dress and said, "I've never seen in all the city, any gal who's half as pretty." With this, Corky was off greeting other new arrivals with his collection box.

Once Fletcher's eyes became adjusted to the dim light, he checked out who was around. There was always a good crowd at Corky's parties, but the printed invitations drew an even bigger one. Young girls with sleek, bobbed hair flirted outrageously. Older women with too much lipstick and fluffed hair smiled seductively at Dandy, who announced he was going to sing a song he wrote. Two couples attempting to dance in the crowded room, bumped others with their behinds to make more space for themselves. In the corner beside the piano, a snare drum and bass fiddle had joined Dandy.

". . . Highbrows, lowbrows, so-and-so brows, shimmy with your Jimmy through the Harlem night . . ." he crooned.

Corky deftly wove in and out of the melee to hand Virginia and Adam a drink. "Gin leads to sin, so let's begin," he sing-songed and then wove away again.

"My goodness! Sure is a mess of people," Virginia said, her voice shaking nervously.

Adam protectively drew her closer. "You ain't skittish, is you?"

"Maybe just a touch," she confided.

They wandered into the next room. It was dimmer and more crowded with bodies than the first room. Couples were dancing closer together, and the smell of food assaulted their senses. They managed to squeeze past the dancers to the kitchen, where tables of collards and chitterlings and potato salad were set up.

A spontaneous outburst of squeals made Billie hold Fletcher's arm tighter, drawing them to the last room at the end of the flat. Once they were inside, Adam spotted what the excitement was all about.

"Can you beat that," he said. "With all these people, there's three crap games going on."

Faces closed in on the players, egging them on with shouts and taunts. There was so little elbow room, Adam wondered how anyone managed to throw the dice.

"I don't like gamblin'," Virginia said above the feverish chanting, reminding Fletcher of his own strong Baptist up-bringing.

He nodded to show he understood, then pushed aside the frenetic bodies that hemmed them in until they were back in the front of Corky's living room again. A plump albino woman was leaning against the piano, singing a sad song in an off-key voice about a mean man who took her money to entertain younger girlfriends, and yet she still loved the bum. Between choruses, the woman ran a fat, colorless hand through her colorless hair when she wasn't gulping gin.

Adam nudged Fletcher. "You'd think she'd get herself another man if'n he treats her that bad."

"Maybe that's what love does to you," Fletcher responded.

"Maybe," Billie suggested, "that's why they call it the blues."

Around them, people swayed to the music's beat, drank their tumblers dry, rushed to Corky's bathtub, which was filled with his homemade gin, returned with replenished glasses, swapped ribald jokes and gossiped, then drank some more. Everyone except Adam, Virginia, and Billie was getting drunker by the minute.

Dandy suddenly segued from the blues to "Ain't Misbehavin'," making each chorus faster than the preceding one, his fingers eventually flying about the keyboard, while his striding left hand pounded out a frantic beat, playing better than Fletcher ever remembered. Dandy had applied for a scholarship to study in Europe. With this display of talent, Fletcher understood why he was so confident of getting a grant. He played brilliantly. By now, the room was still except for the insistent piano. Every face seemed mesmerized by Dandy's playing. Without warning, Dandy finished a final chorus and shouted, "All right, then! You got it! Take it away!" and another musician slipped onto the piano stool and began to play without missing a beat.

"What are they doin'?" Virginia asked.

"Search me," Adam returned with a dumbfounded look.

Fletcher was about to explain when the plump albino woman screamed at the new pianist, "Oh go, Johnny, go! Break it down, baby!" She pulled a ten-dollar bill from between her substantial cleavage and fluttered it in front of her colorless face. "Who'll match my sawbuck on Johnny?" The new player was embroidering Dandy's last chorus, trying to prove he could play better and faster.

"I wish I understood," Virginia said.

"It's a cuttin' battle, whaddaya think?" someone beside them muttered. "The most original player wins."

"Thank you," Virginia said, but the head had turned away with a disgusted expression, and was yelling, "That's the way, Johnny! Make this a shout to remember!" A hand waved money in the air.

"He may call it a shout," Adam remarked, "but to me, it's still jus' an old-time rent party like we got back home."

Then as quickly as it began, the piano competition was over and the music turned sweet and mellow again. The albino woman still leaned against the piano, gulping from a glass, but now, Fletcher noticed, she was arguing loudly with a scarfaced, tough-looking man wearing a bowler hat about who actually won the cutting. Her voice boomed across the room.

"Don't hand me that shit! Dandy won! You owe *me!*"

Adam and Virginia were dancing as well as they could in the crowd to a slow version of "My Blue Heaven" when Fletcher noticed Billie had slipped off to the other room with a friend of Dandy's. He guessed it was obvious how he felt without her at his side, because Adam edged Virginia through the shoving crowd to him and asked, "What's wrong?"

Then Virginia noticed Billie wasn't with him. "Where's Billie?"

Fletcher nodded toward the next room, feeling empty and unhappy. "She's in there. Some guy who says she's wasting her time being my model is bending her ear." There was a sour ring in his voice, but he couldn't help himself. Adam seemed to sense how he felt because he said, "This is her first party up here. Makes a lotta sense if she talks with people besides you."

Fletcher didn't answer. He downed his drink and continued to lean against the wall, feeling lost.

The albino woman chose this moment to toss her gin in the face of the tough man with the scar. "You don't know shit!" she bellowed. No one paid the slightest attention to her. Even the tough man merely patted his wet face with a handkerchief, took the ten dollars from her hand, and walked to the next room. As the clock began to chime the countdown to twelve, Corky ran around turning off most of the blue lights, making Fletcher acutely aware of the winter moonlight outside the windows. More couples started to dance, and Fletcher felt all the lonelier. A muted trumpet added its voice to the band. Sliding feet set up a rhythm of their own. Adam and Virginia rejoined the swaying crowd and danced.

It was early in the morning by the time they stopped.

"Man, oh man," Adam said to Fletcher, slightly out of breath, "I ain't danced that much since Virginia and me started courtin'."

They found Billie in the packed back room. The acrid smell of reefer and body sweat was thick in the airless, smoke-heavy chamber. Billie was throwing the dice. She yelled with delight as she made her point. She merrily waved a wad of money in Adam's face.

"Little Billie's growing up," she laughed, throwing back the hair that had fallen in her eyes.

"C'mon, snake, show me them dots," a voice shouted.

Adam angrily took her arm. "Little Billie's goin' home." He directed her toward the door where Virginia was waiting.

A short man ran up to Billie as they were walking out of Corky's apartment. Fletcher resented the man on sight when

Dandy introduced him. His straightened hair was slicked down
with pomade, and his sharkskin suit as well as his teeth showed
too much gold.

"Don't forget what I told you," the man said to Billie. His
voice oozed hidden meaning.

"Don't worry. I won't," Billie drawled, flirting. Fletcher was
annoyed at himself for feeling jealous.

Finally, on their way upstairs, he frowned, "How'd he know
you modeled for me?"

"From your pictures hanging in the library."

"What did he want?" Fletcher persisted.

"Nothing special."

"I don't like him," Adam volunteered.

Billie shrugged sarcastically. "You don't have to like him.
He's *my* friend."

For a second Fletcher thought Adam was going to reprimand
her. Then Virginia quickly broke in. "I'm tired. What a party!"
She leaned cozily against Adam's chest. "There. That's better."

Once in the studio, Billie continued to jut her chin out rebel-
liously and ignore the men's presence. In no time at all, she
vanished behind her curtained-off bedroom.

Chapter Eleven

Adam loudly apologized to Fletcher for Billie's bad manners, making sure Billie heard him. Then he slammed the door.

"No sense doing that," Virginia told him calmly. "She was asleep before she hit her pillow."

Adam joined Virginia at the high wall of windows that overlooked the Harlem River, wrapping his arms around her tiny waist, softly kissing her neck as they gazed at the lightening sky.

"Look," Virginia pointed. "The sun's coming up. Happy New Year again!" She turned to him, pulled his head down, and kissed him. "Is it too late?" she whispered softly.

Adam knew perfectly well what she meant. "It's never too late," he whispered back, thinking, *It'll make me forget that rotten job and it'll make me forget the trouble Billie is startin' to cause.*

It didn't make him forget, though. Later in the afternoon, his worries came back stronger than ever.

Chapter Twelve

"This is it," Adam said to Chick and Dewey when they reached the run-down Victorian building. "Ya mama and Billie is already inside." He led the boys through the iron grillwork entrance of their new home on 112th Street off Lenox Avenue and ushered them into the hexagonal tiled foyer. He noticed that the boys' faces held the same expressions of pleased surprise his had when he first saw the place, thinking how grand it was. It wasn't until a closer look brought to light the cracked tiles, the painted-over, splintered wood paneling, and broken fixtures that Adam realized how dilapidated the building really was.

The two rooms they rented on the fourth floor were even worse. The five-room apartment had been subdivided into eleven rooms. As they walked up the stairs, Adam wished rents weren't so sky-high, wished he could afford something better.

Once they stepped inside, he seemed to notice more; the seedy furniture, the smell of cooking grease in the frayed curtains, the flimsy, dirty, ill-fitting partitions that were supposed to separate the rooms. He'd bet you could hear every snore of the other boarders. But as bad as the place was, Adam had no intention of letting Chick and Dewey know his feelings. "You fellas gonna have fun here," he enthused. "Plenty more than at Fletcher's."

"I liked it at Fletcher's," Dewey said.

A big, muscular woman with short, curly gray hair stood facing them. She held her hands on her hips. "This is our landlady, boys."

The woman who had turned her apartment into a rooming house scrutinized the boys. "Cute lil' devils, ain't ya. My name's Boss. Do what I tell you an' we'll get along fine. If you don't, you find another place to stay. Understand?"

Chick and Dewey looked at Adam. He hoped they caught the twinkle in his eye that said, "Don't take her to heart."

"As your father knows," Boss continued, "the kitchen and bathroom are public rooms. Each boarder has a schedule for when to use them. The living room is free to everyone till eleven, but"—she wagged a finger at the boys—"I don't want no loud noise, no mess. You understand?"

Chick and Dewey nodded that they understood, then Adam took them to their two adjoining rooms off the middle of a long hall. Billie and Virginia were inside unpacking clothes and putting them in the drawers of a peeling veneer dresser.

"I liked it better at Fletcher's," Dewey said, looking around.

Virginia glanced up from the unpacking. "We can't interfere in his life forever."

Adam added, "Now we got a place of our own. That's bet-ter'n livin' off other people."

"We'll have fun here," Chick said, flashing Dewey a glare.

After the first few days, it seemed to Adam that everyone accepted their new quarters; at least, they appeared to. He and Virginia occupied one room, while Billie and the boys slept on three cots in the second room. He discovered he was right about the partitions. You could hear everyone's snores.

Virginia continued to work at her house cleaning jobs. She had to, she told Adam, when he complained that she was doing too much and her health was suffering. "If I don't, we can't afford to stay here at Boss's." He knew this was true, but he hated to admit it to himself.

In the weeks that followed, Adam still worried about Billie's independent attitude. She never discussed her modeling for Fletcher anymore and hardly said more than hello or good-bye to him. He himself went off every day to the Neighborhood Betterment Company, even though he knew he should quit. The job bothered him more and more. Often, during free time, he looked around for something else, but he discovered jobs were no easier to find now than they'd been previously.

One spring morning while Adam ate breakfast, Boss stomped in. "I don't like the way you been misusing my kitchen. You and your family are always off schedule. Cookin' when you should be eatin', eatin' when you should be in the bathroom, in the bathroom when you should be leavin' for work. The other boarders don't like it none, neither."

Adam wanted to tell her what she could do with her schedule. Instead, he curbed his tongue. "Whatever you say."

She paraded her big, bulky body out of the rancid-smelling kitchen with heavy, deliberate steps. "Get your habits in line," she ordered, disappearing into the living room.

Later that same morning, Adam got word that a major operation was set for the afternoon. Charley and the other white men who ran things at the company gathered everyone into "headquarters" and told Adam and his co-workers to listen to a man named Owney Madden, who was dressed in a fancy suit. They said he owned the Cotton Club. He said that he and the other club owners were adding a fin to each man's pay for the day; that they were sick of colored radicals complaining about speakeasies and campaigning to get bootleggers kicked out of Harlem.

"It's the nightclubs that make Harlem prosperous," he added in a raspy, cold voice that grated on Adam's nerves. "We want the soapbox shits to shut up!" Madden picked his nose for a moment, then abruptly turned and walked out.

Next, a man named Dutch Schultz took over. "Everyone important in Harlem is in on this!" he screeched. He sounded out of control to Adam, reminding him of a newfangled radio whose volume was turned up too loud. "We want youse guys to teach these clucks a lesson!"

The meeting they were supposed to break up was not what Adam expected. Instead of a street corner gathering, the meeting was being held in a wide, wood-framed, two-story building with two small windows on each side of a narrow front door. One of the men said it had been a dancehall at the turn of the century and now it was being torn down. Scaffolding now stood outside the building, part of which already had been demolished. Only the inner rectangular hall remained intact and walled. The rooms around the hall—bathrooms, small offices, the lobby—were half-exposed to the street. Adam and the others went inside. There in the hall they found an audience of colored people, poorly dressed, but well mannered.

A podium faced the audience. Behind the podium was a large poster announcing "The Black Equality Advancement Association." A barrel-chested man with an enormous head was addressing the assembled crowd. He spoke in a clipped baritone voice. "For the few newcomers in the audience, let me say that my name is Leo Mackie, the president of your association."

The crowd cheered as Mackie introduced the association's board of directors. Adam and the others stood patiently to one side and watched as a marching band in green and black uniforms entered playing "Onward Christian Soldiers," parading smartly down one side of the auditorium, across the front, then back down the other side. Once the music stopped, Leo Mackie raised thick arms to silence the applause.

Adam looked questioningly at Charley. These people were just like him and Virginia. He couldn't see that they were doing anything wrong. Charley stared back at him with "do what you're told" eyes.

Mackie's voice from the podium boomed into Adam's ears. "We are ten thousand strong. We want to be one hundred thousand strong! Get your neighbors to join us! Your friends and relatives! Together we can turn Harlem into a law-abiding community!"

"Yes, Jesus!" shouted the audience. The walls seemed to vibrate with voices.

"Arrogant bastard," muttered Charley.

"We will break down barriers to equality!"

"Amen! Amen!" screamed the crowd, chanting their response in cadence with his words.

"The stupid pig," added Charley.

"We'll make our own laws! *We* will police our own streets!"

"Our savior!" shouted a female voice. "We love you!" shouted another. Hands clapped and feet stamped.

The voices and responses reminded Adam of back home. A heaviness settled in his chest.

"All black people will have a chance to work and own homes!"

"We should kill the bastard," cooed Charley.

Feet continued to pound the wood floor. The chanting grew louder. "Yeah!" "Amen!" "Hallelujah!" "Yeah! Yeah! Yeah!" The hall trembled under the impact, creaking and groaning in time to the chanting.

A mob of police under Lieutenant Baxter's command charged into the hall behind Adam and Charley. They carried nightsticks, passing additional billies to Charley and his men. Adam shook his head when one was shoved at him.

"Take it, you fuckin' idiot!" the officer yelled.

Adam was pushed forward by the arm-locked officers. He tried to escape, but he was hemmed in on all sides. The nightsticks slashed and slugged their way through the surprised assembly. Then surprise quickly turned to horror.

Helpless screams filled the hall. Pleading eyes stared back into Adam's, as though he could save them. In front of Adam, a man was knocked down by a swinging club. Blood streamed over his face and out of his mouth.

"Please," he begged, reaching up toward Adam. Adam was bending down to help when Charley gave the man a series of vicious kicks. The man screamed in pain before his mouth went slack. Adam stared, horrified at the stilled body. Then Adam was pushed past him and the man was out of sight, lying somewhere behind Adam under the stampeding feet.

The crowd cringed before the nightsticks, jamming against one another, desperately trying to reach exit doors before being beaten to the floor.

Oh my God, Adam thought. *What in hell am I doing? These are my people.* He fought his way back through the pressing policemen and their nightsticks, knowing he had to get out of there, now, this instant.

Suddenly he heard a sharp crack, then a rumble. He looked back. The platform stage was crumbling in a cloud of dust and splintered wood. The large poster hung suspended from one corner for a second, then the wall toppled over and the banner disappeared into the rising dark cloud.

Bodies were underfoot everywhere now. Screams rang in Adam's ears. Bloody heads bumped against him. Sunlight streamed in from behind the podium over twisted bodies. A side wall began to sway, pulling away from its uprights. Hanging light fixtures swung from the ceiling like pendulums. Specks of plaster and fragmented wood filled Adam's nostrils. He pushed through a side exit as the ceiling fell in with a thunderous crash behind him.

"What happened?" a stranger asked when Adam got across the street. Clouds of dust and fire and smoke still rose from the collapsed assembly hall. The only thing left standing was the scaffolding outside it.

Adam couldn't answer. He was still numb. His eyes wouldn't focus. He managed to get to an alley before his stomach let go. He was sick through his mouth and his nose. The stench he caused came back up at him from the pavement and made his eyes water. He got sick all over again.

By the time Adam could pull himself together, fire engines and ambulances were just arriving. Screams of terror still rang in his ears.

As soon as Adam got home to the boardinghouse, he went directly to the bathroom. He tore off his clothes, which smelled of hate and vomit, and took a long bath in burning hot water. Other boarders banged on the door. It wasn't his time to use the bathroom. After a while, he heard Boss hollering, "You're messin' up the routine!"

Adam let her scream. Finally she went away. He lay in the steaming water a long time before he felt clean enough to come out and look Virginia in the face.

Adam refused to go back to the Neighborhood Betterment Company again, even to collect the back pay he was owed. He knew he couldn't touch the money now, if he had it. *Let Charley come after me,* he thought, aware the company didn't like men who walked out on them.

Too ashamed to tell Virginia what his job had been, or that he was without one again, he pretended he was still working. Each day he'd get up at his usual hour, leave the house on schedule, then wander through the streets of Harlem looking without hope for something else. One day, by sheer chance, he happened across Corky Johnson. He was still throwing rent parties.

"Noticed you moved," Corky greeted him.

Adam nodded, and pointed. "Not too far. We're on Lenox. How's the poems goin'?"

"Not selling much these days. I've stirred up a little bootleggin' trade to stay alive. Whatcha up to?"

Adam shook his head. "Not much. Lookin' for work mostly . . ."

"Why don'tcha come in with me? I could use some help. With two of us workin' deliveries, I can do three times the business."

"You mean it?"

"Do I have to dig out one of my poems to prove it?"

Adam thought, *Why not? What have I got to lose?*

After that, Adam began going to work at four in the afternoon, often not arriving back home until five or six in the morning. He slept during the day, explaining to Virginia that he was assigned to the late shift. He figured there was no point telling her he was now bootlegging. She wouldn't approve of this any more than the previous job.

Soon, Adam and Corky were delivering wholesale gin made in Corky's bathtub to every type of small store and business, as well as to private citizens. Everyone, it seemed, was in the business of retailing bootleg, from beauty shops to tailors and magazine stand vendors. Adam knew it wasn't legal; he also knew nobody really cared. In fact, one of Corky's best customers was a big-time judge who lived on Sugar Hill. Adam got so busy, even his concern over Billie's new grown-up attitude faded into the background. *Besides,* he thought, *Billie spends most of her time with Fletcher, and Fletcher's a man I can trust.*

One rainy late September afternoon, Adam was in Corky's apartment with little to do. Deliveries had been taken care of, and he decided to go upstairs and say hello to Fletcher. The scent of linseed oil seemed stronger than ever when Adam walked in. He was surprised Billie wasn't there. "Where is she?"

Fletcher looked at him strangely. "She hasn't been here in weeks."

Adam's stomach sank. "Why not?"

"Don't you know?"

"If I did, I wouldn't be askin'!" Adam tried to keep his voice from rising.

"She's working at the Cotton Club. Lied about her age. One of the showgirls." Fletcher's usual enthusiasm was gone. "I thought everyone knew."

Anger and an old fear clogged Adam's throat. He was thinking of Billie's lies and how convincingly she told them.

"Have a drink," Fletcher offered. "You look like you could use one."

Adam had three drinks. It took that many before he calmed down.

Virginia was flabbergasted when Adam told her.

". . . and all those men starin' at her," he added.

"Now, Adam, starin' ain't touchin'. Billie knows how to handle herself," she pointed out.

"She's too young," Adam remarked, his anger returning.

"Don't be silly. I married you when I was sixteen," she countered.

"You had me to take care of you," he said.

"I 'spect Billie knows what she's doing."

Virginia arranged for Adam and Billie to spend the following Sunday after church together, to get to know each other again and clear the air. They walked down Seventh Avenue toward 125th Street. The smell of smoldering leaves burning in garbage cans on vacant lots swirled about them.

"You don't hafta lie anymore," Adam told her.

Her slim body seemed to stiffen. "What are you talking about?"

"Virginia and I know where you go every night. We've known over a week." He decided he'd get it all out in the open.

"You could have told me sooner. It would have saved a lot of trouble," she answered. "I know what you're thinking. I quit school, but I plan to go back next term during the day.

An unexpected voice sounded behind them. "Well, hello! How are you?"

Adam turned to see the man with the straightened hair from the rent party. The gold in his teeth reflected the sun.

"Fancy meeting you," Billie said, much too friendly for Adam's taste.

"You two sound pretty chummy," he said after the man walked past them.

"What's wrong with that?"

"You know I don't like him."

Billie stopped. "Look. He got me my job at the club. I gotta be nice to him. I know he's after me."

"You don't know nothin'!"

"I know more'n you think!" she said, closing the subject.

A week later, Adam decided it was high time he and Virginia went to the Cotton Club to see for themselves exactly what Billie did there. Virginia arranged for one of the other boarders to watch Chick and Dewey. Virginia and Adam got dressed up in their best clothes. They hadn't told Billie they'd be showing up as they wanted to surprise her.

Along the way, Adam caught their reflection in a candy store window. In their citified clothes, he noticed they now looked like the other couples who strolled in Harlem after dark. *Who would've guessed we'd change this much?* he thought. He knew they worked a lot more than most people and yet they didn't have what people in Harlem considered much money. Still, for poor farmers who once had to squeeze by on two dollars for as long as four months back in Florida, they weren't doing too bad.

An enormous black doorman in a bright green feather-plumed hat stood at the entrance of the Cotton Club. He wouldn't let Adam and Virginia go upstairs.

"Whaddaya mean?" Adam growled.

"I just follow the rules. I don't make them," the doorman said in a thick Southern drawl.

"We got the money!"

"You folks'll have a better time at the Royal Roost down the street. Take my word for it," said the doorman.

"But we got the money," Adam repeated. He flashed a few bills to prove it.

The huge man shook his head. A wisp of plume floated down to the shoulder of his costume. His Southern drawl vanished.

"Ain't you wised up? Coloreds can't come in here. Not unless you entertain, work the tables, or work the kitchen."

"Please," said Virginia. "One of the showgirls is our relative."

Seeing Virginia's disappointment, the doorman added, "I'm sorry, ma'am, but I'd lose my job if you went up there."

Adam led Virginia away, feeling cheated. He offered to take her someplace where they did let coloreds in, but Virginia said she'd rather go back to Boss's apartment. Besides, she said, she was tired, and tomorrow was another workday.

"What's this Captain Thomas got to do with us?" Corky wanted to know. He and Adam were in his place bottling a new supply of gin.

Adam patiently tried to explain again. "He's colored, that's what. One of the guys I once worked with told me the white bootleggers, the ones in the mob, are afeared the small colored operations like ours'll start gettin' police backup like they do, now that a colored's been promoted to captain. It makes sense."

"Baloney!" shot back Corky. "We're just little guys trying to make a few bucks."

"They says it'll mean more colored cops on the beat and that's gonna mean coloreds in the business like us'll get protection and cut into the mob's money. That's what this guy I know told me, bumped into him on 125th Street. He says they don't want no nigger-run mob in Harlem."

"I still say it's just a whole lotta bullshit. Every six to eight months the mob spreads the word that they're gonna get tough. That's to scare people from getting into the business. But they've got better things to do. It don't mean nothin'.'" Corky returned to pouring the gin through a funnel.

"Okay. Have it your way," Adam shrugged, wishing he knew how to convince Corky that people like Charley and his friends were vicious when they wanted to stop something.

The next day Adam and Corky heard that three of the largest black-owned stills were destroyed the night before. Each day after that, gossip reached them about another black independent being put out of business. Corky continued to slough off the news. "Our little ol' business ain't worth a grasshopper's asshole. They don't even know we exist."

This time Adam refused to let the subject drop. "These guys is real mean. Believe me, I had some dealin's with 'em. Let's jus' shut down for a mite . . ."

Corky's ears picked up. "What kind of dealings?"

"Nothin' much." Adam backed off. He didn't want to go into details. "Jus' take my word." He waited, watching Corky think about it.

"Okay," Corky finally agreed and Adam breathed easier. "But not till after tonight's delivery. I got the stuff all ready to go."

"This ain't no time to be makin' drops, I'm tellin' ya," Adam insisted.

"We ain't important, man. No one's gonna care. Just a little private party over by Mount Morris Park. Ten cases' worth, that's all."

"Can't do it. We need a pushcart," Adam reminded him.

"All arranged," said Corky, sounding pleased with himself. "I'll load the cart. You do the delivery. Okay?"

"I don't think we should," Adam frowned.

"You'll be back in a half hour."

"An' this'll be the last?"

"Agreed. Absolutely agreed. I need a vacation," smiled Corky.

The pushcart lay hidden under a tarpaulin in the alley behind the loft building. Corky often borrowed it from one of their grocery store customers. After Corky loaded it with the ten cases, Adam covered the cases with the tarpaulin, and for good measure, added a few empty valises and an old straight-backed chair on top. He wanted to look as if he were moving his belongings.

"Better get going," Corky urged with an anxious frown. "I promised the goods would be there by seven."

"I'm goin', for Chrissakes," muttered Adam, pushing the cart down the alley and onto the street.

Corky was right, he realized as he hurriedly rolled the cart down Third Avenue and across 124th Street. No one seemed to be paying any attention to him. A few cars slowed as they passed by, but Adam figured that was only natural. Ten minutes later, he reached Mount Morris Park. He stopped for a moment to catch his breath, suddenly aware he'd been hurrying faster than normal. Usually, Adam was not a nervous man. Tonight, though, he was. *What is there to be so jittery 'bout?* he thought, laughing to himself, remembering the nights he and the family had spent in the park across from him. *Thank God those days are over. Thank God we now have a roof over our heads and things are gettin' better.*

He rolled the cart onto the sidewalk across the street from the park and wheeled it slowly from one brownstone to the next, looking for the number of the house where the goods were expected.

Out of the corner of his eye, he thought there was movement in the bushes bordering the park. He swung his head in that direction, but saw nothing. Even so, he quickened his step, deciding this was not the time to take unnecessary chances. The sooner he got rid of the gin, the better off he'd be.

It was a dark night and few people seemed to be on the side streets. In this block, there wasn't a soul besides himself. He stopped the cart in front of the next brownstone, finally finding the number. It was then that he noticed the bulky figure of a man at the far corner of the block ahead of him. The figure was almost out of sight, half-hidden by the last house. Adam turned to look behind him. Was there another man at that end of the block too, or was it his imagination? He was about to start up the steps when a service door to the left of the front stoop was thrown open. "It's about time you got here," a voice called out. Adam rolled the cart through a cast-iron gate and backed it up to the door of a small entry hall. Three men who said they were catering the affair unloaded the cases while Adam watched. One of them added, "If you want your dough, you'll have to go in the kitchen."

Adam edged around the men and stepped inside. Food was being arranged on large serving trays covered with lettuce. Sparkling glasses were lined up along the length of a sideboard. An elderly woman in a long black dress with white ruffles at the wrists and throat was putting the finishing touches on a floral arrangement of gladiolus while ordering the caterers around. Adam decided she must be the maid. "Where do I get my money?" he asked her.

"From me. Who did you think?" She looked at the cases being brought in. "That was ten cases of sherry at five dollars a case." She held out a fifty-dollar bill.

Adam shook his head. "Ten cases of gin is what I brought at ten dollars a case."

"How dare you!" the woman said. In spite of the words, her voice was genteel and even-toned. "Everyone knows I don't allow gin in my house." Her breath came in short spurts and Adam wondered what was wrong with her. She gasped and clutched at her heart. "We'll see about this," she sputtered, moving to the staircase, taking slow steps up it. "We'll just see about this."

When she returned, a shortish, well-dressed, dapper man was with her. Adam guessed he was in his mid-thirties, then he recognized him as the man who'd thrown him out of Geneva's office. He didn't seem to recognize Adam. The old woman called to the man. "Lester," she said, pointing at Adam, "this bootlegger insists we ordered ten cases of gin."

Adam couldn't believe it. Did coloreds own this house?

"Well?" the man said, wiping his brow with a handkerchief.

Adam nodded firmly. "That's the order. Ten dollars a case. One hundred smackers." He held out his hand, thinking, *Of all the goddamn nights to have problems!*

The elderly woman seemed to have recovered from her gasping spell. She stood erect and in control now. Her eyes locked with Adam's, daring him to disagree with her. "Go back and bring us ten cases of sherry. And take that vulgar gin with you. Otherwise, you'll get no money at all."

A clacking footstep came from the staircase behind Adam.

"Oh no he won't!" a voice called. "I ordered the gin because that's what I want for my guests. This is my party, and this is my house, not yours." The elderly woman's rich brown complexion seemed to turn sallow as Adam stared at her. Her shortness of breath returned.

The man looked behind Adam at the staircase. "You must stop upsetting Mother like this." He riffled through a wallet and pulled out two fifty-dollar bills. He thrust them at Adam. "Here you are."

"That's more like it," said the newcomer. Adam turned and saw the fashionable young woman slinking down the last few steps. He couldn't help staring. The light skin, the darting eyes, reminded him of someone. A glittering, low-cut orange gown hugged her body and matched the color of her pouty lips. He realized that it was Geneva.

She was staring at him with equal intensity. Her eyes blinked rapidly. "Adam!" she said, walking toward him. Adam looked around at the others. What would they think? But Geneva came right up to him and grabbed both his hands. "I never thought I'd see you again," she said. "How long have you been here?"

"Who is this man, Geneva?" the elderly woman asked petulantly.

Geneva glanced around disconcertedly, and dropped Adam's hands. "Oh, an old friend from back home. Goodness, it's been so long since I've seen anyone from there that I forget myself. This is Adam Lambert, and Adam, this is my mother-in-law, Mrs. Noble, and my husband, Lester Noble."

"Charmed," grumbled Lester. "Haven't I met you before?"

"I reckon I best be gettin' on my way," Adam said, sensing

the tension Geneva was causing. He turned back to Geneva. "Virginia was wondering what happened to you after you said you couldn't put us up."

"I would have. I just didn't have the space, what with my mother-in-law living with us." Adam could tell she was saying this as much for the others as for him.

"Don't you think you should go upstairs and prepare for your guests?" Geneva's mother-in-law spit out in glacial tones. "As for me, I won't be attending your gin party." She clutched her heart and held her other arm out to her son. "Lester, help me to my room."

After they disappeared up the stairs, Geneva kissed Adam's chin. The caterers stopped what they were doing for a moment to cast covert glances her way.

She ignored them. "I can't tell you how often I think of you," she said. "Tell me where I can get in touch with you."

"You sure your husband wants to be around me an' Virginia?" he asked as he wrote his address down. "He don't seem too obligin'."

Geneva laughed, staring down at the caterers, intimidating them into getting back to work. "Who cares what Lester likes! Or his cranky old mother. If they had their way I wouldn't see anyone or go anyplace. I used to be scared to death of them. But they can't hurt me now." She picked up a tiny sandwich from a passing tray and popped it into Adam's mouth, then swung around enthusiastically with arms stretched to indicate the house. "Can you believe this place? Ever think your little Geneva would end up so grand? I bet those jealous jackasses back in Florida would give their eyeteeth to be in my shoes."

When Adam left, Geneva followed him to the gate on the

sidewalk. The shadowy figures still waited at each end of the block. He pulled Geneva back inside the service door and closed it.

"What's wrong?"

"Can I leave by the back?"

"You'd have to climb a fence."

"That's easy. I'll pick up the pushcart tomorrow." She showed him through the kitchen as the caterers pretended not to notice them. Outside, at the end of her narrow garden was a ten-foot fence. He jumped up and pulled himself over it.

By the time he approached Corky's building with the money, his apprehension had vanished. He was sure no one was following him. He smiled to himself, feeling pleased he'd given them the slip. *They probably think I'm still in Geneva's house*, he decided, *probably still waitin'*. He walked into the building with another pleasing thought. The gin was delivered. As far as anyone was concerned, he and Corky never sold bootleg. And, he vowed, they never would again. "Of all people," he laughed aloud, "Geneva."

The hall outside Corky's apartment was quiet. Adam opened the door, sighed with relief, and shut it behind him.

"What took ya' so long?" a familiar voice cooed. Adam spun around. Charley leaned against the wall beside the door. A cigarette dangled from his mouth. "I was wonderin' when I was gonna see ya' again," he said in the same oily phrasing Adam remembered. "You an' me got three debts to settle. One, I don't like guys who turn me down. Two, I don't like guys who walk out on me. Three, I don't like bastards who muscle in on my territory."

Adam looked about the living room, wondering where Corky

was. "Don't blame the guy who lives here, Charley. He jus' let me use the place. It's only me you got debts to settle with."

"Ya think I'm some dumb fuck who don't know the score?" Charley's voice cooed softer than ever. "We had you an' him fingered two weeks ago, chump."

Just then, Adam sensed movement behind him. Before he felt anything, the blow struck the side of his skull. The light in the lamp dimmed and moved in his head and grew dimmer with each blow. His entire head felt numb. After that, Adam didn't see anything; not the kicks, the pummeling, the pounding— nothing. He only felt them.

Some time later, the smell of bootleg entered his consciousness. It was heavy and suffocating. He moved an arm. He heard the crunch of broken glass from far away. He finally managed to half-open an eye. He was lying in the bathtub on top of smashed bottles. Then the darkness came again. He sank into it, fighting against the descent, finally slowing it, hovering for a while above the empty pit—then forcing himself back up to the foul-smelling reality of homemade liquor and the pile of shattered glass that lay beneath him.

Eventually he worked up the strength to pull himself out of the tub. He pushed himself along the floor with one knee, refusing to let the pain reach him. After a while, he was able to crawl into the next room. The stickiness was everywhere. Each time the darkness came back, he'd let it close over him, then he'd find the energy and pull himself back into the dimness, and the stench. He had to get to the end of the hall, and he began to crawl to the back, to Corky's bedroom. In what seemed to take hours, he finally reached the door. Splintered furniture, shattered glass, torn books, ripped pages, filled the room. Corky's twisted body partially hung over the sill of an opened window.

Adam crawled to him. "You all right?" he tried to ask, but no sound came from his swollen, blood-dried lips. Adam tugged at Corky's trousers. His body fell from the sill and crashed limply beside Adam's. It wasn't until then that Adam realized Corky's opened eyes were empty and lifeless. Adam slipped back into the darkness.

Chapter Thirteen

Charles Payton noticed that paper profits were making everyone think they were millionaires. There seemed to be no end to how high the stock market could climb. It was all he and his friends downtown talked about. Each night when he walked home from the subway stop, he could almost smell gold floating up out of manhole covers and oozing through cracks in the sidewalk. "Money, money, money," the autumn wind seemed to sigh as it kissed his cheek as tenderly as his little girl, Evelyn.

Even the colored people he'd pass on the street appeared to be caught up in the fever, although he doubted any of them had the cash or inclination to buy stocks. The only people who didn't seem affected were the hopeless dark faces he'd sometimes glimpse crouching at the end of garbage-strewn alleys, waiting patiently for something to happen. They looked as desperate as ever.

Nothing, though, not even the poor, could take the edge off his own euphoria. His new importance kept him continually in a state of light-headedness. On Wall Street, he was being called one of the brighter young executives. His personal funds were piling up from shrewd investments as fast as the fortunes of the clients he handled. Already, he'd paid back the mass of debts his dead father had left behind, and in another year he would own the mortgaged family brownstone free and clear again.

Everything is perfect, he thought, until he walked by the old Hingham house. As long as he lived, he knew he'd never forgive Ralph Hingham for what he'd done. Not that there was anything wrong with the colored family who'd moved in. The Nobles appeared to be as fastidious and refined as any white family he knew. *Maybe more so*, he said to himself as he thought about it. The mother was an extremely proper *grande dame;* the son, a genteel businessman; the wife, striking and extremely well educated. *No*, he conceded, *it's not the Nobles that bother me, it's the whole idea of it. This block is supposed to be for whites. In a few years, we'll end up being the only white family among a block of niggers.* He was a strong believer in what he called the "thumb theory."

"If your thumb holds someone down, keep holding it there," he explained once to Rose regarding office politics in his firm. "If you take your thumb off, the next thing you know, that person will have his thumb on *your* head holding *you* down!"

"Like you hold me and little Evelyn down," Rose paralleled. "Is that what you mean?"

"I mean nothing of the sort!" Charles was indignant. Sometimes he couldn't figure what went on in Rose's head.

"You don't like me associating with the nice people next door.

You're suspicious of everyone Evelyn plays with," Rose rambled. "If you had your way, we'd never see anyone but you."

"Stop babbling," he told her. Charles hated it when Rose's emotionalism got in her way, making her misunderstand every goddamn word he was trying to communicate.

Rose ignored him. To his way of thinking, she always did. "Well," she continued, "for your information, I've become quite friendly with Geneva Noble next door and her mother-in-law. Even if they are colored, they're the nicest people on the block. So put that in your pipe and smoke it."

"Do you always have to use those childish clichés?"

Rose glared at him a moment, then flounced out of their bedroom in stony silence to spend another night in the guest room.

Remembering this conversation and others like it, Payton promised himself he'd be more careful tonight in selecting the topics they'd discuss. He felt too good to have unresolved arguments spoil the evening. He walked up the eight steps that led to the front door, deciding to talk about safe subjects such as relandscaping the back garden and possibly taking a place next summer in the Hamptons. For some time now, when he and Rose were communicating a little better, they talked about a summer place, and now it was more than possible. From habit, Charles mentally added up the value of his investments. Recently, it had become one of the things he loved to do most. Just thinking of all that money made him expand with self-satisfaction. *Let's face it,* he thought, *I have money to burn. We could take a trip to Europe. Put Evelyn in a private school. Hell—I could afford a maid and a butler if I sell off some of the stock.*

By the time cocktail hour commenced, Rose was as fired up about Charles's grandiose plans as he. Charles watched her bubble over with excitement as she skipped and twirled around the living room with Evelyn singing "Ain't We Got Fun?" Then, as Evelyn joined in, singing in her thin, high-pitched way that was so endearing, Charles realized he no longer resented the fact that she wasn't born a boy.

It was the best evening they'd had together in a long time, Charles decided, letting a happy smile take over his face as he and Rose fell off to sleep.

The next day, the stock market broke.

JOYRIDE OVER! screamed the headlines.

Panic swept through the banks and brokerage houses that had financed the orgy of extended credit and stock buying on 10 percent margins.

Charles Payton rushed to unload, but by then, as for most of his peers, it was too late. His $535 per share stock had dropped drastically, and the rest of his investments were in no better shape. He went outside the Exchange on Wall Street and sat on the curbstone beside a hydrant and cried. Beside him, other men were doing the same thing.

The next day, Payton heard that Ralph Hingham had jumped from the window of his nineteenth-floor office.

The following week, newspapers began referring to the day of the crash as the blackest of all days.

By the end of November, every day seemed black to Payton. He had forgotten about his scheme to get a summer house, go abroad, and send Evelyn to private school. It was all he could do to get himself out of bed in the morning and shave.

Chapter Fourteen

Things were beginning to go Geneva's way. Ever since the party, Lester's mother had stayed upstairs in her room. Geneva felt that was exactly where she belonged. At least she wasn't always underfoot, criticizing everyone's moves, throwing a wet blanket over everybody's fun. Now, she played sick for sympathy, pretending her heart was bothering her, having Dr. Corey stop by practically every other day.

Geneva had never felt more chipper. She finally had her life with Lester and his mother under control. The house, being a wedding present, belonged to her outright. All of Lester's many bank accounts were also in Geneva's name, for business reasons which Lester kept to himself. On top of that, Geneva was aware that Mother Noble had sold off her investments just weeks before the Wall Street panic, and Lester was her sole beneficiary.

No doubt about it, Geneva smiled in self-satisfaction, *things are going my way at last. I'll never be a little nobody again.*

Her inner being radiated confidence. She now felt completely free to do as she liked. Her unexpected meeting with Adam had been a godsend, and she didn't care who knew it. Furthermore, she was convinced she could win him back. No longer would she have to content herself with old dreams. For a moment, she thought about that summer long ago down home before they had their silly argument over . . . *over what?* Geneva wasn't sure anymore, even though she could still see his angry face when he left her, and she remembered clearly how her world exploded into useless pieces when she'd first heard the news he'd married that simple cousin of hers.

This afternoon, on the way back to her brownstone, Geneva rationalized to herself that Adam had only married Virginia to get even. He couldn't possibly have loved her then, anymore than he could today. *Not after what we were to each other,* she told herself, feeling the old tingling sensation run up and down her body. She was amused at the thought that every time she'd reminisce about Adam, her body responded with a warm rush. She wasn't sure if it was love or lust.

I may have left that two-horse town with my tail between my legs, she laughed to herself, *but it was the smartest move I ever made. If I hadn't, I wouldn't be here. I wouldn't have everything I ever wanted. Everything, that is, except Adam . . .*

Geneva paused on her way up the front steps and looked in her purse. Adam's address was still there. She decided she'd get in touch with him as soon as she had some sensible plan worked out. She wondered for a moment why he hadn't come back for his delivery cart. Lester finally had had to push it out on the sidewalk, where it disappeared in practically a matter of seconds. "Kids ran off with it," Geneva figured. "They steal anything they can get their hands on these days."

Taking her coat off, Geneva heard Esther downstairs rattling pots. Her last duty before going home for the day was to tidy the kitchen after leaving dinner warming in the oven. Upstairs, two low voices were talking. She guessed it was Rose Payton from next door, visiting Lester's mother. Rose was a kind, generous woman who believed everything Mother Noble told her. Geneva couldn't help liking her despite her gullibility. Also, Geneva was awed by Rose's fragile ivory skin with the slight freckling on her forehead, her pale eyes and red-blond hair, her pretty smile. What's more, Rose was the only neighbor around who seemed pleased the Nobles had moved in. Even little Evelyn was friendly; always running to the service door asking for cookies, then coming in and chattering away about any little thing.

The only member of the Payton family Geneva wasn't sure about was Rose's husband. When Geneva invited him and Rose to her party, only Rose had shown up. She said that Charles, unfortunately, had a business meeting to attend and as much as he'd love to be there, he couldn't.

Geneva was having tea in the front bay window of the large living room when Esther left, muttering loudly that she was overworked. "One of these days," Geneva vowed, "I'm going to get rid of that woman and find someone who enjoys her work. God knows I pay her enough!"

Shortly after Esther closed the service door with a bang, Geneva heard Rose come downstairs. "I took the day off to shop, so I got home early. Join me for a cup of tea," Geneva said when Rose peeked into the room.

Rose gave her a friendly kiss on the cheek and sat down. "I'm worried about your mother-in-law," she said while Geneva filled a cup for her. "She doesn't look well and her breathing is atrocious."

Geneva kept any trace of condescension from her voice. "Don't you realize she just puts on an act to get sympathy? She doesn't dare do it with me. She knows I can see right through her little games." Talk about Mother Noble bored her. "You must hear my new record." She wound up the Victrola and put it on.

> *Harlem's jumpin',*
> *Really somethin',*
> *Nothin' beats the razza-ma-tazz*
> *In Harlem . . .*

Geneva could tell by Rose's wrinkled brow that her mind was still on Mother Noble's bid for more attention. She turned up the volume.

> *Highbrows, lowbrows, so-and-so brows*
> *Shimmy through the night;*
> *Highbrows, lowbrows, so'n-so brows*
> *Don't go home till the mornin' light . . .*

Geneva snapped her fingers, hoping to get Rose into a more cheerful mood. "Recognize it?"

Rose shook her head.

"Dandy Reed, the man on the record, played piano at my party. Don't you remember?" Geneva watched Rose concentrate, trying to recall.

> *Hey, good lookin'!*
> *Harlem's cookin'!*
> *You can have the time of your life . . .*
> *Come on up but don't bring your wife!*
> *You can have the time of your life*
> *In Harlem!*

"I remember it now," Rose finally said, but Geneva suspected she was just being agreeable. As soon as the record concluded, Rose leaned forward. "Wasn't the crash awful? . . . I don't know what's going to happen to me and Charles and Evelyn."

Until then, Geneva thought Rose was merely in a gossiping mood. She herself was in such a state of well-being, she wished Rose would get on to something lighter. The last thing she cared to talk about was the stock market mess. She said, "Speaking of Evelyn, I know her birthday was a couple of months ago and I've been meaning to give her a little belated party, if it's all right with you." Actually, Geneva had only thought of it that moment. "If you make a list of her special friends, I'll take care of everything." When Rose didn't perk up, Geneva patted her hand. "Stop worrying. I'll burn some incense for you. It's an old New Orleans custom, and it works. In another month or two, you and Charles will be right back on easy street. Stocks will be selling again like hotcakes. Everything will work out. You'll see."

"I hope you're right," Rose answered, her frown at last disappearing. "And about the party. Evelyn would love it. It's really too sweet of you."

After Rose went home, Geneva couldn't wait to open a small brown paper bag she'd bought during her shopping expedition. It contained a tiny bottle of chicken fat mixed with ground dried leaves. Geneva told herself she didn't believe in this kind of mumbo-jumbo, but another side of her was just superstitious enough to make her go into the dreary store when she passed it. Besides, she rationalized, she also needed incense.

After Geneva gave the peculiar little woman who ran the store fifty cents, the woman handed Geneva an egg covered in cloth and told her to smash it, then chanted a lot of gibberish. When the woman opened the cloth, blood was mixed with the broken egg. Geneva had to laugh as she thought about it. The woman had rocked on short, stubby legs and stared through thick glasses.

"Julia Mae sees evil ahead. The egg is bleeding with sorrow."

Geneva wanted to giggle. She started to leave.

"Wait!" The woman held out the bottle. "Take this home. Burn what's in it. The evil spirits will scatter."

Geneva had to pay the woman another fifty cents for the potion, but she fantasized, *Who knows? Maybe it'll do some good.*

Geneva found a clay saucer in the backyard and began to follow the doll-like woman's instructions. She dumped the contents of the bottle in the saucer. She carried it up to the living room, deciding the rear wall by the bookshelves was the center of the house. The woman said this was the location where evil

spirits always clustered. Geneva struck a match and dropped it
into the thick liquid that looked like glue. A small blue flame
danced about the clay saucer, and pungent whiffs of smoke
floated about it. Geneva couldn't decide if the odor was pleasant
or unpleasant. She still hadn't made up her mind when she
heard the mysterious tapping. Startled, she jumped. Then she
realized it was only Mother Noble knocking on the wall behind
her bed upstairs. As usual, she wanted attention.

Geneva took her time going up there. She waited until the
mixture was completely burned. Then she put the saucer on one
of the shelves, thinking, *What a waste of fifty cents.* She checked
her makeup in the foyer mirror. Finally, she walked up the staircase.

Her mother-in-law's eyes, Geneva noticed, were almost
friendly for a change. Maybe the funny little woman in the voodoo shop had been right after all. Maybe the evil spirits *were*
being chased out.

"I think it's high time you and I had a talk," Lester's mother
said. "We can't continue this way."

Geneva refused to be taken in by Mother Noble's slow
speech, which seemed deeper in her throat than usual, or by the
little gasps between words. Dr. Corey had been there just the
day before and told Geneva and Lester his mother was fine,
considering her age.

Mother Noble's eyes sharpened and bore like knives into Geneva's. "First, I want to know exactly who this bootlegger friend
of yours is. I want you to tell me how you know him. And I
want to know why you refuse to give me the address of your
mother."

"What if I don't tell you anything?" Geneva asked in her

sweetest tones. She decided she would not let this spoiled old woman treat her like an inferior another second.

Mother Noble breathed in openmouthed gulps. "I'll be forced into things I'm afraid you'll regret."

"Things like what?" Geneva asked. A rush of hostility burned her throat.

"That, you'll have to wait and see, my dear." Geneva thought, *As I suspected, she's bluffing again.* She turned and headed for the door.

"Don't you *dare* leave!" cried Mother Noble, all the genteel coating gone from her voice. "You stay here and answer my questions!"

This was all Geneva needed. She was suddenly thrown back to her early days after her mother ran off, leaving her a parentless child requiring the charity of a bad-tempered aunt who resented the responsibility, and who was always demanding this and threatening that. Geneva's anger overflowed.

She faced Mother Noble. "I'll give you the truth. I was once engaged to that bootlegger, as you call him. I used to love him! And I don't come from New Orleans, I grew up in a Florida shack! My mother was a tramp, if you must know!" Mother Noble's eyes were open wide in shock. They goaded Geneva on. "I ran up here to escape. I earned money any way I could." She liked seeing the startled expression on Mother Noble's face. She decided to really shock her. "I even hustled and whored and stole," she lied. "I did everything."

Now that it was all said, Geneva felt winded, as if she'd been running for a long time. On the other hand, she felt purged. Mother Noble's mouth was set in disgust. Her head lay back on the pillow. "Call Dr. Corey. I can't bear to look at you."

Geneva thought, *She's at it again, getting everyone back under her beck and call.*

"I want Dr. Corey," Mother Noble repeated.

Geneva decided to humor her. "What you want is a sympathetic ear, but I'll call him anyway. Don't blame me, though, if he refuses to come." She went downstairs to phone, then she changed her mind. *I will not lick that petulant old woman's boots,* she told herself. *Let her wait. It'll serve her right.* She went below to the kitchen instead, checking out the dinner in the oven, tasting each dish, adding salt here and pepper there until she was satisfied. She made herself a gin fizz and sat with it at the kitchen table, killing time, smoking a cigarette. Finally, she went back up to the parlor floor and phoned the doctor. He didn't sound very concerned, but he said he'd come over anyway.

When he arrived, Geneva walked upstairs to Mother Noble's room with him. She wanted the doctor to realize she was a dutiful daughter-in-law doing her best, considering that she had a cantankerous old woman living under the same roof. "She's sleeping," Geneva whispered, peeking in.

Dr. Corey went to the bed and checked Mother Noble's pulse. He looked back at Geneva. "She's dead, I'm afraid. It looks like the poor woman's had a heart attack."

Geneva knew her face looked dreadful. For some reason, she couldn't make her mouth move. It felt twisted out of shape.

"Don't blame yourself," Dr. Corey told her, his voice filled with fatherly compassion. "You did all you could. Her time had come, that's all . . ."

———

Ben Cannon was thinking, *Harlem's funerals have become major social events, attracting bigger crowds than even the Labor Day parade.* Since Cannon ran his newspaper, the *Harlem Voice*, pretty much as a one-man operation, he covered everything himself. On this particular blustery afternoon, he stood outside Abyssinian Baptist Church, on West 138th Street between Lenox and Seventh avenues, the most important church in Harlem. He was bundled up in a topcoat that was fifteen years out of style, the wind tossing his undisciplined mass of white hair every which way, and was taking mental notes for the story he planned to write.

This funeral, Cannon noticed early on, was as formidable as any he'd reported in years. Considering the current chaos of the country's economy, it was all the more impressive. The exterior of the church, for example, looked even grander than usual. Traffic was stalled for blocks up and down Seventh Avenue, and West 138th Street was an even bigger mess. Shortly after Cannon predicted it would happen, hundreds of extra policemen, some of them mounted, arrived to handle the throng of pushing mourners. Onlookers overflowed from sidewalks into the street, defying the barriers, leaving no room for the guests arriving in rented limousines, edging closer to the church. The police finally cleared a path for the cars to drive up. The walkway to the church was so jam-packed, it took twenty men to keep the crowd parted to allow folks to get inside. That's when Cannon got a better view of the mourners entering Abyssinian. He'd never seen such elegance in his life.

Once inside, Cannon sat in the rear pew that was reserved for the press. He knew all the Harlem papers would be covering the

funeral, but he was surprised to find even a few downtown papers represented. Cannon's eyes counted the number of atten-
dants, the faces in the choir, the baskets of carnations, the rows
of pews at the front roped off for really important personages.
In each category, he'd never counted so many. Watching guests
being led to the front, he realized everyone who was anybody in
Harlem was there—the old elite from the professional, academic, artistic, and political worlds; the new elite of entertainers, musicians, and sports celebrities.

After all the invited were seated, the remainder of the pews
were thrown open to the masses outside who might be lucky
enough to get in. The stampede was a shoving nightmare until
every seat was filled. Then the commotion suddenly subsided.
The doors were closed. A hushed silence fell over the gathering.
The service was about to begin.

That evening, on his worn-out typewriter, Cannon wrote the
story for the next day's edition of his weekly paper: "Mrs. Adelaide Newton Noble was laid to rest in a befitting tribute to one
of Harlem's most generous, most elegant, most compassionate
citizens. She was a woman who never turned her back on the
needy, who never closed her eyes to social injustice, who never
thought of herself at the expense of others.

"The Reverend Adam Clayton Powell's eulogy was both elo-
quent and enlightening, living up to his dynamic reputation in
every respect, urging the well-to-do mourners to follow the late
Mrs. Noble's example and use their ample resources to help
Harlem's poor and desperate in these troubled days."

What occurred to Ben Cannon, but what he didn't feel was
proper to put into his story, was that most of the people in the

unreserved pews weren't there to mourn Adelaide Noble. Most of them had never heard of her. They attended the ceremony for other reasons. One was to see and hear the handsome, loquacious Reverend Powell, who was the idol of the downtrodden and just about everyone else. Another was the love of attending funerals and having a good cry regardless of the deceased's name. The last was to catch a glimpse of the reverend's rebellious young son, who, wherever he went, already had the reputation of being a romantic playboy, scoffing at rules and society, not caring how much his famous father or the deacons of the church objected.

Sitting in front of his typewriter thinking these thoughts, it also occurred to Cannon that regardless of one's reason for being at the funeral, no one left the church unsatisfied. Mrs. Adelaide Noble was put to rest with all the prestige her position demanded. Reverend Powell, the elder, never spoke with more authority or exuded more sensuality. Those who came merely to weep had more opportunity than usual. And Adam Clayton Powell, Jr., lived up to his exciting persona in bucketfuls. He looked whiter than any white man there. His many pictures in the papers didn't do him justice; in person he was twice as handsome. He moved with the assurance of a prince who thoroughly understood his appeal and his function. He was immaculately dressed and much more glamorous than any movie star. Best of all, Cannon chuckled, remembering the gasp that ran through the crowd when he first showed up, he hadn't let a single person down. On each of his arms floated a gorgeous showgirl.

Yes, Cannon concluded with cynical detachment while carefully shrouding his typewriter for the evening, *that funeral was*

exactly what Harlem needed to give it a lift. With unemployment
growing even worse than usual, it was better than a funeral. It was a
preseason mardi gras.

A week after the funeral, Geneva decided to
lay some facts on the line with Lester. She
said, "Now that your dear mother, God rest her soul, has been
taken away from us, I think there's a few things we should talk
about."

"If you wish." Lester's face still looked bloodless. Geneva had
no idea his mother meant this much to him. They were finishing dinner in the formal dining room at the rear of the parlor
floor overlooking the garden. Geneva noticed he had hardly
touched his food.

"Perhaps this isn't a good time . . ."

"No bother," he assured her.

"Well there are certain things I lied about to you. Nothing
important, just small things . . ."

Lester's face lifted from his untouched plate to look at her.
The lifeless gaze turned to curiosity. "Oh?"

"I never told you I had relatives in Florida. It was the side of
the family we were always ashamed of. Dirt poor sharecroppers,
uneducated, living from hand to mouth. But from the very beginning, I felt sorry for Virginia, my cousin. It wasn't her fault.
Well, she and her husband, and two kids, wouldn't you know
. . . They moved up here just before we were married. I hadn't
seen or heard of them in seven or so years. That was her husband who delivered the gin for my party. I didn't dare tell you

who he was then, when your mother was alive. But I can tell you now . . ."

Lester laughed. His spirit seemed to pick up. "So that's who he was. I thought he looked familiar. And to think I was put out. *And* a little jealous. I thought maybe you were getting tired of me."

Geneva knew she was over the first hurdle. "I'd like to do something for them. I feel it's my duty . . ."

Lester reached across the table, placing his hand over hers, rubbing his soft forefinger across the antique engagement ring embedded with the tiny diamonds. "You sound more like Mother every day. Always trying to help . . ." He thought for a moment. "We could fire the gardener and hire your cousin's husband . . ."

Geneva quickly pointed out she liked the gardener they had. "Besides, I think Adam's bright enough for something better."

Lester pursed his lips. "Maybe there's something in the office he can do. Some simple bookkeeping, things like that . . ."

This was exactly the conclusion Geneva wanted Lester to come to. "You really think so?" She kept her voice dubious.

"He can learn. I'm sure we can work it out . . ."

Geneva jumped up and ran around the table and kissed him, just as she had the night he put the engagement ring on her finger. "Lester! You're great! I'll get in touch with my cousin as soon as possible and have her send Adam over." She ran to the phonograph and put on Dandy Reed's record:

Harlem's jumpin',
Really somethin' . . .

She ran back to the dining room and pulled Lester to his feet. "And there's another thing. We're giving more parties and starting tonight, we're going out to the clubs more. We're both going upstairs and dress ourselves to the teeth. We'll have fun like everyone else."

Lester frowned. "But the funeral . . ."

Geneva led Lester upstairs. "A few days of mourning is all that's required these days. You're so old-fashioned . . ."

Late that night, after an evening of club-hopping, Lester and Geneva fell into bed, exhausted. Dandy Reed had kept her laughing all night with his naughty stories. He'd flirted outrageously with Geneva, who returned the favor wholeheartedly. Lester was such a cold fish, sitting back from the table, eyeing everyone haughtily. It was time he learned to loosen up and have some fun. If Dandy weren't such a fly-by-night in terms of women, Geneva might have considered having a fling with him.

As she pulled the covers over herself, Dandy's newest song kept humming through her head. Suddenly she thought of Adam, remembering her first time with him in the sultry, breathless night with the cicadas screaming from the weeping willows overhead. She glanced over at Lester's sleeping bulk. Since their marriage he'd become quite chubby, almost fat. She turned over in distaste.

Chapter Fifteen

Billie's feeling of guilt didn't hit her until she rounded the corner and faced the forbidding iron gates of the apartment house. It wasn't the first time she'd stayed out after the last show, but the sun was coming up and she didn't know what she'd say if Adam was awake. The jolting start of the grilled elevator seemed to sound noisier than ever as it creaked up four flights. She tiptoed down the narrow hall that led to the room she shared with Chick and Dewey, holding her breath until she quietly shut the door behind her. She leaned against the wall near her bed and wondered how much longer she could keep up this act. She hated Boss's rooming house. She was reaching for her bathrobe when she spotted the note pinned to her pillow. She knew something was wrong. Whatever it was, it was punishment for going to Duke's party.

She threw on her robe and took the note to Boss's living room where a dim lamp glowed. Billie seldom used the room. It always smelled like mildewed velvet and dust. People usually saved good news to tell in person, she thought, as she held the note up to the light.

"Terrible thing happened," she read. "Be back when I can." Virginia's normally neat penmanship was scribbled, signed with a scrawled "V."

After reading it, Billie didn't even try to sleep. She looked into the other room and saw that Adam was gone, too. She returned to the living room, hugging herself to keep warm, worrying about Virginia and Adam, wishing they'd come back. Finally, she went back to her room, thinking she must do something, but she had no idea where to go find them, or what there was to do.

A while later, she put on her coat and went outside. Anything was preferable to just sitting in that musty room waiting. She wandered aimlessly through the cold dawn-tinted streets. She forced her mind to think of other things. The new routine at the club was easy enough. She thought of the hours she had posed for Fletcher. She thought of the watercolor he'd done of her that appeared on the cover of the *Saturday Evening Post* and how everyone raved about it.

The newsstand was opening, and Billie bought the *News*. The little man behind the counter returned Billie's nickel. "My first customer smiles like an angel and you want me to charge her?" She thanked the nice Jewish man and promised to always get her paper from him. She returned home, praying Virginia and Adam would be there. Their room was still empty. Boss was up, though, and she gave Billie an evil stare. "You're supposed to sleep all morning since you work all night," Boss ordered in her martinet voice.

"And you're supposed to mind your own business," Billie snapped.

She woke up Chick and Dewey and made them breakfast. "It's not your time in the kitchen," one of the other boarders complained, tapping her foot impatiently beside the table.

"Tell it to the police," Billie muttered.

"Oh no. I'm tellin' it to Boss," the boarder said with an evil smile, rushing to the door.

"Suit yourself," yawned Billie.

Chick ate his farina in silence, but Dewey was curious. "Where's Mama? You're supposed to be asleep."

Billie tried to joke in spite of her deepening concern. "Don't you start. You sound just like Boss."

Boss marched in. "If you're not careful, I'm throwing you out for good!"

"Oh, really," Billie taunted. "Considering how filthy this place is, you'd be doing us a favor."

Boss, unaccustomed to confrontation, stormed off.

Billie dropped Dewey off with Mrs. Davis, one of the boarders who had a little girl of her own, and then walked Chick to school, although he said he'd rather go alone. "I feel like it and I'm going to," she argued, trying to keep her voice lighthearted, pretending nothing was wrong.

"The kids'll rib me," Chick complained.

"Let 'em. What do you care?" Billie was determined not to return to Boss's until Virginia and Adam were back. After dropping Chick off, she walked to a drugstore on Seventh Avenue and got a cup of coffee. She dawdled over it for what seemed hours, but when she looked at the clock behind the counter, only twenty minutes had passed. Restless, she left the store anyway. She slowly meandered about until she found herself before the rusty iron grillwork of their building. She stood there, trying to decide whether to go inside or not, when Fletcher came running out of the entrance. "I've been waiting for you," he called.

Billie hadn't seen him in a long time, and she'd forgotten how soothing his presence could be. She ran to him, grateful to see him. "Something's wrong," she cried, letting her bottled-up fears spill out over his chest.

"I know, that's why I'm here." He gently rubbed her back, making her feel somehow safer.

"Where's Virginia and Adam?" She clung to him closer, not wanting to find out, still knowing she had to.

"Virginia's all right. It's Adam. I found him in Corky's place. I think we got him to Harlem Hospital in time . . ."

"In time?"

"He was beat up pretty bad."

"Beat up? Who would beat him up?" Billie tried to make light of it, "A jealous husband?" Then the reference to Corky sank in. "How was Corky mixed up in it?"

Fletcher's sad expression filled her consciousness. "By the time I got there, it was already too late for Corky . . ."

"Dear God! Will Adam . . . ?"

"It's touch and go," Fletcher told her.

For three days, Virginia stayed at Adam's side whenever she was allowed in the ward. Billie got Chick off to school and dropped Dewey off with Mrs. Davis each morning and watched over them when they returned until Virginia showed up again. On the fourth day, the hospital pushed Adam out, saying they needed the bed, so Virginia was forced to bring him home to Boss's.

Billie was shocked when she first saw him. His broken ribs were taped, he had a bad limp in his left leg although the doctor told her and Virginia it would disappear in time, and his body was covered with nasty bruises and bandaged knife wounds, which were supposedly healing. Both of them had difficulty getting Adam's battered body into the bed. The sedative the doctor had given him was working, and he soon fell asleep.

"They said he's gotta stay in bed another week or so," Virginia whispered. "It means I won't be able to work."

"Of course you can," Billie assured her. "I'll take care of him during the day and you'll be here at night."

Virginia shook her head. "I can't 'spect you to do that."

"You don't have to. I'm doing it." Billie was firm. She'd already figured out just how they'd handle it, and she didn't believe in changing directions.

O ne night, while Billie was showing off her body and best smile on the horseshoe-shaped floor of the Cotton Club, life began to change. It started with her first glimpse of the man sitting alone at the club's center ringside table. Dimples Frazier, the showgirl next to Billie in the line, pointed him out. "He's the one who sent you the flowers last night." Billie had to admit he was the best-looking man she'd ever seen. A shiver ran through her that she explained away to herself as a draft of cold air.

"What did ya think?" Dimples asked in her raspy voice once they were back in the dressing room.

"Nothing special," Billie lied, hoping to sound blasé.

After the show, Billie received another box of orchids from

the same man. This time, though, there was a handwritten note. "Have supper with me. Please! I'll wait outside in my car for you after the show. Lloyd Harrington." Dimples grabbed the note and the girls passed it from one to the other.

"Have you hit the jackpot, girl!" Sally exclaimed in breathless panting. "Harrington makes Rockefeller look like po' white trash!"

Her sister, Laurelle, added, "But get what you can out of him fast. The first week, men are so hot for those cookies they can't spend enough on you. The second week you're lucky if you can get subway fare. By the third, they're sending flowers to a new cookie jar."

Dimples took Billie aside. "Don't listen to her. She's a troublemaker. Although I must admit she's right this time. Remember, honey. These rich guys come up here thinking we're jungle bunnies who's gonna cure what ails 'em. Then they pull down our drawers and realize we ain't got no more cure than the girls downtown."

"Yeah, but we give 'em better pussy!" Sally screamed.

"Don't listen to her, neither. She's got the morals of an alley-cat in heat."

Billie shrugged indifferently. "Thanks, Dimples. But I can handle myself."

"Sure ya can, honey. Are ya going out with him?"

"No," Billie said, strong and definite.

Billie was well aware she was considered the most beautiful of the current crop of Harlem showgirls. She knew everyone who came into the club had heard of her. Prints of Fletcher's paintings of her sold all over the city. The latest Cotton Club poster featured her in a feather costume. This wasn't the first time flowers had been sent backstage to her, either, or that some man had begged her to have supper. It happened all the time. But Billie always refused. Right now, she wasn't interested in forming an attachment, legitimate or otherwise. She was a realist. She didn't want to be an easy mark like so many of the other girls. She wasn't someone with her hand out, the kind who'd go along with any invitation provided the money and presents made it worthwhile.

Billie considered the money she earned, combined with Virginia's, quite sufficient to cover their family's requirements for the time being. She had learned by now that it *was* all right to dream about living better. There were quite a few coloreds who lived elegantly on Strivers' Row or Convent Avenue, so she knew it was possible. And new moneyed coloreds were continuing to push white families off Sugar Hill into Washington Heights. *Colored people are really coming into their own*, she thought, pleased.

Her dream was to someday live on Sugar Hill, a long stretch of luxury apartments that lined Edgecombe Avenue. They were situated at the edge of the hills that loomed over uptown tenements with an imposing view of downtown skyscrapers and the Harlem River. She also knew dreams took time and perseverance, and she wanted them to come true through her own ability, not from someone else's.

She left the club that night and walked down the alley to the street. Lloyd Harrington's note had said he'd be waiting there for her answer. The usual clusters of thrill-seekers cluttered the sidewalk, despite the Depression. Billie figured Lloyd Harrington would be off by himself, waiting where he could easily spot her. She acted nonchalant, showing no sign of interest in whether he spotted her or not.

A second later, she saw him jump from an open Packard and hurry to her. "I hope your answer is yes." He laughed, slightly embarrassed, sounding like a young boy. "Hey, I should introduce myself. I'm Lloyd Harrington." He held out his hand.

No white man had ever offered to shake her hand before. For an instant, Billie was thrown off balance. "I know who you are," she said.

"Well?" he asked. His eyes were agate gray, his hair light brown, and a pleasant scent of lemon floated around him.

"I liked the flowers," Billie stalled.

"I thought we might go over to Tillie's Chicken Shack." His eyes were hypnotic. "The food's swell, and they've got the best fried chicken and corn bread anywhere, and a great blues singer."

"Sounds terrific, but . . ."

Lloyd Harrington's face fell.

She felt obliged to offer an excuse. "I always go straight home."

He quickly added, "Tillie's is a lot of fun. Can't you break your rule this once?"

Billie was almost tempted, but she knew Adam would have a fit if she accepted a white man's invitation to supper. Even Virginia would side with him. "It's just not possible." She turned away and started toward Boss's apartment.

"Let me drive you home, at least," he called.

She looked back, smiled, then shook her head.

As Billie passed through Boss's living room heading toward

the room she shared with the boys, she was surprised to find Virginia there, sewing in the dim light. Boss refused to put higher wattage bulbs in any of their lamps. "I'll have to raise everyone's rent," she threatened when Billie once complained.

"What are you doing up?" Billie asked.

"I couldn't sleep." Virginia looked more tired than ever.

Billie's stomach tightened. "Is Adam worse?"

Virginia shook her head. "Other than the limp, he's almost mended. It's my cleanin' jobs. I lost one yesterday 'cause I wasn't working fast enough. Today, the other people said they can't afford me no more. Their store went bankrupt."

Billie went to her, gave her a consoling pat and a kiss on the forehead. "Don't worry none. I make enough. Besides, you'll get better jobs and Adam will be working again soon, too."

"You think so?" Virginia's voice sounded hopeful.

"I know so. Now go back to bed."

Billie didn't leave until Virginia put away her sewing and went to her room. Then she undressed, careful not to make a noise, and slipped quietly into her bed so she wouldn't disturb the boys in theirs.

The next night, Billie saw Lloyd Harrington at his usual table. All through the show, whenever she was on the floor, she felt his eyes following her. She was afraid there'd be another box of flowers with another note in the dressing room. This time she might not be able to resist the temptation.

But when she got there, neither flowers nor a note appeared. By the time she was dressed to go home, she began to feel a queasy emptiness, a feeling that was new to her. *Perhaps Harrington's interest wasn't as keen as he pretended,* she thought. When she reached her room and fell into bed, she convinced herself she was lucky. Going out with Lloyd Harrington would only be asking for trouble.

The following night, when Billie paraded past Lloyd's table, she was at first pleased, then deflated, to find it occupied by a strident foursome who were said by the other girls to be Broadway stars. Billie let Dimples ramble on about how important the foursome was, glad to get her mind off Lloyd Harrington's absence. After Dimples ran off, Billie's disappointment in not seeing Harrington returned. The next night, when Harrington again didn't show up, her frustration grew stronger. By the end of the week when he still hadn't reappeared, Billie had become edgy.

"What's eatin' you, kid?" Laurelle asked after Billie made a particularly caustic remark.

"Nothing." Billie pulled on her tiny fringed costume.

"You don't fool me none," Laurelle said with showgirl wisdom. "You're hooked on some guy and he's givin' you the business."

"You're nuts!" said Billie, adjusting her enormous headpiece, wondering if Laurelle was right. Maybe she was getting hooked. Maybe Lloyd Harrington was giving her the business. She made up her mind then and there, she'd drive the man out of her thoughts.

The following afternoon, she ran to the sanctuary of Fletcher's loft. The linseed-and-turpentine-soaked air of his studio was stronger than she remembered.

"How's Adam?" he asked, concern showing on his dark brow.

"Better than we hoped. He's looking for work starting tomorrow."

"And you . . . ?" His expressive eyes searched her face.

"I need a friend," she blurted out.

Fletcher's hands touched her arm. "I've missed you. You don't know how much."

She moved her arm away. "I want us to be friends, Fletcher, not sweethearts." Billie couldn't help noticing the sadness in his face. She felt bad about it, but she couldn't help him. It was an awkward moment for them both.

Her eyes roamed the studio and avoided his. His most recent work leaned against the walls. They were portraits of her that she'd never posed for. She knew they were better than anything he had done before.

Finally, Fletcher pulled himself together. "I want us to be what you want us to be." His face broke into a wide smile.

After that, Billie saw more and more of Fletcher. He often stopped by Boss's in the afternoon, or she'd stop by his studio. And each night after work, Billie'd find Fletcher outside the club waiting to walk her home. She felt protected and comforted. Furthermore, she always had a reason why she couldn't attend the parties thrown occasionally by Owney Madden, whom she wanted to keep away from. Fletcher never let her down. Not once did he step over the carefully drawn line of friendship she had placed between them. Even better, one morning she awoke to find all thoughts of Lloyd Harrington completely erased from her mind. It was as if he'd never existed.

Nights when she was onstage, Billie wasn't conscious of the audience at all anymore. Then one evening it all came to an end. The last show was nearly over when Dimples bounced up to her. "Did you see who just came in big as life and sat down at his old table?"

Billie figured her blank face was enough of an answer.

"The center ringside, dummy! You never notice!"

Dimples didn't have to say his name. During the last number, Billie was unable to resist looking. Lloyd Harrington sat there at the table watching the floor show, not paying the slightest bit of attention to her.

After the show, Billie thanked heaven his infatuation with her was over, and vice versa. She changed into her street clothes, said good-bye to the stragglers, and went outside to meet Fletcher.

For the first time in weeks, Fletcher wasn't there. Three quarters of an hour later, Billie still waited. A cold wind had come up, making her wish she'd worn something warmer. After an hour, Billie concluded it was foolhardy to wait any longer. Obviously something unexpected had held him up.

She was halfway down the block when the open Packard caught her eye. Lloyd Harrington was behind the wheel, smoking a cigarette. She realized he must have been waiting for her all this time. He stepped out of the car when she drew near. "Hello," he said. His face had a sheepish grin. He looked embarrassed.

Billie decided the situation was out of her hands. She was cold after the long wait. She was annoyed Fletcher hadn't shown up. Harrington, she noticed, was more attractive than ever. She liked his bashful demeanor. He seemed sincere. Being practical, she went straight to the point.

"You still want to take me to Tillie's Chicken Shack?"

"You know I do," Harrington said, immediately appearing less shy.

"Then let's go."

"I can't."

Billie stiffened, dumbfounded for an instant. Then she broke into howls of laughter. She couldn't believe it.

Harrington was confused. "What's the joke?"

Billie managed to get out, "You. Me. This whole situation."

He laughed with her, self-consciously, still not sure what was funny. "I thought maybe you'd let me drive you home."

Billie's laughter stopped. "Is that why you came tonight? To drive me home?"

"Since you stick to that rule of yours, I reached the conclusion driving you home was the only solution."

Billie laughed again. "When you said hello, I suddenly decided maybe it was time I broke it."

Harrington said, "I wish I could break it with you. How about tomorrow night?"

Billie ignored the question. "I'm freezing. Do you still want to drive me home?"

"Hey, I'm sorry." He helped her into his car.

She settled into the plush leather. It smelled wonderful, as only leather can. It was Billie's first exposure to those special pleasures the wealthy take for granted and ordinary people don't even know exist. She gave him directions to Boss's place, then luxuriated in the comfort of the car.

Harrington broke into Billie's reverie. "You haven't answered me . . . About supper tomorrow night."

"Well . . ." Billie heard Dimples say one shouldn't be too available.

"Was tonight just a spur-of-the-moment breaking of your rules?"

"I wouldn't say that . . ."

Harrington faced her. "Is there someone else?"

"Not at all. I didn't say I wouldn't."

The boyish smile came back. "You certainly know how to torture a guy."

The car pulled in front of the wrought-iron entrance. She climbed out quickly. "Tomorrow night." Then she ran into the building, hoping no one saw her.

Billie, as was her custom, arose that noon to discover Virginia in Boss's kitchen preparing breakfast for her.

"Sit down," Virginia directed. "I haven't made you a proper breakfast in ages." She placed a plate of scrambled eggs, fried ham, and grits in front of Billie.

Billie filled her mouth with eggs. "This is so good," she said. "What's the occasion?"

Virginia sat down. "Good news, I think. Remember Cousin Geneva? She sent a note to Adam. She wants him to stop by her husband's office. It seems she's married into money, and they have a job for him. What do you think about that?"

Billie hesitated. It seemed odd that Geneva would send Virginia out to starve on the streets one time, and then offer Adam work the next. "What's in it for her?" Billie asked. "Geneva doesn't strike me as the generous type."

"I guess she's decided she's not too good for us, after all. Maybe her conscience got to her," Virginia said. She looked sharply at Billie. "It does seem a little odd, doesn't it?"

"Well, who are we to question good luck? If he can take her money, why not if she's got lots of it," Billie replied. It struck her as odd that Geneva knew where they lived, but she decided not to mention it. Maybe Adam had gone back to Geneva's office to beg for work and just didn't want Virginia to know.

"I guess you shouldn't look a gift horse in the mouth," Virginia said. "He felt so good when he went to see them, his limp hardly showed. At least if he gets a job, we won't be hanging over your shoulders to help pay for stuff. Don't think we don't appreciate it."

"You and Adam took care of me long enough. It's what families do. Besides, it's no problem."

Virginia disagreed. "It ain't right . . . You can't go to school no more like you should. I'm gonna get me some more cleaning jobs soon as I find 'em."

Billie couldn't understand Virginia's insistence on working every minute. "You should take it easy for a while. You don't look so good, if you ask me."

"I gotta do my share, and there's so much . . ."

Boss barged in, interrupting. She clapped her hands. "Your time's up! OUT! Miss Gardner's scheduled now!"

Billie imagined Boss as a prison guard, thinking they must sound exactly the same way. "You know what you can do with your lousy kitchen," she mumbled under her breath, wishing Boss would somehow vanish in a puff of smoke.

Boss inflated herself into a furious rage. "What'd you jus' say?"

Billie pushed her chair back. "Can it! We were leaving anyway." She took Virginia's arm and jauntily walked into the living room with her. A number of other roomers sat crowded around the new radio Boss had bought, listening to a voice mixed with a barrage of static.

"It's the responsibility of each of us to handle unemployment locally," Billie could hear the singsong voice saying. "My responsibility is to balance the budget and then we'll all have jobs again . . ."

"It's President Hoover," one of the roomers whispered to them. "All the way from Washington, D.C."

Later in the afternoon, Billie walked over to Fletcher's. She looked the other way as she passed by the door where Corky once lived. She often wondered about Adam's beating, and his explanation to Virginia. He'd said that Corky was heavily in debt to a numbers runner, and Adam accidentally became involved when he happened to stop by while the runner's henchmen were evening up the score. She suspected Adam was holding something back, and that he didn't want to upset Virginia more than he already had.

On her way up the stairs, new thoughts pushed aside the old memories. Billie's mind jumped to the night before, when Fletcher hadn't shown up. Because of him, she was now committed to supper tonight with Lloyd Harrington. She still wasn't sure whether she was pleased or annoyed, but somehow she sensed she was complicating her life unnecessarily.

Once inside the studio with its homey disarray, Billie relaxed. She found Fletcher sitting cross-legged by the wall of windows, his eyes concentrating on the rooftops across the street. He didn't seem aware of her presence. She said the first thing that came into her mind. "You weren't there last night."

Fletcher turned. He looked apologetic. "I meant to be . . ."

"We had no arrangement." Billie wished she'd said something else. "I guess I was just getting used to the habit."

"We were having a few drinks at Small's and I lost track of the time. Dandy Reed got a grant and was talking about moving the whole niggerati to Europe."

"It ain't funny to call yourselves that. It's degrading . . ."

Fletcher laughed without humor. "It hurts less when you joke about it. We knew when we were all the rage, it wasn't going to last forever."

Billie decided he was still hung over. "Want me to make some coffee?"

He shook his head. "On Broadway they want Noel Coward instead of Harlem high life. Publishers have lost their interest in our stories and poetry—as if we've told all there is to tell. All of a sudden black artists can't give their paintings away. Except for music, the Renaissance is over."

Billie put her hands on her hips. She hated this kind of talk. "If I were you, I'd get off my ass and stop feeling sorry for myself. Your work is better than ever."

Fletcher stared at her. She was beginning to regret hurting his feelings when he broke a long silence. "You grew up without me even noticin'."

"I was born grown-up," she said, still irked by his attitude.

"Are we on for tonight at least?"

She shook her head. "No, it's . . ." She was about to tell him the truth, then changed her mind. "There's a birthday party for one of the girls. I promised I'd hang around . . ."

As Billie left the studio that afternoon, she began thinking of the evening ahead. She imagined herself lost in a maze of expensive furs and wallowing in exotic perfumes, enveloped by soft laughter and hot saxophones, letting herself sink into the pinks and scarlets and purples of the evening, waiting for the hand that would touch hers when the right moment came along.

B illie noticed that Virginia's new excitement had taken on a deeper intensity. Chick and Dewey, too, seemed to sense the importance of the occasion, as if they understood instinctively it meant the bad days following Adam's beating were ready to be forgotten. Adam suddenly was like his old self. His limp disappeared overnight. He held his head high. The only reminder of the beating, and one that would always be visible, was the scar on his forehead.

To Billie, the others' contentment meant even more as weeks went by. Now, she didn't feel guilty about the happiness building up inside her. The girls at the club were the first to notice it.

"My, my, but ain't we all sweetness an' light for a change," Laurelle taunted after one of the performances. "Whatever happened to that evil little tongue you were cultivating?"

"Leave Billie alone," a protective Dimples shouted back before whispering in Billie's ear, "He sure is pretty, honey. And all that dough!"

Billie kept her secrets to herself. She had no intention of gossiping with the girls or even Dimples about her personal life.

Back at Boss's rooming house flat, though, if anyone noticed Billie's gentler manner, it was assumed to be caused by Adam's recovery and his job.

"I figured Cousin Geneva would come around eventually,"

Virginia said to her one afternoon. "And I can see by your smile that you knew it, too."

Billie wasn't aware she was smiling, but she knew it had nothing to do with Virginia's cousin. Her thoughts were on Lloyd. He was a real gent in the best sense of the word, well mannered, kind, and considerate. At first she kept telling herself, *This is impossible. It can't be happening.* Then the good night kisses began to take longer and longer, despite her thinking, *I'll break it off tomorrow night.* But tomorrow night would come and go, and she'd still be seeing him. Finally she told herself, *There's nothing wrong with us being friends. It's no different than me and Fletcher as long as Adam doesn't hear about it. But it won't go any further.*

Then one evening, Lloyd took her across the Hudson on the 125th Street ferry and drove north up through the New Jersey countryside. Shortly before dawn, he pulled off the road and parked high above the river.

"It's beautiful!" Billie exclaimed.

Lloyd seemed to savor her enjoyment more than the view. After a long silence, he said, "I love you, you know. I guess I don't have to tell you."

It was what she'd been waiting to hear, and what she also dreaded. "I feel the same way," she said, hating herself for not being able to hold back the words. Then his lips touched hers, tender at first, then warmer and more passionate, then hotter.

"Do you want to wait?" he asked.

"No," she said.

They made love in the front seat of the Packard while the sun was coming up, oblivious to the chilly morning air, the cramped space, or a man who passed twenty feet from the car on his way to fish in the Hudson below.

It wasn't until their breathing returned to normal that Lloyd realized her condition. "You should have told me . . ."

"It didn't matter," Billie said, feeling somewhat embarrassed.

"I didn't think anyone was a virgin anymore."

She laughed, all her self-consciousness gone. "Maybe no one is, now."

After that night, Billie spent more and more evenings after work with her friend, Dimples, who lived closer to the club. At least, Billie explained her absences that way to Virginia and Adam, who were so wrapped up in their own new life, they didn't think to question it. The truth was that Lloyd had rented a small flat on Edgecombe Avenue at the foot of Sugar Hill so he and Billie would have a place to go when they wanted to be alone.

During the months that followed, Billie gradually became accustomed to the gifts and luxuries that Lloyd showered on her. At first, she felt slightly dirty about the whole thing. Up until then, she'd kept herself from becoming someone's paramour, telling herself she was just working in the club because it was the easiest way to make money. But now she was really living the life of a showgirl, lover and all—not to mention that he was white.

It was awkward going around Harlem with Lloyd. Even though they were driven around in limos, ate the best food in the best restaurants, and left outrageous tips, still they were glared at by waiters, hatcheck girls, cabdrivers, people passing by on the street, black and white. Billie had never paid much

attention to mixed race couples before, but now she always noticed them, looking to see how others reacted to them, because
now she, too, was one of these pairs. Sometimes she wondered
if it was worth the dirty looks and nasty comments that she
heard no matter how hard Lloyd tried to drown them out with
his laughter or loud conversation. But then she'd step into the
flat, furnished sparsely but elegantly, and she'd breathe a sigh of
relief at the cleanliness and quiet. *It's high time I did something
like this*, she told herself one morning after Lloyd had left the
apartment and she was luxuriating in bed before she had to get
up and return home to Adam and Virginia's place. *I'm a sucker
for not having done this earlier.* So far, Lloyd seemed to be considerate, not taking her for granted, not seeing other women on
the side. *And at least he's good-looking*, she thought, thinking with
a shudder of some of the men she'd seen Laurelle and Sally
with. All in all, she was very lucky. *And best of all, no one at the
club knows*, Billie thought.

"Of course, everyone knows," Dimples said when Billie eventually asked if she'd heard anything. "They know you got a
place somewhere too, but no one's exactly sure just where." Not
long after, the *World Sun*'s gossip column ran a blind item,
"What rich, make that *very* rich, heir to what famous railroad
fortune is up to his dollar signs in love with what beauteous
Harlem showgirl?" Dimples had pointed the column out to Billie.

"That could be anyone," Billie frowned, and by the next day,
she'd fooled herself into thinking her affair was known only to
the girls she worked with.

Seven days later, Billie received a note from Fletcher. "Meet

me at Small's tomorrow. At five. I want to say good-bye." Billie
was still wondering what this meant as she walked into Small's
the following afternoon and found Fletcher at a table in the
back. A guitar player was softly playing the blues to himself in
one corner of the bandstand. Fletcher looked better than the
last time she'd seen him. His eyes had their old sparkle back,
and the slump had left his shoulders. She held out the note.
"What's this business about good-bye?"

Fletcher pulled out a chair. "Sit down and have a drink with
me."

Billie seldom drank. She'd seen how quickly liquor cost
showgirls their jobs. Even the faces of the young ones soon
couldn't hide the cocktails. Today, however, she felt she had to
join him. She sat down and waited until after he'd ordered before saying, "You don't have to say good-bye to me. I . . ." She
was about to explain why, when he held up his long arms.

"Not just to you, Billie. To everyone. To Harlem."

She wasn't prepared for this. "I don't understand." An emptiness began to form in the pit of her stomach. The waiter
brought their drinks.

"Dandy Reed, Howard Dobbins, me, and a couple of other
guys . . . we're leaving for Paris tonight. The Negro cultural
boom may be over here, but they say it's goin' great guns over
there." Fletcher raised his glass. "To you," he said. "My perfect
model, my perfect friend."

For an instant, out of guilt, she thought he was being sarcastic, then his smile told her he wasn't. She lifted her glass, deciding it wasn't the time to tell him about Lloyd. "Good Luck,"
she said. "I'll miss you."

Fletcher kissed her in a brotherly way. "I'll be back. Maybe then, my timing will be better."

"Maybe," Billie said, wishing he wasn't going, feeling somehow lonely already—knowing, though, there was nothing she could say that would change his mind.

Then Fletcher was gone.

Chapter Sixteen

M ost of Billie's co-workers hated rehearsal. If they were dancers, they were constantly limbering up at the barre, or going over steps with the choreographer. If they were musicians, they were expected to be perfect even during rehearsal, no more, no less. But showgirls, Billie discovered, only had to look good. Very little else mattered.

Rehearsal on this particular day was more chaotic than usual. Owney was berating his kitchen staff in such a loud voice, Ethel Waters couldn't continue her song. The bass player lost his tempo. Ethel threw her music on the piano, strutted over to the bar, ordered a double sloe gin, sat down, and propped her shapely legs on the bar.

Owney Madden walked out of the kitchen's service doors with a wad of papers in his hand, red-faced from anger. The stairwell leading to his office was located behind the bar. He marched up to Ethel, belligerent, glancing alternately at her face and then at her legs still propped up on the bar.

"What the hell is this?" he barked at Ethel. "I thought you needed to rehearse!"

Laurelle, who sat at one of the ringsides with Billie, Dimples, and a couple of the other girls, leaned over and whispered, "Oh-oh. He's messin' with the wrong bitch this time." Even some of the help stopped doing their chores to see what she'd do.

Ethel slowly moved her legs from the bar and slithered down the bar stool. Her large breasts met Owney's nose. "Now let me tell you what I really need, Owney. I need a drink!" She tossed her bobbed hair back and poured the rest of her drink down with the flourish of a Spanish dancer. "Now I don't need one anymore." She flicked Owney's tie with a well-manicured finger that sported a large, sparkling diamond.

"But," she said, striking a dramatic pose, "I do need a man." She glanced over her shoulder at the bartender, who returned a wide smile. "And, sugar, evidently, that's taken care of too." She pulled Owney's tie out from behind his vest and drew him closer. "So why don't you get off of your cheap ass and go to the florist, 'cause what I *really* need is a dozen orchids for my opening tonight, you cute little devil." She kissed him on the forehead. Owney's face turned crimson again, only this time from a blush. "And now I need to get on with my rehearsal, sweetie, without your filthy-mouthing, loud-talking interruptions."

Owney smiled back, looking like a little schoolboy since Ethel was a good foot and a half taller. She'd handled him like an expert, melting his foul tongue into butter with one, quick silly gesture and yet maintaining her status as a star.

That night, after Ethel sang her first number, carrying a bouquet of a dozen orchids, she told the expensively dressed crowd of first-nighters what had happened during rehearsal. But that was just the beginning, she said, pulling her microphone to Owney's table. Billie, by now, had seen many opening nights from the wings and although she'd heard lots of fanciful introductions of Owney Madden, she'd never heard one with a story.

"You liked that story?" she asked the audience in a friendly manner, as if they were old friends. "I thought it would be a fun way to introduce Owney tonight," Ethel explained to the slummers over their applause. "So, earlier tonight," she continued, "I went to his office to see if he minded if I told it. You know how easily men's feelings get hurt. And he said, 'Of course not,' I mean he was real good-natured about it."

"But he was busy with some papers on his desk and I wasn't sure if he was listening to me or leveling with me, so I asked again if it was all right to introduce him with the story."

Owney began to shake with laughter. He was finding it difficult to compose himself.

"So Owney asked me what did he have to do to apologize to his star, and I told him he should seal our little spat with a kiss. 'But you're too tall,' he said, and suggested I bend down and close my eyes. So I did. Then he hopped around and kissed my behind."

" 'Don't be embarrassed,' he told me. 'My last star act was a trained dog—and I had to kiss her ass too!' "

The audience was in stitches. Ethel was too much of a pro

not to take advantage of the moment. She spontaneously took an orchid from her bouquet and presented it to Owney. The crowd applauded her as the spotlight followed her return to the piano; then a few gasps starting at the back of the audience that seemed to work their way toward Ethel made her turn. Each of the eighteen waiters and four bartenders carried two baskets of orchids and placed them at Ethel's feet. It took her by surprise. She looked at Owney in bewilderment. He blew a kiss to her and gestured with a sweeping arm that he appreciated the capacity group of worshipers her talent had brought there.

When Ethel couldn't control her tears a second longer she turned to Duke Ellington at the piano. Billie and Dimples could see her from the wings. "Got a hanky?" Dimples whimpered.

Billie laughed between tears. "In this costume?"

Duke played a key chord for Ethel when she thought she had composed herself, but when she turned back toward the audience and the orchids, a new flood of tears welled in her eyes. She started to laugh to ward off the tears, and the audience laughed and applauded and cried with her for a good ten minutes.

Finally, Ethel held up her hand. An obedient hush fell over the audience. Even the kitchen help had stopped their work. She nodded to Duke, then sang a sad love song Dandy Reed had written for her just before he left for Paris called "The Note He Left Behind."

When she finished it, there wasn't a dry eye in the house.

A few weeks later, while Billie and Duke were sharing a cab on their way to the Apollo to catch an afternoon show, she teased him about that night.

"I saw you," she said taunting him. It was a hot and sticky

summer day, and traffic was jammed due to floods from open
fire hydrants ahead. The cabdriver kept staring back at them
through the rearview mirror.

"Take a side street," Duke impatiently directed the driver.
Then he turned to Billie, who was nudging him. "You saw
me . . . ?"

"I saw you wiping your eyes at the piano that night with
Ethel and all those orchids," she teased as they headed downtown on St. Nicholas Avenue.

"That was one of the most memorable nights I have ever
had—but I didn't cry." He laughed at his obvious lie. "Yeah, I
cried, but so did Sonny Greer and all those tough guys in the
brass section."

Duke treated Billie like a sister. He was a neighbor at the
Sugar Hill apartment, and was one of the few people she and
Lloyd socialized with. Duke took her to parties and recording
sessions, introducing her to famous people she admired. He
shared his intellect, his secrets, his philosophies. Billie was
thinking how lucky she was when he asked the cabbie to stop.

"I'll only be a minute," he said, getting out of the taxi. He
approached a drunken woman who was having difficulty climbing the five steps that led into a neglected tenement house. The
woman's hair was unkempt, matted from equal neglect. Her
legs were swollen from booze and her dress looked as if it had
been slept in. Billie couldn't hear what Duke was saying, but he
handed the dazed woman some money and returned to the cab
with a frown of concern on his brow. He didn't say a word for a
full block.

"She used to sing with my first band," he explained. "In college. Good voice, real sweet."

"So how did she end up like that?"

Duke shook his head sadly as he patted his perspiration away. "I don't know what makes people pour their talent down a drain with cheap hootch. She never believed she had anything to offer. Always apologized for doing something I would never notice. Just before we'd play at a school dance, she'd fall apart and she'd run to the bathroom, and after a few minutes she'd come out fresh as a daisy." He lit a cigarette and threw the match out the open window.

"I used to joke with her a lot to try to calm her down. She was always sick, throwing up, nervous. Lena used to be that way when she first started. I never dreamed this innocent little gal was putting away a quart every night."

"Couldn't you smell it from her breath?"

"She stayed her distance. And since I thought she was vomiting all over the place, I kept far from smelling range. Then one night at a Kappa dance, in the middle of a serious song, she raised her arms and a bottle she was concealing under her dress dropped to the stage. Then, as if the loud crash wasn't bad enough, the bottle rolled off the edge of the bandstand and splashed on the Dean of Women's shoes."

He looked out on the sweltering streets as he thought of that night. "I felt so bad for her. Keep in mind, I kept strict rules for my band. So, a few of the boys caught on to her bathroom routine and she was blackmailed into going to bed with them— each of them—to keep it quiet."

"How rotten."

"It was quite a scandal on campus. A few of the guys were expelled, including her. She kept in touch with me for a while, then . . ."

"Booze did her in," Billie concluded.

"No," he corrected, "lack of confidence did her in."

The taxi pulled over to the curb on 126th Street, where the most notable backstage in Harlem was located. A few of the local kids playing stickball spotted Duke and scrambled to get his autograph.

"I thought I recognized you," the cabdriver said as he gave Duke his change. "You're my wife's favorite singer, Mr. Calloway."

That weekend, Billie and Lloyd had their first argument. She had gone over the reasons why it was better to meet him somewhere other than her neighborhood, but as she stepped out of her apartment building, there he was, leaning against his Packard, reading the *Harlem Voice*, looking like a well-scrubbed, well-dressed, spoiled, rich man who was oblivious to the crowd's admiration of his car. *How could I ever explain this to Adam or Virginia?* she thought in a mental scream as she ducked into the car as quickly and as inconspicuously as she could manage, waving weakly at neighbors who knew her from the building, hoping none of them knew the rest of her family.

"How could you park there!" she complained when they reached Lenox Avenue.

Lloyd kept his smile. "It was easy. I drove."

She hated it when he teased her.

"You look lovely."

She pretended to be interested in the newspaper he'd placed on the car floor. She held it up between them.

"I bought a present for you."

She ignored him.

"Duke has a surprise for us." She pulled the paper down. Curiosity had replaced her annoyance. "I knew that would get a rise out of you. He'll tell us at the Park Casino. I've been wanting to take you there."

The Park Casino was a private club that occupied the top two stories of the tallest building on 110th Street. It catered to a privileged class of politicians, celebrities, sports figures, gangsters posing as ordinary businessmen, and, as Lloyd put it, "ordinary businessmen posing as savvy gangsters who spend extraordinary sums of money to impress perfect strangers."

A small elevator that was inlaid with yellow silk taffeta panels carried Billie and Lloyd to the top floor where they were greeted by the owner, a loudmouthed woman in her forties who wore a great deal of jewelry on her bare arms and what seemed like a full bottle of perfume on her ample body. Her yellow dress matched the panels in the elevator.

"Looks like a colored Mae West," Lloyd whispered.

The woman led them through an art deco hall with spotlighted sculptures and avant-garde impressionist paintings, past a crowded, smoky room of gamblers at gaming tables, and finally to two padded yellow taffeta doors. Billie was stunned when they entered the main ballroom. The place was magical.

They were on a landing of thick dark blue carpet surrounded by a shiny silver and gold railing. A sweeping wide staircase spiraled down to an elegant restaurant of candlelit tables under two-story windows and stars and a full moon and Central Park below. The owner advised Billie to take her shoes off because high heels had a tendency to get caught in the carpet.

"Thanks," Billie said, walking down perfectly poised, "but this is what I do for a living."

The owner didn't understand, but when they joined Duke and his current girlfriend at their table they all enjoyed a good laugh from it. Billie could always tell when he had a good story to tell or something up his sleeve. He would dawdle. This time he dawdled with Lloyd and Billie over the first round of drinks, making a *very* long story out of his surprise. First he described the concert he gave in Chicago where the band performed some of his more serious compositions. He didn't mind that some of the critics didn't understand what his new music was all about, but he was disappointed when some of his fans in the audience seemed restless, as if they'd rather dance.

"Some of them weren't even listening," he complained. "Just because it wasn't something they could pop their fingers to. A one, a two . . . Anyway, Larry Brown and Sonny and I went to the bar at Du Sable." He paused after his exaggerated pronunciation of the hotel that was similar to the Hotel Harlem, where Negro musicians hung out, indicating he was getting to the heart of his story. "And I got a phone call."

"And?" Billie impatiently prodded.

"And Paramount accepted my terms."

"You're going to make a movie?" Lloyd asked.

Over dinner, Duke explained why he was so pleased. The studio wanted him to play a bandleader who would lead a studio orchestra in the film. He refused the part unless his own band was in the movie too. He was excited about the role, although he had no deceptions about his career as an actor, a subject he found laughable. The part called for a colored hero who had a pretty girlfriend—like in the Oscar Micheaux films—and, he emphasized, he wasn't asked to act like Stepin Fetchit. "Funny," Duke mused, "Oscar called me a few years ago, wanting me to be in a one-reeler of his. I decided it wasn't worth the time it would take."

"Why?" Billie wanted to know.

"Well, first of all, he doesn't pay much. He can't afford the kind of salaries the studios give out, poor guy. I think he does everything but paint the scenery—writes, directs—and he puts a lot of creative energy into his work, but he's poor. He's got to haul ass all over the country with his film under his arm, going to all the colored theaters to show them for a week to earn enough money to make another one. It's like selling Fuller brushes from town to town. So a handful of people in each town and city gets to see me in one of Oscar's movies. But if a major studio makes the same movie, it gets played in lots of theaters all over the country."

Lloyd wasn't following his drift.

"All I'm saying," Duke continued, "is, if *I'm* accepted by the audiences, America is ready to accept *real* colored actors playing real people who laugh and cry and love and die like everybody else."

Billie applauded him and kissed him on the cheek.

"So let me tell you what the movie is all about . . ."

A coarse voice coming from behind a potted palm interrupted their chatter. It was Laurelle, the girl from the club, making sure her portly gentleman friend saw her socializing with Duke. They were on their way to the gambling tables. She stopped at their table, chatting with Duke and treating the rest of the group as if they were part of the tableware. When Laurelle left, Billie turned to catch a glimpse of the girl's new love interest.

The man and Laurelle had halted at the foot of the staircase to talk to Judge Andrew, a friend of Duke's from Washington. "I've seen that guy before," Billie said. When the judge scanned the room as he and his party were escorted to their table, he caught Duke's signal to stop by. The judge was a charming man with a rich coffee complexion and silver hair framing a youthful face. Duke asked him about the man with Laurelle.

"Lester? He comes from an old line of money. Rarely see him with his wife. He's trying to get me to invest in some renovation scheme of his. Sounds pretty interesting."

Billie then knew where she'd seen him. Virginia had cut out a picture from the *Amsterdam News* several weeks earlier, showing Geneva and her husband, Lester, stepping out at the Renaissance Ballroom. Before the judge left to rejoin his table, Billie asked, "Is his last name Noble?"

"Yes. Friend of yours?"

"No. But he's close to someone who used to be."

Several days passed before Billie had a chance to talk to Virginia alone. They were walking from the Donato grocery store, each carrying a package of groceries, on an ideal summer afternoon of marine blue skies and billowy clouds. Virginia seemed happier and prettier than Billie had seen her looking in a long time. That's when Virginia brought up Geneva.

"I sent Dewey by her office with an invitation to the church social tonight. They prob'bly won't come 'cause it isn't fancy enough."

Billie started to tell Virginia about seeing Lester at the Park Casino, but she realized she'd have to explain who she was with, why, and all the other information that would go along with it. She decided to keep it to herself.

Later on, while Virginia was ironing a dress in her tiny bedroom, Virginia brought up Geneva's name again, talking on and on about her generosity and how much nicer she seemed now that she was happily married. Billie's lips felt numb. Lester Noble's infidelity seemed less important to her.

As Virginia put the last finishing touches on her dress, Billie studied her sister-in-law's angelic face. She didn't have any more right to tell Virginia about Lester's carrying on than she had a right to tell her about Geneva's chasing Adam in Jacksonville, and probably all over Harlem. It was pretty obvious to her why Geneva got Adam the job. Then a feeling of guilt engulfed her. Her family needed money, but she couldn't give them much. Adam had a fit whenever she bought even the smallest item for them. Her salary from the Cotton Club alone could take care of the family, but Adam wouldn't hear of it, and he definitely wouldn't accept any money from Lloyd. She had deceived poor Adam and Virginia as much as Geneva had. And although she'd never forgive Geneva for the shabby way she treated them when they first got to Harlem, after seeing Lester slobbering over Laurelle, she couldn't help feeling sorry for her.

Chapter Seventeen

Geneva stood at the large window that overlooked the street, watching Dewey disappear around the building, wishing Virginia would stop sending her home-cooked dishes. If she was firm enough with Dewey, she wondered if he'd tell Virginia about the "special diet" she pretended to be on. Dewey looked just like his father, and was probably just as headstrong.

She left the view of 125th Street and went into the inner office, wondering if Lester had any suspicion of her feelings for Adam. If he had, he certainly showed no signs. He never questioned the night she lost her head, affectionately greeting Adam in front of everyone. Still, Lester treated Adam as nice as could be.

Remembering made her smile. It was almost like old times. She and Adam against everyone else. Geneva's mouth relaxed as the memory took over. She went back to her desk and took a small mirror from her handbag. She studied her face, letting it go soft. For a moment, she felt innocent and young again. *I was pretty then*, she told herself. *Pretty* . . . Her face reverted to its newer, more sophisticated expression. . . . *and dumb.* She decided she preferred the way she looked now.

Geneva put the mirror away, letting her thoughts return to Adam. So far, he remained the perfect gentleman, never outwardly implying that his attraction for her ran as deep as ever. But Geneva knew it did, as only a woman could know. She knew by the way his eyes avoided hers, by the care he took never to stand too close to her, from the unspoken expectancy hovering in the air whenever they were together. If only he didn't have that old-fashioned sense of morality ingrained in him, holding him back, she fumed. Wasn't he aware times had changed? That life here was different from down South? That marriage meant next to nothing these days, and fidelity even less? Frustration unsettled Geneva's stomach.

She heard the hall door open and close. Footsteps crossed the linoleum floor. She knew it was Adam; Lester's steps sounded entirely different. She pulled the mirror back out and gave her face one final check. "Who's there?" she called, keeping her voice low and interesting.

"Me."

"And Lester?" Her heart stopped as she waited.

"He said he had something to take care of," he responded in the new, careful voice Geneva had been teaching him.

Geneva breathed again. A lighthearted mood replaced the cramped tenseness. She walked into the next office, momentarily at peace. Adam was putting papers into the top drawer of his desk. "How did it go?" she asked, trying not to appear too interested in Adam's first outside meeting with Lester. Adam seemed to look everywhere, except at her. "Lester got the deeds turned over to us, so I guess it went okay."

A look of concern crossed Adam's face. She'd seen the look before, and had assumed it was worry over learning business procedures and saying the right thing. Now it all became clear in her mind. The job wasn't causing it, Virginia was. Geneva suspected Virginia had no understanding of what he was going through at the office. How could she? Most likely, she resented Adam's new responsibilities. Geneva decided to get it out into the open. "She doesn't fit in anymore, does she?"

Adam's eyes were curious. "Who?"

"Virginia," she said.

"What makes you say that?" His voice was guarded.

Geneva was convinced she was on the right track. "It's obvious she can't adjust to city life. She's holding you back."

Adam smiled, amused. "You don't know what you're talkin' about."

Geneva guessed he was speaking more out of loyalty than truth. "You need someone who knows the score," she said, stepping closer to the desk, wishing he'd look at her. "Adam!"

Now he did. Their eyes locked. Geneva felt encouraged. She moved around the desk and took hold of his arm. "Look in my eyes! Can't you see what's there? What's always been there? You should have married me, not her. You still love me. I can tell! I know it! Don't try to hide it!" Her heart pounded frantically. She'd been waiting so long to say this.

Adam removed her hand. "You shouldn't say things like that."

"Why not, for God's sake, if they're true? I'm not afraid of them!"

"I love Virginia," he said. "Anything between you an' me is out of the question."

Her ears pounded now. The room closed in. "It isn't true!" Her voice rose. "You're just saying it because . . ."

A voice behind her cut off her words. "What's wrong?"

She swung around. Lester was coming in from the hall. She ran to him, as if he were the only thing on her mind. "Nothing . . ."

Lester pecked at her cheek. "I could hear your voice in the hall . . ."

"She doesn't like the way I answer the phone," Adam said.

"Oh, is that all?" Lester went into the inner office.

Geneva remained, watching Adam study an opened ledger. He seemed oblivious to the interrupted conversation, as if it never took place. Lester's door stayed open. Her unfinished business with Adam would have to wait. *Damn Lester!* she thought. If only he'd stayed away longer. She would have cleared the air with Adam. Instead, she was left with this void inside her.

She moved back toward Adam's desk, catching a glimpse of Lester's eyes as she crossed in front of his door. She picked up a pack of Adam's cigarettes lying beside the ledger and helped herself. "Light?" she asked. Without looking up, Adam struck a match and held it in her direction. "Thanks," she said with a tinge of sarcasm, becoming as annoyed with him as she was with Lester. "You and Virginia don't get out much, I take it."

"Not much."

"I didn't think so. Otherwise you'd know all about it . . ."
Geneva was determined to get a rise out of him. "Lester and I
were at Tillie's Chicken Shack last night after the show at the
Harlem Opera House."

"Uh-huh." Adam signed another paper.

"I couldn't believe my eyes when she walked in. She was such
an awkward little girl . . ." Geneva paused for a puff. "But she
really is gorgeous now . . ."

He looked up, finally. "Who?"

Geneva felt she was beginning to strike paydirt. "Her friend
is so handsome. They go everywhere together."

"Whose friend?"

Adam's attention was riveted on Geneva and she basked in it.
"I really shouldn't say anything," she said. She wanted him to
get angry, to shake the information out of her. The scar above
his eye reddened. A scowl creased his forehead. At that instant,
Lester called out from the other office.

"Geneva!" His voice was more insistent than usual. Geneva
threw Adam one last teasing look before reluctantly joining
Lester.

"You shouldn't bother him," Lester reprimanded.

"I was trying to tell him something he should know." She
jabbed out the cigarette in an ashtray Mother Noble had given
Lester.

"He has a lot to do," Lester said, dumping the contents of
the ashtray into his wastebasket. "You can tell him later."

"Don't think I won't," Geneva snapped.

Chapter Eighteen

A dam did his best to concentrate on the pa-pers in front of him, but his mind kept re-turning to his conversation with Virginia the night before.

"She ain't never around anymore," he complained. "This place ain't no more to her than a closet to hang her clothes in." It was another humid night of stifling heat. They'd been sitting on the sidewalk on two wooden chairs left behind by a recently evicted family. People all up and down the block were fanning themselves with anything they could find, hanging about, on the stoops, out on their windowsills and fire escapes.

Virginia poured another glass of lemonade for him from the pickle jar she'd brought down with her. "Don't fret 'bout Billie. She feels cramped up in Boss's place. Besides, she's a grown-up young woman."

"I don't like her stayin' all the time at that Dimples's apart-ment."

Virginia's thin hand patted his cheek as if to smooth away any fears. "If I could find me another cleaning job, we'd have enough for a real apartment of our own. A place we can use like we want instead of like Boss wants us to."

Adam glared at her. "You were workin' yourself to death before, and you're not goin' back to that again."

They were still there, listening to the music coming from a nearby window, enjoying any slight breeze that found its way to them, when Boss came through the grillwork entrance. "Hot enough for you lovebirds?" Her voice had a whine in it.

Adam ignored her, but Virginia nodded. "In Florida this time of year, it's twice as hot," she smiled. "Sometimes you can hardly breathe."

"Hotter'n this? No wonder so many niggers runnin' up here, straight out of the country, messin' Harlem up."

Adam had to speak up then. "You're lucky Harlem's gettin' so crowded. Otherwise you couldn't skin us with your high rents for what ain't worth half the price,"

Boss's voice went testy. "If you don't like it, you know what you can do." When he didn't answer her, it turned snide. "Don't see much of that fancy sister of yours, Virginia."

"We get along so well, people think we're sisters," Virginia said, "but she's Adam's stepsister."

"I should've known," she said, turning to leave. "They both got sassy ways." She went back inside.

After a long silence, Adam rested his lemonade on the sidewalk, and said, "See? Everyone thinks it's funny Billie ain't 'round much."

Twenty-four hours later, plaguing thoughts of Billie still

gnawed at Adam. Nagging little references and clues kept cropping up. Now, this from Geneva. He knew perfectly well she'd been baiting him, trying to get attention for herself. But it didn't soften the realization that Billie was hiding something she was ashamed of.

Usually, Adam stayed longer in the office than Lester or Geneva, reading documents, looking up words he didn't understand, checking entries in the ledger. However, this afternoon, he went home before they did. Their voices were droning on in what sounded like a serious discussion when he shut the hall door behind him. He had decided it was time to have it out with Billie. If he were lucky, he'd get home before she left.

He was just rounding the corner of the last block when he saw Billie running out through the grillwork entrance. It was still hot and the stoops and sidewalks were crowded. "I want to talk to you!" he yelled.

She darted around a cab to the other side of Lenox Avenue. "Can't," she called back. "I'm already late. See you tomorrow."

Adam started to run after her, then changed his mind. He didn't want them to look like trash, talking their business in the street, but he was more bothered than ever now.

After supper, Adam treated Virginia, Chick, and Dewey to a ride down to Washington Square and back to Harlem on an open top deck of a Fifth Avenue double-decker bus. It was one way to get the kids cool and one way to cool himself down.

The next morning, Adam decided to question Geneva, but she remained in her office with Lester. Occasionally he'd hear her voice rise, and he knew they were having another argument. Recently this had become a habit. It wasn't until just before noon that the door to the inner office opened and Lester stormed out. "I'll be back later," he said, slamming the hall door, rattling the frosted glass.

Geneva came out soon after. "I wish his mother had taught him better manners," she said, half-sarcastically. Her eyes flitted around the room. "I hate eating alone. How about having lunch with me?"

Adam ignored the invitation. "Let's talk about Billie."

"We can talk about it at lunch."

"Let's talk about it now!" Adam felt a nerve twitch in his neck. "Who's she messin' with?"

Geneva's tone turned coy. "So you're finally waking up."

His temper exploded. He couldn't control it. He didn't care about the job. He went to her and roughly grabbed her shoulders. The need for Geneva's goodwill slipped from his mind. He pressed his fingers into her flesh, feeling her body shudder between his hands. "What do you know?"

Her voice lost its confidence. "They call her the Cinderella Showgirl."

"What's that supposed to mean?"

"It means she's involved with a wealthy man. It means everyone envies her. It means . . ." Her voice broke off. "How do I know what it means?"

Adam let his grip loosen. "What's his name?"

Geneva pulled away. He watched her turn, start for her office, then stop and face him again. "She's his mistress. He took an apartment for her on Sugar Hill. Anyhow, that's what they say." She turned away once more. "His name's Lloyd Harrington."

"Harrington," Adam repeated. His voice sounded hoarse in his ears.

"I haven't told you the best part," Geneva said, standing at the door of her office, her voice cool again.

"I can guess it." Adam knew full well what she meant. As soon as Geneva said *wealthy*, it was clear. He left without looking back, going into the first gin mill he saw. Three hours later, Adam felt subdued enough to go to Boss's apartment. Chick and Dewey were in the living room listening to the radio with Virginia. "Where's Billie?" he asked.

"She stayed with Dimples last night. You know that." Virginia's eyes showed him she didn't want to talk in front of the boys. "Why don't you two go outside and play."

They scrambled to their feet. After they ran off, Virginia led Adam into their room, away from Boss's nosy roomers, who were staring from their open doors, sniffing gossip. Once alone, she said, "What is it?"

Adam didn't trust his voice. He finally managed to get out, "Billie's sleepin' with some white man."

Virginia's hands shook. "What are you going to do?"

"I'm gonna pack her belongings," he said, feeling he couldn't let Billie disgrace them and not do anything about it.

After a long time, Virginia said, "You've got to give her a chance to make a choice."

"She already made it." He got out one of the old straw valises from under the bed and carried it into Billie's room. As Virginia sobbed, he methodically went through the drawers of the chipped veneer dresser, taking out Billie's things. When everything was packed, he returned to Virginia and set the valise and a shopping bag by the door. "We'll just wait," he said.

Billie came in shortly after seven. "Oh, there you are," she said to Virginia, seeing her first in the brilliant summer dusk that blazed through the window. "Don't bother to fix dinner for me. I'm changing clothes and running right off again." Her face turned in Adam's direction. "Hello," she smiled. "You're home early." When neither spoke, she asked, "Why so glum?"

Virginia sniffed. "I'm sorry. Adam won't listen to me."

Adam watched Billie's eyes move to the valise. When she looked back at him, he could see she understood. "I guess I've been expecting it," she said. "I couldn't help it. I didn't mean to make everyone feel bad." She walked over to the valise. Adam wanted to say a lot of things, but he couldn't put them into words.

Virginia ran to Billie, embracing her. "If only it had been Fletcher . . ."

"Unfortunately, it wasn't," Billie said. She picked up the valise and walked out.

Virginia sat at the edge of the bed crying softly. "You shouldn't have let her go." Her voice was barely audible.

"I had to."

After that, Adam refused to discuss Billie's disappearance. Whenever Chick and Dewey wanted to know where she was, he told them, "She ain't part of us anymore." To Boss's inquiry, he said, "None of ya damn business." To Geneva, he said, "She made her bed, she'll have to lay in it."

Without Billie paying some of the expenses, Adam was just able to squeeze by. On Sundays after church, he and Virginia would take the boys on the pretense of a stroll, while they searched for a cheaper place to live. They could find nothing Adam liked.

Adam knew Virginia was still looking for a cleaning job, although he told her not to. One evening, she told Adam not to worry. "Getting around sure has opened my eyes. We should thank the Lord and Cousin Geneva that you go to work every day."

Adam looked lovingly at her small, chiseled face. Then, a feeling of uneasiness came over him. Perhaps it was the mention of Geneva's name. He knew he'd have to make a decision soon. Either way, it meant things would be different. He wasn't looking forward to the day.

At the job, all Lester could talk about was how bad the real estate business had become. "You don't know the games I have to play to keep afloat," he confided to Adam one afternoon. They'd just called on a nervous owner of a Strivers' Row house who had made his money selling insurance. Lester had to talk a blue streak to get the owner to assign him a piece of recently foreclosed property. After getting the man's signature, Lester was visibly worn out. He'd said he was in no mood to go back to the office, insisting Adam join him for a few drinks. They went around the corner of 137th Street to a speakeasy on Seventh Avenue.

A huge carved door swung open, and Lester was greeted by a colored man as if he were the King of England. He took their hats and handed them to a sleepy-eyed hatcheck girl, then led them into the fanciest room Adam had ever been in. His weight sunk into a soft dark green carpet, making the soles of his new shoes slip as he approached the mirrored bar. He admired the expensive-looking paintings along the opposite wall. He was amused that he'd passed this place many times before and never given it a second thought. It was a just a plain gray building with an ordinary stoop and rickety wooden steps that led to the basement.

Looking at Lester on the next bar stool, Adam noticed beads of sweat accumulating on his pale forehead. Probably worried about Geneva's high-spending ways, he surmised.

Lester lifted his double scotch. "Cheers," he said.

Adam's eyes wandered about the empty room of crystal chandeliers and large paintings and burgundy wallpaper.

Lester must have read his thoughts. He said, "This place is too expensive for riffraff. You should be here 'round midnight. Piled to the ceiling with important people."

Lester drained his glass and signaled for another. "Geneva always complains about my bills from here," he said, "but she doesn't seem to understand how much it costs to entertain clients these days. She doesn't realize you've got to bend a little if you want to keep your money." He patted his forehead with a handkerchief he lifted from his breast pocket. A business card dropped from it. Before he could get off his bar stool, a waiter seemed to appear from nowhere, handed the card back to him, then disappeared equally as quickly.

"She'll see the light eventually," Lester concluded while he tucked the card back into his coat pocket. "She's a pigheaded woman, but she'll stop complaining when the bucks start rolling in. She likes money as much as I do."

When they got back to the office, it was only a few minutes after five, but the door was locked. Geneva wasn't there. Lester shrugged. "At least I won't have to listen to complaints until I get home."

Chapter Nineteen

Geneva had grown accustomed to Lester's bad habit of making social engagements without consulting her, like the Gavel Club Dance that evening at the Renaissance Ballroom, but she hated when he'd wait to tell her until the day of the affair. Luckily, she'd taken the precaution of having her dressmaker stitch a few new ball gowns for last-minute notices. Worse was his habit of taking ill on the day of the affair, sending her off to represent the family, entering on the other arm of a friend's husband.

As Judge Andrew and his wife, Thelma, drove her home from the formal, she promised herself she'd never go to another dance without an escort ever again.

Despite every man at the table asking her to dance at least once, she had had a miserable time. It was embarrassing for her to lie over and over about Lester's sudden toothache. She didn't believe it, so why should they? And it was so humiliating to be left alone at the table when the band played the "Sweetheart's Waltz," she left for the ladies' room.

While she was in a toilet stall, staring at the blue and pink tiles beneath her rhinestoned slippers, she heard a familiar voice.

"Of course he's cheating on her. I thought everybody knew that," the voice said.

"Poor Geneva, and she adores Lester."

At that moment, Geneva flushed the toilet. She didn't want to hear anymore. She stayed in the stall until her two friends left, not wanting to cause any more embarrassment for herself. She was thinking of this horrid little moment when they reached Mount Morris Park. The judge left Thelma in the car and accompanied Geneva to the front door of her house. "I can't remember when I've enjoyed a dance more," she lied as she searched for her key.

"Is everything all right with you and Lester?" he asked. His genuine concern seemed to reinforce her fears.

"Right as rain," she responded instinctively with a kiss on his cheek. "Things couldn't be better. Tell Thelma I'll call her tomorrow."

She waved from her opened door until the car rounded the corner, then she quickly shut the cold late evening breeze outside. Her feet were tired and while she leaned over to remove a slipper, she noticed a light was on in the kitchen downstairs. After removing the other shoe, she went down the stairs. Lester was sitting at the kitchen table, staring into a cup of tea, still dressed from work.

"How's your tooth?"

He hadn't heard her come in and reacted with a startled look, as if someone had caught him doing something bad. "It's not hurting anymore. Guess I won't have to go to the dentist after all."

She opened a cabinet near the sink and pulled out a glass. She looked at Lester, as if for the first time, and decided he was loathsome. She also decided to have a little fun at his expense. "Why didn't you come home this afternoon?"

Lester gulped from his cup. "Couldn't. I had to meet the Brockingtons. They're thinking about selling their place in Flatbush. I think they'll like the brownstone on 136th Street."

Geneva savored this moment. She took her satin jacket off and twirled her sparkling slipper by its strap around her index finger. "Oh? How are Bea and Jacob?"

"Fine. They said to say hello."

"Save your breath, Lester. The Brockingtons were at the dance tonight. Their attorney is a Kappa, it turns out. Oh, and by the way, they told me to say hello to *you!*"

Lester wiped his upper lip, got up from the table, and poured a cup of scotch from the pantry bar, not saying a word, turning his back on her.

Geneva slammed her slipper against the tabletop in anger. "You're fooling around with another woman, aren't you?" She waited for an answer but he offered none. "Is that why you're out all the time?"

"You've had too much to drink," he said, turning around.

Geneva picked up the saucer from the table and hurled it at him, grazing his arm. She looked around for something else to throw when she spotted a pot the maid had left on the sink. Lester rushed to restrain her, forcing the pot out of her hand, sending it clattering to the floor.

"Let go of my arm!"

"Not until you stop this ridiculous jabbering!"

"You've been lying to me all along! No wonder I get funny looks when friends ask where you are. Everyone in Harlem knows where you are except me!" She jerked her arm away from his grip and ran upstairs.

A half hour later, after Geneva had calmed down and undressed, Lester appeared at the bedroom door. She snatched her dressing gown from the bed and covered herself. "Under the circumstances," she said in a cool, detached tone, "I think you should sleep in the guest room." She moved to her vanity and began to comb her hair.

Lester went to the bedroom closet and removed a suitcase and a couple of dark suits. He dumped the contents of a dresser drawer in the suitcase, then finally spoke. "Under the circumstances, bitch, I should've left you a long time ago. I wouldn't sleep in the same house with you if they paid me. In a short period of time, Laurelle has shown me more affection . . ."

"So that's the name of your whore."

He snapped his suitcase shut. "She's more of a lady than you'll ever be. At least she doesn't lie about rich relatives in Europe and New Orleans and all that crap about being proper. I found out all about you a few months after the wedding. I never told Mother. It would have killed her."

Geneva's heart thumped, but she acted nonchalant and continued to comb her hair.

"I wanted to annul the marriage, but practicality stopped me. We had our good name to protect. You were nothing but a cheap farm girl from Jacksonville before you met me, and you probably screwed every man you could until you found one with money. So if Laurelle's a whore, what the hell does that make you?"

Geneva looked at him in her mirror. "Smarter. I've always known how to take care of myself." She turned to face him. "I never knew how to cuss before I met Dandy Reed. And I remember him saying one night over dinner that sometimes the most profound words ever spoken are 'Fuck you!' " She put her comb down. "I helped you build your business and I've provided a lovely home and I've tolerated your bad breath and your bad manners . . . Well, fuck you, Lester Noble! Fuck you!"

The next morning, Geneva found a note in the bathroom. Lester wanted his mail and phone calls forwarded to the Hotel Harlem. She was amused that he'd pick the most expensive hotel in Harlem. After a light breakfast, she phoned the hotel and left a message which read: "I am pregnant and desperate. Please call." After the desk clerk repeated the message with a nervous stutter, Geneva asked him to sign it: "From Laurelle, with love."

Chapter Twenty

Over the next several days, Adam wondered why Geneva didn't show up for work. Lester made no effort to explain. He was sullen, and hardly spoke. He stayed in his office behind a closed door. From time to time, Adam heard him on the telephone. He sounded peeved. Adam kept himself busy and tried to pretend everything was fine.

On Saturdays, the office closed at noon. On this particular Saturday, by eleven-thirty Lester still hadn't arrived. A few minutes later, the phone rang. Adam expected to hear Lester's voice. Instead, it was Geneva. "Lester won't be coming in today, nor will I," she said in pinched tones. "As soon as you close up, will you come here to the house? There's something I must tell you."

Geneva clicked off and Adam sat at his desk for the next twenty-five minutes, trying not to think. Then he locked the office door and arrived at Mount Morris Park five minutes later. The park brought back memories of when they first arrived in Harlem, huddling together to stay out of the rain. This led to sad thoughts of Billie. Apprehension filled him as he climbed the granite steps to Geneva's front door.

When he rang the bell, he heard voices inside. She wasn't alone. His spirits improved. Maybe he had nothing to worry about, after all. She opened the door, and he was surprised at the change in her appearance. The sleek bobbed hair had vanished into rows of marcelled waves. The rosebud mouth seemed wider and less full. A pale blue dress hung nearly to her ankles in the latest style.

"Well, here you are," she said. Her eyes danced as they glanced over him. "Come in, come in."

He followed her to the living room where two women sat on a plump sofa. Pungent incense burning in scattered clay saucers drifted about their heads. Adam looked for Lester. He wasn't there.

"This is my neighbor, Rose Payton," Geneva said, pointing to a pretty, red-haired white woman who nodded a smile. "And this is Julia Mae Hopper." Geneva gestured at a woman in thick glasses who sat on the edge of the sofa, her feet hardly touching the oriental rug.

Julia Mae pushed her spectacles further up on her nose with red fingernails that seemed longer than her fingers. Adam guessed that even with her platform shoes and varnished hair piled on her head, she didn't reach more than five feet. "Nice meetin' ya."

"Don't go on my account." Adam had hoped they were staying.

"*Our* meeting is over," Julia Mae said with emphatic innuendo.

"Yes, we must go," the white woman said. "It was nice meeting you."

The two women hurried behind Geneva to the foyer. After a few moments of frantic whispering, the front door closed and Geneva was back in the living room with Adam. "Would you like a drink?"

"Where's Lester?" Adam hoped she'd say he was upstairs.

Instead, she said, "Gone for good, thank God. He's at the Hotel Harlem." Geneva sat herself in a chair facing the sofa and crossed her legs. "You look surprised."

Adam thought of the rent at Boss's place, the cost of food, the lines of unemployed. The incense, bitter yet sweet-smelling, made his head woozy. "I'll have that drink."

Geneva indicated the portable bar. "Help yourself." Once he was settled, she went on. "Half of everything Lester owns belongs to me. It was easy. He never checks anything. This house, of course, is mine outright. At the same time, I've separated myself completely from the real estate company. I want no part of it." She smiled, looking proud of herself.

Adam guessed she expected him to say something, but he knew whatever he said would be wrong.

Geneva leaned toward him. "Adam, I'm a rich woman! There's plenty for both of us. You don't need that job now. Don't you see? I have a better proposition for you, anyway . . ."

The moment he'd been trying to avoid had arrived. "Geneva . . ." He hesitated. "I'm married. I love Virginia. I've loved her ever since Jacksonville. You don't want nobody like me. I ain't got no money, couldn't buy you things . . ."

"I don't care about all that! Besides, I told you I have enough money for both of us now. I'm free! You can come live with me. It'll be like the old days, but much, much better." Geneva raised her arms alluringly.

"No, Geneva," Adam said calmly. "I tole you. I can't be with you 'cause I love Virginia. She's my wife."

"You need me, not her! What has she ever done for you but drag you down?" Geneva yelled.

She was staring at him. Adam stood up and walked out. Once on the sidewalk, he looked back and saw her watching him from a window. At first he thought she was crying, but then he realized she was screaming at him. Judging from her expression, he was glad he couldn't hear it.

Chapter Twenty-one

Charles Payton sat in the bay window of the house next door to Geneva's. "He left," he called out, without much interest. He was in a depressed state of mind. He kept telling himself that things would change, that business would pick up, that he'd soon have a job. He knew he was kidding himself, and he ended up feeling more defeated than ever.

"Who left?" Rose came up from the kitchen, where she was fixing lunch.

"The relative. The one you just met." Payton wondered why Rose couldn't keep anything in her thoughts for more than a minute.

"If he doesn't want to work with Geneva, we'll just have to find someone who does," she said, not paying attention to him, starting toward the kitchen staircase.

"I'd think the least you could do is let me have the money,"

Payton called, louder than was necessary. He'd been furious ever since he first found out about it.

Rose looked back at him with that weary look she reserved for lecturing on drinking too much. She finally said, "If you need money, Charles, we can rent rooms. What my mother left me is mine to use as I want. Going in with Geneva and Julia Mae is what I want."

"You're throwing it down the drain. What the hell do the three of you know?"

"You're in no position to talk about throwing things down the drain. Geneva and Julia Mae know a lot more about business and life than most of your cronies. They're all out of work, too! As for me, I'm learning. And I've decided I'll be just fine. If you can't earn any money, perhaps I can." Then she was out of his sight.

Payton started to yell something back, but it was too much of an effort. He went to the liquor cabinet and removed a bottle of whiskey. He was on his second drink when Rose called upstairs that lunch was ready. He knew she didn't like it, but he brought his drink down anyway.

"You're drinking too much," she said, seeing the glass. "Can't you at least wait until evening?"

"I'm going to sit with you," he said to Evelyn, ignoring Rose's comment.

"I don't like the smell of liquor," Evelyn said. She moved her silverware to the other side of the round oak table. Payton decided he couldn't eat the food Rose placed in front of him. He drank his whiskey and watched his wife and daughter eat. He noticed how much alike they looked, although Evelyn's hair was brighter and shinier.

Rose glanced at his plate. "Aren't you eating?"

"I don't like baked beans."

"I made it because it's cheap," she said, exasperated.

"I still don't like it." Payton took his empty glass upstairs and replenished it. *She thinks she's going to make a fortune bottling creams and lotions,* he thought. The whole idea was so ludicrous; he wanted to laugh.

He took his drink to the chair in the bay window and stared across the street at the park. He thought back to when he was a small boy, when the park was a racetrack. From the same window, he would watch the horses round the bend, circling the park. He remembered how wonderful it had been over there when he was growing up, playing ball, sledding, chasing friends with snowballs, kissing young girlfriends on top of the hill. But that was all different now. He closed his eyes. He felt he had no one.

Chapter Twenty-two

Billie tried to wake up, but her dreams of making love had a sweetness that made her savor a few more tender moments. Instead of answering the telephone, she snuggled deeper into the pillow that was covered in smooth cotton and smelled of fresh gardenias.

She was in Lloyd's arms. They were at her apartment on Sugar Hill, only they seemed to be higher than the fourteen floors she'd grown accustomed to. They were dancing in her living room without their clothes on, and the french doors which led to the narrow brick terrace that overlooked downtown and the Empire State Building were missing. Everything else—the white baby grand, the curved satin settee, the antique Chinese chests, even the standing ashtray Lloyd continually tripped over—was there, but not the walls. Instead, they were surrounded by evening stars, and Fletcher Henderson's orchestra was playing a romantically slow rendition of Lloyd's favorite song, "I've Got a Feeling I'm Falling," from behind a dark curtain suspended in air.

Lloyd's arms felt stronger and tighter, and he began to breathe hot life on her cheeks as he kissed her. They floated in mid-air under the double door frame to the bedroom, where the moon spilled silver strands over them. He parted her thighs and slipped inside her private soul.

Then the stars around their bodies started to form into pairs of eyes of all colors, in different size and shapes. They were spying on them.

"Whatcha doin' wid dat white boy?" a deep masculine voice whispered.

"Who do you think you are?" another voice chimed in.

"So this nigger comes up here and thinks she can get away with anything she wants," said a screeching voice that sounded like Laurelle at the club. Then Billie realized the whole family was there. Chick and Dewey were laughing at her. Virginia looked sad, and Adam looked mean. Hands unattached to arms or bodies popped out of furnishings near the bed, from the gold clock, the parquet table. The hands pointed accusing fingers at her, waving clenched fists, and that's when Billie heard the phone ring for the second time.

She jumped out of bed, relieved to be free from the dream that had turned sour. She tried to focus on the clock, but the afternoon sun had filtered through the venetian blinds and glistened brightly against the gold numbers, making them unreadable.

She interrupted the next ring. "Good morning, sweetheart," she murmured.

"How did you know it was me?" Lloyd asked. He sounded irritated instead of surprised.

"Who else would be calling me at this hour?"

"I was just about to ask *you* that."

Billie's eyes sharpened on his photo across the room. "If that's supposed to be funny, I'm not laughing."

"Who else has your number?"

Billie couldn't believe what she'd heard. "You can't be serious."

"Damn right I'm serious!"

She slammed the phone down on its hook, threw a robe over her shoulders, and went to her window. She snapped the venetian blinds up and forced herself to stare out over the park that was fourteen stories beneath her bare feet. She took a deep breath and let her eyes wander across the Harlem River and out onto the smoky horizon of the Bronx. She quietly tapped her manicured fingers across her silk sleeve, annoyed at herself for getting so upset with him. She tried to relax the tightness she felt in her lips, folding and unfolding her arms.

"The nerve!" she blurted out loud as she went into the bathroom.

She sat on the small bench near the etched-glass shower door and left the bedroom door open a crack so she could hear the phone. When it started to ring again, she smiled to herself, turned the shower on to its fullest power, inspected her body in the full-length mirror behind the bathroom door, and after a nod of self-assurance, took a long, hot shower.

When Billie turned the shower off she heard the downstairs

buzzer to the intercom, signaling a visitor. Her building, the
Roxbury at 409 Edgecombe Avenue, considered the best on
Sugar Hill, was the first building to install one in Harlem. It
always excited her when she heard it. She wrapped herself in an
oversized towel, ran through the hallway that led to the front
door, and instructed the doorman to let Dimples up to her
apartment. She continued to ignore the ringing phone.

"Aren't you going to answer it?" Dimples wanted to know
after Billie had shown her in.

"Let him stew," she responded, still shivering, not yet dry
from the shower.

"I thought you two patched things up last night."

"I thought so, too." She hoped the hurt she still felt didn't
show in her voice.

Dimples seemed to wince every time the phone rang. "If you
don't let me answer this goddamned phone, girl, I'm gonna
scream."

"All right, all right," Billie said with a toss of her hair, "but
I'm not speaking to him."

Dimples sighed heavily and answered the phone. It was the
grocery store around the corner. They were all out of Cheddar
and wanted to know if she'd like Muenster instead. When she
hung up, she went to the closet where Billie stood thinking
about what to wear.

"Don't let him bounce you around, honey. You ought to get
out more on your own."

"That's exactly what I had in mind. Let's go shopping," Billie
said as she picked a crisp linen suit and began to dress.

"That's not what I mean. Go out and have fun when you're

not seeing him. He's making you afraid to look at another man. He doesn't own you."

Billie buttoned her jacket before responding. "I didn't think I'd ever say this, but . . . I love him." The phone rang. "And I'm still not speaking to him."

Dimples picked up the phone. "No, Lloyd, she's not speaking to you. He says he's sorry," she reported. "Okay. Yeah, okay, I'll tell her." Dimples opened the movie magazine she'd brought with her and flipped through it. "He said he wants to apologize, and he just picked up his apology for you. He'll pick you up in the limo after the last show." When Billie didn't respond, she added, "Sounds like he means business, girl."

Billie finally laughed at it all, and they were off for their shopping spree.

While they waited in the hall for the elevator, Dimples ran her finger against the heavily brocaded texture of the maroon wallpaper that was joined at the ceiling by ornately carved mahogany moldings. Then she turned from the wallpaper and whispered the latest rumor about the club. "I heard Owney's looking for a place downtown."

They stepped back for the janitor, lazily pushing a carpet sweeper over the thick beige carpet.

"I heard Owney sold the club to a bunch of hoods from Brooklyn and it's gonna be a swanky restaurant," she continued in a hushed tone behind her cupped hand.

"Why are you whispering?"

Dimples shrugged. "I don't know. 'Cause it's so quiet up here, I guess, like I'm in a library."

As the elevator operator brought the mahogany-paneled elevator to an easy stop, a distinguished-looking woman and a short, worried-looking man brushed past Billie and Dimples as if they didn't exist. Billie gave Dimples a signal to ignore their rudeness.

"I'll explain later," Billie said.

While the elevator slowly brought them down, Billie thought about her next-door neighbors and how nice they were when she first moved in; how they kept inviting her over for cocktails; how they tried to match her up with their forty-year-old son; and then how they saw her and Lloyd coming out of her apartment a few days ago and stared at her with such intense hatred, it made her look the other way.

"Let's walk," Billie suggested as the doorman scrambled for the door. The fresh air felt good and a vigorous breeze was coming off the river. She liked walking and talking with Dimples. They were almost the same height and they both always wore high heels, so keeping pace with each other was easy. She admired Dimples for her innocent beauty, but most of all she liked her honesty.

"Wasn't that Dr. Knox and his stuck-up wife?" Dimples asked.

The baseball fans at the Polo Grounds let out a deafening roar as Billie attempted to answer. It wasn't until they passed the candy store on 153rd Street that Dimples brought up the snubbing again.

"Why did Dr. Knox and that cross-eyed bitch give you the cold shoulder?"

Billie was still amazed sometimes that someone as virtuous-looking as Dimples could have such a foul tongue. "I don't know," Billie instinctively answered, wishing she could be as open with Dimples about her feelings as Dimples had been with her about men when they'd first met. She hated the namby-pamby way she answered, then for a moment, she remembered how Virginia would often forget her good English rules and would sound more colored than anyone. She wished she could get Virginia and Adam off her mind.

They stopped at the drugstore on Seventh Avenue to pick up some headache powder. As they were leaving the store, a white woman outside was drunkenly pulling on a dark-skinned man's arm, pleading for forgiveness.

"Oh no, Daddy, I didn't mean it!" the woman tearfully begged. "Don't leave me. Don't leave!"

"I wish they'd stay away from our men," Dimples said as the mixed couple lurched back into the restaurant next door. "They oughta' stick to their own kind."

Billie started to ask her how she felt about Negro women going out with white men, but the double decker bus was approaching the bus stop. By the time they reached a seat on the top deck, Dimples was complaining about her new shoes and Billie decided not to question her. Instead, Billie explained why they were ignored by Dr. Knox.

"That ol' hypocrite," Dimples hissed. "That nigger's had a white girlfriend for years! She lives on 112th and Lenox. I know 'cause I had a boyfriend in the same building. I used to see him sneaking in and out of the place all the time."

Dimples had a way of gathering up momentum when she was angry, like a pumped-up sewing machine running too fast. By this time, she was livid. "That bastard cuts babies out of women for a living and he has the fuckin' nerve to ignore you? When he's nothin' but a fuckin' butcher?"

A man sitting a few seats in front of them seemed horrified at what he heard and went downstairs with a frown of disapproval on his brow. Billie's face must have shown the embarrassment she felt, but Dimples was oblivious.

"I thought everybody in Harlem knew that, honey." Then she touched Billie's wrist, looked at her with genuine concern, and said, "I never realized how tough it must be for you and Lloyd sometimes. You two get those drop-dead stares from the blacks and the whites."

They got off at 125th Street and while they window-shopped, they talked about men and gossiped about the club and looked for new hats. After a dozen or more hats that didn't please them, they decided to go to the Hotel Harlem's Coffee Shop for lunch.

The usual crowd was milling about in front of the ornate marquee of the hotel. Billie and Dimples were seasoned veterans and knew how to avoid undesirables in a crowd. There were the fashionable young men who looked as if they never shaved and spent their time idly under the marquee hoping to run into someone important, hustling nickels from strangers as they flirted with every pretty, unescorted woman who passed. There were the shoe shine boys who were old enough to be Billie's grandfather, who never looked up into anyone's eyes and purposely kept their hands polish-stained to discourage customers from taking their change. But coming in and out of the Hotel Harlem were some of the most famous names in the world, and Billie enjoyed being a part of the glamour.

As she and Dimples stepped into the lobby from the shiny brass revolving door, the photographer from the *Amsterdam News*, assigned to catch well-to-do visitors entering the lobby, snapped their photo. The entrance to the coffee shop faced the hotel's long front desk. The best seats in the restaurant were the booths adjacent to the door that overlooked the lobby.

As usual, the short-order restaurant was bustling with busy waitresses and lively conversations. Impatiently looking at their watches, prominent businessmen and society ladies waited in a line for tables in a small area in front of the cashier's stand. Fortunately, a group of four people left a prime booth and Dimples turned on her charm.

"Hey, good-lookin'," she said to the handsome cashier with a wink, "we're expecting two more friends. Why don't you give us that table?"

The cashier ignored the complaining customers in line and led Dimples and Billie to the large booth. He kept looking back at them as he returned to his station at the door. "They had reservations!" they heard him say in a loud, condescending manner to the irate customers. He returned shortly after with two menus and a wide grin.

"I didn't know there was a beauty convention at the hotel," he said, smitten with Dimples.

"I bet you say that to all the girls," Dimples responded with her tiniest voice.

The cashier's flirtation was interrupted by a tap on his shoulder. It was Laurelle. She looked nervous. Without asking either of them whether it was all right, or even saying hello, she pushed Billie over to the end of the booth nearest the window, sat down, and began to pour out her problems. "My boyfriend's giving me a hard time. He doesn't want me to move downtown with the club."

"So it *is* true," Dimples interrupted. "Owney sold the club."

Laurelle turned to Billie. "I thought surely Duke would've told you by now. He must've known months ago."

"I just heard about it today," Billie said, taking a sip from her glass of water, trying to get the waitress's eye. "I was quite surprised."

"Oh, c'mon, Billie, you don't have to lie to me. Everybody knows he put you up in that ivory tower on Sugar Hill. You sure didn't get a place like that on the salary Owney's paying."

"You don't know what you're talking about," Dimples said, waving at the waitress.

"The hell I don't," Laurelle defended herself. "I have friends who live near the Roxbury. I've seen the two of you going inside. And I know for a fact that's where Duke stays."

"We both live in the same building," Billie explained.

"And the same bed, too?"

Billie was tempted to spit the sip of water she'd just taken into Laurelle's eye, but she controlled herself. Dimples laughed so hard at Laurelle's misinformation, she knocked her glass across the table and into Laurelle's lap. The waitress quickly ran over to give Laurelle several napkins to mop her dress, then, noticing she didn't have one, handed Laurelle a menu.

"That won't be necessary, dear," Dimples instructed the waitress. "The bitch was just leaving."

Humiliated, Laurelle got up and left.

After the waitress took their order, Dimples leaned over the table and said, "I've been wondering all along when you and Duke would get it on."

The two friends laughed throughout their lunch, unaware of

the men staring at them, unmindful of the women who were envious of them, enjoying each other's company as they cattily tore Laurelle apart.

A tapping at their window interrupted their chatter. It was Ethel Waters. They rushed to the entrance to greet her and brought her back to their table, causing a great deal of commotion among the gawkers in the lobby. Billie loved Ethel. She was warm and friendly and understanding, just like family, and when she smiled at her, Billie felt she was back in Jacksonville where things were much simpler and people had more love for each other.

The waitress nervously poured a cup of coffee for Ethel and backed away as if she had just served royalty. Ethel brought them up to date on *Rhapsody in Black*, the Broadway show she was rehearsing, but as conversations with Ethel always went, her work in the church and the newest boyfriend quickly became the subject.

She pointed through the window at a handsome young man in the lobby. He wore a mustache thinner than Duke's and an expensive suit. He was handing a valise to a bellboy as he looked around for Ethel. He seemed several years younger than she was.

"Well, what do you think? Isn't he gorgeous?"

"Whatever happened to the bartender?" Billie asked.

"He slipped me a mickey one night and ran off with some little hatcheck from Asbury Park and my diamond bracelet."

"The one you bought in London?"

"Don't fret, Dimples, he earned every penny—the hard way."

Ethel's laugh boomed through the coffee shop and spilled out into the lobby. It attracted the attention of her boyfriend. He straightened his tie and beckoned Ethel to rejoin him, pointing at his watch.

Before leaving, she invited Billie and Dimples to a small party she was throwing that evening at the Hotel Harlem's Skylight Ballroom. "Then you can meet my new man," she said with the breathlessness of a bride.

When they got back outside after lunch, neither Billie nor Dimples could decide which direction was best to continue their shopping. While they were making up their mind, a one-legged man leaning against the hotel wall thrust an open cigar box containing a few coins at Billie.

"Can you spare a little change, pretty lady?" he said in a whiskey-soaked, gravelly voice.

Billie reached in her purse and donated a dime to the unfortunate man before the doorman chased him away. That was when she saw Adam. He was crossing Seventh Avenue on 125th Street and had reached the Tree of Hope in the middle of the island when the traffic light began to change. He lightly touched the tree stump Harlemites superstitiously rubbed for good luck and rushed across the busy street before an oncoming bus and downtown traffic could reach the corner.

Billie stood in his path. He looked her in the eye, but he passed her as if he hadn't seen her. "Adam!"

He didn't answer.

For an instant, Billie thought she might have been mistaken. But she could tell his walk in the dark. She moved through the crowd and caught up with him. She grabbed his coat sleeve. "Don't be this way," she begged.

Adam turned. His face seemed even angrier than it had appeared in her dream. "Leave me alone, Billie!"

A crowd began to gather.

"But you're my family."

"No woman in *my* family sleeps with a white man! I don't know you, lady." He ran behind an old Ford truck that belched black smoke into the air and hopped on the streetcar that was moving west. Billie watched the clanging trolley disappear across Eighth Avenue before turning back to the corner where she'd left Dimples. She saw the sneers and dirty looks of some people who evidently had heard Adam's comment about a white man. She had the impulse to quicken her step and look down at the sidewalk, but she was determined to hold her head up as high in public as she did at the club. She strutted all the way back to Seventh so alluringly, it caused drivers to slam on their brakes. Her heart felt heavy, though. Adam was mean, she decided, and although her eyes felt moist, she refused to cry.

"Let's go get that blue hat you liked," she said to Dimples when she reached her. "My treat."

They arrived at Billie's building in a taxi filled with shopping bags and packages. The doorman carefully placed them on a luggage carrier, and sent them up to her apartment on the service elevator. Before going upstairs, Billie checked her mailbox. She never received anything other than bills, but it was a daily routine she dearly needed. To her surprise, a postcard from Hollywood was waiting for her.

"It's from Duke! He says he'll be back on the twenty-first."

"Today's the twenty-second," Dimples reminded her.

"Then he's here!" She hoped she didn't sound as excited as

she felt. She was revitalized by the news. Later, before she left for the club, she tried to reach him on the phone, but there was no answer. Duke was always on the go, always working. She wasn't surprised not to find him home, but she was disappointed. She wanted to invite him to Ethel's party. It would've given her a real kick to invite him to something for a change. He was always inviting her somewhere. She was putting the finishing touches on her hair when the intercom buzzed. The doorman informed her there was a delivery on its way up. The doorbell rang shortly after. The package was from Saks, and it required her signature.

She tipped the delivery boy and took a bulky, heavy box into the living room. She opened it and had to sit down on the setee when she saw what was inside. Under what seemed like yards and yards of tissue paper was a sable coat. She sank her fingers into it and immediately realized why it was considered the best kind of fur. She ran her hand over it. It was soft as a kitten.

The enclosed card was from Lloyd. "Sorry," it said in his careless scribble.

She put the coat on, went into the bedroom, and stood in front of the brass full-length mirror near the closet. She was looking at someone new. She realized she hadn't actually changed, but she looked as rich and pretty as any movie star. Even the inside label from Saks was classy. *In fact*, she thought as she inspected her reflection again and noticed the furnishings behind her, *everything here is terribly expensive, and Lloyd bought it*. The thought bothered her for a moment, but she didn't know why.

She wanted to call Lloyd to thank him and to tell him how much she loved him, but she had promised she'd never call him at home. She decided she'd convince Lloyd to take her to Ethel's party, if only for an hour, so she could meet Ethel's new boyfriend, show off Lloyd, and show off Lloyd's generosity. Then she'd bring him back to the apartment and they'd make love all night. A few minutes later, as she stepped into a taxi and headed toward 142nd Street and the Cotton Club, she couldn't tell if it was the coat or her plans for later that evening that made her radiate with good feelings.

Normally, walking through the club to the raised stage that led to the dressing rooms was as routine for Billie as getting up in the afternoon, but this evening was out of the ordinary. The stagehands, the busboys, the bartenders, the waitresses, even the poker-faced wardrobe mistress—everybody—smiled or gazed or hooted their appreciation for how good she looked. The glaring exception was Laurelle, who ignored her and ducked into the ladies' room.

Cab Calloway, looking handsome in his white tuxedo, was standing by the spiral staircase talking to some of the boys in his band and another man in street clothes. When Cab saw her, he waved at her to join them. The other man turned out to be an old friend, Bill Robinson, who was the star at the club the day Billie was hired. Whenever he was in town, if he wasn't working there, he'd stop by.

"You look like a million dollars," Bill said, giving her a warm embrace.

"With that coat and that fine, brown frame you're draping it on," Cab added, "I'd say maybe twenty to twenty-five *billion* dollars." Then Cab's face turned serious. "Your dancing partner had another fight. And this time, he broke his arm."

Cab was referring to Otto, the dancer who would move

around her as she sat on a glittery country wagon while Cab sang a romantic tune. Ever since Otto caught his boyfriend cheating on him, they'd been constantly fighting. Billie had known it was simply a matter of time before matters got worse.

"Luckily," Cab continued, breaking into his magnificent smile, "Bill here has volunteered to fill in for him at the broadcast tonight." Performing three to four numbers over the radio was relatively new to the club, and it was considered a temporary experiment. But recent glowing newspaper reviews and the increase of out-of-towners coming to the club convinced Owney to renew the broadcast contract with CBS for another six months.

Billie left the group of men wondering why Lloyd couldn't be more like them. They were pleasant; Lloyd wasn't. *At least not with me recently*, she thought.

In the dressing room, Laurelle was having a temper tantrum. She was throwing her makeup and personal belongings into a straw shopping bag, mumbling incoherently between screams of anger, tossing half-used jars of cold cream noisily into the trash basket, flinging her costumes to the floor, cursing Owney Madden.

Billie noticed she was favoring her right arm and shoulder, and when she reached her dressing table Billie could see a discolored bruise under Laurelle's left eye.

"You poor dear," Billie said out of concern, going to Laurelle. "What happened?"

Laurelle snatched her arm away. "A lot you care. You never liked me in the first place."

Realizing it was no use, Billie turned back to her own table. Two of the other girls continued to dress in their costumes, stepping over rolling jars as if they weren't there. Billie decided they had the right idea. Laurelle tossed the last item in her shopping bag when the wardrobe mistress came by for Billie's coat.

"I'm locking this beauty up in Owney's vault," the ex-singer said in her low, gritty voice, then she picked up the costumes Laurelle had thrown on the floor. "And I 'spose I'll fumigate these."

Laurelle left without saying a word, pushing Dimples to one side as she went through the door.

"I heard she got knocked up by her boyfriend," Dimples told Billie while they were waiting backstage to go on. "They had a big fight in his room at the Harlem over it, I mean a real loud one with cursing and broken lamps and stuff. A few people called down for the detective to quiet them, and a few minutes later the boyfriend booted her out of his hotel room. She showed up in the lobby with the mouse under her eye. Then that cheap fucker threw her clothes out of his tenth-floor window, but kept all the jewelry he'd given her."

"How did you find out all this?" Billie asked, impressed with Dimples's resourcefulness.

"Remember the guy at the coffee shop? Well, while you were chasing after that damn brother of yours, he came out of the hotel and asked me for a date."

"He works fast," Billie teased.

"He sure does," she agreed. "He's taking me to Ethel's party tonight."

The radio broadcast had begun when Bill Robinson, wearing a tattered shirt and pants that had been glamorized with sparkly sequins to match Billie's scanty slave-girl outfit, joined them.

The announcer introduced Cab, who was already onstage. It wasn't until then that it occurred to Billie she was only moments away from appearing with two of the greatest talents in show business.

When Owney took the spotlight and the CBS microphone, a slight tingling sensation began to run through Billie's fingers.

"The next number," Owney said in his ringmaster's voice, "will be performed by two stars and one angel. Guess who?"

The crowd buzzed with excitement. The radio executives who clustered near the curtain backstage seemed nervous at the time he was taking as he played with the audience.

"C'mon, Owney. Who ya got back there?" a voice yelled.

Owney held up his hands for a little patience from the crowd and said, "I've already introduced Cab, and he's certainly one of the stars . . . and my angel is none other than Cotton Club's most beautiful showgirl, Billie Lambert. And here with them, making a special appearance direct from starring in a smash Broadway hit—one of the greatest dancers in the world—a *big* star—the one and only . . ."

Cab's drummer rolled his drum to a climax.

". . . Bill 'Bojangles' Robinson!"

The audience applauded wildly as the houselights went down and Owney slipped back to his table.

Billie rode in the wagon as two stagehands wheeled it in place. The number had Cab singing a romantic ballad from the bandstand behind the stage, while Bill interpreted the lyrics that described the torment of lovers on the verge of being separated. Consistent with every other number she was in, all Billie had to do was to be beautiful and look aloof.

After Cab sang a chorus, Bill danced out to a thunderous

ovation. It was interesting for Billie to compare Otto with Bill, but after Bill started to counter Cab's smooth instrumentals with machine-like taps of amazing accuracy, she decided to drop the comparison. Robinson was the consummate performer, and although he was best known for his dancing, he was also a good actor.

Then, to Billie's surprise, Bill ventured away from the original choreography, took her by the hand, and led her off the wagon. He swayed her body to the deep mournful cries of Cab's trombones and the wailing altos as if the number was always done that way.

She felt like a schoolgirl at her first dance. Bill glided her around the wagon and led her downstage, which jutted out into the audience. He made her feel graceful and light. She could tell from the strength in his arm and the confidence in his moves that no matter where he led her, she'd be able to follow.

He smoothly lifted her back onto the wagon by the end of Cab's last chorus, then threw himself on the stage to show his desperation as the wagon was slowly pulled offstage and behind the curtain.

The audience seemed stunned by the drama of Cab's singing and Bill's dancing. It took a moment before the first patron started applauding, then another—then they were all standing at their tables, clapping in unison until Bojangles stepped back on-stage in his confident yet humble strut.

The radio executives nervously tried to quiet the club so they could get their sponsor's message on the air, but time ran out while the audience continued to whistle and clap and hoot and scream Bojangles's name.

Billie was watching from the wings when Bojangles returned,

grabbed her arm, and pulled her out onto the stage with him. "C'mon," he said when he felt her resistance. "They're clapping for you, too. You were terrific out there."

She could feel her knees trembling, but Billie managed to walk gracefully back on the stage with Bojangles and take her first solo bow to an audience.

"Billie Lambert, ladies and gentlemen. Billie Lambert," Bojangles repeated. It was such a thrilling moment, she gasped for breath when they reached the wings, thanking him for his kind words.

He squeezed her hand as they passed dancers in their animal skin costumes and feathered headpieces rushing by to get onstage. He said, "I didn't know you could dance like that."

"I can't," Billie laughed, heading for the dressing room, ignoring the compliment. "You're good enough for the two of us."

But she couldn't hold back her excitement once she closed the dressing room door behind her. "Dimples, I danced with Bill 'Bojangles' Robinson!" Dimples and the wardrobe mistress were the only women in the room. The rest of the girls were doing the jungle number. "Didn't anybody see me?"

"I hung your coat up in Owney's closet, child." The wardrobe mistress nervously unhooked Billie's costume, and, mysteriously, looked embarrassed when she rushed out of the room.

Billie turned to Dimples. "Was I that bad?"

Dimples hugged her. "Honey, you showed them how. She was just a little upset for you. So am I. Whenever he wants to break a date he sends you one of these." She gestured to a transparent flower box containing a deep magenta corsage. A note was pinned to it.

"Can't meet tonight," the note said, but it didn't explain further. Billie angrily handed the note to Dimples.

"The hell with him," Dimples finally said after she glanced at the note. "I don't suppose you'll want to go to the goddamn party now."

"Why not?"

"You mean you'd really do it? Without Lloyd?"

Billie took the note back and flipped it into the trash basket along with the flowers. "He's been bouncing me around all day. First I'm bad, then he's bad, then he's sorry, then he can't see me. Sure, I'm going. And we're going to have a damn good time!"

It seemed as though everyone at the Cotton Club knew about Ethel's "small party." Fats Waller had stopped backstage after the first show and said he was on his way to the party with W. C. Handy. Cab and practically the whole band were going. By the end of the last show, Billie began to feel excited about dancing on top of one of the tallest buildings in Harlem.

Mike, the nice young man from the coffee shop, had a taxi waiting for Dimples and Billie when they left the club. As the taxi reached the Hotel Harlem and a new doorman opened the car door, Billie noticed that the evening crowd gathered under the famous marquee was quite different from the day crowd. Instead of well-to-do visitors going through the revolving doors, sporting gals pranced from corner to corner in bouncy steps, looking at their watches, pretending they were waiting for a late date while eyeing unattached men entering and leaving the hotel. Instead of businessmen, there were overly dressed pimps with custom-made beaver fedoras and five-and-dime shirts acting aloof as two or three of their girls draped themselves over each arm. And there were always one or two men in dark suits who lurked in the darkened alcoves of the closed shops that lined the hotel's lobby walls, pretending to be looking at the window display while watching the richly dressed couples coming and going. Mike knew them. They were house detectives.

A crowd of partygoers swept Billie away from Dimples and Mike into another elevator, which took her to the top floor. As she stepped off the elevator and entered the French Provincial splendor of the Skylight Ballroom on the twenty-fifth floor, she experienced a strange sensation that relaxed her shoulders. It was only when she entered the grand foyer and made her way toward the hatcheck that she realized she was feeling what Duke once called, "a sense of presence," particularly after overhearing someone whisper, "That's Billie Lambert."

Dimples and Mike arrived in the other elevator and shortly after reuniting with Billie disappeared, heading toward the dance floor. Ethel had arranged for everything from catered home-style food to champagne and wine. None other than Louis "Satchmo" Armstrong, who had just finished a stint at Connie's Inn, brought his band as a gift to Ethel, and as Billie wove through the well-dressed crowd of people who danced and laughed and looked as if they were very happy to be there with one another, she felt a little sad that she couldn't share this moment with Virginia, Adam, and the boys. Then a deep, soothing voice brought her back to the party.

"I've been looking for you."

Duke seemed handsomer than ever with his dreamy eyes, dark brows, and neatly trimmed mustache, debonair in his tan gabardine suit and alligator shoes. Billie hugged him tightly, unable to talk, choked up with surprise. They found an empty table near the bandstand, but people they knew kept interrupting their conversation, even when they danced. Duke was trying to tell her about his time in Hollywood when Satchmo swung into a loud, brassy song. So he led her out to the grand foyer where they could talk, but Fats was in one corner telling risqué jokes, and it was noisier than the dance floor.

"Let's go to my place," she said. "I've got some new things I want to show you."

Duke liked the idea. While they waited for a nearsighted hatcheck girl, who was nervously scanning the racks, to find Billie's coat, Duke asked how she and Lloyd were getting along.

"Who knows. We argue, we make up." The hatcheck girl, looking relieved, brought the coat to her. "I used to be flattered by his jealousy. But now it sounds like he doesn't trust me. He's changed, and I don't know why. Things just ain't what they used to be."

"I can see that," Duke said as he helped her into the sable, handing a generous tip to the hatcheck.

During their ride uptown to Sugar Hill he told her a little about his trip to Los Angeles; how nice the studio was to him and the band; how surprised he was to see so many mixed couples, "But I knew it was too good to be true."

"What went wrong?"

"Nothing. Absolutely nothing. I'd get to the studio for an

early call, perform for the director, and each time, no matter
how rotten I was, the scene would be acceptable. 'That's a take,'
the director would say. Not once did we have to redo a scene."

"You were probably very good and they didn't need to redo
any of them."

"With all those wonderful actors and actresses out there who
have to shoot take after take, I find that hard to believe. Now
don't forget, the only reason why I accepted the role in the first
place is because I had a girlfriend in the script and I kiss her in
three different scenes. It was going to be a breakthrough for
Negro actors. Ha! They didn't use a single scene."

Billie could see the disappointment in his eyes. "None of
them?"

"You'd never know I had a girlfriend, or that I had any lines
to speak. I was suckered into thinking we were going to be
treated differently from that Stepin Fetchit movie I made, but
all they ever wanted was a colored bandleader leading a colored
band. They never intended to put those scenes in the movie. It
was all a bunch of jive."

The white cabbie smiled through the rearview mirror at
Duke. He recognized him, but seemed too shy to say anything.
He pulled the taxi to the curb and the night doorman rushed to
open the car door. Duke took out an alligator wallet that glistened in the night light and gave the cabbie a five.

"Keep the change," Duke said, flashing his confident smile.

Then all hell broke loose.

Lloyd rushed from behind a shaped evergreen tree that
flanked the entrance and pushed the doorman away. He
grabbed Billie's arm and pulled her out of the taxi. Duke

jumped out of the cab and shoved Lloyd away from Billie. Lloyd fell backward to the sidewalk.

"You don't treat our women like that, Lloyd!"

"I can handle this," Billie said, trying to calm things.

Lloyd got up from the pavement and dusted his suit jacket. "I always thought you two were screwing."

Duke's fist landed between Lloyd's nose and upper lip. His face was bloodied. He backed away

"If you ever hurt Billie," Duke warned him, "I'm going to personally kick your ever-lovin' ass!" He handed the cabbie another five-dollar bill. "Take this chump where he belongs."

In the elevator, on their way upstairs, Billie decided she'd find another apartment, one that she could afford to pay for herself.

Duke broke the silence when they reached her door. "He isn't worthy of you, Billie. I'm sorry, but I've bit my tongue long enough." He kissed her on the forehead after she stepped inside and said, "Think about it. All he's got is money. Without that, he'd be a bum." Then Duke left for his apartment.

Chapter Twenty-three

M onday, Adam went to the real estate office as he always did, even though he
wasn't sure he still had a job. He was glad to find Lester already
there. "Want me to keep on with you?" he asked.

Lester looked up from a cup of coffee. "Of course. Why?"
He picked up a deck of cards and started aimlessly shuffling
them.

Adam hesitated. "Geneva told me you two broke up."

"It doesn't bother me if it doesn't bother you," Lester said,
putting the deck down and taking another sip of coffee.

Adam said, "I was hoping you'd feel that way." He went to
his desk, relieved. There wasn't much to do lately, but any job
was better than none, he thought. At least he wasn't out on the
street, trying to find work that didn't exist.

When he returned home for supper and told Virginia the
good news, she was overjoyed. She said she'd been worrying

about it ever since he left that morning. He had told her the day before that Geneva had left Lester and the company.

"I hope Geneva's all right. She's been so nice to us," Virginia had said in her thoughtful way. Adam hadn't told her of Geneva's wild behavior with him the past Saturday. He decided he'd keep it to himself.

Tonight, throughout dinner, Virginia's mind seemed to be only on Adam's good news. "It's going to be okay. We're so lucky!" she said, smiling, her face warm and loving.

Seeing Virginia happy like this made Adam feel good. He suddenly was more optimistic than he'd been in months.

Chapter Twenty-four

As time passed, Ben Cannon gradually accepted the fact that neither he nor his fiery editorials nor his newspaper had the strength to improve the plight of Harlem's needy. *Maybe, with the way the world is, nobody has*, he thought. In this resigned frame of mind, he covered Harlem's latest scandal. Before the trial came up, he interviewed the man's separated wife, Geneva. He had at first suggested meeting at the YWCA, but instead, at her suggestion, they had tea in the bay window of her brownstone. They talked first of how self-sacrificing her mother-in-law had been. Then Cannon brought up the reason for his visit. "You have no idea where he is?"

"He moved into the Harlem many, many months ago, and I haven't been in contact with him since. I can't imagine what made him do it."

She gazed at Cannon with sad, straightforward eyes that

melted his heart. He thought how hard it must be for her. "Are you familiar with the Paytons next door?" he asked. "Charles Paytons's father was one of my best friends. I often played in that house as a young boy," he explained.

She smiled as she rose to pour herself another cup of tea, and he was glad he changed the subject for a moment. "His wife and I are very close," she said. "As a matter of fact, after Lester moved out I had to do something to support myself. So Rose and I are taking a flier on a new business venture with another woman who has secret beauty formulas. Keep your fingers crossed."

"I will," he said, adding, "But back to the story at hand—you saw no signs of anything going wrong?"

"Not a thing. It must have started after I left the company." She nervously twisted the pearls that hung from her neck. "I had no idea he gambled or was in financial trouble." She sat back in her chair. "I realize now, I didn't know him at all." She paused a moment. "Then those other things! I'm shocked! He must have been under someone's influence."

Cannon jotted a note in his pad. "And he's made no effort to contact you?"

"Not once. He knows I'd turn him in immediately." She poured him more tea. "Selling houses he didn't own, forging deeds, cheating people out of their money, out of their homes . . ." She shook her head in dismay.

When the case came to trial, Cannon made it a point to travel down to Lower Manhattan each day by subway to the Criminal Court Building. Every paper in Harlem seemed to be covering the story. He understood why. The Noble name lent glamour to an otherwise sleazy tale of greed; everyone loved to see the mighty fall from their ivory towers; and besides, it gave readers a moment of respite from the stultifying effects of the Depression. Topping it off, Cannon thought, there was the element of mystery. Lester Noble had vanished without a trace after checking out of his hotel a day before police searched his office. There was also the question of the missing twelve thousand dollars.

Geneva Noble took the stand on behalf of the prosecution.

"And why do you think your husband left the Hotel Harlem?" the prosecutor asked Geneva.

"I have no idea. When I was told, I assumed he was out of money."

"And his accomplice? Why didn't he disappear?"

"Your Honor," the defense lawyer said in a loud voice, "I don't think the witness is qualified to answer that question."

"Let me rephrase my question," the thin, balding prosecutor said. "You told us earlier in your testimony that *you* recommended his alleged accomplice for his job."

She spoke so softly, Cannon had to strain to hear her admit that, yes, she did originally recommend his alleged accomplice for the job as a favor to her cousin.

"Did you think he was honest at the time?"

"At the time."

"Meaning, you don't think he's honest now."

"I didn't say that." Cannon felt sorry for Mrs. Noble. He noticed how she nervously twisted a handkerchief she was carrying in her lap.

"Objection!" shouted the defense lawyer.

"Overruled," the frowning judge said.

The prosecution seemed friendlier toward Mrs. Noble the

following day. "Did you have any idea the accused was cheating?"

"No. I was never invited to their meetings." Then she added, "I don't know what they discussed at their meetings . . . but I'm sure Adam had nothing to do with cheating."

The crowded courtroom mumbled varied sighs over Geneva Noble's response. It implied to Cannon that the lovely Mrs. Noble had been duped into thinking everything was aboveboard, just as the victims had been duped into thinking everything was legitimate.

"Is this the defendant's signature?" The thin prosecuting attorney stepped closer to the witness stand and showed Geneva Noble a document. She looked away after a glance.

"Yes. I suppose so."

He turned from her and, with a victorious smile, addressed the dour white faces that stared back at him. "I could produce fifty-six such documents with the same signature, ladies and gentlemen of the jury. This tells me, as I'm sure it must have told each of you, if the accused co-signed all these documents, and never questioned them once, he must have known what he was doing."

A scuffle broke out in the court. Cannon watched the accused spring from his chair. "It ain't true! I didn't know!" he shouted before being pulled back down. It was Cannon's first good look at the man. Afterward, he remembered the scar over the eye, the twitching nerve in his neck, the angry eyes. *The man's guilty as hell*, Cannon decided, lying in bed that night, thinking about the outburst and his uncontrollable temper.

The next day Cannon watched the jury file out, only to return in what newspapers would call "record time." Cannon

stood at the back of the court. The defendant's eyes were fixed
on the floor. Cannon stared at him over the heads of the seated
assemblage as the man was pronounced guilty on all counts. His
expression didn't change. When the judge sentenced him to ten
years in a penal facility, there was a moment of stillness in the
mahogany-walled room before it was broken by a woman sitting
in the last row, just in front of Cannon. He watched her fall
forward to her knees, sobbing.

The prisoner looked toward her for a moment, then returned
his eyes to the floor as guards led him from the court. The
woman continued to sob while the courtroom emptied. Cannon
had never seen anyone so devastated. He heard someone say she
was the prisoner's wife. Someone else corrected the voice and
said she was his girlfriend. A third party corrected them both,
saying she was neither, that she was Lester Noble's girl and was
crying because he had skipped out with the money and left her
behind.

Whoever she was, when Cannon wrote his story of the ver-
dict that night, he couldn't get the sound of her woeful sobs out
of his thoughts.

Chapter Twenty-five

Virginia's world had disintegrated. Only her responsibility to Chick and Dewey kept her from falling apart. She wasn't aware that Roosevelt had been elected, or that the Eighteenth Amendment had been repealed. She moved through the streets of Harlem like a sleepwalker, not noticing curtains being torn down from speakeasy windows, signs advertising beer and liquor going up, bars opening everywhere. Her entire being was concentrated on two things. She must get a job, and she must find them a cheaper place to live. The little money she and Adam had managed to save by careful scrimping would be gone soon.

One day, feeling especially desperate, she swallowed her pride and went to her cousin Geneva's house. She wished she looked better, that her thin coat wasn't so shabby or her shoes so scuffed. When the door opened, she saw Geneva's eyebrows raise in surprise.

"I want to talk with you," Virginia said, keeping the anger out of her voice. She once was in awe of Geneva, but she realized she wasn't now.

Geneva's eyes stared at a spot above Virginia's head. "I have a meeting going on."

Virginia mustered her strength and pushed into the foyer. "We can't talk in the street. I need money to tide me over."

She heard Geneva let out her breath. "Well, really, Virginia . . ."

Virginia was determined to overcome Geneva's high-handed ways. She'd been thinking about this moment ever since the trial. "You helped them put Adam away. You did it out of spite." She'd been afraid her voice would shake, but there was no sign of nervousness.

"We'd better go down to the kitchen," Geneva said, her eyes darting behind her. "I have someone in the living room . . ."

"I'm not going in to the kitchen," Virginia said. "We'll talk right here!"

Geneva seemed to stiffen at the new firmness in Virginia's voice. She stepped to the double door of the living room and called inside. "Rose, would you mind going down to the kitchen and making coffee? I'll be there in a jiff." Virginia heard footsteps tap across a wood floor. Geneva looked back at Virginia. "Now. What is this? Embarrassing me in front of my business associate . . ."

"I already told you."

Virginia waited while Geneva went into the living room and returned a few moments later. She held out some bills. "Here's thirty dollars."

Virginia put the money in her purse.

"Don't get the idea I owe it to you. I have nothing to feel guilty about," Geneva said.

"You lied about Adam. It's your doing . . ."

Geneva opened the front door. "You don't know what you're talking about." Her voice quavered.

Virginia, pleased to see that Geneva was nervous, walked down the steps to the sidewalk, clutching the purse. She didn't look back. She told herself she'd manage somehow. Chick and Dewey were going to get their education and their chance for a better life, even with Adam gone. The thought of him momentarily took away her resolve, making her legs weak again. She had to convince herself: *Time will fly by. He'll be home any day.*

Mr. Donato, owner of a local grocery store and father of Dewey's best friend, Aldo, helped solve one of Virginia's immediate problems. The Donatos had been sending Dewey home with bowls of food ever since they heard of the family's plight. One late afternoon, Dewey arrived with a dish of spaghetti and the news that Mr. Donato had uncovered a cheaper place for them to live. Dewey explained, "He knows you don't have a job. It's right near where they live, too . . ."

"You shouldn't've told him. He's got worries of his own," Virginia chided. Secretly, she was grateful. The sooner they moved, the better.

The one-room apartment was on the fifth floor of a run-down tenement building on 119th Street and Third Avenue, with litter-strewn hallways and rickety stairs that creaked when Virginia climbed them. The room was dingy and badly needed paint. Its single window looked into an airshaft. Standing against one wall was an old stove; next to it was a deep sandstone tub for washing dishes and clothes, and taking baths. In many ways, it reminded Virginia of the shack they'd left in Florida, except the water closet was a foul cubbyhole down the hall instead of an outhouse in the backyard.

The neighborhood outside was equally shoddy. Children's chalk marks and candy wrappers covered the sidewalks. Debris glutted the gutters. Many of the tenement stoops lining the block had half-broken steps and front doors that wouldn't close. Looking about, Virginia hid her dismay for Chick's and Dewey's sake. She knew she had to take the place. It would cut their expenses almost in half. She went to the superintendent's apartment on the first floor and paid two weeks' rent.

That afternoon, Virginia, Chick, and Dewey packed their belongings at Boss's. When they walked out, Boss yelled, "Soon as I saw ya, I knew you was no good. Actin' so high and mighty! Sniffin' like honey wasn't sweet enough! Ha! I'm glad to git rid of the lot of yas!"

Mr. Donato sat outside in a horse-drawn wagon borrowed from the potato storehouse. He had insisted on taking them to their new home. Virginia, feeling tired, was now glad he had. She and the boys piled their things in the back before climbing onto the front seat with him. "How's Mrs. Donato?" Virginia asked, wanting to sound cheerful even if she wasn't. Virginia hadn't met his wife, but she felt she knew her.

Donato shook his head. "She not so good. She feel bad all the time. Too many bambinos. She listen to priest 'steada me . . ."

Hearing this made Virginia ashamed of feeling sorry for herself. She, Adam, and the boys had their health, at least.

Once settled into the miserable one-room apartment, Virginia spent her days looking for a job, and convincing herself things were fine. She pretended not to notice the rain that seeped into the walls that made the place smell mildewed. She covered her ears when the rent parties went on all night. She tried to ignore the drunken fights across the hall, and the cockroaches and mice that scurried from one wall to the next when she turned on a light.

Every day, her savings sank lower. She wondered how much longer her family could last. To take her mind off the worries that consumed her, she began baking sweet potato pies again when she could afford the ingredients. Baking them gave her a sense of security. One day, she was taking two out of the oven, when the boys came in from school. "I want you to carry one to the Donatos," she told Dewey.

"Christ!" Dewey said. "I got a lot to do."

"Don't talk like that," she scolded. "They've been nice and I want to do somethin' back." She noticed Chick's dirty face and clothes. "What happened to you?"

"Nothing." Chick looked sheepish.

"He was fighting, but he ain't smart."

"Don't say ain't. What do you mean, he ain't smart?"

"He loses." Dewey sounded smug.

"And you don't?"

"Not yet."

After Dewey left with the pie, Virginia felt sorry for Chick with his hangdog face. "You shouldn't fight," she sympathized. "But when you do, it's better if you win."

"Some kids said Pa's a swindler," Chick told her. "He ain't . . . I mean, he isn't, is he?"

Virginia hugged him. "Your pa never did nothin' wrong. He got tricked by Lester Noble. You remember that." Her eyes felt wet. She wiped them with the hot pad she still held.

"Next time," Chick said, "I'll fight dirty like everyone else."

On Sundays after church, Virginia took Chick and Dewey to Riker's Island where Adam was locked up. Adam hardly looked at them when he was brought into the visitors' room. Virginia knew he was still ashamed of being made a fool by Lester Noble. "Get over it," she said to him one Sunday. "Your pride'll be the death of you."

"They ain't gonna keep me here!" he vowed, pounding his side of the table. "I'll get out somehow."

Virginia stared, her stomach sinking. "You're not going to do nothin' to make things worse. If you do, I swear, Adam Lambert, you're never seein' me or your sons again. We'll make the best of this and everything else that might happen. Chick and Dewey are gonna have the chance you and I didn't. No matter how much it costs."

That night, Virginia was unable to sleep. She could make out the figure of Chick tossing about on his cot. Dewey, on his, was dead to the world. She swore through clenched teeth, "I'll make enough to support them, if it's the last thing I do."

Virginia continued her job hunt each day. "I'll take anything," she'd tell people, but there never was anything for her.

Every two weeks, Virginia went to Mrs. Sontag's, hoping her old job might be available.

"Things haven't quite jelled yet," the jolly woman would say. "Here. Take some gefilte fish. It's good for you. Meanwhile, come back in another few weeks." As regularly, Virginia and the boys visited Adam on Sundays. Virginia was determined to hide their hardships from him. She made Chick and Dewey promise they'd pretend everything was fine. "It's like a game," she'd explain. Then later she'd say as they walked into the prison, "He's got enough worries."

She was pleased Adam didn't speak of breaking out anymore, but a cold expression in his eyes disturbed her. "Please try to get along," she said to him one day, holding his hand on top of the board in the center of the long table that separated them. "The better you behave, the sooner you'll be back with us."

His grip hurt her. "I feel like I'm in my grave," he said.

"Well you ain't, thank the Lord," she smiled, wishing she could find some way to cheer him up. Then the guard blew his whistle and they had to leave.

Shortly after that, something unexpected happened. Aldo, nearly frightening her to death, banged on the door of the tenement flat, calling frantically, "Mrs. Lambert! Mrs. Lambert!" His father needed her right away, he said. Virginia threw on her coat and rushed to Mr. Donato's grocery store. She was sure his wife must be feeling worse. Instead, a beaming Mr. Donato waved to her. A man stood with him by the cash register. "This is Gino," he said. "I sell him the cigarettes cheap. He says there's job when I tell him you need one."

Virginia was so overjoyed, she hardly heard Gino explain he was the bookkeeper at the Lafayette Theater and he knew they needed someone to mop up the lobby and rest rooms after the last performance. The woman who had the job had died last night.

Virginia gratefully kissed Mr. Donato, then went with Gino to see the manager who did the hiring.

The manager eyed her up and down. "A little thing like you can't have much strength . . ."

"Please," she begged. The job didn't pay much, but Virginia wanted it desperately. "I'll keep things so clean, you won't believe it."

"Well . . ."

She went to work at midnight, except on Fridays and Saturdays when there was a midnight show. On those nights, she went at two-thirty. She'd fill a bucket with water and ammonia and mop each floor twice. It took her three hours. When she'd get home, it was still dark and she'd fall in bed exhausted. Then, she'd get up at seven in time to make a hot breakfast out of whatever she could find for Chick and Dewey before they went to school.

"We can get our own breakfast," Chick said one morning. "You don't have to get up." Dewey was in the bathroom down the hall.

"I had plenty of sleep," she said. "Besides, I like fixin' your breakfast."

"You don't look so hot. You're coming down with something."

Virginia felt tired all the time lately, but she didn't want Chick to know. "Nonsense. I'm fine." She hummed a tune to prove it, but she could see Chick wasn't taken in. He continued to look disapprovingly as she put fried bread and Karo syrup on the table. Then Dewey came in and they all sat down to bless the food.

That afternoon, she walked aimlessly along a windswept 125th Street, knowing she needed more than her job at the Lafayette to keep food on the table, but not knowing where to look. The clang of trolleys rang in her ears like the jabs of an icepick. Ahead of her, a line of marchers paraded noisily in front of Blumstein's Department Store, blocking traffic on 125th Street. They held up signs saying, DON'T BUY WHERE YOU CAN'T WORK! Other coloreds were clustered near the store entrances, persuading everyone to stay outside.

Virginia asked a woman next to her what was going on. "Reverend Powell's boy—he got folks together and told us not to buy nothing in stores that don't hire us." She pointed at an impressive-looking man. "There he is! Ain't he somethin'?"

People flocked around him chanting, "We want jobs! We want jobs!" The woman beside Virginia ran off to join the group, pushing through street barricades of policemen with their nightsticks out, barking orders to keep on the sidewalk, yelling when marchers held up pedestrian traffic, ordering shoppers to move on. The crowd behind Virginia pushed her closer as a string of paddy wagons pulled up to the curb. More policemen hopped out and began pulling marchers from the sidewalk, throwing them inside the vehicles.

One of them grabbed Virginia's shoulder and shoved her toward the nearest wagon.

"I didn't do anything," she tried to explain, but no words came from her mouth. Another officer shouted, "She ain't one. Just the marchers, I tol' ya!" The large hand released her. Virginia's head throbbed and her feet were numb with cold. She thanked God for her good luck. She and Chick and Dewey might be hungry and cold most of the time, but there were worse things. *We'll pull through!* she promised herself with tight lips, hurrying back to the tenement.

Virginia's meager earnings from the Lafayette Theater continued to be her only help in postponing the day they'd be thrown out of their one-room flat. The cold winter months went miserably on until March finally arrived with a warmish rain that washed away the gray slush from the streets. The only reminder left of the grim winter was Virginia's nighttime cough, which she couldn't shake off.

Virginia nervously cleaned the breakfast dishes in the sandstone tub that always smelled of bleach no matter what she did to it. Her job at the Lafayette had abruptly ended the night before because she accidentally got soapy water on the manager's shoes. She was worrying about the rent that had to be paid tomorrow, wondering how to raise the money. "I've got to go to the Sontags' this afternoon," she said to Dewey.

"That's okay, Ma. I'll be home late anyway." He headed for the door.

"Not today," she said. "I want you to scrub this floor while I'm gone."

"Can't, Ma," Dewey called. "I'll do it tomorrow." Then Virginia was left alone with what seemed like a thousand problems, problems she knew could all be solved by money. Money would pay the rent. Money would put food on the table. Money would buy clothes.

That afternoon, Virginia made the long trek once more to

the Sontag apartment. This time, Mrs. Sontag said she had good news. "Well . . ." she qualified, "I'll know for sure in a few days."

Leaving, Virginia felt encouraged. Then she remembered the rent. A few days would be too late. Virginia had one last possibility. She had sworn never to go there again, but today she went anyway. A half hour later, Virginia was at the door.

When Geneva answered the bell, she said, "You're not getting inside my house."

"I need more money." Virginia's threatening voice sounded unfamiliar in her own ears. She thought, *My God! What's become of me?*

Geneva's eyes were on the sidewalk beyond Virginia. "What is this? Blackmail?"

Virginia stubbornly persisted. "I'm in trouble because of you. I need money . . ."

Geneva's fluttering hand patted her marcelled hair. Her voice turned shrill. "And then more and more money? I won't have you upsetting me! I'll call the police if you come here again!" Geneva slammed the door in Virginia's face.

Virginia walked away more dejected than before. By the time she was back on 125th Street, she was so wrapped up in her self-concern she didn't notice the people running past her until a mass of bodies surrounded her, sweeping her with them. She tried to free herself. More bodies were behind her, pushing her forward. "What's going on?" she screamed at the faceless crowd. An angry face emerged. "They got a colored kid inside and the clerks are beatin' him up. They says he stole a li'l ol' pocketknife. Well, they ain't gonna get away with it!"

Virginia realized her legs had stopped moving. She and the

crowd were now in front of Blumstein's Department Store. She felt tension seep into her body from the bodies around her.

"Let the kid go!" rang out a shout that broke the silence.

"Let him go!" shouted Virginia, not knowing what made her shout too. She looked about self-consciously, thinking people were staring, but no one paid any attention to her. Eyes were riveted on the store entrance. The breathless silence took over again. *What is everyone waiting for?* ran through Virginia's head. She found the suspense unbearable. Her worries left her, and she joined in the mutual frustrations of the crowd. "It isn't fair," a voice—was it her own?—shouted.

The siren of an ambulance could be heard nearby. The motionless crowd was now so large, it spilled into the street, blocking traffic, pushing the police barricades back. All eyes swung toward the ambulance when it arrived.

A voice near Virginia cried, "My God! I hope they didn't kill him!"

Hearing this, another voice cried louder, "They killed him! They killed the kid!" The cries repeated themselves over and over, up and down the street, echoing for blocks.

It was what the crowd wanted to hear. Bodies swarmed into the store's entrance, moving Virginia with them. The manager and three clerks blocked the doors. The manager had an arm up. "Everything's all right," he shouted through a megaphone. "The kid is fine. We sent him home . . . the back way."

"How come the ambulance?" someone shouted back.

"The kid bit a clerk, that's all," the manager explained, but few heard him, or wanted to. The chant went on, louder. "They killed the kid! They killed the kid!"

Virginia and the crowd surged forward, receded, then forward
again, like a pulsating artery. A policeman ran toward them
swinging his billy club, blowing his whistle. Someone on the
fringe pulled his club away.

A man beside Virginia waved a rock. "Now they're killing our
kids!" He threw the rock. The manager and clerks fled inside,
barring the doors. It seemed like a lifetime before the crash of
breaking glass penetrated Virginia's ears. After that, other windows shattered in quick succession. Hands reached into broken
windows, bringing out merchandise. Virginia forgot herself.
Dazed, she did what the mob did. Her hand slipped into a window, removing the first thing her fingers touched, unaware. Instead of feeling guilty, surprisingly, Virginia felt elated. She was
getting away with something. She was getting even for the in-
justices festering within her. The mob carried her to the brownstones across from Mount Morris Park. She was in front of Geneva's house, watching a rock crash through the bay window.
Then she was back on 125th Street. The entire black community seemed to be there, running, shouting, grabbing things out
of shattered windows, cursing the invisible sources of their mis-
eries. Every window in sight had been broken. The street was
layered with splintered glass. Bonfires erupted in empty lots and
vandalized stores. Men with flaming torches passed Virginia, so
close the smoke filled her nostrils and the heat warmed her
cheeks. A wagon was set ablaze. "For the jobs we don't get!" the
men shouted. Across the street, a car was overturned. "For the
lynchings in Georgia!" the men there responded.

Virginia picked up a shattered barrel stave. She pounded it
against the hood of a deserted car at the curb. "For Adam!" she

yelled. As soon as she said his name, she dropped the stave and sank to the curbstone, emotionally exhausted. Her head started to clear. Behind her, a row of stores burst into flames.

"You gotta get out'a here!" A hand was on her arm, yanking her up, dragging her down the street. Then, in the shadow of a doorway, its owner said, "Let's you and me have a drink,"

Virginia pulled away. "I gotta go home," she said, in control of herself again.

"Jus' one." The hand returned to her arm.

Virginia shoved the hand away and ran in the direction of her neighborhood. At every turn, she saw crowds still climbing in and out of store windows, looting and setting fires. *I must've gone crazy*, she thought first, then she remembered Chick and Dewey, praying they were safe at home. She hurried faster.

By the time Virginia climbed the five flights, she could hardly breathe. She heard the radio playing a new rendition of "Sweet Georgia Brown," and Chick's and Dewey's voices coming from inside the apartment. Relief flooded her. They were all right, after all. She leaned against the door, waiting to calm down before opening it. But even as she lost her worry about Chick and Dewey, her other worries came rushing back. She knew the superintendent wouldn't let them stay. His rule was, "Out of money, out on the streets." He repeated it to Virginia and other tenants every time they paid the rent. Virginia's hand was moving to the doorknob when she heard Chick say, "Ma'll hit the ceiling if she finds out you took it."

"She's never gonna," Dewey said.

Virginia's mind jumped back to the afternoon. An emptiness formed in her throat. She knew Dewey was capable of getting into trouble. She opened the door.

Dewey was seated at the table across from Chick, who held one of his schoolbooks. They looked startled. She saw Dewey lower his hand to a small box in front of him and close the cover.

Virginia turned the radio off. "What am I not going to find out?" she asked.

Dewey carried the box to his cot and put it under his pillow. "We were just kidding," he said.

Virginia was afraid of the answer, but she had to ask. "Where were you this afternoon?"

"I was here," Dewey said, sounding too innocent.

Virginia walked to the cot and took the box from beneath the pillow. She handed the box to Dewey. "You got a pocketknife in there?"

Chick kept his eyes on his book while Dewey put the box on the table and took out some money.

Virginia pulled the money from his hand. She counted furiously. "Eighty-seven dollars! What else is in there?" Dewey handed her a wallet. "Where'd this come from?" she demanded.

Chick and Dewey looked at each other. "I found it," Dewey said, too off-handed. "The money was in it."

Virginia stared at the wallet, her hand shaking. "Where'd you find it?"

"Downstairs in the garbage. Someone musta thrown it there."

"You weren't in a store on 125th Street this afternoon?" Virginia asked. "You didn't steal a knife there?"

"I don't steal, Ma," Dewey said. "Besides, I was here." He pointed at the floor. "See. I decided to scrub it today 'stead of tomorrow."

Virginia looked at the polished floor, suddenly relieved and ashamed of herself for thinking the worst of Dewey, yet she was still filled with mixed emotions.

"You should've given this to the police," she said, thinking at the same time with gratitude that she now could pay the rent.

"They'd only keep it for themselves," Chick said, being practical.

"I 'spect you're right," Virginia had to concede. She was taking off her coat, beginning to feel better, when a small bottle fell out of the pocket. Puzzled, she picked it up. It was an ornate blue glass bottle. "Midnight Magic," the label said. "Perfume for Tan Beauties from Julia Mae Cosmetics."

"Now where did I get this?" Virginia asked as she broke the seal and took a whiff. Then she stopped short. A distorted image of a hand reaching into a broken window raced into focus. She sat weakly at the table, laughter beginning to form in her throat. Once it started to come out, she couldn't stop it. *And here I was, accusing Dewey,* she thought. Tears formed in her eyes and ran down her cheeks.

Chapter Twenty-six

Virginia was at the kitchen sink late one afternoon when there came a hesitant knocking at the door. *Wonder who this is?* Virginia thought as she dried her hands on a dishrag. They didn't have too many visitors, except for bill collectors. When she opened the door, Billie's face was smiling at her.

"Oh, girl . . ." Virginia cried, and hugged her. "You're a sight for sore eyes."

Billie nodded, tears streaming down her cheeks, overcome with emotion. She took a seat at the table and blew her nose. "I tried to find you everywhere. I had mumps right before Adam's trial, and just couldn't get out of bed. That bitch Geneva! I can't believe she let him go to jail for Lester's doings. How is Adam?"

"As well as he could be, I guess. It's horrible in there," Virginia replied.

"Do you think he'd let me come visit him?"

Virginia hesitated. "I don't really know, Billie. Let me ask him next time I go."

"Well, don't push it. Maybe in time. Anyway, after the trial I went to Boss's place and you all were gone. Nobody knew where you were, and I went to Geneva's office but it was all closed up. After that, I didn't know where to look." Billie started to sob again.

Virginia patted her arm. "You found us. I kept thinkin' you would. I missed you, gal."

Chick and Dewey ran in from the street. "Billie!" they exclaimed, racing over to hug her.

"How are my boys?" she said, smiling.

"How did you find us?" they wanted to know.

"Finally I remembered you all played with the Donato kids. The storehouse gave me the address of his new market. After I found him, I came straight here. Lucky day!" she concluded.

"Let me get you something to eat," Virginia said, standing up. "I don't have much, but I can make up some soup."

"No, let's go out. Let's go to Regents. My treat," Billie said. "It's so good to see you all."

She took a good look around the dark, crowded apartment. She was going to get them out of this place, no matter what Adam had to say about it.

Chapter Twenty-seven

Virginia's spirits were higher than they'd been since Adam went away. The money Dewey found in the wallet was almost gone, but it didn't matter now. To Virginia, it felt like Christmas. First, Billie had bought them clothes to replace the well-mended garments they wore, and pushed enough money into Virginia's hands to allow them to eat properly once again. Then, a week later, Mrs. Sontag excitedly opened the door when Virginia showed up at her apartment. She pulled Virginia inside to the living room where Dick Powell was singing "Everything I Have Is Yours" on the radio. Mrs. Sontag turned the volume down.

"It happened! My husband made connections," she said, happily hugging her. "We can afford you again."

Virginia beamed. She felt a miracle had taken place. All but one of her prayers were being answered at the same time. Mrs.

Sontag wanted her four mornings a week and a full day on Fridays. It was more than she hoped for.

"Starting Monday," Mrs. Sontag added. "The neighbors will be so jealous."

Then, as if that weren't enough, just before Virginia left for Mrs. Sontag's, Billie showed up at the tenement with more good news. "I'm moving to a bigger apartment," she said, eyeing the bleak room with its stained walls and scarred floor. "It's over on Hamilton Terrace and it has a nice sunny living room and three bedrooms."

"Oh my," sighed Virginia. "It must cost a lot."

"I make more than I need from the club," Billie quickly explained. "I want you and the boys to move in with me."

Virginia's heart leaped. It meant she could get Chick and Dewey out of this miserable place. Then her mind swung to Adam. She was sure he wouldn't like the idea.

Billie seemed to read her thoughts. "There won't be any problems," she said. "I need you and you need me. It's as simple as that."

"When do we move in?" Virginia asked, not needing more coaxing.

"Next Thursday," Billie had told her.

A tremendous load had been lifted from Virginia's shoulders. All her old energy came surging back. First she scrubbed the floor. *Whoever moves in after we leave*, Virginia thought, *will know decent folks lived here.* Then she put three sweet potato pies in the oven. When Chick came home, she had him take two over to the Donatos, feeling one wasn't enough for so large a family. She'd heard Mrs. Donato was still not feeling well.

"What are we celebrating?" Dewey wanted to know. When Virginia told him, he put an arm around her waist and danced her around the table. When Chick came back, Dewey yelled out the news and the three of them danced.

Virginia thought, *We haven't had this much fun since God knows when.* She felt almost as if Adam were laughing and celebrating with them, too.

Finally, Virginia fell exhausted into a chair. "Oh my goodness," she sighed, "it's almost like before . . ." She paused. "I know everything's gonna get better an' better from now on." She pushed the wish for Adam to be with them to the back of her mind. "It's only gonna get better."

Day by day, Virginia's enthusiasm continued to build. By Wednesday, the day before the move, she could hardly control her excitement. *Thank God for Billie,* she repeated over and over to herself, looking at the room. *Thank God we won't have to live here anymore . . .*

She got up before six, unable to sleep longer, and started packing the few belongings they had. She cooked Chick and Dewey a big breakfast of French toast and sausage, their favorite, and the wonderful smell of the food made the dreary room seem less mean. After everyone had eaten their fill, Virginia dropped Dewey off with Mrs. Davis and walked Chick part of the way to school. While they were walking up Third Avenue, Chick said, "The principal told me I should go to vocational school when the time comes, instead of regular school where most of the white kids go."

"Why'd he say that?" Virginia asked, not sure what vocational school was.

"He says that way we'll be ready for the only kind of jobs they give Negro kids when they get out of school," Chick explained.

Virginia slowed her pace, not liking what she heard. "When did they start pushin' colored kids into these . . . vocational schools?"

"The principal told us it's some new government plan. He said it'll teach us a trade and how to work with our hands . . ."

Virginia stopped. "You and Dewey are goin' to learn to use your *brains*, not your hands. You can work with your hands in the cotton fields. No matter what *anybody* says, you're both goin' to get a regular education like they give white kids. That's why your pa and me brought you up here. If that principal or anyone else says anything more about vocational school, you tell me and I'll straighten them out. We've been through too much trying to give you a decent education to have someone try to take it away! They act like they're doing us a favor! Afterward, if you're too dumb to use what you learned in school, then it's your fault. But at least you had your chance." Virginia kept her eyes on Chick, hoping he understood what she meant.

"Actually, Ma," Chick said, "that's more or less what I planned to tell him."

When they reached 125th Street and Lenox Avenue, Virginia kissed him good-bye. "I haven't walked you to school in a long time, even if it isn't right to the door." She waved, watching him cross the street when the light changed to green, admiring how grown up he was. Then she headed west on her way to the Sontags.

Morningside Heights was many blocks away, but Virginia had plenty of time. She looked in the windows of Blumstein's as she passed. Some of the smaller stores were still boarded up and some were in the midst of repair, but not Blumstein's. Not only had all the broken windows been replaced, but for the first time, they were using a colored mannequin in the window. As Virginia imagined how she'd look in the red gown that was draped on it, her hand touched the plate glass. It brought back a twinge of guilt. She still carried the fancy blue bottle of perfume in her purse. For weeks she'd been meaning to return it, but so far, she hadn't. She was afraid they'd arrest her if she did. She decided maybe it would be safer to secretly leave it on one of the counters in the store. That way no one would be the wiser. Maybe she'd drop it off on her way back from the Sontags' place.

Virginia was finished with the Sontag apartment by one. She stepped out into the warm afternoon sun, feeling more excited than before. Things were looking up. Tomorrow their life in that miserable little tenement would be over. Maybe Adam wasn't with them, but in a little while, all he was going through would be over. They said when he was sentenced, if he was good he could be out in two years. Then, the bad times would be quickly forgotten.

Instead of walking the long distance back, she decided to take a trolley. Normally, she hated wasting the three cents, but today she felt she could afford to give herself a treat. She headed north to 125th Street. She hummed snatches of a popular song Dewey had been teaching her. She noticed people passing by, glancing and looking friendly, as if they were as pleased with her good fortune as she was.

Despite the warmth of the day, she snuggled cozily into the pretty new scarlet spring coat Billie had given her. It felt good. She imagined everyone must think she was wealthy. The very idea of it made her smile even more. Then she quickly thought, *But I am wealthy. I have Chick and Dewey, and Adam . . . and Billie . . .*

Thinking of Adam, she told herself, *Next Sunday I must say something to him about Billie.* She had planned to tell him last Sunday, but she hadn't been able to see him. He wasn't available, they had vaguely explained. She crossed 123rd Street where Chipper's, a new music store, played colored music through a loudspeaker. In front of the store, a group of teenagers danced the Lindy Hop to Andy Kirk's swing version of "Sweet Georgia Brown," Dewey's favorite new record.

On 124th Street, she passed the vegetable stand, forgetting she planned to buy cabbage, not conscious of the increasing amount of people hurrying out of the subway onto the sidewalk, wrapped in her own thoughts of Sundays. She was seeing herself beside Adam one Sunday, in front of the minister, at a small church in the colored section of Jacksonville. His hand was fumbling with her finger. It could have been yesterday, it seemed so clear. She was seeing her mother's pineboard coffin being lowered into a freshly dug pit one Sunday morning; her father's impatient tapping of his foot when she last tried to get him to talk to her; Chick's and Dewey's expectant faces as the bus drove them out of Florida; all of them huddled together under the monument staircase in Mount Morris Park, trying to sleep while the heavy rainstorm pelted down a few feet beyond.

A momentary rush of sadness from the thought of Adam swept over her, then it was quickly replaced by a new surge of excitement. A vivid picture of Billie's apartment came to mind. She couldn't wait to move in. Each of the three bedrooms had a large window and was flooded with light. Chick and Dewey would have the biggest room, she and Billie decided, because there were two of them. The bedroom with the ivy wallpaper would be Virginia's; the one with the big closets would go to Billie. Virginia could see them having Sunday dinner in the room with the wood paneling that went halfway up the walls. She could see herself taking a freshly baked cake out of the large oven, and serving it for dessert.

She was near the jewelry store at the corner of 125th Street and Seventh Avenue, across the street from the Hotel Harlem. The trolley, in the center of the street, was clanging its bell, announcing it was ready to head east. Virginia hurried toward it, oblivious to everything but the pictures in her head. She was so absorbed in her thoughts, she didn't notice the car careening recklessly around the corner, swerving drunkenly in her direction. It happened so quickly, so unexpectedly, the smile was still on her face when it hit her. Her body was thrown a good fifteen feet, flying haphazardly, arms and legs akimbo, like a rag doll tossed across a room by a spoiled child, landing in front of a milk truck approaching from the opposite direction. The truck driver, people said, did his best to stop, but his front wheels had already rolled over the body before his brakes took hold.

By the time stunned observers came to their senses, the speeding blue sedan was down the block and out of sight. By then, it was too late for anyone to take down its license number. No one could even agree on the make of the car when the police arrived and began questioning witnesses.

One of the officers located Virginia's purse containing her name and address, a crumpled one-dollar bill, a handkerchief, and a small ornate blue bottle of perfume. He took off his jacket and discreetly placed it over Virginia's head and shoulders.

"Now what did she have to be so happy about?" people heard him mumble as he covered up Virginia's smile, which still clung to her even in death.

Chapter Twenty-eight

It was a gray, overcast Friday morning when Virginia's funeral service took place at the Metropolitan Baptist Church on Seventh Avenue and 128th Street. It was a large square-faced church with a huge circle of biblical figures on stained glass in the front of the walnut-brown stone facade, a church Virginia had admired from the outside, but never attended. It was a small funeral; only the first two pews were filled.

Billie, with Chick's and Dewey's help, made the necessary arrangements and contacted the few people who knew Virginia. Her cousin Geneva was absent. She did, however, send a basket of white carnations and a hastily written note that read: "My deepest sympathy to all."

Billie couldn't convince herself Virginia was gone. Chick and Dewey were numb. Mr. Donato came with Aldo and Angelina and her friend, Evelyn. He placed a bouquet of pink roses by the casket and told Billie he'd grown them in his backyard behind the store, apologizing that his wife was too sick to come. His sad, round face reminded Billie of a wilted head of lettuce. "My wife, she never met Virginia, but she feel bad for her just the same." Then he mumbled something in Italian and, going back to his pew, started to cry.

While the organist played the closing hymn, "God's Tomorrow," Billie's eyes wandered about the empty pews. She wished there had been more people to invite. Somehow it didn't seem right, Virginia's life ending so soon and so few people here to say good-bye.

The morning after the accident, she'd desperately tried to get word to Adam, thinking naively that through some act of God and humanity, he'd be allowed to attend the funeral. She'd gone to Riker's Island, but they told her he was in transit and to come back later.

Billie felt she'd fallen into a bog of quicksand. Not knowing what else to do, she sat down and wrote him a letter, carefully explaining about Virginia and that she was caring for Chick and Dewey. She knew by then there was no chance for him to attend. The letter would never reach him in time.

When the service was over, the mourners left the church with wet eyes. Billie, Chick, and Dewey went along with the minister to a plot Billie had hastily bought at the Long Island Cemetery, one of the few places near the city where Negroes could be buried. After the casket was lowered, they each dropped a handful of soil on the lid. Then, the gravediggers hurriedly shoveled in the rest of the earth. A small, gray marker stood at the head of the new grave. "Virginia Lambert, wife of Adam—1906–1932. Always With Us," it said.

Then Billie took Chick and Dewey home. *Whatever they're feeling*, Billie thought, *they're still managing to hide it.* She couldn't, though. On the way to the apartment, tears kept spilling from the corners of her eyes.

Chapter Twenty-nine

A heavy downpour cascaded off the edge of the poppy-red canopy of Julia Mae's Beauty Salon and splattered against Geneva's stockings as she stuck out her umbrella with urgent jabs to an oncoming taxi. The vacant cab never slowed down.

Her mind urged her to be practical. *Wait for the storm to subside like any sensible person would do,* she told herself. If she went back up to the office, she reasoned, she could find out what Rose was so anxious to talk about, and perhaps she'd tell Julia Mae how crude her language had become recently. All of these were good reasons to get out of the biting cold wind that was now blowing under the canopy, but she stubbornly looked down 125th Street toward Madison, wondering why taxis and policemen alike were never around when you needed them.

Only a fool would stay out in this weather, Geneva thought, and she abruptly turned back toward the building, bumping into a man passing under the canopy.

"Why don't you watch where you're—"

She recognized his face and grabbed his arm. "Dandy! Dandy? Is that you? When did you get back?"

Dandy Reed seemed embarrassed to see her. His greeting was weak and lackluster. Out of all of Lester's card-playing friends, Dandy was her favorite. He was the best dancer, the best dressed, and told the funniest stories. She felt slighted not knowing he was back from Paris.

"You didn't write. You didn't let anyone know you were in town . . . I'm not letting you get away without having a drink with me," she insisted, pulling him by the arm through the driving rain to a bar two doors down from the salon.

She had always been a little curious about the Shanghai Bar, with its green lacquered door and three long, yellow lanterns hanging above it, but it had a reputation for attracting brawls and she would never go to any bar unescorted. The inside wasn't as she'd imagined. Instead of dark red carpeting, there were clumps of sawdust chips that clung to her wet boots. Instead of incense, she was overwhelmed by the cloying odor of stale beer. A large-bosomed woman with uncombed hair appeared from the back of a long mahogany bar. Geneva and Dandy shook the rain off their coats as they approached two backless bar stools.

"What can I do fer ya?" the woman asked, tying a stained apron around her waist. A cigarette dangled from her mouth.

Dandy nudged Geneva and pointed to a large cockroach scampering out of a used beer mug.

"Absolutely nothing," Geneva answered without hesitation, putting her coat back on, swinging toward the door.

"My car is right down the street," Dandy offered.

"And I know where you can get the best cocktail in town," she added.

"Hi-falutin' motherfuckers," a raspy voice mumbled out of the corner as the door closed behind them.

Much to Geneva's surprise, Dandy's "car" turned out to be a long, gray funeral limousine. When he got back to town, he explained, he took the first job he could get. The limo belonged to the Jones Brothers, owners of the largest funeral parlor in Harlem. Geneva didn't like either of the brothers. The younger one danced too close at socials, making the bulge in his pants obvious, brushing it against every woman he passed. The older brother was only slightly better behaved . . .

Geneva's "best cocktail in town" was at her house, a short ride from where they were. Dandy seemed nervous when he got inside, although she couldn't think of a reason why. They went into the living room and she lit the gas fireplace as he poured them both a brandy. It wasn't until he brought her her drink that she noticed how he had changed.

Gone was the clean-shaven cocoa face and the devilish schoolboy smile. He now wore a raggedy mustache that almost covered his upper lip. Gone were the dapper English-cut suits with creases so sharp they seemed to slice the air. His pants were now wrinkled, his coat tattered. He smiled as he toasted her with his glass, but he seemed defeated.

"You haven't changed a bit," he said, sitting in the easy chair in front of the fireplace while Geneva turned on a few lamps.

"Except maybe you're prettier," he added after another sip of brandy.

"Skip the flattery. I'm a little peeved at you. Why didn't you let me know when you were coming back?"

"I had things to tend to."

She stepped in front of him. "I thought we were friends."

"We are."

"Then why the *hell* haven't you called since you've been back?"

Dandy was surprised by Geneva's outburst. "Actually," he said, while loosening his collar and tie, "I've been avoiding everyone, including myself."

When he'd first arrived in Paris, he explained, he'd been convinced he and his buddies were right—that they all had a better chance to make it big as artists over there. It didn't look like Jim Crow was ever going to change in America. He felt he was on top of the world at the time, and with good reason. The Davies Foundation had just given him a grant to write a folk opera under the tutelage of Guilliame Debrineaux, a famous composer in Paris, and Josephine Baker, who had been in *Shuffle Along* with him on Broadway, was a good friend and the toast of Paris.

"Josephine took me everywhere—to parties, to Bricktop's, castles, dinners . . ."

"Bricktop's?"

"The owner's name. She has bright red hair. She's a blues singer from Harlem with a great sense of humor. She changed her name from Ada Smith and became the rage of Paris. She said there were too many Smiths singing the blues in Harlem to suit her. I hear she's opening another place in Rome. And like I said, Josephine took me with her all the time. Every night there was something exciting to see, a new place to go. Once, I even showed a duchess how to play the boogie-woogie."

"My . . . A real duchess?"

"Gen-u-wine," he exaggerated. "Dripping in diamonds. But partying that hard took a great deal more money than I could allocate for fun."

"Bring your drink. I've got a few things to do."

Dandy followed her up the stairs describing a particularly funny night when a jealous dancer at Le Club Pierrot was caught vandalizing Josephine's costumes by sewing the arms together and loosening seams. After the spiteful dancer was fired, she threw a bottle of bubble bath in the club's water tank.

"You should have been there, Geneva. Bubbles were rising out of faucets, coming out of sinks, toilets—everywhere."

Geneva and Dandy ascended another flight, laughing. It felt like old times.

"I usually open the window a crack in this room," Geneva explained as she did so. "It draws the heat upstairs and through the entire house. C'mon, let's grab a bite to eat," she said impulsively. "I'm hungry and we've got lots more to talk about." She led him past the living room floor down the narrow staircase to the kitchen. He sat at the wooden table and reminisced about old times with Lester.

"What happened to you and Lester?"

"He found a whore to play with."

"And you?"

She let her eyes tell him she didn't like the impertinence of his question, but decided to answer him.

"I found money to play with."

"Did you ever love him?"

"At the wedding," she said after a thoughtful moment, wondering at the same time why she was being so honest with Dandy. "I convinced myself I was doing it for love, that Lester was in love with me."

"What happened?"

"We went on our honeymoon," she said, taking a few casserole dishes out of the icebox. "For Lester, making love meant two quick stabs in the dark. For me, it was getting stuck under an overweight slob who rolled over after he moaned in my ear and snored the rest of the night in my other ear."

"I'm sorry. I didn't mean to pry."

"Yes you did!" She softened her voice. "That's what friends do. They pry. Now it's my turn to pry. Tell me about Paris."

While Geneva prepared a meal from leftovers, Dandy talked about Duke Ellington's concert; how Duke was an inspiration to every Negro in Europe. Frenchmen were waving in the street at them, shouting *Vive le Jazz!* It was an exciting time to be a Negro in Paris.

"Then they took that goddamn picture with Josephine."

"The one where you're looking down her dress? It was in all the papers. I clipped it out and saved it."

"So did the Davies Foundation. Believe me, Geneva, it was all so innocent. It was Bastille Day and everything was wild—people dancing in the streets, drinking and carrying on. I picked up

Josephine after her last show at the Folies-Bergères and we went to Bricktop's. It was like Times Square on New Year's Eve—jammed to the rafters. Bricktop came out of the back with a bottle of her best champagne. Someone spotted Josephine and the crowd pushed to get a better glimpse of her, bumping into me, spilling my drink down her bosom.

"A week later, the head of the Davies Foundation sends me the by-now-famous photo—only this one appeared in the *New York Mirror*. A note was scribbled on it in red ink. 'Isn't this *our* boy?' It was accompanied by a letter that questioned my intentions toward music and said they were not providing the grant for slumming, nightclubbing, or womanizing."

For a while, Dandy remained silent. Geneva turned away from the stove, seeing the pain in his face.

"They were looking for somethin' to pin on me, Geneva. I realize that now. For several months I had been going 'round and 'round with them about the story of my opera. They wanted me to do another version of *Porgy and Bess*. I wanted to do a contemporary love story about a colored couple in Paris, but they said the story didn't lend itself to serious music. I said it was high time people saw Negroes wearing something other than overalls and bandanas. They didn't like this uppity nigger telling them what he wanted to create. So when that photo hit the front pages, they hit the ceiling.

"They took it away from me. Just like that." He snapped his fingers.

"They didn't let you explain about the drink and the crowd and all?"

He shook his head and chuckled sardonically. Geneva wished

the old, fun Dandy was back; his new sarcastic manner wasn't very entertaining. "Well, I'm sure you'll get things going again now that you're back in New York," she said.

He looked at her, frowning. "Maybe so," he said. "But I'm not counting on it."

Chapter Thirty

Geneva was disappointed with the way her impromptu supper turned out, but Dandy kept refilling his plate, and he gave her several compliments while they washed the dishes. She was enjoying the evening. She was so accustomed to being alone, she'd forgotten how nice it was to have a man's laughter in the house—although Lester seldom laughed, and Dandy's laugh grated with irony.

When they returned to the living room, Geneva decided to freshen the air in the room for a moment. When she reached the bay window, she couldn't believe her eyes. She called Dandy to take a look.

He was amazed. While they were downstairs having dinner, the rain had turned to snow. The limousine was completely covered, looking like an inverted bathtub glistening in the light of the street lamp.

"No traffic at all," she said.

"No one on the street neither," he whispered.

"Not a sound."

It was as if a gentle blanket of peaceful quiet had fallen on the city, and everyone was in for the night.

"I've gotta call my job," he suddenly remembered. "I gotta get the car back to the parlor."

"You can't move that car tonight."

After looking back at the mound of snow he'd have to dig out, Dandy agreed and called the Jones Brothers, explaining he was snowed in. He ended the conversation by saying, "For goodness' sake, man, be reasonable!" Then he slammed the phone down and returned to Geneva in front of the fireplace.

"What was that all about?"

"That sucker wanted me to find a shovel, dig out his car, and glide his cadaver over to him."

"There's a body down there?" The idea of riding in that limo with a dead body sent shivers up Geneva's arms.

"I didn't want to spoil the fun."

The conversation began to give way to Dandy's long, tired yawns. Eventually, he closed his eyes and dozed off in the blue armchair.

Geneva went over to him and gently tugged at his shirtsleeve. "Wake up, Dandy. You can stay with me tonight."

Dandy's eyes opened with renewed brightness. A sly smile crept up to his cheekbones.

"Oh no," Geneva laughed. "That's not what I meant. I'll get you some blankets and clean sheets. You can sleep in the guest room."

———

Geneva woke up the following morning to the smell of food cooking downstairs—bacon, coffee. "Could that be biscuits?" she wondered out loud as she slipped on her long quilted robe. She hurried downstairs to investigate.

Dandy greeted her with a broad smile at the foot of the basement staircase with a steaming hot cup of coffee.

"How do you like your eggs?" he asked, placing golden brown biscuits on the table.

Geneva was stunned by all this. No one had ever cooked breakfast for her.

"Hope you don't mind me takin' over your kitchen like this, but I wanted to show my gratitude for last night's supper and warm bed. I took a place over on St. Nicholas and they haven't sent up heat once."

"How long have you been there?"

"Two weeks."

"It must be a shock to be back here after living in Paris. Tell me what you did after they took away your grant," Geneva said.

"I was pretty frustrated. I felt like I was up against a stone wall. I hooked up with a couple of ragtag trios on the Left Bank, since that wasn't near where I was staying. I didn't want my pals to see me."

"Why not?"

"I dunno . . . Maybe it's a pride thing. I started it all, y'know. I was the only one going to Paris with a guaranteed income. What would they think if they found out I was gigging at the sleazy greasies?

"So for a couple of months, it worked. I jived everyone into thinking I had some chippie in the rich part of town. Then one night, at an especially filthy dive by the river, Booty, one of the guys who went over with me, staggered in with two other friends. Booty's big mouth didn't stop until the entire population of Paris knew I was playing the piano to pay the rent. It was an honest living, but I guess I was ashamed of not going straight to the top, up there with Duke.

"One morning I woke up in a cold sweat. I dreamed I was out of stuff to hock. Y'see, I was still putting up a front with Josephine, trying to party, trying to keep up. I didn't have a dime for breakfast. So the dream was pretty close to the truth. I had started taking some things to the pawnshop, and it was becoming a weekly visit. But when I woke up—the dream was so real, I jumped out of bed to see if my clothes were still in the closet. They were still there and I had a good laugh at myself.

"But then I got to thinking, 'Why not?' Maybe the dream was some kind of vision. So I hocked *everything*—suits, dinner jackets, cuff links, cigarette cases, even some of the records I took with me. And I sold a couple of songs to the Peters Sisters—so I bought a car."

"Wait a minute," Geneva interrupted, pouring herself another cup of coffee. "You just said you didn't have a dime for breakfast, yet you went out and bought yourself a *car?*"

"I've never been practical. Anyway," he continued, "I felt I had to get away from it all—away from borrowing money from Josephine, away from the excuses and lies, pretending everything was okay. I suppose I left Paris with the same feeling I had when I left Harlem. I felt betrayed!

"So I ventured out into the country, taking every dirt road I could find that was heading south, wanting to get lost in another world, hoping I'd find it changed overnight for Negroes, wishing the Foundation could see things from our perspective. I lived on wine, bread, and cheese and whatever meals I could drum up with a secondhand guitar I managed to keep. Then I stumbled across Le Cheval Bleu, on the southern outskirts of Limoges, before reaching Toulouse.

"I knew it was special when I first saw it, a pretty little restaurant and inn I was checking out for lunch and gas money. Y'see, I always waited until a busy hour when people were eating, then I'd stroll in strumming my guitar, singing a peppy song . . . Funny, I didn't mind being a minstrel when I thought I was free from acting like one. So I sang for my supper like a real trouper and it worked every time.

"When I met Jacques and Thérèse, they were married and owned the place—I could tell they were my kind of people. They loved jazz. They spoke English. They read a lot and they *loved* to talk. I sang during lunch and supper for a couple of days. They put me up in a room that overlooked a long, beautiful lake, and it had the softest bed I ever slept in. When it was time to go, they didn't want me to leave, but I wanted to get to the next big town before dark, and after an embarrassing amount of sad farewells and extra loaves of bread and wine and cheese, I took off in my little car. But as luck would have it, by the time I reached the end of the lake, my car started overheating. I pulled over to the side, deciding I'd better take a look under the hood. That's when I first heard the screams.

"In the middle of the lake an old woman was reaching out to someone with an oar, screaming desperately for help. Naturally, I dived in the water and swam out to her."

"With your clothes on?"

"Didn't have time to take them off. I found out later the ol' gal was trying to save her five-year-old granddaughter. She was playing with her dolly and she got up to retrieve it and . . . splash! But that was shortly before I arrived on the scene. By the time I got to the boat, all I could see was a hysterical woman pointing beneath the boat. The water was muddy. I could hardly see anything. Then I caught a glimpse of something shiny on the other side of the boat sinking to the bottom, but I had to go up for air. I prayed whatever I saw would still be in the same spot. I grabbed some air and dove down again.

"Somehow—I found her. By the time we got her in the boat, her little body wasn't moving. I pushed on her stomach again and again. Finally she started coughing up water and part of a sandwich. I rowed them back to shore while her grandmother kissed her, muttering things in French, repeating the little girl's name, Kiki. A few of the villagers were waiting at the shoreline. One offered me a blanket and drove me back to the inn. Kiki turned out to be the daughter of the owners of the inn I told you about, Jacques and Thérèse. I was kind'a like a hero.

"You should've seen it, Geneva. It was like in the movies. After I got into some dry clothes, everyone in town came by the restaurant, toasting me, hugging me, shaking my hand—and for the first time since leaving Paris, I wasn't conscious of being the only colored person around. They were just real nice people. Jacques insisted I stay at the inn that evening. I'm telling you, those people know how to party. After we ate, we went up to the inn, which sits on a hill above the restaurant, where there was a grand piano. I played and we danced and drank wine and boogied all night long.

"The following day, Jacques and Thérèse took me on a tour of the town and their grounds. Lots of battles were fought there during the Franco-German War. Behind the restaurant was an unused stable. That's when I got the bright idea to work on my opera there, if they'd give me a job. I had fallen in love with the place, Geneva. I would've found any excuse to stay."

"And they went along with it?" Geneva asked, getting up from the table with a stretch. "Let's go upstairs where it's more comfortable."

After they settled, Dandy in the blue chair and Geneva curled up on the sofa, Dandy returned to his story. "They converted the old stable for me. In less than a week, I had my very own studio. They moved the piano down to the stable, put furniture in it, the works. 'Stay as long as you want,' Jacques told me."

"Sounds wonderful."

"It was. I worked on my opera every day. I ate garden-fresh food every day. And then, after helping out in the kitchen, I'd play the piano to entertain every night and earn the rest of my keep. You know I'm a big ham, and the word was getting around among the tourists about *Le Jazz* at the inn. We were beginning to turn people away on the weekends."

"How long did you stay with them?"

"Almost a year. And then I left them and France in a hurry."

"What happened?"

"It was quite funny at first. A large party of rich Southern crackers from Mississippi blew into town. When they spotted me, I was sitting outside the kitchen peeling potatoes for Thérèse, who promised to make me some potato salad from my Lenox Avenue recipe. Well, as you can guess—those crackers figured I was the hired man and insisted I lug their baggage up to the inn.

"Now I don't know what got into me—but I acted like Stepin Fetchit. Shuffled my feet, stuck out my lips, acted dumb and grinned a lot, but I wasn't ready for what went down next. They assumed I *was* Stepin Fetchit, and proceeded to talk about me like I was a dog in French to a Parisian couple who was showing them the countryside. Anyway, it gave me a terrific opportunity to hear bigots firsthand. I bowed and scraped and widened my eyes appropriately when they spoke French."

"What did they say?"

"They said nasty, stupid things. Things like colored people had small brains and couldn't be taught too much beyond working in the fields or the kitchens, but we seemed happier that way."

"Did you get mad?"

"Not at all. I was enjoying their nastiness more than they were. I'd run down to tell Jacques and Thérèse. *They* got mad. But I reasoned with them to go along with my little masquerade because I wanted to know more about racists and what they say, how they think. So I got Jacques, Thérèse, Kiki, even the grandmother, in on the act. Every time those crackers came up with another myth about colored folks, I'd nonchalantly do something when I was sure they were watching, to quietly dispel the lies and make them look like the fools they were—bless their souls.

"Like the time they said colored folks all had bad feet and weren't too well coordinated." He rushed to the fireplace, picked up a pair of candleholders and some framed photos, and began to juggle them. "I was doing this when they passed me on the way to the dining room, only that night I was using a couple of sharp knives and some cabbage."

He carefully put the candleholders and pictures back in place and returned to his seat. "This went on for almost a week until the son, a smart-ass mama's boy if there ever was one, started one night while I was playing a little Ellington."

Dandy's eyes narrowed. "That son of a bitch started talking 'bout how primitive we were; that as long as coloreds have been away from the jungle, the jungle was still in our blood, and it wasn't safe for women—especially white women—to be out at night when one of us primitives were around.

"And as if that wasn't enough, the mother got into the bull-shit after polishing off another goblet of wine, loudly declaring niggers never could learn to read music. She said that's why the poor devils can never play classical music. Their brains can only comprehend native rhythms. The French couple kept listening to them, then looking at me. This was one nigger who was getting so hot under the collar you could fry fish on my shirt—but you would have been proud of me, Geneva. I kept my cool.

"To them, I was just another nigger hustling in the kitchen, incapable of learning anything, especially a foreign language.

"Well," he said, stretching his legs out, "I decided it was time to teach them a lesson, and that's when the brown stuff really hit the fan. Instead of going on my break, I began to sing a few songs in French—very good French I might add. Those crackers almost fell off their chairs when they heard my French. The father's bald head turned red as a tomato. We had a big crowd that night, and they made me stand and take a bow.

"Then I sat back down and blew them away with Bach, Chopin, Mozart—anything classical that leaped into my head—and I played better than ever."

"How did they react to that?"

"The French couple looked like they were amused at the Southern crackers' embarrassment. All of the other guests stood up at their tables and applauded. Some of them brought money to the piano, some came by to shake my hand. Others cried. It almost made me cry."

"What did the crackers do?"

He laughed. "They left their table without dessert with their tails between their legs. I didn't see them again until the next night. They were talking in German. I know five languages. German is one of them. And every time I was within earshot, they'd be talking about me, pouring more poison into the French couple's minds.

"Now for a while, playing dumb was fun. I could find out what these vile, horrid, little people were up to. In a certain sense, it was quite academic. I had never experienced blatant prejudice firsthand in my life. Sure, I've seen stares before and I've heard whispers before and I've been in a few fights in high school caused by some remark before, but nothing like this. I could examine my oppressor up close while he was doing his dirty work. That's what made it so sweet. But it finally got the best of me."

Geneva folded her arms across a pillow and squeezed it. *This,* she decided, *is what made him change.*

"I was at the piano, talking to Thérèse, when Kiki, ready for bed in her pajamas, ran up to me and gave me a big hug and kiss, which by now was as much of a ritual at the inn as singing the French national anthem before closing. And just like every other night, some customers applauded or laughed at this cute French Shirley Temple."

"The son—the mama's boy, that bastard—was telling another couple at the next table I was an ex-convict and they'd better lock up their valuables. Then he said I was screwing three generations of whores—Thérèse, Kiki, and the grandmother. That did it!"

"What did you do?"

"I lost my cool. I saw red. And then I don't know what I saw—a whole mess of fists flying and women screaming and Jacques pulling the ol' man off my back who was trying to pull me off his son, the mother yelling for the police, Thérèse trying to calm the others down—and through all this, I somehow managed to get that loser out in the alley, alone—just the son and me.

"One thing I give Harlem credit for, Geneva, it sure taught me how to fight. I clipped him with a solid left and got the advantage. I held him by his collar and banged his fuckin' head against the wall—each time, I'd tell him a little bit 'bout myself, sort of like a ten-minute crash course about his fellow American—the one he was fucking with!

"In French, I told him how I grew up in Harlem; how my mother was a trained opera singer and light-skinned enough to pass for white and how she taught me five languages before I reached four—then I banged his head against the wall.

"In Italian, I asked him why he was spreading those vicious lies about me and Jacques's family. He didn't seem to understand Italian, but I banged his head against the wall with each of their names. He seemed to understand that.

"Then I told him how I had to play at rent parties for piano lessons; how I finally got a scholarship to Julliard—I don't re-member what language I used by this time, probably English, but I remember beating him and telling him why."

Dandy got up from his chair as if reliving it, and lunged close to Geneva, which was somewhat frightening to her.

"Ordinarily, I'm not a violent man, but I will always remem-ber his teeth loosening under my knuckles for putting my fore-fathers into slavery. I will always see the blood streaming over his brow for the lynchings his kind of thinking caused.

"And I remember telling him my name because I wanted him to remember *who* gave him the whipping as well as why."

"Did you kill him?"

He seemed too engrossed in his story to answer. He paced in front of the fireplace. "Every time I cracked his head against the wall, I told him who it was for. 'This one's for Kiki! This one's for Bessie Smith.' I pulled names out of a hat by then. I don't know how long I was beating on him before a couple of friends and Jacques pulled me off him. His face looked like raw meatloaf."

"Did you kill him?"

"I don't know. He was rushed to the hospital while Jacques hid me in Kiki's room, under her bed, until the police went away. Everyone in the village said they didn't know who the Southern crackers were talking about, claiming they'd never seen a colored American in the village. It was wonderful. Even the other tourists who were dining had varying reasons why they couldn't give the police an accurate description of me.

"In the middle of the night, Jacques brought me a change of clothes." He looked down at the wrinkled suit he was wearing. "These clothes. Mine were too bloody. Jacques found out the

Île de France was leaving for the United States that morning. He gave me money for passage. I gave him my car. He drove me to the docks that night. I didn't even have enough time to grab my ol' guitar . . . or say good-bye to Kiki."

Dandy seemed exhausted and sat back down in the chair. "I'm going to write that opera, Geneva." His voice was stern, his lip stiff with determination. "And it's gonna show bigots like that how they can't keep us down. It's gonna show the world what colored folks are really made of."

Geneva hated to bring up practical matters, but she felt Dandy needed to be more realistic. "What are you going to do for money?" she asked in as sweet a tone as possible.

"An artist never knows where his next meal is coming from. All I know is I had to come back. I had to come back home to Harlem. And now I know why.

"While I was on the ship, I did a lot of thinking. I kept wondering why someone with money—like those southern crackers—would be so preoccupied with putting me in my so-called proper place? Why were they even bothering?

"And I decided they were just poor white trash, just like the poor black trash or any other color trash that tries to denigrate other people's lives to make themselves look better. And even more to the point of the lesson I learned, I decided they weren't worth worrying about. That led me to think about my own situation with the Davies Foundation. They destroyed every idea I had.

"Take my opera, for instance. They said it was too modern; people weren't ready for love stories between colored folks, or they'd use words like 'too progressive,' and 'daring.' Now what the hell's so daring about a love story between two people? It made me realize Davies was spending a whole lot of time and money to convince me I should base my work on times when darkies knew their place—and what they were really telling me was to stay in *my* place!

"Then I figured this whole goddamned racial prejudice out. Y'see, the Mr. Charlies with money dangle dreams in front of the poor Mr. Charlies. They point to a millionaire's estate, a fancy country club, a college education for their kids, and they tell these gullible souls, 'This is yours, but you can't let *them* have any. That would mean your skin color doesn't make you extraordinary, and that would mean *I'm* not extraordinary.' But they make it just as hard for poor whites to achieve anything as it is for us. That's how the rich stay in control. That's how the American pie is sliced up.

"They keep pointing at us as reasons why the poor Mr. Charlies are still poor. It's the niggers or the Jews or the Chinks—anybody but themselves—and that keeps the poor son of a bitches looking in the wrong direction. Instead of getting a piece of the pie, they're getting pie in the face!"

Dandy slumped back in his chair. His face became longer with despair. "Funny," he finally said, "I had to go halfway around the world to realize beating the crap out of some ignorant white boy wasn't the answer to anything. They're just as much victims of discrimination as we are. They'll have to live with their feelings of inferiority for the rest of their lives, too. The real fight was back here—back in Harlem."

"I don't suppose the Jones Brothers are paying you too well. They have a reputation for being cheap."

"I barely make enough for rent."

"You can stay here if you like." Geneva surprised herself with her spontaneous, but genuine offer. "Instead of rent, you can help me fix things, get stuff done around the house—maybe even work on your opera."

Lines formed on his forehead. He looked confused.

Geneva decided she needed to make her offer easier to accept. "We'll tell our friends I decided to take in a roomer and felt more secure having a friend of the family in the house. With prices being what they are these days, everyone's taking in roomers."

Like before, Dandy clammed up. He didn't say anything.

"We'll clean up the room downstairs. It has its own entrance from the street, except of course when it snows this much . . . maybe pick up a secondhand piano for you."

"You're sure you want me here?"

"Of course! You're too talented to be driving dead bodies all over Harlem."

Dandy eyed her for a moment. A slow smile formed on his lips. "Well, if you're serious, I'll take you up on your kind offer."

Chapter Thirty-one

If her eyes outshine the skies
of bright new twinkling stars above her . . .
she's a Cotton Club Girl.

If she finds you with her style or pretty smile
for awhile she makes you love her . . .
she's a Cotton Club Girl.

The baritone was a little wobbly, Billie thought, and it felt strange wearing an evening gown instead of a flimsy costume onstage, but she was caught up in the moment. Dimples stood in front of her, waiting for her name to be called.

"Just think, honey," Dimples said in her raspy voice, wiping a tear from her eye, "this'll be our very last time here."

"And now," the baritone announced, "Miss Dimples Frazier!"

Dimples turned to Billie. "Godammit! I think I'm gonna cry." She went out through the curtain with a face full of tears.

Billie thought about the good times she'd had with Dimples and the rest of the girls; the exciting times, dancing with "Bojangles" or hearing Ethel sing the blues on opening night or recognizing the smiles of Sophie Tucker and Jimmy Durante in the audience; the happy times, parading in her costume to Duke's orchestra or hearing Duke compose a tune or tapping her foot to the Nicholas Brothers clowning around after hours when the club had closed. She felt grateful for being so lucky.

> *Why don't you take a chance?*
> *Maybe she'll want to dance.*
> *This might lead you to romance . . .*
> *with a Cotton Club Girl.*

Billie's was the last name announced. She didn't lose control like Dimples, but she wasn't prepared for the emotions that swept over her. As she walked down the edge of the stage, hearing the applause, seeing the familiar faces, smiling at the other girls who had vamped before her, she prayed for the tears not to flow until she got backstage.

When she reached the front of the stage, Baldy, one of Owney Madden's henchmen, signaled to Billie. Baldy was a short, stocky fellow who had a face that resembled a bulldog, but he was always very sweet to her, and his smile postponed her tears.

"Owney wants to see ya upstairs," he whispered. "Gee ya look extra pretty tonight."

Billie kissed him on his bald spot. The audience cheered and laughed, and after completing her promenade, she wove through the crowd to the staircase which led to Owney's office. Owney was in the room adjacent to his office where he kept his icebox and pool table.

"Come in, Billie. I must say . . . you're taking the last night quite well."

"Dimples is taking it pretty hard, but I'm okay."

"I know you decided some time ago not to come downtown with us, but I thought, maybe you changed your mind. I jus' want you to know the job's still open for you."

"Thanks, Owney, but Lloyd was talking about moving to San Francisco, and we haven't made our plans yet."

Owney stared at her. "You're still seeing each other?"

"Sure. You know that. He's supposed to meet me here."

Owney laid his cuestick down on the table. "I don't think he's going to show up tonight."

"What are you talking about?"

Owney went into his office and returned with a newspaper under his arm. He patted Billie on the shoulder. "Take a look at this. Sorry you had to find out this way, kid."

Vague images appeared before Billie as she read the article at the top of the folded paper. A picture of Lloyd with a plain-looking woman . . . Engaged . . . Celebrating at a private club . . . Wealthy heiress . . . Next June . . . Her heart pounded. She didn't have to read any further; she was mad enough.

Billie stood up and left the office, snatched up her coat and a bottle of champagne backstage, and was halfway out the door when Dimples caught up with her.

"Hey! Where do you think you're going? We're supposed to go to the Nicholas Brothers' party. I told them we were comin'."

"I'll meet you there," Billie said, racing down the steep staircase that led to the street below.

She went across to a drugstore where there was a phone booth
and called Lloyd's house. When the phone was answered she said
she had flowers for delivery to the party, but had misplaced the
address. The butler told Billie to have them delivered to the
Union League Club, and gave her the address on Park Avenue. It
was a stylish men's club that was established during the Civil War
to send Negro men off to battle in the name of eligible, wealthy
white men who stayed home. She took a taxi downtown.

When she arrived, the doorman was too stunned to question
her entering the building. A round-figured dark-skinned Negro
maid was helping an elderly gentleman with his coat when she
caught sight of Billie.

"Can I be of service?" she said in a loud what-are-you-doing-
here tone.

"Child, I'm tonight's entertainment," Billie said as she rushed
up the wide staircase that led to the private dining rooms. A
waiter appeared from one of the rooms.

Billie held out the bottle. "Could you open this for me,
please?"

The waiter looked at Billie as if she weren't real. He popped
the cork and handed the bottle back to her. She asked him if he
knew where the Harringtons were having their party. He pointed
to a door at the end of the long, gilded corridor.

When she reached the door, she took a swig from the bottle
and entered the room.

It was an airless little room lined with brocade fabric and angel
sconces holding candelabras along the walls. A large group of

people were sitting at a table filled with half-empty glasses and dinner plates. Lloyd's father was standing, making a toast to Lloyd and the woman whose photograph Billie had seen in the newspaper. He stopped when he saw Billie. The room turned quiet in an instant. No one seemed to be breathing.

"This is a private party," the father said.

"I trusted you, Lloyd," Billie said, brushing past his father, moving closer to Lloyd. "I loved you."

A stern-faced woman with a large mole on the side of her neck asked, "Is this some sort of joke?"

"I guess the joke's on me," Billie retorted.

"Someone call a guard!" a voice whispered.

"That won't be necessary," Billie snapped. When she reached Lloyd, she slapped him so hard the imprint of her hand remained red on his face.

The expressionless fiancée stiffened. "I know who you are. Lloyd told me all about you."

"Oh no he didn't! He couldn't! He doesn't know me at all." She swung her head to Lloyd.

"You're going to marry her?"

Lloyd mumbled a few words and nodded yes.

"Well, for your sake," Billie said, heading back to the door, "I hope she fucks better than she looks!"

Billie didn't realize she had left her purse in the taxi or dropped it shortly after she'd gotten out of it. She had no money. Still carrying the bottle of champagne, she took a few more swallows, pulled her coat collar up to her ears, and walked several long city blocks to the subway, talking the old man at the change booth into letting her go through the gate for free.

While she waited for the uptown train, a panhandler approached her. He was tattered, wearing three layers of clothes, and dirty. So dirty, Billie couldn't tell if he was colored or not. She gave him what remained in the bottle and waited until a train pulled into the desolate station. She got on, and when the door closed, she allowed herself to cry. Billie wept through the next several train stops.

As the train pulled away from the Ninety-sixth Street platform, Billie became aware of eyes staring at her. She wiped her own, and saw the panhandler sitting opposite her. The train was empty of other passengers. He was holding the bottle out to her this time. The idea of drinking behind his filth made her feel nauseous. She smiled appreciatively and shook her head. After a brief moment of staring at each other, the panhandler stood up and held the bottle out to Billie again.

"No thanks," she said. "Enjoy it."

The panhandler returned her smile, revealing an array of crooked, yellow-stained teeth, then he emptied the bottle, but he didn't return to his seat.

"You been dancin'?" he asked in a loud, gargling voice to overcome the rumbling of the speeding train.

Billie decided not to answer him. *He'll go away eventually.*

"What's the matter, cat gotcha tongue?" he slurred. A frown formed on his smudged face of pimples and hairs. He wiped his nose on his threadbare sleeve.

Billie got up from her seat and moved to the other end of the train. Half a minute later, he moved to another seat opposite her.

"Stop it! You're bothering me!" He was beginning to frighten her.

"What's yer fuckin' problem? I ain't good enough for ya?" He took out his penis and waved it at her.

She ran back to the other end of the train and into an adjoining car through two sliding doors. She locked the second door. He took the bottle and smashed the window. She screamed and ran through the empty train to the last car, but the lock wouldn't catch on this door. She was trapped.

He grinned as he forced his way into the car. He fondled himself and displayed his erection.

"You gonna get it like you never got it before," he growled.

She dodged around a pole and ran back toward the front of the train. He chased behind her, but a sharp curve threw him onto a seat. Her heel got caught in the middle of two cars. He was catching up to her. She left the shoe behind and kicked off the other. She screamed, but no one was there to hear. She could see a conductor in the next car, but he obviously couldn't hear above the screeching wheels. The panhandler's grimy hands grabbed her. She held onto a pole in the middle of the car, but he pulled her away from it, dragging her back into the car. He managed to hold her by the throat while he squeezed her breast with his other hand, and was slowly working his hand down her body when the train took another deep curve, swinging into the next station, throwing her attacker against the steel door. The opposite door opened and Billie, too hoarse to scream any more, ran for her life.

She didn't see an empty trash container near the exit and crashed into it, sending her sprawling to the platform, inches from the edge of the downtown train tracks.

The dirt-encrusted hand grabbed Billie again. She desperately looked around for something to hit him with. A train was coming. The rumbling noise distracted him. She squirmed out of her coat and his grasp and ran toward the exit, but she cut her foot on a piece of glass and couldn't continue.

A bedraggled arm wrapped around Billie's neck from behind. He was choking her, almost squeezing the wind out of her. They banged against an upright steel girder. She tried to kick him but his grip was too tight. They toppled to the platform and rolled several feet before stopping. He hit her, bloodying her lip. He pounced on top of her and held her shoulders against the concrete. Then he released the grip of one hand and reached under her long gown while holding her down with the other.

With all her might, Billie kicked up her knee, clipped him on his bearded chin, and poked a long fingernail in his eye, drawing blood from it. The bum grabbed his eye, fell back, rolled over the trash container Billie had knocked down, and tumbled onto the track in front of a speeding downtown express.

The following morning, every newspaper in town featured a picture of Billie, some in her Cotton Club costumes, with headlines boasting BEAUTY BEATS THE BEAST. Overnight, Billie had become a celebrity, the unofficial beauty queen of Harlem, and only a few people knew how sad she really was.

Chapter Thirty-two

Ever since Virginia's death, Geneva had become particularly frightened of heavy traffic. Waiting on the corner of 125th Street and Fifth Avenue, she took a careful step behind the lamppost while trucks and cars of every assortment roared by. She wondered how Dandy's big meeting was going. He had looked quite handsome this morning, wearing an old blue serge suit of Lester's she had the tailor alter for him. Although he claimed he wasn't nervous, she could tell he was.

Geneva lifted the tail of her coat with a sweep of her arm and maneuvered gracefully around a knee-high mound of snow that had frozen overnight. A large-framed woman smiled at her. It was a habit of Negroes to nod or smile a silent greeting as they passed. Geneva had never much liked this habit, it seemed too countrified. But now, she thought, reaching the sidewalk, looking back at the woman who had reached the other side, she was beginning to like the whole idea. It was friendly, civilized.

Geneva went into the corner drugstore to pick up a pack of cigarettes. It was uncomfortably warm inside. The owner, a nice Jewish man, was sprinkling sawdust on the tiled floor but it did little to prevent people from slipping.

Rose was already at the back counter and motioned to the cashier to ring up another pack. It had become a morning ritual to see who'd get there first.

"It's official," Rose gushed with a big smile as she handed Geneva a pack of Wings. "City Culture wants me to speak at their graduation. In Poughkeepsie."

Geneva was pleased for her. City Culture was one of the few accredited schools that taught beauticians how to properly care for Negro hair. She knew how important this invitation was to Rose.

They left the stifling hot air for the crackling cold that whipped down the wide promenade. After a few steps, Rose stopped abruptly.

"You suppose they know I'm not colored?"

"If they don't," Geneva teased, "they're in for a big shock when you step off the train."

They laughed much of the way to the salon, ignoring the relentless wind that pushed against them. They hurried to the revolving door that was protected by the red canopy and pushed their way inside to get away from the weather. It reminded Geneva of when Julia Mae had had a rough time convincing her and Rose to open a salon downstairs from their office. "Don't you think women of color want to look beautiful for their men?" Julia Mae had asked them. "And there ain't nobody on

125th Street that's offering anything like our cosmetics to the colored woman. Our beauty products work, and it's high time we showed them how!" Geneva smiled at the memory. The salon not only boosted sales, it was making a great deal of money on its own. When they got upstairs to their offices, Julia Mae beckoned to them from her office door with a stick of incense. "Gotta see you two right away!" Then she lit it and ducked back into her office to take a phone call.

When Geneva and Rose walked in the dark room Julia Mae was on the phone, waving the incense stick like a bandleader's baton. Julia Mae's office always reminded Geneva of her store. Both office and store had apothecary jars and herbs on shelves and in corners, both were darkened with thick draperies at the window, and both had an intoxicating blend of smells in the air.

Julia Mae was talking in her high-pitched, girlish voice; the one that usually meant she had some new scheme up her sleeve. She punctuated her questions with a light tap of the incense stick on several jars of herbs and lotions on a narrow table behind her.

As Rose took off the red scarf Geneva had given her for her birthday, she asided with a wink, "Sounds like this one's going to be juicy."

Geneva agreed. Judging from Julia Mae's cuteness, this one promised to be outlandish.

Julia Mae tapped her carefully manicured, long, fire-engine-red fingernails on her ornately carved teakwood desk. The desk had been built to her specifications. It was constructed on a platform to make her appear taller when she sat behind it.

"Call me as soon as you find out where she lives," she cooed as she hung up the phone with a playfulness she usually reserved for tidbits of gossip. She tossed a copy of the *Daily News* in front of Rose and turned on a brass lamp on her desk.

"Henry showed it to me this morning. They're calling her 'Harlem's Cinderella,' " she said, standing up behind her desk to emphasize her words. "Right now—right this very minute—people are buzzing in every store, every school, every subway train in Harlem about that gal!"

Rose handed the newspaper to Geneva.

She was shocked to see a picture of Billie on the front page. Her evening gown had been torn and soiled. She was getting into a police car.

"At the newsstand this morning," Julia Mae continued, "that's all I heard. 'She's so pretty. She's so brave. She's this. She's that.' And then Henry got himself a brainstorm. He thinks she's an answer to our goddamned prayers!"

Rose and Geneva glanced at each other, wondering where this was leading.

"Don't you see?" she explained. "Everybody knows her. Everybody loves her. We've gotta make her our exclusive property!"

Julia Mae sat back down in her chair with a self-congratulatory flop. She lit another stick of incense with a long wooden match. "Whenever folks talk about Billie Lambert, girls, I want them to think of us."

"How do we do that?" Rose asked.

"By giving her the highest salary a colored model ever got. By making her Miss Brown Beauty of Julia Mae's Beauty Products!"

"That's a wonderful idea," Rose offered.

"Well, I don't think so," Geneva interjected. "It says here she was almost raped by some wino. I don't think that's the kind of reputation we want. We don't want our customers to think they'll get attacked if they use our product."

"That's *exactly* what we want women to think! Don't be silly, Geneva." A small wrinkle formed at the corner of Julia Mae's pouty lips. "We want them to think a splash of our perfume and a dab of our lipstick are gonna make them into hot stuff—*just like her.*"

She pointed the incense at the front page. "Get a load of that picture. Her hair is a mess, her gown is ripped, and she still looks like a million bucks."

"I say no. She'll cheapen our name." Geneva felt panic creep into her throat. This was no time to be exposed by Billie. She knew she'd never be forgiven for letting Adam go to prison. She turned to Rose for support.

"I'm afraid I agree with Julia Mae," Rose said. "Quite honestly, we could use the publicity, not to mention any extra sales it might generate."

"That settles it," Julia Mae declared. "You're outvoted this time, Geneva. Henry would've voted with us."

On her way home that evening, Geneva wasn't feeling as chipper as she had earlier. First there was the argument between Julia Mae and her secretary, and moments later, the secretary leaving the office in tears. Secretaries didn't last too long with Julia Mae. But that wasn't what really bothered Geneva. She had worked too hard and progressed too far up the social ladder to have some cheap little chorus girl cause her to fall. *Somehow,* she reassured herself as she rushed home to get out of the harsh wind, *I'll convince Julia Mae to use someone else.*

D andy hurried Geneva out of the house so fast she didn't have a chance to freshen her makeup or change her clothes. They were heading uptown in a large yellow cab when he explained what the rush was all about.

"The meeting didn't go too well this morning. In fact," he said, his handsome face turning serious, "it was a disaster."

"It's my fault. I shouldn't have put you up to it."

"Please don't feel that way. I needed to talk to them, face to face."

"What happened?"

"The same ol' crap. The Davies Foundation represents big money—I mean *big* money. They told me a white audience would never want to see a colored love story. They said I was making my hero too brave, my heroine too modern, too smart. One of them said no one could identify with a colored band-leader—a position only a handful of Negroes ever achieve. I suppose they wanted a sanctified Uncle Tom falling in love with a prostitute. I told them it was only a matter of time before someone set 'Amos and Andy' to music to satisfy the minstrel show fantasies bigots have of us. *That* got their goat!"

He gazed sadly out the cab window and watched a family help one another cross a mound of snow. Geneva could tell he was still upset by the meeting, and she decided to remain quiet until he spoke again. When his eyes returned to her, though, they looked mischievous.

"Before I left those pompous bastards, I told them to go to

the devil and then I took a good, long walk through Central Park."

"In all this cold?"

"It wasn't bad. I had things to think about. A few hours later, I found myself in front of the Lafayette Theater. It was like someone had led me to it. I hadn't been there since leaving for Europe and . . . well, I guess I was sort of lonely for the place."

"So why are we going there now?"

"I heard a band rehearsing upstairs. They were playing nice and tight, real pros. So I went around the back. Ol' Snakelips was still on the door, still getting drunk, cursing like a sailor, teasing all the young gals. He remembered me when I was struggling. I used to play two shows a night and four on weekends for six bits a throw, then I'd run over to Corky's—he gave some wild rent parties—and I'd grab a plateful of food and an armful of women and play all night on his old upright. I never got tired.

"Seems like a million years ago. Anyway, I really wanted to hear this band up close and although he wasn't supposed to let me go upstairs, Snakelips let me in. So when I get upstairs, I find out it's an old buddy of mine, Jimmy Lunceford—"

"You know him?"

"And most of the guys in his band, too. They even played an old arrangement of 'Sleepy Time Gal' I did for them five years ago."

"Sounds like the good old times. I bet that was fun."

"It was. But that's not all. We started shooting the shit about making records and going on the road and one-night stands, and I told them about working on the opera and one thing led to another and before I knew it, Jimmy called some friends of his and they've all agreed to come hear my opera tonight."

Geneva was impressed. "You've finished already?"

"No. But if they like what I've done so far, they might back me so I can complete it without starving to death."

"But I don't know anything about music. Why bring me?" she asked.

"I need someone I can trust; someone I don't have to impress. Don't be nervous. It's merely a tryout."

The cabbie pulled in front of the historic Lafayette Theater. Stage plays were performed there before Negroes were allowed in the audience. Vaudeville followed soon after. Geneva admired the large marquee that extended to the curb and imagined how grand opening nights must have been once.

Dandy didn't have any money, so she slipped five dollars into his glove. He paid the fare and rushed her around the corner of 132nd Street to the back entrance of the dark, old Victorian theater.

Geneva was the only woman there. Two of the seven well-dressed gentlemen were white. After introductions and a small amount of polite chatter, Dandy sat at a grand piano and began to tell the story of his opera while playing a beautiful melody. It made Geneva wish she had a piano in the house.

The tryout was nothing like she expected. The rehearsal hall was a large barren room with plain walls and windows that overlooked the noisy traffic below. Stacks of wooden folding chairs were in one corner and folding music stands in another. But. Geneva was mesmerized by Dandy's ability. When he got to a particularly dramatic moment, he'd strike a chord on the piano, or sometimes he'd sing a lyric or two of a song.

She was enchanted by his singing, his music, the love story. She imagined what it would sound like in a real opera house with a real orchestra playing.

When Dandy finished, the men all stood up and applauded. They loved his idea, especially the white men, but one of them suggested putting his play on Broadway and the rest of the group agreed. Dandy seemed genuinely pleased. Geneva didn't understand. She felt embarrassed for him, knowing how strongly he felt about making it into an opera, but she declined to say anything in the taxi on the way back home.

Geneva decided to be direct. when they got inside the house.

"That was crummy of them!" she said, showing more emotion than she intended to.

"What do you mean?"

"Telling you to forget about it as an opera. What nerve! They didn't tell Gershwin to forget about *Porgy and Bess.*"

Dandy crossed the room after carefully hanging up Lester's old overcoat and gave Geneva a gentle hug. "That's real sweet of you, Geneva, but I think it's a terrific tip. Let's face it, people are likely to avoid going to an opera, but a Broadway show . . ."

"You actually like their idea?"

"Like it? I *love* it!" He picked Geneva off the floor with the enthusiasm of a high school athlete and swung her in a circle, making the living room spin around her. "That means I've got backers now! I can start putting my show together!"

"Hmm, I'm surprised in a way you didn't think of it before.

You seemed so set on writing an opera," Geneva commented. *Had all that business about an opera just been an act?*

Dandy's eyes narrowed, then he smiled. "I didn't, but I wish I had. Guess I had my sights set too high. But I'd settle for a Broadway show if these people give me the backing for it. I'd imagine anybody would."

"You're right. Let's have a toast to your new show," Geneva said. As she walked over to the cabinet that held the liqueurs, her heel caught in the rug and she tripped, twisting her ankle. Dandy was beside her immediately.

"Are you okay?" he asked, helping her up. Despite herself, Geneva grimaced. The ankle was very sore.

"Here, let me help you onto the couch," he said. When he had her stretched out, he began to massage her ankle gently. "Why don't you take your stocking off so I can make you feel better," he suggested.

Geneva pulled an afghan over herself as she rolled her stocking down, then uncovered her foot. Dandy began his gentle rubbing again. Soon his hands were on her calves, then when they met no resistance, moved up to her thighs. Geneva felt too good to care. *It's been so long,* she thought to herself as Dandy began to unbutton the front of her dress. *I deserve this.*

Chapter Thirty-three

Adam didn't get Billie's letter until some five months later. It was delivered to him after numerous reroutings: from Riker's Island to Central Files on Broad Street, to a correctional department in Brooklyn, to a jail in the Bronx, to a prison on Long Island. Finally, it reached Ossining, where Adam had ended up because of his refusal to knuckle under to authority and after the last in a long series of fights. His file was now stamped "Unredeemable."

After he read the letter, Adam sat for days in a numbed state, unable to eat or sleep. He blamed everyone for Virginia's death, but most of all, himself. *If I'd been there. If only I'd been there,* he repeated over and over through dry lips. When they forced him out of his cell, he walked catatonically, doing what they made him do without expression. Then one night, he let out a moan that started low in his body and gradually rose to his throat, becoming an unearthly screech, so nerve-shattering, other prisoners shook their cell doors, scraped metal objects against the bars, stamped on the concrete floors, and screamed along with him.

From that moment on, Adam behaved like a madman. He smashed everything within reach and swung out at anyone who came near him. Each evening the moan would start, rising in pitch and volume, continuing until the guards threw buckets of cold water on him. After four nights, he was dragged from his cell and thrown into solitary confinement where he wouldn't incite the other prisoners.

A week later he was brought before the assistant warden. "You haven't learned anything," the man said while picking his nose. "We'll handle you another way."

Adam was taken to the prison hospital. Sedatives were pushed down his throat. Finally, he was injected with drugs that a doctor said would erase from his mind whatever bothered him.

Adam remained strapped to his bed for three months, but he wasn't aware that any time had passed. Then, one day, the doctor and an assistant unbuckled the straps and he was returned to his old cell. The guard told the doctor Adam was more submissive than he'd ever seen him. The assistant warden came by to have a look, too. "Maybe we can now mold him into a responsible citizen," he said, pointing his pipe at Adam through the steel bars.

That evening, Adam sat on his bunk, his eyes fixed on the wall across from him, not caring that his cell door was still open before "Lights out." He was seeing Virginia's body lying on the street. He imagined it being comfortably at rest on a sidewalk that was soft and clean. His mind refused to see her any other way. She looked sweet and innocent, as if she were asleep, so much alive that her eyes might open any minute.

His mind took him to her. Her eyelashes began to move, but then a loud argument from a cell in the corner snatched him back. It was just before the guards made the rounds to close the cells for the night and some of the prisoners were still taking last-minute showers. Charley, the little white guy Adam worked under with the Neighborhood Betterment Company, had landed in the same jail a few weeks earlier. Now he had put his hands on the wrong convict, and the man was beating Charley to death. While the guard was distracted by another argument on the other side of the oval, without really thinking what he was doing, Adam pulled the man off Charley, saving his life.

Three weeks after, a lawyer showed up. He wouldn't tell Adam who had hired him, but he said there was a good chance of beating the rap, if only Adam would try to behave. Adam figured Charley's connections had something to do with it. In less than a month, Adam was sent to the warden's office.

"Evidently, you have some pretty important friends," the balding white man said when his secretary closed the door behind her. "You've got one of the best lawyers in town working on your behalf. And if he says he can get you off, he can get you off."

After serving three years and two months, Adam was released from prison on a "technicality" he didn't understand. The warden said the lawyer found out Adam never dated his signature, so it couldn't be verified what date the documents were signed, a simple thing like that. Before his release, he asked Charley if he'd paid for the lawyer, but Charley just shrugged it off, calling

Adam crazy. Nevertheless, Adam was still convinced Charley
was responsible.

As the gate of the prison opened and Adam stepped outside to
his freedom, everything was clearer to him. He knew from the
beginning who was to blame. It was never his fault, it was Lester
Noble's. Lester had tricked him into jail. Lester was the reason
he hadn't been at Virginia's side, protecting her. If he'd been
there, she'd still be alive.

Chapter Thirty-four

Geneva was late for Thursday morning's staff meeting. She wasn't sure if her slow pace was caused by her bruised ankle or Dandy's lovemaking. Rose was first to notice her limp.

"How'd you do that?"

"I slipped on some ice."

"Where?" Julia Mae wanted to know. "Can you sue 'em?"

"Unfortunately, no," Geneva said in a voice that sounded too cheerful. "It happened in front of my own house."

Julia Mae quickly turned the meeting's attention to their up-coming fashion show. "I think we can do it in a month if we bust our butts. The sooner we capitalize on Billie Lambert's popularity, the better."

Geneva decided to be tactful. "I think your idea of a Miss Brown Beauty is a good one . . . but, don't you think we're making it a little too easy for Miss Lambert?"

"That gal still buggin' you?"

"I have nothing against her. In fact, I think she's very pretty. I just feel you ought to let our *customers* select Miss Brown Beauty."

Julia Mae's face opened with surprise. She shoved her round figure away from the conference table and gave Geneva an enthusiastic hug.

"That's the best goddamned idea you've ever had!"

"It is?"

"Honey, you should know me by now," she said in her tiniest singsong voice. "I don't bullshit."

Julia Mae bellowed out the door for Eunice to come take notes. In less than an hour they had organized the contest and had hired Miguel Covarrubias, one of Harlem's most popular artists, to design a newspaper ad for contestants.

Geneva decided Billie would be less of a threat if there were other beautiful girls to choose from, so she became an active part of screening the contestants. After only two days, she had to withdraw the ad. They received over two hundred entries cut out of newspapers, accompanied with snapshots, from young women who desperately wanted to be Miss Brown Beauty. As Geneva triumphantly pointed out to Julia Mae, Billie wasn't one of them.

The fashion show was beginning to catch on. Julia Mae called every business on 125th Street and sweet-talked most of them into taking an ad in the program. She charged them ten dollars for a full-page ad, and got away with it. The program promised to be at least one hundred and twenty-five pages, and it was fast becoming a considerable source of income. Julia Mae took full advantage of every opportunity that knocked at the salon's door. First, to accommodate the overwhelming crowd of contestants and their supporters, she rented the Lafayette, knowing she could get it at a cheap price because it was rumored the theater would be closing down by summer. Geneva had fancy satin-finished tickets printed up for admission to the preliminary contest, which would select twenty-five finalists. Each contestant was expected to sell at least ten tickets, so this became another source of income for the company.

That night at the Lafayette, Rose was in charge of briefing the contestants. An hour before the contest, they gathered backstage where dressing rooms were assigned and the rules of the contest were reviewed. Geneva and Julia Mae were going over proofs for the main event's souvenir program in the theater's small office. At ten dollars a page, the advertisers would surely complain if there were any mistakes. Geneva's eyes had just wandered to a performer's face she recognized in one of the photos on the yellowed wall when Rose burst into the room, excited with news.

"She's here!"

"Who's here?" Geneva asked.

"Billie Lambert!"

"She has some nerve," Geneva snapped, "Why didn't she send in an application like everyone else? No, I'm afraid she's too late to enter." She returned to her proofreading.

"But she was invited," Julia Mae interjected.

"Who in the hell took the goddamned liberty to do that?" Geneva wanted to know.

"I did," Julia Mae answered in a dignified tone.

"I did, too," Rose reiterated.

Chapter Thirty-five

It took Geneva a full week to forgive Rose for conspiring with Julia Mae, but as much as she hated to admit it, they were both right. Billie brought glamour to the affair. When the *Amsterdam News* reported she was one of the finalists, the downtown newspapers and movie newsreel companies started calling the office for information, wanting special favors and arrangements at the Savoy Ballroom, where the show would be held.

"We're clicking," Rose said. "Business is way up. The show is a sellout, and Count Basie's agent signed and sent back our agreement. This is turning into the social event of the year. Too bad I've got to miss it."

Julia Mae seemed upset. "Why? What's the matter?"

"Nothing's wrong. But I just realized yesterday I'm committed to address the graduation class at City Culture, and it's on the same day. I'd never make it back to town in time. So I expect to hear all about it, Geneva, when I get back."

Later that day, an argument broke out between Julia Mae and her secretary. She could hear Julia Mae cursing and slamming something against her desk. She heard the secretary shout a profanity back and scream something inaudible. Geneva rushed to the front office to find out what was going on, but they stopped talking when she opened the door, sitting across the desk from each other, looking perfectly composed. Geneva was curious, but she didn't say a word, quietly reclosing the door.

That evening provided a few surprises of its own. Dandy nervously handed a letter to her when she walked in the door.

"It's from Lester. This isn't the first time he's written. He's probably after money."

Geneva poured herself a gin and one for Dandy, lit a cigarette, and gave Dandy a reassuring kiss before she opened the letter. She read it, feeling no emotion, and said, "He's picked up a new habit. Race horses. He's run out of money. What did he expect? He wasn't working, as far as I could tell. What a fool."

"What a relief. I thought he might be planning on moving back."

Geneva let out a derisive laugh. "He doesn't want to go to jail. They've still got a warrant out for his arrest. He's been in hiding ever since the trial. Don't worry. He's a coward. He'll stay in hiding."

"Actually, I was more concerned about who gets to dance

with you at the Savoy," he teased. He took the letter from her hand, tore it in half, and threw it in the trash basket.

After that, Dandy was in exceptionally high spirits, talking about the play, flirting. Then a phone call put an end to his good mood.

It was his backers, the men they'd met at the Lafayette, he explained in a subdued tone after he hung up. They'd just agreed to back some other show about voodoo, and they wouldn't be able to take on two new productions this season.

"They told me I should call them next fall," he said in an almost inaudible voice. Then he excused himself and retired to his room downstairs.

It was Friday, March 27, 1934. With only one week to go before the show, the pace inside Julia Mae's Beauty Salon was keeping up with the frantic pace of shoppers outside on 125th Street. Contestants had to be fitted and given new hairstyles. Flowers had to be ordered, a rhinestone crown still had to be purchased. Geneva's schedule was becoming tighter as the big event drew nearer each day.

Perhaps it was the reminder about getting a crown that prompted Geneva to insist they place a ballot in the *Amsterdam News* to assure their customers the contest wasn't "fixed." She wasn't sure why she conjured up the story, but it lit the proper fuse.

"Fixed?" Julia Mae was furious. "Do you know how much time it takes to count ballots? Besides, who's gonna know?"

"A few contestants have started to ask why Billie Lambert gets to be the bride at the end of the show. I told them she was picked at random, but I don't think they believed me." Geneva's lie worked on Julia Mae. She barked at Eunice to call the *Amsterdam News* for an emergency ad. Then she turned to Geneva.

"You're on the ball, Geneva. Although I could swear you only brought this up to try to spoil Billie's chances of winning, I think it's good publicity—a way of saying we're on the up-and-up."

Two days after the ad appeared, the salon was inundated with mail.

Perhaps it was the delivery of the grand piano Geneva bought from the Lafayette, or perhaps it was the tears of surprise in Dandy's eyes when he saw it, that prompted her to call Julia Mae into her office. Nevertheless, Geneva started to review her net worth as an officer of the company.

"This is no time to sell, honey. We're doing better than ever now."

But Geneva was determined to liquidate her interest. She was resolved to put Dandy on Broadway.

"Why don't you wait until after the fashion show. This is a big decision you're making."

"I know what I'm doing."

"Our by-laws says we gotta take it up at our regular staff meeting."

"Since when?"

"Since I thought of it. You've lost your heart, but you don't have to lose your pocketbook, too."

"What on earth are you talking about?"

"Everybody's talking about you and Dandy. It's all over town. I hope you haven't fallen for him."

Geneva wasn't prepared for Julia Mae's candid remarks. She left the office earlier than usual, and took a long leasurely walk home. By the time Geneva reached the front door of her house, she admitted it wasn't love, but it was close.

Chapter Thirty-six

Whenever Geneva and Dandy made love, he would leave her bedroom without saying a word, never a "good night," never a compliment. This time she pulled him back into bed.

"I need to talk to you, Dandy."

"It's late."

"It's really important," Geneva insisted. She settled back into her pillow and covered her breasts with the blanket, then turned on the bedlight.

"Could you raise two thousand dollars toward putting your show on Broadway?"

"We've been through this before, Geneva. That's easy. It's the other eighty-five percent that's hard to dig up."

"What if I told you I have the eighty-five percent."

"Honest?" His smile, and then his kiss, told her he already knew the answer.

The show was only two days away and Julia Mae was a nervous wreck. She didn't like anything—everything was wrong. To calm her down, Geneva and Rose decided they'd take her to lunch at Trixie's, a former after-hours joint that had a reputation for serving the best pork chops in Harlem and the strongest Manhattan in Manhattan. Rose ordered a round.

"We could all use a break," Rose said, taking a generous sip of her Manhattan, offering Geneva a cigarette. She switched the subject from smoothing over Julia Mae's ruffled disposition to Geneva's impending departure.

"Julia Mae told me you're bailing out of the company. Is that true?"

"Now I get it," Geneva laughed. "This was just a plot to get to *me*."

"Not exactly," Julia Mae confessed. "I've been a bitch all morning and that was for real, ever since you told me what you wanted to do. But I planned to pressure you into staying."

"We broke records yesterday," Rose said, getting back to her point. "At this rate, Geneva, we'll double last year's profits by the end of July. You'd be a fool to leave now."

Julia Mae went over the publicity they received from the fashion show and how it had become an enterprise in itself. Depending on how much money they netted, it would probably become an annual event. "You said you wanted to do something more constructive. Well, here it is! This show is beating the crap out of me and it could use someone full-time to work all the angles. We'll fix up your office nice and cute . . . you probably could use your own secretary, too."

"What do you say?" Rose coaxed. "We'd hate to lose you."

Geneva never realized how close she had become to these two women and how important she in turn had become to them, but she'd already made up her mind. She asked them to please understand. They said they understood, but she could tell they didn't.

Julia Mae insisted on having the last word when they returned to the office. Before calling the lawyer to bring the cash and the necessary papers, she said in an uncommonly low voice, "Girl, he must be puttin' down some real good screwin' to make you throw your money down the drain like this."

That night, Dandy had a taxi waiting for her outside the salon. She had more money than she ever imagined she could make on her own, all in a leather overnight valise.

"I thought we might catch a movie tonight," he said.

"Okay by me, but I want to change into something warmer first."

Dandy was amorous the moment the door shut behind them. He didn't give her time to take off her coat before his lips were smothering hers. They made love in the middle of the living room floor with half their clothes still on. Before leaving, Geneva locked the money up in her closet safe.

By the time they reached the Alhambra on Seventh Avenue, only the last movie, a musical about the Sahara, remained to be shown. In it, a movie-star blonde played a sultry dark-skinned beauty. Each time the movie showed a close-up of her blue eyes, Geneva and Dandy, feeling in a giddy mood after their impromptu encounter, laughed.

When they got outside, it was raining. They couldn't get a
cab, so they dodged in and out of the storefronts on 125th
Street like teenaged lovers until they reached home. She
couldn't remember the last time she had had so much fun.

"That's odd," he said to her as he entered the house. "I could
have sworn I locked the door when we left."

"And the lamp is off . . ." Geneva's heart sank. "The
money!" she screamed.

Out of the darkness came a massive body that lunged at
Dandy and knocked him down. Geneva screamed again and
rushed to help Dandy, but she was pushed away. Dandy yelled
for help, gasping for air. The intruder was choking him, banging his head against the wall, knocking down mirrors, crashing
into the bookshelves. Geneva flicked on the hall lights, ran to
the fireplace, and hit the stranger on the back of his head with a
poker, knocking him out.

"Call the police," Dandy wheezed, standing up. "I'll beat the
shit out of him if he moves an inch."

Geneva ran upstairs and saw that the safe was still locked.
Trembling with relief, she returned downstairs to call the police.
The man on the floor began to regain consciousness. He
moaned and rolled over onto his side. As Dandy grabbed the
poker and held it over the man's head, Geneva suddenly realized who it was.

"Don't hit him," she cried. "I know that man."

Chapter Thirty-seven

As Geneva was applying hydrogen peroxide to the cut on the back of Adam's head, she became unsettled by how much he had changed; the graying hair, the unkempt mustache and beard, the deep furrowed lines in his brow, the scowl on his face.

"Let's get him on the sofa, Dandy."

"Who is he?"

"He married my cousin. Come help me lift him."

Adam, still dazed, resisted Dandy's assistance and jerked his arm away. "Who is this guy?"

"I'm the guy you just tried to kill, nigger!"

Adam attempted to stand up, but stumbled against the wall. He managed to make it to the sofa. Dandy stared at Geneva as if she were crazy.

"When did you get out of jail?" she asked Adam.

"A little while ago. I came after Lester."

"Well, as you can see, this isn't Lester. I haven't seen him since before the trial."

"Where is that son of a bitch? I'll get him if it's the last thing I do. You sure didn't put yourself out to clear my name, either," he said, glaring at Geneva.

She backed away from him, thinking fast. "I was confused," she said. "You've got to believe me. Lester told me the night before he left that you were in on the whole thing. I didn't blame you, but I was afraid to perjure myself in the trial."

Adam stared at her. "You should've known I didn't know anything about any fraud. I was jus' followin' orders from you an' Lester. I've been wonderin if *you* were in on it all along, and jus' bailed out right in time."

"Oh, that's ridiculous," Geneva said, glancing over at Dandy, who was drinking all this in. It was time to get rid of Adam. "But if you want to find Lester, you're in luck." She fished Lester's letter out of the wastepaper basket and handed it to him.

"There's his address. Go ahead and find him if that's what you want!"

Dandy had retired to his room early with an upset stomach. As hard as she tried that night, Geneva couldn't get to sleep. She tossed restlessly in bed, turning on another radio station when a song didn't match her mood, although she wasn't quite sure what her mood was. She got up, went to the window and stared out into the park. Back in bed, staring at the ceiling, listening to Ellington's piano . . . more memories.

Adam floated in and out of her mind like a lazy balloon. She saw his naked body that first hot night they made love by the riverbank under the weeping willows. Then she snapped out of her reverie, pulled down her nightgown, and turned on the bedlight. She angrily lit a cigarette.

Why the hell did he have to show up now!

Chapter Thirty-eight

Rose and Geneva were at the Seventh Avenue Florists selecting small bouquets for the runners-up.

"It doesn't seem fair," Geneva said, noticing how tired Rose looked. "Doing all this work and not getting a chance to see the show."

"I don't mind. In fact, it's a lot of fun. If I was at home all day facing Charles and his bottle, I'd probably take to drinking myself." She laughed at her joke, but Geneva could tell there was a great deal of hurt in her words.

As they headed back to the office, sitting among the bouquets of flowers they'd stuffed into a cab, Rose asked Geneva if she ever suspected Lester was having an affair.

"I probably thought he was too dumb to cheat. Why?"

"Just curious."

Geneva noticed a frown of pain on Rose's forehead. "There's more on your mind than that."

"It's just . . ." She hesitated, then she blurted it out. "Charles has been acting rather strange recently. I think he's seeing another woman. He goes to a lot of late night card games and he never tells me about it until the last minute. The other day, I found a blond hair on his jacket."

"Did you ask him about it?"

"I started to." She snapped a flower from one of the bouquets and smelled it, then she continued. "At the time, I was beginning to get a headache. So I went to the medicine cabinet, still holding this strand of hair between my fingers. I felt so silly, I threw it away. But I've still got these suspicions . . . and the headache's back today, a real nagging one."

"Poor dear. All this rain . . . probably affecting your sinuses."

"Perhaps. Maybe I'm allergic to flowers. How would I know?" Rose said with a wry laugh, her frown returning. "Charles never gives me any."

"Why don't you cancel the graduation? You've worked too hard on the show not to see it."

"Well . . . I must admit I'm tempted, but I wouldn't want to disappoint the students."

She patted Geneva's gloved hand and squeezed it. "I wish you weren't leaving. Who am I going to buy cigarettes with now?"

Later that evening, while Geneva was getting ready for the show, Dandy returned to her bedroom with a curious look in his eyes. He waited until she turned from the vanity mirror.

"That was your business partner."

"Which one?" She went back to her face powder.

"The white one."

"Is she waiting downstairs?"

"No. She had to catch a train."

"And . . . ?" She noticed a smudge on her lip line.

"She forgot to tell you she's providing a security guard to escort you to your bank Monday."

"That's nice."

"What are you taking there?"

Geneva looked up from applying her lipstick with a sly smile. "I'll tell you Monday."

The taxi stopped with a skid at 140th Street in front of 596 Lenox Avenue—the Savoy Ballroom. Despite the rain, a crowd of young music fanatics were outside grooving and dancing to the music that poured out of the large partially opened windows upstairs.

From the moment Geneva stepped inside the Savoy with Dandy, she knew the show was going to be a success. As they rushed up the wide marble steps to the ballroom, the sound-proof doors allowed only a whisper of a drumbeat to penetrate Geneva's ears, but when the doors pushed open, her senses pulsated to Fletcher Henderson and his Rainbow Orchestra. The block-long mahogany dance floor was already jammed. The dancers in Cats' Corner were already in a deep sweat, some so exhausted they could hardly keep in step, while other couples bounced and jumped and stomped and shouted to the band to never stop this moment. And Henderson showed no mercy.

The band swung into another tune, another favorite, and the crowd shouted with delight.

Geneva's table was in the front near the bandstand, which was outlined by blue and orange neon strips. Getting to the table meant she had to pass almost every other table before reaching hers. She couldn't help noticing the stares she and Dandy got as they wove through the crowd of revelers. Julia Mae was the first to greet them.

"I'm so glad you're here. We've got a thousand things to do," she said as she whisked Geneva away from her party and Dandy. When they got backstage, Julia Mae, out of breath, sat on a wooden crate, pointing to a shabby dressing room door behind her.

"She wants to see you," she managed to say, fanning herself with a long handkerchief, pulling Geneva toward the door with the other hand. "And don't take long. 'Cause, girl, we've got a show to put on."

Geneva didn't know what Julia Mae was up to. Inside the small room that smelled of damp plaster, crammed with dresses and boxes, was Billie, sitting at a makeshift dressing table, adjusting her stockings.

"I wanted to talk to you before the show, Geneva."

"What on earth is there to talk about?"

Billie stood up from the chair. "Isn't it time you stopped playing games, Geneva?"

"What are you trying to tell me?"

"I heard you've been trying your damnedest to disqualify me from the competition. Why?"

"I didn't even know you were competing," Geneva lied.

Billie took a deep sigh. "Okay, Geneva, despite everything

that's happened, I just wanted you to know that I'm not holding a grudge against you, and since I'm the only family you have up here I think we should at least be able to speak to each other. Don't worry, I won't tell your fancy friends we're related if that's what's bothering you, and I'll never say anything to anyone about Jacksonville."

Billie checked her dress in a dusty mirror that hadn't been cleaned in years. "There. I've got that off my chest. We don't have to be friends, but I just want you to know we're still family."

Geneva stood there, stunned for a moment. Her mind had been so overwhelmed by the events of the last several days; the nonstop preparation for the show, Adam popping up, Dandy and the money. She was startled by Billie's clarity. Geneva slowly moved over to Billie, finally patting her shoulder.

"Thanks, Billie."

When she returned to the table, almost all of her guests were dancing on the burnished maple floor, bathing in tiny, twirling blue lights, swaying to a slow, romantic song. Dandy was the only one sitting at the table, emptying a bottle of Old Overholt into his tumbler.

"Wanna' wet your whistle? The gin's gone but there's another pint of this bourbon left," he said, adjusting his new silk tie.

She needed to get her mind off Billie and what had been said. "I'd rather dance."

"It's too crowded. Let's sit this one out." He toyed with his drink. "Tell me, Geneva, what's all this hush-hush backstage with you and Julia Mae? What are you hiding from me?"

"Nothing that concerns you." He was starting to get on her nerves.

"What happened to all this moolah you were supposed to be coming into?" He pulled his shirtsleeve down so his cuff links would show. "C'mon, whatcha hiding?"

"I told you I'll let you know Monday. Let's dance."

"I heard you scream something about money when that bum tried to kill me. Did you bring a lot of money into the house? Did you change your mind about investing in my play? Is that it?"

Geneva tried to treat it lightly, but Dandy was obviously drunk and argumentative. She leaned over and kissed him. "I'll tell you all about it on Monday after things clear at the bank. Now can we please dance? We're missing all the slow numbers."

He moved away from her. "What's the matter? Don't you trust me, Geneva?"

"You're picking a fight! What's your problem?"

"I don't like ol' boyfriends who just happen to show up." He staggered away from the table, knocking over a few empty bottles, and disappeared into the crowd.

Geneva was peeved. Her pride wouldn't allow her to go after him. She poured herself a bourbon, thinking again that Dandy had become somewhat of a pain in the ass.

Chapter Thirty-nine

Rose had stayed at the Savoy as long as she could. She enjoyed seeing the girls in their first outfits with all the accompanying chaos and hustle and frenzy that goes on backstage, but she had to leave before the actual show. Rose arrived at the train station in plenty of time. She bought a *Look* magazine to keep her mind away from her headache. But when the train was just five minutes from the station, the pounding at her temples became almost unbearable. She hurried across the street to the drugstore to get a pack of Stanback powder, the only headache remedy that seemed to work for her, but by the time she returned to the platform, the train was heading for Poughkeepsie without her.

Her first thought was to grab a taxi and intercept the train at its initial stop in the Bronx, but she decided it would be too difficult to find a taxi in the rain. Her next option, she decided, was going back to the fashion show. But she would need to change into suitable evening clothes, and there wasn't enough time. She wandered into Trixie's and ordered a gin fizz at the bar, then she went to the phone booth where she called City Culture and tearfully apologized to the chancellor for not being able to address the students.

She couldn't get a cab, so she walked home in the drizzle, only adding to the pain of her headache. She wondered how her poor mother managed with migraines. By the time she reached home, she was drenched. Charles had planned to take Evelyn over to her grandmother's in Brooklyn, so he wouldn't be home yet, she reasoned as she stepped out of her wet shoes and dress in the front hall.

It wasn't until she turned on the gas in the living room that she first heard the sounds coming from upstairs. She put the matches back in her purse and cautiously climbed the stairs. When she reached the second landing, she stopped, leaning against the wall, hoping it wasn't what she'd been suspecting all along. The noise, as she quietly approached the foot of the stairs leading to the third-floor guest room, was almost discernible. Charles's voice was certainly one of the two she heard.

She carefully climbed the next flight. He was too busy having sex to see or hear her. When she saw the woman, a slim blonde, she wanted to scream, but a stinging acid rushed to her throat and she quickly went down a flight to the bathroom to vomit in the sink. She seemed to purge herself of every mouthful she had eaten that day. By the time she finished, her forehead was covered with a perspiration that mixed with her tears and flowed saltily into her sour mouth. She made her way down to the basement kitchen, covering her mouth, holding her stomach, so weak she barely reached a kitchen chair.

Her sobbing was uncontrollable. She stared at the back door, wanting to get up and run away, but something stopped her. Eventually Rose went to the sink, wondering how long she'd been crying, and nervously drank a glass of water. She found an old pack of Wings in the cupboard and lit a cigarette.

Chapter Forty

Geneva couldn't believe she and Julia Mae were actually standing on the stage of the Savoy Ballroom.

"And the winner is . . ." Julia Mae said in a trembling, nervous voice.

The building shook.

Someone in the audience said, "Earthquake," and it echoed throughout the crowd.

"Calm down everyone, that ain't no earthquake. How many of you ever been in an earthquake?"

A few people raised their hands.

"See what I mean? Most of you wouldn't know an earthquake if it kicked ya' in the round ones!" The drummer added a quick one-two roll and cymbal kick.

The crowd laughed at Julia Mae's joke, and then she became

serious. "Ladies and gentlemen, it gives me great pleasure to award this crown to . . ."

The drummer rolled his snare with a flourish, punctuating it with a crash of the cymbal.

". . . *Miss Billie Lambert!*"

The band played *"I've Got a Feeling I'm Falling."* Flashbulbs and bright lights blinded the room, while cameramen scrambled for the best angle as Billie ascended to the stage to receive her flowers from Geneva and her crown from Julia Mae. She made a beautiful winner.

Since Julia Mae was so short and stocky, she had to stand on a chair to place the crown on Billie. The ballroom erupted in laughter. Basie and his men returned to the bandstand and lured the dancers back onto the polished floor with a smooth swing version of "Star Dust." Margo Washburn, never a favorite of Geneva's, cornered her at the bar.

"I was surprised to see you with Dandy," Margo said with an air of disapproval. She was well into her cups and slurring. "Let me buy you a drink. We can drink to those old songs of Dandy's. Which one did he use on you?"

"What are you talking about?" Geneva said.

"Didn't he write a song for you?"

"No."

"Maybe he's using a different line these days. When we first started going together, he wrote the most beautiful song for me. I was so thrilled, I bought him a diamond ring. Then I found out the son of a bitch had written the song a couple of years earlier and had used it on lots of other women. We each paid a small fortune for that song, and since we have so much in common, we're all the best of pals now. When did you two get together?"

"Dandy and I are just good friends," Geneva said sharply.

"You should join us. We could have a little convention. We could compare how good he's been in bed. Now that I think about it, he was just as good out of bed."

"Why are you telling me this?"

"Just a little girl talk between friends. You'll love this: One night we were making love in the kitchen and—"

"That's enough!"

Geneva pulled away from her. She wove her way through the dancing crowd, away from Margo. Julia Mae's hand emerged from the crush and grabbed Geneva by the arm. The band shifted into a fast piece and the dancers began to swing hard. Geneva and Julia Mae sat at an empty table, both glad to get off their high heels, both pouring generous drinks.

"I got to hand it to us, girl, we really pulled this one off. I got it all planned. Billie's gonna get her hair cut at the shop Tuesday and in a week's time, you watch, *everybody's* gonna want us to cut their hair the same way. Look at 'em smotherin' her with attention."

"I thought surely Henry would be here tonight."

Julia Mae poured herself another drink and lit another cigarette. "Geneva, there is no Henry, I've been meaning to tell ya. I had a schoolgirl crush on a guy years ago, but the only thing I could latch onto was his name. Kinda like protection."

"You mean . . . you just made him up? Pretending? Then it was always you with the ideas. Why did you tell us Henry made all the decisions?"

" 'Cause I'm a woman. People don't listen to women. Not even women. Let's face it, a man speaks his opinion and no matter how stupid it is, the whole world quotes him. But let a woman have an opinion, and right away, people ask for her qualifications. So I decided a long time ago to give Henry all of the credit, give him all of the qualifications, but none of the cash. *You* deserve a lot of the credit for my thinking."

"Me?"

"When I met you I didn't have any class. I was always smart, mind ya, but I was afraid to show it. You encouraged me to get out of my country ways. You encouraged me to dress up. You inspired me to read books. You told me I had a good head for business, and you treated me with respect. You and Rose got me out of my voodoo store. I'd still be there, mixing potions and talking a whole lotta mumbo-jumbo. You showed me how to change my style, and I'm grateful." She snapped her fingers to the beat of a new Basie tune.

"By the way," she continued. "I'm having a little get-together at my place. Why don't you and Dandy come on over?"

"I don't know where he is. I've been wanting to ask you this for a quite a while. You've known Dandy longer than I have. Who was he involved with before he went to Europe?"

"I was hoping you wouldn't ask, honey. My, my, doesn't she make a lovely queen," Julia Mae said, looking at Billie, trying to change the subject. "Y'know, I met her when she first came to Harlem. When she was just a girl. She and a lady came into the voodoo shop looking for work. I knew Billie was special even then. And she remembered me, too."

"Was he ever involved with Margo Washburn?"

Julia Mae stirred her drink with a long fingernail. "I'm afraid so. Fooled around with Jeanette Miller, too. Now don't go poking in the past. So what if he broke a few hearts? Sure he's gigoloed around, honey, everybody knows that, but that was a long, long time ago and I can tell he's crazy 'bout you."

"Or crazy about my money." The thought of her money, unguarded, stashed in the house, combined with the realization that Dandy had yet to return, made her heart pound.

"What's the matter, child? You look as if you've just seen the Holy Ghost."

"My money! Dandy knows I've hidden something in the safe. Rose told him about the security guard this morning. He knows the combination, and he's been gone for some time now."

"You don't think he's—"

"I don't know," she said, standing up. "But I've got to find out."

"Wait for me!"

Geneva hurried toward the exit door, her heart pounding harder. Although she tried not to think of the possibility, there was a good chance Dandy, at that very moment, was helping himself to every dime she'd saved.

"Why did you insist on cash?" Julia Mae wanted to know when they got inside a cab.

"I wanted to wrap it in a box and have him open it at breakfast, I wanted him to come with me to the bank and see me deposit it in a joint account. I was going to back his show, become a famous producer . . ."

Geneva looked away from her partner. "If you and Rose can ever forgive me, I'd like to buy back into the company."

"Of course. Rose and me never thought you'd go through with this Broadway thing, anyway."

"I've been such a fool."

"Now, now, honey. Think of it this way, he's just another notch in the crotch. Sometimes your heart pushes you right into the fire. Don't blame yourself, blame it on Cupid."

The cabdriver told them he'd take them as close as he could to Mount Morris Park. Traffic cops diverted cars and buses back uptown. They had to get off on 125th Street and walk the rest of the way in the light drizzle that still persisted. Shattered glass covered the sidewalks. Faraway sirens could be heard rushing toward them. An ambulance sped up a sidestreet. Julia Mae asked a young girl what happened. She only knew there was a big explosion across the street from the park.

"That's *my* block," Geneva said, clutching Julia Mae's arm.

They rushed to a barrier where a young policeman stopped them.

"I'm sorry, ladies," the young Negro officer said with a polite smile. "No one's allowed beyond this point."

"But I live around the corner." Geneva felt panic lodge in her throat.

"She's a property owner, for cryin' out loud. Let us through!" Julia Mae demanded.

He quickly moved the barrier to one side and allowed Julia Mae and Geneva to pass. "Sorry, ma'am. I didn't know. But please don't get in the way of the firemen."

When they turned the corner firemen were everywhere—rushing, running, pulling hoses, climbing ladders. Sirens, police cars, floodlights were everywhere. Fire surrounded grotesque black skeletons of buildings, casting a sinister orange glow on the cascades of water being poured into them.

When Geneva realized one of the buildings on fire was hers, she screamed. It was a long, shrill scream that drew attention from even the firemen. She moved closer to make sure.

"Dandy's in there! Someone's got to save him! My money. Somebody save my money! She screamed again. She ran toward her house, but two policemen stopped her and helped Julia Mae sit her on a bench on the side of the park. Julia Mae wrapped her arm around Geneva's shivering body.

"Did he burn up with my money?" Geneva asked, sobbing on Julia Mae's shoulder.

"I imagine he got out in time. He strikes me as a back-door kinda man," said Julia Mae. "But it don't look like Rose is going to have a stick left of her house when she gets back from making that speech. Good thing Evelyn's at her grandmother's."

A newspaperman spotted them and hurried over to the bench. "Is she one of the tenants?"

"Can you just leave her alone?"

"I just have a few questions," he insisted. "There was a gas leak in 1532. Was that your house?"

"Get away! Can't you see she's in no condition to answer your stupid questions?"

"The fire chief said windows must've been open on the top floor for the fire to spread so fast. Know any of the dead people, miss? They found three bodies in 1532 and the blast—"

"Get out of here!" Julia Mae yelled angrily, scaring off the reporter. "Three bodies?" she said, looking at Geneva.

"Dandy burned up with all the money," Geneva said, drying her eyes.

"Don't say that, honey. I just hope Rose was where she was supposed to be."

Geneva sank deeper into her own world. She didn't have to worry about the house anymore. It was gone. She didn't have to think about Dandy anymore. He was gone, too. Everything was gone.

Harlem's flyin'

Electrifying,

Drink your booze and hear

our jazz,

Dance real close . . .

Razz-ma-tazz.

Come on down and we'll do the town . . .

In Harlem.

Music and Revised Lyrics by Dandy Reed

Epilogue
June 29, 1942

THE HOUSE ON STRIVERS' ROW HAD BEEN BUS-
tling with activity all morning. Billie cleaned out Dewey's old
room and freshened it up with flowers. She was a little annoyed
at the last-minute arrangements Julia Mae had made, but
shrugged it off as an opportunity to finally fix the room up for
guests. After all, Dewey had been away in the Army for over
four months now.

She was putting clean linen on the bed when Adam tapped on
the open door.

"I bet it's a lot hotter outside than it is in Jacksonville." He
grabbed the other end of the sheet.

"I doubt that. Plus you've got twice as many mosquitoes," she
pointed out.

"Why don't you come down and see for yourself, Billie? It's changed down there."

As she handed him two pillowcases, she thought to herself that she couldn't imagine living anyplace else. "I don't want no part of the South. I'll stay in Harlem, thank you."

"Why don't you and Jimmy come down for a vacation? I've got plenty of room at the house, but you don't have to stay with me. The colored hotel's been fixed up real nice and—"

"What would Jimmy and I do down there? We've got our home here, he's got his practice here, and I want my children to go to school here. I'm sorry, but I have no desire to go back and see the creek or the river or those Southern crackers who have nothing better to do than give us a hard time."

He followed her down the three steps that led to the kitchen. She poured them each a cup of coffee and they sat on the outside steps overlooking the neatly manicured backyard. It was another scorching June day and although she was beginning to feel uncomfortable on the hard concrete, she sensed this was the time for the talk they'd never had. She brought out a bowl of fruit, lemonade, and two pillows to sit on.

"If it wasn't for Julia Mae," Billie said, peeling an apple, "I don't know what would've happened to Geneva. She stuck by her when the only word Geneva said was your name."

His widened eyes told her he didn't know this. "Well, a long time ago I decided to let bygones be bygones. Besides, it don't make sense to hold a grudge against someone who's lost their mind. By the way, who took care of all her doctor bills?"

"Julia Mae. She took care of everything connected with the hospital. She's been a good friend to Geneva."

"Did they ever find her roomer?"

"Julia Mae and I often wondered what happened to Dandy. The police never found his body. They spent a couple of days rummaging through the ruins, but they told us they had too many real bodies to take care of, so I guess they stopped looking for him. He kinda' disappeared into thin air."

"Maybe he was one of the bodies in the fire."

Billie gave him a slice of an apple. "Who knows? He disappeared, like Lester Noble."

She noticed Adam's change of expression. "Do you know what came of Lester?"

Adam lit a cigarette, a habit Billie still couldn't get accustomed to seeing. "Well . . ." he said. "Remember that night I waited for Geneva at her house? I must've waited in the dark for three hours. That was after waiting in the rain across the street in the park for over two hours."

"You waited that long? In the rain?" she asked.

"I would've waited until hell froze over, Billie. I hated Lester. All I could think of was revenge. Kill Lester. Make him pay. Kill the bastard!" He took a long draw from his cigarette and allowed the smoke to seep from his lips as his mind drifted back into the past.

"That night, Geneva gave me his address, and I went to find him. He was on 112th Street in a run-down place. One of the people in the building took me down to the basement. She pointed to a door that had piles of old newspapers up to the ceiling and half-empty cans of food and bottles all over the floor. She said there was a Lester that lived there. The walls was crawlin' with roaches. The door was open, so I walked on in.

He didn't recognize me. I hardly recognized him, for that matter. When I told him who I was, he knew it wasn't social."

"Did he run away?"

"No, he was eating in bed. He'd gained so much weight, he could hardly move. I don't think he ever left his bed. His face looked like a balloon with extra skin hanging off it. And he smelled real bad. The whole place smelled bad, like a dirty toilet. He said he hadn't had a bath in months because he couldn't get in his bathtub."

"He weighed that much?"

"Not only that, he had sores all over his face. The dirty sheet he was wallowin' in had spots of blood all over it. He told me he had syphillis. Then I took out my gun and told him why I was there. He said I'd be doing him a favor if I killed him."

"And . . . ?"

"That's when I realized how dumb I was to spend all my time looking for this miserable bastard, when I could be spendin' it with my sons. I put my piece back in my coat and told him he'd have to clean up his own mess. That night I got a job, and," he said, lighting another cigarette, "the next night I found you and the boys."

"I guess Harlem can be tough at times."

"And it's getting tougher," Adam said in a serious tone. "It's not safe here anymore, Billie."

"It never was. No place is completely safe. Jacksonville wasn't safe. That's why we left. I swore to myself the day we saw the Statue of Liberty I'd *never* go back . . ."

"But it ain't natural here. You can't grow tomatoes or corn or beans or . . ."

"We grow brains and talent here!" Her voice was harsher than she intended. *Poor Adam*, she thought, *he's just lonely*. She leaned over and kissed him on the forehead. "We haven't done too bad for a couple of dumb farmers," she chuckled. "You seem to manage to have money all the time. What's your secret?"

Instead of another wisecrack, Adam regarded her seriously. "That's really what I wanted to tell you 'bout. When I was in prison, I met up with a white guy who used to be my boss. That was a long time ago. I told Virginia and you and the boys I was in the import business."

"I remember."

"Well, it wasn't no kind of legal business. He worked for the big boys."

"I should've known when you got beaten up."

"Anyway, I saved this guy's life one day, after he tried to kill me."

"He did what?"

"Me and Corky was musclin' in on his bootleg action. I was just another guy to get rid of at the time."

"How could you save his life after he almost killed you?"

"I just kinda reacted without thinking. Anyway, a few weeks passed and the guard tells me there's a new lawyer working on my case, so I better be on my best behavior. Charley wouldn't fess up to it but I know he had it fixed, because I got out of the slammer in no time. I'm tellin' you this now, Billie, 'cause if you ever came down to Jacksonville, you'd find out what I did, 'though I done retired from that."

"Retired from doing what?"

"Bankin' numbers. This guy Charley worked his way up with

some big people. He loaned me money and set me up in Jacksonville. His connections got me out of the can, and his connections put me in my own business back home."

"So *that's* what you've been doing down on the farm," she teased.

His eyes turned sad. "I had to, Billie. It's not easy for an ex-con to get a job. Couldn't work the land. Most of the farms have houses on them instead of carrots. I didn't have much choice. I didn't want to come beggin' to you or anyone. I only lied 'cause I didn't want you or the boys to be 'shamed of me."

In a way, Billie admired him. As far as she was concerned, he did whatever he had to do. "All those secrets . . . Well, at least you're out of harm's way now. Retired, thank God!"

"Well, not exactly retired from workin'. The numbers is a tough business. I got tired of lookin' over my shoulder. I want somethin' respectable now. I'm thinkin' 'bout openin' up a small place to eat."

"A restaurant? Imagine that! I guess things *have* changed a lot down there. And you've changed, too. I just can't picture you cooking . . . or collecting numbers." She couldn't help laughing.

Adam laughed with her for a minute. Then their mirth was interrupted by the front doorbell.

It was a sweating cabdriver who looked too young to drive. He was at the door carrying a large suitcase and a matching hatbox. His passengers were making their way up the stairs.

Julia Mae, whose arthritis now forced her to walk with a cane, wiped her brow with a handkerchief as she and Geneva reached the top landing of the brownstone steps. She stepped aside for Geneva to enter first while she caught her breath.

Geneva's face seemed fresher, and surprisingly somehow younger, although she had entirely too much powder on to suit Billie's taste. Billie noticed the simple cotton dress she had bought for Geneva, and for a brief moment, she was reminded of how Virginia looked when they all first came to Harlem.

Geneva stood shyly in the doorway. It was an awkward moment. What do you say to a woman who's been in an asylum for 8 years? Fortunately, she broke the ice as she admired Billie's beautifully decorated rooms. Once they settled down in the living room, Geneva said to Billie in a soft voice, "You've put on a little weight."

Adam said, "She's heavier because she's two months pregnant. She and Jimmy's gonna have a baby!"

Billie was only slightly annoyed at Adam for spilling the beans, but Geneva's happy response and Julia Mae's squeals of delight couldn't have been more earnest or spontaneous.

"Before I forget to tell you," Geneva said, carefully placing her glass in a coaster on the mahogany cocktail table, then nervously twisting a handkerchief in her hand, "the doctors want me to talk about the past. They say it's good for me. If I'm going to stay healthy, I've got to face certain things."

"God knows we've all got a lot of past to face up to," Adam said.

"If we're going to catch up, let's go outside and get comfortable," Billie suggested.

They sat on folding chairs out in the backyard shade and talked. Billie noticed that Geneva could not take her eyes off Adam. Eventually, Geneva brought up Lester's name.

"That reminds me," Billie said, trying to change the subject,

"I've decided to renew our contract, Julia Mae. One more year. This one's for the baby."

"Good, I'll tell the photographer before you get too plump."

Geneva waited patiently, then she asked Adam about Lester again.

"Did you ever find him?"

"Who?" Adam asked.

"Lester."

"You know, Geneva, I . . . I lost that address you gave me. Never did get a chance to catch up with him."

"Oh . . ." Geneva said. "I had wondered about it lately. Adam, I am sorry I lied in that trial. I was just doing it to protect myself. I've seen a lot of things about myself more clearly since I've been away."

"Forget it, Geneva. It's all water under the bridge, now. We've all done things we regret," Adam replied after a pause.

They all avoided one another's eyes for a minute. "Well, I gotta be goin'," Julia Mae said, standing up. "It was good to see you all again. Don't get up, I'll let myself out." She waved and made her exit quickly.

"She's been so good to me," Geneva said. "I owe her everything."

Billie stood up. "I'm going to get dinner ready," she said. "Holler if you need more lemonade."

When she'd gone into the house, Adam looked carefully at Geneva. *She don't look like someone that's been locked up*, he thought. Actually, she looked pretty good for someone who'd been through what she had.

"It's sweet of Billie to let me visit her," Geneva said. "I've never met her husband. Is he colored?"

Yeah."

"This place is so fancy, I couldn't tell," she laughed.

"He's a lawyer. Doin' well. They met at a party at Duke Ellington's place and got married two weeks after. One thing's for sure, they both seem to love Harlem as much as they love each other. I can't even get them to visit me. . . . How often do you have to go back to the clinic?" he asked.

"I don't have to ever go back. That's all behind me now."

"What are you going to do?"

"I don't know. Julia Mae took such great care of the business while I was away, I really don't have to work if I don't want to. After the fire, they found the money. It was still in the safe. Can you believe that? Julia Mae put it all in the bank for me. Poor Rose, I often think of her. What a horrible death she had. Julia Mae has offered me a room in her house, but I don't think I want to settle in Harlem again. Too many sad memories. I've even thought of going back to Jacksonville, at times."

"Well, if you ever do go back, look me up," Adam said kindly. "It's changed a lot too, but which one of us hasn't?"

Geneva smiled. "You've got a point. Guess I'll go in and see if Billie needs any help," she said, rising.

"Believe I'll follow you," Adam said. Together they went up the steps and into the house.

It was six o'clock.